burning
bridges
laura anne gilman

LUNA™
www.LUNA-Books.com

LUNA™

BURNING BRIDGES

ISBN-13: 978-0-373-80274-6
ISBN-10:   0-373-80274-9

Copyright © 2007 by Laura Anne Gilman

Author Photo by: Peter R. Liverakos

www.LUNA-Books.com

Printed in U.S.A.

Praise for the Retrievers novels of

laura anne gilman

STAYING DEAD

"An entertaining, fast-paced thriller set in a world where
cell phones and computers exist uneasily with magic,
and a couple of engaging and highly talented rogues solve
crimes while trying not to commit too many of their own."
—*Locus*

"Gilman delivers an exciting, fast-paced, unpredictable story
that never lets up until the very end.... I highly recommend
this book to fans of urban fantasy, especially [the works of]
Jim Butcher, Charlaine Harris, Kim Harrison, or
Laurell K. Hamilton. This is an extremely strong start,
and I hope Gilman keeps it up."
—*SF Site*

"What's a girl to do now that *Buffy*'s been canceled?
Read Laura Anne Gilman, of course!...
If Nick and Nora Charles were investigating *X-Files,* the result
would be *Staying Dead.* These 'Retrievers' are golden."
—Rosemary Edghill, author of *Met by Moonlight*

CURSE THE DARK

"Fans of Tanya Huff will cherish *Curse the Dark,*
a fabulous romantic fantasy that showcases
how talented Laura Anne Gilman is."
—*Affaire de Coeur*

"Gilman maintains the standard set in the first volume of this
series.... Gilman has managed the nearly impossible here:
a cleverly written and well-balanced fantasy with a strong
romantic element that doesn't overpower the main plot."
—*Romantic Times BOOKreviews* [4½ stars]

"With an atmosphere reminiscent of Dan Brown's
The Da Vinci Code and Umberto Eco's *The Name of the Rose*
by way of Sam Spade, Gilman's second Wren Valere adventure
(after *Staying Dead*) features fast-paced action, wisecracking
dialog, and a pair of strong, appealing heroes."
—*Library Journal*

For James: Even now

ACKNOWLEDGMENTS

The IM Brigade:

Arwen Rosenberg

Tom Powers

Sarah (Bear) Wishnevsky

Kathy Kimbriel

Nea Dodds

Jules Lee

"A safe place for all the pieces that scattered/
learn to pretend there's more than love that matters."

—"Love will come to you"
Indigo Girls

one

January 23rd 6:25pm

Fresh snow could make even the dingiest, most urban part of Manhattan into a magical place. The colors and noises all faded away, the city's usual frenetic pace slowing to a more studied waltz of snow falling, white against the bare black limbs of trees and outlines of buildings. Drifts pushed up against maildrop boxes, covered fire hydrants, and shut down traffic except for the unstoppable city buses and madman-driven taxi cabs zipping through the night.

It might have been lovely, but Wren Valere wasn't paying attention to the scenery. She was a professional working her craft. Or trying to, anyway. Two new high-end locks had hit the market, supposedly proof against the "bump-and-enter" method, and she wanted to make sure she understood how they worked before she actually encountered one in the field, when time might be against her. In her particular profession, you didn't get many second chances, and Wren was pretty sure the past twelve months had used up all the ones she was going to get in a lifetime.

Sometimes, honestly, she didn't know what got into her. For a mind-her-own-business Retriever, she'd spent a hell of a lot of time muddling around in things she should have left alone. Curses and politics and *meetings*, for God's sake.

Never mind that she'd done it to save her own skin, after the Mage Council tried to use her and her partner, Sergei; never mind that she'd done it to help out her friends among the fatae, the nonhuman members of the *Cosa Nostradamus*. All of that might have made what happened inevitable, but none of it made it smart.

"Hey, Valere." The voice came from the other side of the room, about three feet to the right and a foot down. And speaking of fatae....

Wren Valere didn't sigh, but she wanted to.

Retrieval wasn't easy. She had studied her craft, learned from masters, and kept up-to-date on all the most recent developments, not only in her own field, but anything that might come in handy. In addition to mastering the current-magic that flowed from within her, she had trained her body, as well; toning and strengthening her muscles, increasing her lung capacity, maintaining her flexibility. She had forced mind and body into partnership, more than once spending hours waiting in a cramped, close situation, anticipating the perfect moment to move on a job. She knew all about patience. About focus. About dedication.

And that focus and dedication was being destroyed, not by a stubborn client, or impossible mark, or even the weight of the snow outside and what was happening in the city beyond, but by her companion.

She didn't bother looking in the direction of the voice, not wanting to encourage him.

"Valere," the voice said again. "What does this do?"

She looked, then, briefly. "Opens locks."

The room's other occupant—and the subject of her irritation—put the tool back down on the small table next to him and picked up another. "And this?"

She reached for patience, found it. "Opens a different kind of lock."

"And this one?"

Patience threw up its hands in disgust and fled the room. "It gets the gunk out from between my teeth. Damn it, P.B., will you please leave my kit alone? Those extremely delicate tools you're paw-handling cost me a fortune, and half of them are custom-made." She reached up from her cross-legged position on the floor, and snagged the instrument in question out of P.B.'s paws. A thin ceramic shape with a non-reflective black coating, it actually did look like something that might be found in a very trendy Goth's toothbrush holder, except that the fiberglass pick at the end was attuned to more delicate vibrations than enamel generally gave off.

"Sheesh. Someone's snappy." The short, white-furred demon settled on the padded bench under the room's single window and stared at her with his dark, dried-bloodred eyes. He wandered over to the corkboard that hung above her desk and tapped one curved black claw on a color pencil sketch tacked there. "This the bansidhe-horsie you been chasing? How long you been working that case?"

"Five years." She refused to look up from her notes, hoping against hope he would finally take the hint and go elsewhere.

P.B. snorted, a wet, vaguely disgusting noise his flattened snout of a nose seemed designed to make. "That's dedication. You get paid for any of that time?"

"Five years ago, yeah," It wasn't always about money. A lot of the time, it was about reputation. The Wren never gave up. Never left a job unfinished. No matter what.

Okay, maybe some of it was about money. Her mother had spent most of her life worrying about money: how much, never enough. Having money-savvy Sergei Didier become her manager when she was a teenager had given Wren the opportunity—and the education—she needed to change that. Over the years, her reputation—and her fees—had grown. If she was careful, and kept working, her savings would be enough to buy her apartment when it finally—inevitably—went co-op. More, Wren was now in the position of being able to have ego spur her to do things, rather than need.

Financial need, anyway.

The demon and the human were occupying the spare bedroom/library of Wren's East Village apartment, surrounded by three stacks of books, a scattering of papers, and the remains of two pizzas. The air was heavy with the scent of pepperoni, cheese, and a dry heat coming up through the building's ancient radiators, making her sinuses itch.

Ego had its own need in it, too. The bansidhe—Old Sally—was the one job Wren hadn't been able to close. Yet. Her clients—descendants of the original owner—had, she suspected, long since written off their initial deposit, but she couldn't let go.

No, the whereabouts of one taxidermied warhorse, no matter that it was a portent of doom, didn't really matter a damn to her. But professional pride was involved. With her last dying breath, if need be, she was going to bring that damn sawdust-stuffed equine doomsayer back in. Someday. When everything else got settled.

The thought made her laugh, bitterly. The *Cosa* was in the middle of a battle for survival against enemies it hadn't been able to identify, who were determined to wipe them out of the city. Her partner's former employers had screwed them over and left them to hang. The Mage Council was playing their usual we-know-nothing, did-nothing game with the rest of the *Cosa*. All in all, "settled" wasn't something Wren expected to see anytime soon.

Although these past few weeks of the new year had been oddly if pleasantly calm: nobody had set a psi-bomb off anywhere near her; nobody had tried to bribe, threaten, hijack or otherwise annoy her or any of her friends; Sergei was off on a legitimate business trip for his gallery; and she was actually catching up on her filing, bill-paying, and her exercise routine. The entire city seemed to have come to a pause.

Hell, the entire city had come to a pause, thanks to the weather.

"It's still snowing." P.B. had given up staring at her, now

looking out the window, one white-furred, black-clawed paw pushing aside the dark green drape. His short muzzle, which—along with the plush white fur and rounded bear-like ears—had been the cause of his nickname of "Polar Bear," pressed up against the glass, his breath causing the window to fog over.

"It's been snowing for the past seven hours," Wren said as patiently as she could manage. "This isn't a news flash." After two months of winter, snow of any sort wasn't news.

The constant curtain of white was making her stir-crazy, too, but she could live with it. Without the snow, Wren had no confidence that the agreement she helped broker—that the Eastern Mage Council and tristate lonejacks would sit down and shut up and play nice together, at least while they had murdering bigots out for their blood—would have held together longer than a week, much less the month-and-counting.

It helped that attacks by those bigots who had been trying to "cleanse" Manhattan of anything supernatural had all but stopped. She didn't think they were gone, though. The threat of the *Cosa* finally working together, in however limited a fashion, wasn't enough to work that miracle, no matter what some of her fellow members might want to believe. No, it was far more likely that frostbite was a hell of a deterrent—as was the fact that their prospective victims were wisely staying inside, where it was warm.

No matter. She'd take whatever reason, if it gave them a breather.

P.B. turned away from the window and hopped down off

the bench, kicking the pizza box with one clawed foot as he moved. "Hey. There's still a slice left."

"Yours."

"I'm full," he said, by his voice, borderline perturbed by that admission.

"You're full?" That got her to look up. She stood, creaking unpleasantly in the knees, and went over to look out the window, as well. "The Stomach that Digested Manhattan is full? Damn. There's the fourth horseman, riding past."

"Oh, shut up," he snarled, uncharacteristically. "I wanted kung pao chicken, remember? But you didn't want to order Chinese. For the first time ever, speaking of the end of the world."

Wren didn't snarl back at him, but only because she could feel current coil in her core, the power looking for an excuse to get funky. Control. She needed to maintain control. P.B. knew why she didn't want Chinese food. Or he should know, anyway. With Chinese food came Chinese fortune cookies. Fortune cookies, in this city, had an unpleasant tendency to be written by actual Seers. Sometimes, not knowing what was about to fall on your head was a blessing.

Wren counted backward from ten in English, then up again in Russian, the only thing she knew in that language except for a few useful swear words. Stay calm, Valere. He was cranky. She was cranky. Stir-crazy didn't look good on either one of them.

This was the third day of snow this week, snowing hard since dawn the day before, and P.B. had been bunking with her for two days of it. She would have told him to go home, but Sergei had been caught out of town when the airports shut down, and she had been glad enough for the company at that point to tell the demon that he could stay as long as he liked.

Apparently, he liked overnight.

Besides. She had no idea what P.B.'s home was actually like, much less if it was currently livable. The law said landlords had to provide heat when it dropped below a certain temperature, but the demon was unlikely to call the tenant complaint hotline, much less appeal to a disciplinary board.

"We need to get out," she said. "Do something." Something other than eat and prod unruly paperwork, anyway. She wasn't able to focus properly on the lock schematics, so long as P.B. was restless.

"As you just pointed out, it's been snowing all day. There's, like, a foot of snow out there. This, in case you missed it, is a problem for me."

Wren turned and looked at the demon, all four feet of him standing upright and reaching. The vision of him lost in a snowbank, only the black tips of his claws and the black tip of his nose visible, made her laugh for the first time in days. She didn't think he would appreciate her sharing the image, though.

"Let's get out of here," she said again. "Come on."

It only took a few minutes for Wren to lace up her boots, pull on a sweater, and grab her heaviest coat out of the closet. The cold air was like a slap against her face, after the dry heat of her apartment, and she stuck out her tongue to catch a snowflake, just because she could.

P.B. promptly went out and measured himself against the nearest plowed-in snowbank, coming out about six inches the victor.

Her street hadn't been plowed in hours, and the sidewalks were impassible. They trudged through ankle-deep snow in the middle of the street, watching their breath crystallize in the night air.

Most of the population was safe indoors, watching out windows, catching updates on the television, or determinedly pretending that this latest storm Wasn't Happening. But a few equally snow-loving souls were out and about: Wren saw a couple of teenagers building a scraggly looking snowman wearing a Yankees cap; a young gay couple walking slowly glove in glove; and at least three groups of kids, dashing about madly as though they had never seen snow before.

Maybe they hadn't, not on this scale. The Winter of Snows was a long time ago now, for all that she remembered it vividly, and the past few winters had been pretty dry.

Her brow furrowed under the wool watch cap as she thought about that. Was there anything potentially worrisome about that, other than from a drought perspective? No, after the heat wave of the summer past, it would make sense they'd be due for another extreme winter. No need to assume anything more sinister—or supernatural—than that.

Anyway, other than the occasional thunderstorming, lonejacks and Council both knew better than to mess with the weather. Mother Nature was a bigger badass than any ten Talents, and less predictable than your average blissed-out, neurotic, brain-fried wizzart.

Spring would come. Eventually. In the meantime, she should just be thankful for the peace and quiet the storms were bringing to a city that badly needed it. Having to layer blankets at night was a decent trade, for that.

All right, the rest of the city, unaware of what was going on, might not know that they needed it, but she did. Wren had been starting to feel worn decidedly thin by all the new demands on her: the endless Negotiating and Line-walking and Behaving when all she wanted to do was kick everyone out and lock the door behind them.

She was not good at playing with others. Not at all. In fact—

"Hey, Valere!" P.B. called.

Wren turned in the direction of his voice, and got a faceful of cold white powder smack on the left side of her face.

"Argh!" Tears came to her eyes, but she was grinning, ear to ear. Wiping away the stinging cold snow, she shot back, "You're dead meat, you polar bear wannabe!"

Bending down to scoop the snow into her fist, she whispered a soft incantation she had memorized as a kid, to melt the snow just enough for it to pack easily. But before she could do more than sight on the spot right between the demon's black-lashed eyes, his wide mouth grinning at her from over a snowbank almost as tall as he was, the soft shushing noise of falling snow was overridden by a deep, jagged scream.

"What the hell?" P.B. yelled, clapping furry paws over his rounded ears as though that would do anything to stop the sound.

Wren staggered and slipped in the snow, unable to mimic P.B.'s actions as the wave of current associated with that scream slapped into her like a windstorm, almost knocking her over. "Over there," she managed, forcing herself back up and forward. "It came from over there!"

They moved as quickly as they could through the snow, but by the time they got there, it was too late.

"Oh, damn." It was less a curse than a brimstone-fueled prayer, coming from her companion's mouth. He rubbed his palms against his fur in a nervous reaction, wanting to look away but held by the gruesome display.

Wren had seen an angeli die before, left to bleed out in a back alley after being beaten and abused by human bigots. It wasn't a sight you forgot, one of the angeli brought low.

This was ten, a hundred times worse.

"Jesus wept for mercy," she said softly, feeling a long-gone impulse to cross herself.

"Much as I hate them, individually and as a tribe," P.B. muttered, then said again: "Damn."

Angeli were the oldest of the winged fatae, the nonhumans. Despite being part of the *Cosa Nostradamus* for almost two decades, Wren had never seen one with its wings completely displayed. The great feathered muscles of this angeli stretched out almost seven feet tip to tip, near as she could estimate. It was difficult to tell for certain, though, since the angel was hung upside down, its feet tied together with rope and strung from a lamppost in front of a tall, non-descript office building. Its front had been cut open, messily, from groin to chest: only an empty cavity remained, slowly gathering snowfall.

Blood dripped from a slash in the neck, falling to the snow-covered sidewalk, staining the white a deep crimson black.

"It's started again," Wren said.

So much for the storms keeping people safe.

two

December, one month earlier

Wren Valere was spitting mad. Literally. She rinsed her mouth out again and spat into the sink, watching the red foam mix with the green of the mouthwash into a truly disgusting mess before being washed down the drain. The taste of mud and blood remained. Her arms ached, her leg muscles still burned, and she could feel the adrenaline still running in her body like a drug, despite having been home, safe, for twenty minutes and more.

"I hate my job, some days."

She was speaking to her reflection only, and it didn't even bother to look unimpressed.

Her partner was down the hall in the office, actually one of the three tiny shoe-box bedrooms in her apartment, and so he didn't hear her words. She rinsed again, and, this time, satisfied that there was more mouthwash-green than bloodred, reached for a towel to clean her face off, and went down to bitch to him in person.

He was sitting at her desk, a white cardboard box the size of a small cake in front of him, his cell phone pressed to his ear. Sergei was taller than she was by almost a foot, and he looked oddly scrunched in her chair. His long legs were stretched in front of him, resting on an old, beat-up leather hassock under the desk. Middle age was starting to show in the strands of silver in his hair, and the lines on his face—not to mention the slight thickening of his waist—but he was, still and all, an impressively elegant figure, and a pleasure to watch.

He saw her standing in the doorway and held up a hand to keep her from coming in. She stopped and waited, not at all put out to be barred from her own office. Being a Talent—witch, mage, magic-user, in more superstitious times—meant that electronic objects often had total meltdowns in her presence, especially when she wasn't in complete control of herself.

She was pretty well locked down right now, but that hadn't been the case when she came home half an hour ago, dripping with the now-washed-off mud, blood, and hellhound feces. Wise, for her partner to be cautious. He'd already gone though half a dozen cell phones because of her, not to mention three PDAs, to the point where he claimed it would be cheaper to hire a scribe to follow him around everywhere with a quill and paper.

"Yes. I understand," he was saying into the phone. "Excellent. Much appreciated."

Wren snorted, but softly. Sergei had a way of sounding urbanely pleasant even when he was ripping someone a new one. When he turned the charm on, men and women both had been known to slide out of their pants before they knew what was going on. Only she could see the way his face was still a little gray, his hand still a little shaky. He hadn't quite recovered from seeing her walk in the front door, that no-doubt lovely snapshot the instant before she dropped the white box in his hands and went into the bathroom to scrape the gunk off her skin and brush her teeth. It wasn't a visual she had wanted, either.

Her partner was getting slammed with, she suspected, a combination of fear—for her safety—and anger—at her, at the client for not warning them, at the universe in general—mixed with just a dash of envy. As he said as she came in, with only a little bit of irony, she always got to have all the fun.

She would have gladly given him all the "fun" of this job, if he really wanted it. She'd stay home and work the clients—

All right, no. She wouldn't. They'd tried that and it hadn't gone all bad but it hadn't gone all right, either.

"Yes, of course," he continued, his voice smooth but his eyes hard. "And we will complete the transaction tomorrow morning, as planned. Pleasure doing business with you."

He *had* been talking to the client, then. Good. She waited until he had turned off the phone and put it away before coming completely into the room. "Is he gonna cough up more money to cover the cost of my slicks?" Her specially treated bodysuit, the most overpriced piece of gear she owned, had been torn into shreds by hellhound claws. While she had been able to seal up the cuts in her own flesh so that, although not healed, they already looked several days old, Talent weren't very good at mending fabrics.

And the way the cabbie had acted when she got in his car, she was pretty sure word had already spread never to pick up anyone matching her description, ever again. Not that anyone could remember what she looked like, from day to day— that was part of the innate talent that made her a natural Retriever.

Her partner/business manager smiled the way that flashed dollar signs in the ether, and his almost-too-sharp nose practically quivered…okay, that last bit was her imagination. But if his nose *did* twitch, it would have been twitching now. The smell of money was in the water. "Enough to get you that fabric upgrade you were lusting after, even."

"Oh, good." No wonder he sounded so pleased with himself. Still, it was no more than she deserved. "Easy job" her aunt 'Tunia. The Retrieval had been a bitch and a half, way beyond what they'd been promised, and she'd earned every penny of that bonus. "And, partner, before you throw something out, patting yourself on the back? That's twice now I've run into targets with 'hounds. Unpleasant, and unfun. Let's make that a standard check in the background file from now on, okay?"

Sergei didn't flush easily, but he did now. Background checks were, mostly, his responsibility, and her getting almost torn to bits by the massive, nasty-tempered hellhounds was not something either of them thought of with pleasure. At least this time there had only been one of the bruisers. Last time, she'd faced off against an entire pack, and she never ever wanted to even think about that again.

"Right. Sorry." His pale brown eyes looked honestly remorseful, but he was a salesman with a heart of granite when it came to business. And, as she'd be the first to point out in any other situation: she'd gotten the job done, hadn't she?

Only this time, he wasn't the one who had faced down a slavering beast almost twice her size, with less brain and more teeth, she thought sourly. Her mood clearly communicated itself, and he added:

"The client was impressed—a lesser Retriever wouldn't have finished the job."

She waved her hands as though swatting flies away, then reached up and started undoing the pins holding her hair in a tight knot. She had cut a good six inches off, so it barely reached her shoulders, and her old French braid didn't do the job anymore. "Yeah, yeah, I'm the best, that's what he was paying for. Flattery will get you everywhere, but I'm still angry." She wasn't, exactly. But she had Right on her side in this argument, and wasn't about to let it go. "You can start making it up to me by taking me out to dinner."

He coughed, then shook his head. "Some other time, fine. Right now, you need to go take a shower and get ready."

"What?" She looked at him, her righteousness overtaken by befuddlement.

He pinched the bridge of his nose, and didn't look at her. "It's Tuesday. Tuesday night?"

Wren had to backtrack a bit, then shook her head, coming up blank. Her head was still filled with the specifics of the Retrieval. "What?"

He didn't even bother sighing, a decade of experience with her having trained him to lower standards. "You ran late on this job. We're supposed to be uptown at the *Cosa* meeting in—" he checked his watch "—ninety minutes."

Wren blinked, then made an explosive gesture with both of her hands. *That damned meeting!*

"We can always cancel…"

Wren didn't even bother responding to that as she ran back to the bathroom, shedding the remains of her once-sleek black working slicks in the hallway as she went. There had been a time when she'd had weeks off between gigs. Time to hit the gym, go shopping, hang out, sleep in…

"Get me something to wear!" she shouted back over her shoulder, even as she was turning the shower on. "And more coffee! I'll be ready in fifteen minutes."

She didn't wait for the water to run to her usual heating standards before she was soaping up her hair, muttering to herself. This meeting had been scheduled two weeks ago; circled in red, for God's sake, on the calendar in her office. And she still managed to forget about it, totally out of her head like it never existed. That wasn't like her. Not at all.

This job had come on the heels of another one, a museum snatch-and-grab, and if she hadn't been so twitchy from the dry spell of the summer, she would have had Sergei turn it down. Her preference was to take downtime between jobs, recover and rest. But being blacklisted by the

Mage Council last year had made her aware of how fine the line between "comfort" and "concern" was, financially. And in the crush of all that, she'd forgotten—clean-wiped it off her slate—that she had other obligations.

Stupid meeting. Stupid, essential *meeting.*

She heard the door open and close, the steam in the bathroom cooling slightly. The click of ceramic on tile was Sergei placing the mug of coffee on the counter; the swish of fabric was him taking the towel off the towel bar, and the silence that followed was him standing there, towel in hand, waiting for her to finish up and get out.

She tilted her head back into the hot water one last time, even though the soap was totally rinsed by now, and let her skin soak up a little more warmth before reaching down to turn off the flow.

"Dry first, then coffee," Sergei said, his hand reaching around the shower curtain to give her the towel.

She took it, not even bothering to growl. So long as the coffee was waiting for her, she'd be okay.

Truth was, she'd *wanted* to forget about this other obligation. She'd wanted it to not exist. She had wanted the entire scenario—Mage Council, her fellow lonejacks, the fatae, hate groups, political backstabbing, murders and suspected murders—to all disappear into a bad dream, so that she was just Wren Valere, thief-for-hire and girl-about-town. She had wanted time to actually sit down and figure out where her relationship with her partner was going, now that they'd added sex to the list of options. She'd wanted time to sit at a coffee shop, drink way too much café americano, and gossip about nothing more important or dangerous than rent or fare increases or what fatae breed was pissing off what other fatae breed this week.

What she wanted, and what she was getting these days, had a really annoying gap between them. There had to be somewhere to lodge a complaint....

"Valere." Sergei didn't quite tap his watch, but the implication was clear in his voice. Ninety minutes included travel time from her apartment in the Village up to the meeting site in midtown, and with their luck, every minute she lingered was another minute the trains would probably be delayed.

"Yeah, yeah." She wrapped the towel around her and went into the bedroom to get dressed.

The trains behaved, for once, and they actually made it to the designated meeting place before anyone else except Michaela. The lonejack representative had picked the short straw and had to attend this meeting, while the other three were off doing God knew what. Four representatives—three original and a replacement for the late, unlamented turncoat Stephanie—for the four sections of lonejack life in the Metro NY area: city-dwellers, NJ/NY/PA commuters, Connecticut, and the gypsy population, the lonejacks who didn't have a fixed address. Wren had never realized that there were enough gypsies to warrant their own representative, before all of this, but the general disdain for authority that made a Talent become a lonejack seemed to extend to paying rent and taxes, too. Reportedly, there was a family that lived out of a huge-ass, stripped-down RV, using the rubber wheels as insulation from the kids' occasionally misdirected current. Wren still wasn't going to believe that until she saw it, but she didn't doubt the probability of it, now.

Michaela was the gypsy's representative, but today she spoke for the entire lonejack community. She was seated in a chair off in one corner, clearly meditating when they came in. Wren and Sergei took their place at the table without disturbing her.

Wren sat down gingerly in her chair, trying to determine if she could sit all the way back and still have her feet touch the floor. She couldn't. As usual, she had the choice to either be comfortable, or feel like a ten-year-old swinging her legs under the table.

All right, so five-foot-nothing was short, even for women, but it annoyed her nonetheless. She wasn't about to get on her hands and knees in order to see if the chair's height could be adjusted, though. With her luck, she'd be halfway under the table the moment the others walked in, and that was no way to create a serious impression.

Instead she continued the discussion they had begun on the ride up from her apartment. "The real problem is there are too many civilians in the City."

Sergei Didier leaned back in his own chair and raised one extremely well-manicured eyebrow in a move his partner had been trying to achieve for years. "And by civilians you mean...?"

"Humans. Non-Talents. All right, yeah, Nulls. Okay?"

Wren tapped her fingers on the table in front of her in irritation. "Something's going to blow, and it's going to blow soon, and there are too many...God, what's the term...?"

"Incidental casualties. Collateral."

"Right." Wren tried again to get comfortable, then gave up and pushed away from the table a little so that she could slump. It didn't look professional, but it hurt her calves a lot less. She looked around the room—gray flannel wallpaper and subdued lighting—and then stared down at her booted toes, wondering if she shouldn't have worn something dressier than slacks and a sweater. Even if the weather outside was threatening to turn ugly with more snow. No. Nowhere in any of the small print did it say that she had to wear a skirt. Or, God help her, a suit. Sergei had picked this out for her, and he was way more of a stickler for appropriate clothing, so she was okay. Or maybe he just knew they didn't have time for a fight over pantyhose. Not that she actually owned any.

"Not to mention," she went on a little bitterly, "several thousand fatae who, for whatever reason of stupidity have no idea what's going on."

"I thought the Quad was taking care of that?" he said, clearly taken aback by that intelligence. "Wasn't that the entire idea, that they would pass word along, whatever was happening, whenever?"

Since her hair was, for once, actually coiled neatly at the back of her head and gelled into submission, she settled for slapping the table one last time, rather than running her fingers through her hair, then looked up at her companion.

Sergei looked every inch the well-heeled businessperson: expensive white button-down shirt tucked into dark gray wool slacks, a just-ever-so-slightly-artsy tie knotted under his collar, and his hair trimmed back in a fashionable cut that had obviously been rumpled more than once by an exasperated hand raking through it, but still looked good. Clearly, his hair product was better than hers.

She snorted at Sergei's comment. Now and again she forgot how little he knew about that side of her life. "What, you think humans have the lock on Don't Know, Don't Care? Half of the fatae are convinced it's a human plot, anyway, and the Quad's just a tool being used to herd them to their doom, etc. etc. grassy knoll, bleat bleat bleat."

The Quad were the four fatae—nonhuman—representatives for the area, each with their own constituency to match the four lonejack leaders. Wags within the *Cosa* quickly started using "the Double-Quad" when referring to both sets of leaders—and it was just as often "that *damned* Double-Quad."

Wren still marveled not only that the fatae had managed to elect leaders without too much obvious politicking among the hundreds of breeds, but that in the months since, nobody had—to the best of her knowledge—tried to change horses midstream. They were trusting their chosen leaders.

Trust. What a simple word, Wren thought, not for the first time. What a deceptively simple, shrapnel-laden word it was. And how little of it there was to go around, even on a good day.

There hadn't been many good days in Manhattan, lately.

In the past year, factions had formed, gotten paranoid, and turned against each other; all fueled, as far as anyone could tell, by the double-edged sword of antifatae thugs killing anything even vaguely nonhuman, and the Mage Council trying to strong-arm lonejacks, unaffiliates, into joining their lockstep union. It had all gotten too bloody to allow. Hence, the Quad, and the Double-Quad. And hence, this meeting, where all sides were going to put cards on table, eggs in basket, pick your cliché.

"Okay, good point," he allowed. "So what do we do about it?"

Wren slumped even further. "I haven't a goddamned clue. All depends on what happens here."

"Here" was a rented conference room, complete with a huge fake mahogany table, a whiteboard, pads of paper and pens, and a sideboard filled with pastries and large urns of coffee. All the teleconferencing materials typical to such rooms had been removed prior to the meeting time. Wren approved whoever had thought of that, and then wondered uneasily if that was supposed to have been her job. Nobody had ever been able to tell her exactly *what* she was supposed to be doing as the so-called lonejack advisor, other than "observing and advising" the lonejack leaders.

They had wanted her to be one of the leaders, back when this all started. Only the fact that she had become a Retriever, partially because people consistently and completely overlooked her, had saved her from that fate: tough to follow a leader nobody could remember seeing!

She had never been so damn grateful for that particular quirk of Talent and genetics before.

Michaela finished her meditation, and quietly moved her chair back to the table, looking over last-minute notes and pretending not to hear anything Sergei and Wren were saying to each other. The lonejack representative was dressed in her usual posthippie, protogypsy style, only now the skirt and soft, flowing top were made of a thick, nubby, warm-looking material, rather than the silks and gauzes she favored in the summer, and her feet were encased in practical boots. She should have looked ridiculous, sitting in that corporate setting. Instead, she looked cool, confident, and powerful. All of which she was, and then some. Bart, Rick, and Susan, the other three members, were all strong Talent, and with other skills that made them the right choice to speak for their respective areas, but Michaela could outpower them, on sheer current.

She also kept her temper better than any of them, which was the true reason she was in the room today, and they weren't. There was no such thing as a fair straw-pull among Talent.

"I mean it, Sergei," Wren went on. "Things are way too tense right now. Everyone's walking cross-eyed and pigeon-toed from trying to predict the next move."

Manhattan was a huge city, even if it didn't technically qualify as more than a borough. It was also a very small island, especially when filled with paranoid paranormals.

Sergei had nothing to say in response to her words, and so they sat in silence while his outrageously expensive gold watch ticked off another minute, then another, and the door to the conference room opened to allow two more humans to walk in.

"Ayexi. Jordan." Wren rose to meet them. Sergei stayed seated until she kicked him in the shins, at which point he rose, but remained silent.

"Valere." The dark-haired, middle-aged man named Jordan didn't seem happy to see her, but the other, a slight, almost frail-looking man in his eighties, came forward with a delighted smile on his face. "My dear, my dear. Ah, you look so well. John would be so proud of you."

"Neezer would kick my ass for getting conned into this," Wren retorted, kissing both offered cheeks, European-style, and receiving the same in turn from the elderly Talent. "And you. Gone all Council. The shame!"

Ayexi had been her mentor John Ebeneezer's mentor more than four decades earlier. Lines of mentoring were the closest thing Talents had to a family tree, and although she had not seen Ayexi since she was a teenager, and then only infrequently, the bonds remained strong.

"What can I say? The body grows old and weak. The health-care benefits begin to appeal."

"They bought you, you mean."

"And paid very well for the privilege, I assure you." His gray eyes twinkled, and Wren shook her head.

It was impossible to be angry at Ayexi. He simply deflected negative energy, and returned only good humor. It was probably the only reason he was still alive, considering the trouble he used to get into. Neezer used to say that the mischief gene had clearly skipped a generation, as he—the middle generation—was so well-behaved.

Neezer was also the only one who had wizzed, who had been overwhelmed by his current and driven mad by it. Someday, when she actually had some downtime, she might do a little research into that fact. Or not.

"Ayexi, my partner, Sergei Didier."

For all that Sergei had partnered with her for more than a decade now, he still didn't know most of the major players, not even on their own team. Hell, being honest, *Wren* didn't know most of them, either. Just the ones she had used, or had used her at some point.

Introductions made, the two men sized each other up and down, and she could practically see both of them file the other under "ally, for now." About as much as anyone could hope for, these days.

The two Council members nodded with significantly less enthusiasm at the lonejack representative also seated at the table. Ayexi was there to support Jordan, the same way Wren was there to support Michaela. Sergei was there because nobody had said a Null *couldn't* attend, and ever since the Council had accepted him as her proxy for a meeting during that damned Frants job, everyone pretty much took the two of them as one player. She wasn't complaining: since she had gotten involved in *Cosa* politics, getting attacked by a slavering hellhound intent on protecting his master's property seemed like small change, dangerwise. Sergei was a good man to have at her back. Or at her front…

She shoved those thoughts down as being totally inappropriate and distracting, but a faint smile twitched her lips upward, anyway.

"Who are we waiting for?" Jordan had taken a seat on the opposite side of the table, resting his hands palm flat on the table. His fingers matched the rest of him: squared-off and well-manicured. Ayexi, by contrast, was disorganization personified: his hair looked like current had run through it and his clothes as though he had just come from an assignation, with the tails of his shirt not quite tucked into gray wool slacks, and his leather shoes scuffed around the toes.

"The fatae representative. I don't know who they are sending." She had hopes, though. If only it weren't winter, Rorani would be awake and the obvious choice. But in winter she was dormant, and even if they could coax her from her tree, the dryad would be too groggy to handle negotiations.

The door opened again, and a young female human held it open for the newcomer. "Good afternoon, gentlemen, mademoiselle," the fatae entering said, nodding to them all inclusively.

Wren let out a sigh of relief. "Good afternoon, Beyl."

There was a God, and he did listen to prayers. Wren took her seat next to Sergei, allowing Beyl's assistant—a gray-skinned, flat-eared gnome—to clear a space for the griffin to crouch at the table.

Griffins were born negotiators—the breed was herd-based, so they thought in terms of group benefits, but they were also meat-eaters, so they had a predator's instinct.

And Beyl had led her herd for longer than Wren could remember, so she knew how to face down challenges.

Plus, her claws and hooked beak kept opponents wary and a little nervous. Making a Council member nervous was never a bad thing, in Wren's book. Even if they were all supposed to be on the same side, right now. Or coming to the same side, which was what this meeting was all about.

Wren closed her eyes for a moment as the greetings and seatings went on, feeling a headache threatening. It was the kind her mother used to complain about on really bad days, the kind with the little man with a sledgehammer standing on the bridge of her nose.

Oh yes, she told the little man, this was going to be so very, very ugly. The Council had tried to intimidate lonejacks into Council-approved behavior, the fatae were skittish around *all* humans, and lonejacks never behaved well under stress, ever.

And you have nobody to blame but yourself for being stuck in the middle of it all. She could have walked away. She could have said no when the lonejacks had asked her—cornered her—to help represent them. She could have said no when the fatae asked her to bring the Talents to discussion. She absolutely should have said no when the Council started to make inclusionary noises.

She seemed incapable, these days, of saying no. Not to jobs, not to personal appeals, not to anything. She was going to have to have a word with herself about that at some point, when she had another one of those near-mythical spare moments.

Michaela went straight to the chase, while Beyl was still getting her tail set in the chair. "Thank you for agreeing to meet here today, gentles. Here's the deal— we've been faced for almost a year now with the reality that there is a strong, scary group out there, going after supernaturals. We've been calling them vigilantes, after their own advertisement, but in truth they are nothing but bigots with baseball bats. And while they're confining the bulk of their bloody activities to the fatae *at this moment,* the assault on the All-Moot last month is a strong indication that any member of the *Cosa Nostradamus* will be considered fair game to them."

There were nods of agreement all around the table. Council members had given the All-Moot—the *Cosa's* version of a town hall meeting—a pass, but even they knew what had happened; someone had given word to the vigilantes that there would be a gathering of fatae that night, and they hadn't bothered to pull their blows when a human lonejack got in the way. Part of the reason the Council had come to the table now was a desire not to be blamed for that disaster by the rest of the *Cosa.* The other part had to do with more internal politics: the head of the Council was trying to protect her own ass in the wake of some less-than-stellar behavior on her part, and she couldn't afford to have enemies on the outside of the Council, as well.

"In short," Michaela went on, "if we don't stop chewing on each other's tails, they're going to have us all by the throat. So it stops. Here. Now. At this table."

A little blunt, but Wren couldn't argue with the approach.

If you're going to hit them over the head with an ax, might as well get it over and done with in the first stroke, right?

Bad analogy—the little man with the sledgehammer took another whack, and she tried not to wince too obviously, for fear of being seen and misunderstood by others at the table.

"As the individuals most directly menaced by these humans," Beyl said, her beak creating an oddly clipped, almost British colonial-sounding accent, "the fatae have come to the table willingly, looking to create an alliance which will—"

"Save your feathered posteriors."

"Protect us all," Beyl said, ignoring the Council snark. Ayexi looked as though he was kicking Jordan under the table, were he so ill-bred as to do such a thing.

"Indeed," Michaela said, as though Jordan hadn't spoken. "And we thank our cousins within the *Cosa,* both for their aid in recent days, during the All-Moot and the days since then, *and* for their assistance in years past." A reminder to lonejacks and Council alike, that the fatae had been there for humans before in days of war and danger, here and in other continents, other times.

"The Council has officially gone on record as being dismayed and disgusted by the attacks on our fatae cousins," Jordan said. "And we have agreed to call a cessation in recent developments, in light of this external threat."

The general mental snort at that particular word-weaseling was audible to everyone, and Jordan went on quickly, as though to drown it out with his words. "However, we have yet to see any reason to believe that this is more than the actions of some confused, if hostile Nulls, acting against individuals they see as being dangerous."

"The Omaa-nih are dangerous?" Beyl sounded as angry as Wren had ever heard the fatae. "Startling-looking, yes—" the four-legged 'nih had almost-but-not-quite-human faces, which tended to freak Nulls out, if and when they noticed "—but peaceable to a fault. They eat grain, do not use weapons, and yet three of them alone have been killed in the past year!"

"To us, no," Jordan said, shaking his head in a manner that Wren supposed was meant to convey some kind of deep, paternal sadness and, well, didn't. "To a Null who sees nothing other than—forgive me, honored representative—a speaking beast? Especially a Null who, for whatever reason, has let their sense of wonder lapse? Indeed, then dangerous an Omaa-nih is."

Wren never wanted to agree with Jordan on anything, but the bastard was right. The Omaa-nih were the size and shape, mostly, of elk, and most humans didn't want their reindeer to talk, no matter how popular Rudolph and the rest of Santa's crew might be this time of year. Jordan was also missing—intentionally, she suspected—the point. She tapped her finger on the table, catching Michaela's gaze.

"The vigilantes did not discriminate when they attacked the Moot," Michaela said, picking up the current-whiff of suggestion Wren sent her. "Human Talents were harmed, and killed, as well. If they were not aware that the fatae had human connections before, they do now—and have shown no hesitation to attack."

"A onetime event, in the confusion of battle…"

"Council member!" Beyl had the best mock-shocked voice Wren had ever heard, like a fourth grade schoolteacher. The Retriever stifled the totally inappropriate urge to giggle. "Are you *defending* these vigilantes?"

"Of course he is not," Ayexi said, so smoothly Jordan didn't even have a chance to get huffy at the accusation. "He is merely playing, dare I say it, devil's advocate. We must be aware of all possible interpretations, in order to make the best countermoves in our defense."

Ayexi was good. He was cool, and smooth, and on the surface you might think he was discussing china patterns, or the price of something he had no interest in buying. But Wren could see the faint twitch over his left brow, the one that meant he was sweating inside. The Council was taking this seriously. Good. It was their fat in the fire, too: you didn't get a stamp on your forehead that said "council" when you joined; anyone gunning for Talents wouldn't discriminate based on your internal allegiances. That much, Wren was pretty damn sure about. More, Madame Howe, the head of the Eastern Council, was pretty damn sure about it, too. Enough to cover all her bases, by sending her people to this table for parlay even after doing her damnedest to break the local lonejack community to the Council's yoke. It might only be for appearance's sake, but if Jordan and Ayexi were willing to take it seriously, they could maybe accomplish something despite the politics.

"No matter their reasons, by attacking indiscriminately, both human and fatae, these…vigilantes showed that they do not distinguish. They *chose* not to distinguish." Beyl was definite on that.

"The associate of my enemy is my enemy," Ayexi said.

"Exactly." Beyl's feathered head gave a decided nod of agreement.

Wren could feel Sergei wince, beside her, even though he didn't move. The answer to that was *not* to be the associate of the enemy, an answer they couldn't afford the Council to make.

So far, everyone was falling into their preconceived roles: the fatae calling for attack, the Council wanting to hold the status quo without too much risk, and the lonejacks wary of either position—and of making any decision at all. Time to shake things up a bit.

"There have been reports." Michaela looked down at the material Wren had given her before the meeting started, all the details she and P.B. could recall, from all their meetings and discussions and overheard conversations over the past twelve months. "There have been reports of these… bigots taunting fatae. Calling them animals, yes… but also calling them on their use of magic."

"Fatae do not use magic!"

Jordan sounded almost outraged at the thought, as though a fatae had dared snitch something of his own possession. But he was right. Fatae, for the most part, *were* magic, deep in their bones and sinews, but they didn't *use* it. They weren't designed to channel current the way Talents were. In their own way, they were as Null as…as Wren's mother.

Okay, she amended that thought. Nobody *is as Null as my mother.*

"You're missing the point," Michaela said.

"You're pushing the point. And I'm not entirely sure I buy into your argument."

Beyl leaned into the table, a feather coming loose and floating, slowly, to the floor. Wren found her attention focusing on that, and had to bring herself back to the discussion at hand—and talon—with an effort.

"We are the *Cosa Nostradamus*. If that is to mean anything, it must mean something now. It must mean solidarity. It must mean accountability. It must mean that we can count on each other—for support—and for shared defense. In their eyes, we are all one, and worthy of disdain, fear, and violence. We must show them that we are also one in our response, and that response must be worthy of respect—and teach them to leave us alone."

Beyl built a pretty good case for a counterattack against their enemy—except that she couldn't, for certain, say where the attacks were coordinated from, assuming they had any single source at all. Any attack the *Cosa* made would be based on reactive information, not proactive. Wren wouldn't have wanted to go on a Retrieval with such sketchy info, ignoring the fact that she already had, once.

And see where that landed you? Learn from it!

"We can't afford that sort of attack." Michaela was parroting what Wren had been beating into their heads from the beginning: that without something concrete and significant, any large-scale act of aggression would be met with even fiercer aggression and even more justification from their enemy. She had been talking about the Council at the time, but it was even more true here.

Although lonejacks were better at violence than they were at organization, as a rule.

"We can't afford not to, either." Ayexi looked surprised to be agreeing with the fatae—almost as surprised as Jordan looked, to hear his advisor taking the lead. He went on, undaunted. "You are correct, Michaela, Madame Griffin. If this threat is to all Talents—to all the *Cosa*—then we need to take action. Before it spreads beyond this city."

Wren got it. From the exhalation of breath from her partner beside her, he figured it out at the same moment, as well. Michaela was a little slower, but she got there. Beyl's feathered eyebrows rose in puzzlement. The fatae were clearly not as au courant—pun intended—on Talent politics as they should be.

The de facto leader of the New York City-area Council, KimAnn Howe, had just brokered a significant—and tradition-breaking—merger with the San Diego Mage Council, bringing their leader into a subordinate level to her own. It was a risky, distinctly ballsy move that, if it hadn't been for the attacks, would have been the primary concern facing the lonejacks—had, in fact, been the primary concern just a few months earlier, when the Council was being twitchy while she made her moves.

If Madame Howe could not now prove to the local members of the Council—and the other Councils across the country—that she could control things in her own city, then she would lose the power amassed by that merger.

KimAnn Howe did not let go of power easily, if at all. Especially not after what she had gone through to get it.

"You are proposing...?"

"A truce. A...cessation of any probing for weaknesses, or maneuverings, or any kind of hostilities, overt or otherwise. On all sides."

Wren, by sheer force of effort, didn't roll her eyes in disgust. In other words, do nothing.

"Too passive. And entirely within your best interest, but doing nothing for the fatae. What can you give to us?" Beyl asked.

Jordan started to spread his hands, as though to say he was out of ideas, when a new voice piped up.

"What about reinstituting the patrols?" Beyl's assistant, the until-now silent gnome, poked his head up over the tabletop and peered at them all, black eyes sparkling with interest. "They did the job proper, they did, back then."

Wren almost fell off her chair. Oh, perfect! Damn it, as one of those former patrollers, she should have been the one to think of that! They'd done it twice, actually; once when the piskies decided to take their pranking to near-dangerous levels, and had to be sat on, and then again more recently, when there had been a series of attacks on the fatae—attacks that, in hindsight, were probably the first inroads of vigilantism, the early attempts of the so-called "pest exterminators" to clear the city of what they perceived as an infestation of nonhumans. So it had the value of precedent, wasn't so proactive as to unnerve the Council, but gave the fatae something real to work with....

"It was only a short-term cure," Michaela was saying, dubious. "A preventative…"

"A deterrent," Beyl said, warming to the idea as though she'd been proposing it all along. And perhaps she had. Wren admired griffins in general and Beyl in particular for many reasons, and sneaky maneuverings was high on the list of why. "Earlier, we used volunteers, whatever was available. It was lonejacks, mainly, then. Here… we can recruit specifically, from all the Talent. Match partners together, Talent and fatae, to create an effective pairing, as your Wren Valere and the demon P.B. have created such an effective team on their own."

Ouch. Zing. Yeah, they had clearly thought this out beforehand. But that didn't make it any less a usable solution for being tricksy.

"A pairing that will scare the hell out of any would-be assailant?" Jordan sounded like he rather enjoyed that idea, as well.

"Long enough to give us a chance to trace their source. Find out who is funding them—and why. Who is behind all of this."

Wren sat back in her chair, and reached for the diet soda she had placed on the floor next to her feet, popping it open with a hiss that earned her dirty looks from Jordan and the gnome. Now they were getting to the meat of the problem….

"Well. That was fun."

"It was?"

"Zhenchenka. Hush."

They were standing in the lobby of the building, pulling on gloves and wrapping scarves before going out into the wintry weather. It wasn't snowing, but the wind was fierce, and the bare limbs of the saplings outside looked to be shivering. Sergei had bought her a pair of fleece-lined leather gloves when the first snap of cold weather hit, and while they were an almost decadent buttery lambskin, she was still breaking them down to a usable flexibility.

"I was useless in there," she continued, flexing her fingers inside the leather. "I came up with nothing, contributed nothing... I might as well have stayed in the shadows, for all the good I did."

"You were extremely useful in there." Michaela was firm on that. "Both in the briefing you gave me beforehand and the advice you were able to give me ongoing, about our esteemed companions."

True, Wren had been able to head off a few potential missteps, as Michaela had never worked with griffins before, and made the usual errors of thinking of them, however subconsciously, as smart animals instead of peers.

"And now you will be even more valuable. To us, and to the *Cosa* overall."

Sergei's managerial antenna perked up, and he looked at Michaela, his eyes squinting suspiciously at her too-innocent tone.

"How valuable?"

"Beyond price."

"By which she means, beyond payment." The two women grinned at each other, more a grimace of stress than real amusement, and then Wren sighed, resigned again to her fate. "All right, what are you about to sign me up for, now?"

"Keep the lines of communication open."

"Huh?"

"Keep them talking to each other," Michaela elaborated.

"Keep who what?"

"Don't be dense, Valere." Michaela pushed the door open and went outside, leaving the other two no choice but to follow her. Wren gasped a little as the cold air hit her face. You forgot, sitting in an overheated conference room, how *cold* cold actually was. "All three sides of the equation—lonejack, fatae, and Council. The idea of a truce, while we figure out what's going on, is all well and good, but we need to also be able to figure things out. Which means communication. They're going to need a push, all of them, to remember why it's important to play nice. We need someone who can get close enough to make that push."

"You can do that," Sergei said, nodding. He took her arm, and then crooked his other so that Michaela could slide her hand under his elbow, which she did.

"Do what?" Wren felt like an idiot, but she had lost them at the last sharp turn in the conversation.

"Keep everyone talking," Michaela repeated, as though speaking to a child. "You and the demon. You started that, created the first bridge, with your friendships among the Council, your familiarity with the fatae breeds. Now we need you to maintain it." Her voice softened. "It's what Lee—"

"Michaela. Don't. Go. There." She might be willing to be

manipulated, in a good cause, if they really needed her, but she would not allow them to use Lee's memory to do it. Not yet. Not ever.

Lee had died during a Retrieval gone wrong—not because of the Retrieval itself, but because a fatae got stupid, and Lee had to be a hero. His widow still refused to speak to Wren.

"Think about it," Michaela said. It wasn't a request. Wren didn't dignify it with a response.

The three of them walked down the street to the subway station in silence, heads down against the wind. The Council members had been picked up by car service, of course. Ayexi had given a faint wave as he folded himself into the sedan, while the moment they left the conference room Jordan had acted as though the others had disappeared from sight. Typical. Ayexi was never going to survive in the Council, if he kept being friendly like that.

Beyl had been bundled into the back of a van in the loading bay, and her gnome companion had driven away, heading uptown, doubtless heading out of the city to wherever her herd was based for the winter.

Wren bit back a sigh. Michaela was right, damn her. This had started long before today. Before she attended her first Moot. Before she had gotten the first flyer advertising a "pest removal" company that was the vigilantes' first cover for their activities, when they were soliciting and recruiting new members. Before P.B. and Lee had used her apartment as a meeting place, to get the fatae talking about what was going on, to get them to open up and trust someone outside their closed, clannish communities.

It had started the first day she had met her first fatae, and called him "cousin," as Neezer had taught her. It had started the afternoon P.B. brought the first courier package to the then-newbie Retriever, and she merely handed him a napkin when he snitched a slice of pizza.

The fatae trusted P.B., despite the fact that demon were generally not among the most outgoing or social of the fatae breeds, and through him, they trusted her. The lonejack didn't trust her, exactly, but the Troika, as Sergei called the leadership, was relying on her, and that was more weight on her shoulders; weight she didn't want, didn't need. And the Council…well, that was going to be the unknown they were solving for, wasn't it? What reminders, what nudges would keep the Council at the table?

She knew Ayexi. She knew people on that side of the river. More, KimAnn and her Council flunkies knew her, Wren. Knew and maybe possibly a little bit respected her, by now. Listened to her, they'd proven that, as much as KimAnn listened to anything other than her ego.

Michaela got on the uptown 5 train. Wren and Sergei caught the downtown 6. The moment they were inside, and the doors closed behind them, Sergei wrapped his arms around her, pulling Wren into an awkward, but oddly comforting embrace, resting his chin on the top of her head. The hair that had escaped the pins holding the coil in place tickled against the back of her neck, under her scarf, and she was sweating in the stale air of the overheated, overcrowded subway, but she didn't move.

"I don't know if I can do this." Her words were muffled against the wool of his overcoat, but he understood her.

"They hired you. Why?"

Damn his oh so logical, analytical habits… "They didn't hire me, I volunteered. Because I'm a moron."

He didn't sigh, but he might as well have. "Work with me on this, Genevieve. They brought you on board to do the job because…why?"

"Because I'm the best." Best Retriever, yeah. This wasn't a Retrieval. It was…

"It's the same." Like he was reading her mind. Which he couldn't. Except somehow he did. "It's about seeing the details and creating a plan. About adapting to situations as they change. Playing the scenario as it evolves, bringing back—Retrieving—the information the Troika needs. You can do it. Just finish the job."

His ever-repeated advice, in every situation. The magic mantra. Finish the job. The act of finishing the job proves it's possible. So long as you're focused on the job, the practical details of the job, you don't have time to panic over the magnitude. The potential pitfalls. The ramifications.

She knew the logic behind the magic. Somehow, it wasn't as reassuring as it used to be.

And he left something out of the equation. Payment. Everything costs. That was his mantra, as well, what he had taught her better than any community college business course. Value for value, preferably in their favor. And Wren couldn't help wondering, as she snugged closer into his embrace, what the cost of all this would be, when the blood and dust all settled.

three

When Wren got to the landing of her fifth-floor walk-up apartment, the phone was ringing. Odds were it wasn't Sergei, who had stopped at the bank on the corner to hit his ATM, sending her on ahead. Teller machines normally ignored all but the most overt current displays, but she was, as he indelicately pointed out, a bit tight-wound from the meeting, and likely to be twitchy with current. Better safe than sorry when her partner was down to a handful of singles in his wallet.

Wren never used ATMs, herself. It wasn't about the risk, however minimal, of frying the machine; she just liked to have a face to go with the figures who had their fingers all over her money. Sergei, on the other hand, never used anything but, despite constantly griping to anyone who would listen about not being able to get anything smaller than a twenty-dollar bill. It wasn't as though he couldn't get to the bank during their normal hours—what was going to happen, the boss would yell at him for being late? But no, he was never willing to take the extra few minutes it took to go into the lobby and deal with a teller in person, during actual work hours.

Some days, she really didn't understand her partner at all.

Locks undone and door opened, no rush, and the phone was still ringing. It was either someone who was very determined, or someone who knew a. that she didn't have an answering machine and b. that she was home.

Or…

"Hello?"

Or it was her mother, a woman of determination, certitude, and the stubborn conviction that her daughter wouldn't dare not pick up the phone if she was on the other line.

Her mother was, of course, completely right in that assumption.

Wren dropped her keys into the dish on the counter, and shoved her gloves into her coat pocket. "Hey Mom. How's Seattle?"

Her mother had, at her request, gone on an extended vacation back in September, when things first got significantly ugly. Wren hadn't been sure when things were going to break open, but she knew she wanted her totally magic-Null mother as far away from it as possible. It would have been unthinkable, previously, to consider someone going after a Null relative in order to injure a Talent…but there were so many other unthinkables suddenly being thought that Wren had figured better safe than sorry.

Some days Wren thought it would be better—certainly easier—if her mother moved out of the area entirely, to somewhere that the name "Valere" wouldn't raise an eyebrow in any circles. Hell, some days she thought *she* should move....

Fortunately, her mother had found that trip so enjoyable that it had turned into a series of cross-country relative visitations, a new one every few weeks as Margot could get away from her job. The fact that it also made Margot into a moving—and therefore less appealing—target was something Wren wisely kept to herself.

In payment for that peace of mind, Wren was now getting the color commentary blow-by-blow by phone. Currently, it was cousin Jeanne's turn for a Royal Visit, out in not-so-sunny Seattle.

"Uh-huh. Yeah?"

Wren shrugged out of her coat one arm at a time, transferring the phone from ear to ear as she did so. Measuring the distance to the closet against the length of the phone cord, she draped the coat on the counter, and dropped her bag and keys on top of it. Sergei would put everything away when he came upstairs.

"And the kitten?" she asked her mother, having reached the end of a recital on Jeanne's present condition, which was fine, loving her new job, still not dating anyone new after dumping her most recent significant other.

The kitten was Jeanne's son, Kit. He would be... Wren searched her memory, coming up blank. Ten? Eleven? There wasn't all that much family on her mother's side, and none that she knew of on her male genetic donor's side, that she should have such a blank spot on that information.

Not that it mattered. Her mother, hopeless when it came to seeing or remembering anything odd or unpleasant in her daughter's life, had excellent recall for things familial, and a willingness to share it at the drop of a hint. All Wren had to do was make interested noises until the older woman ran down.

Wren perched herself on one of the stools, and settled in, reaching across the counter for a pen and scratch paper to write down her thoughts about the morning's meeting, while she listened.

Nothing like a little multitasking to keep your mind off how impossible her to-do list was. *But hey, look on the bright side,* she thought. *At least you know the depth of the kimchi you've been thrown into, right?*

"Isn't that a little young?" she interrupted her mother. "No, I don't remember what I was like at that age, sorry."

1. get feedback from Beyl on meeting for Quad
2. talk up the idea of Patrols on the street, see who jumps. Esp. fatae.
3. …

Sergei came in through the door before she could think of a third thing. He heard her talking on the phone, obviously made an instant—and correct—evaluation of who was on the other end of the line, and waggled his fingers in greeting to her mother, with whom he had a rather strained, you're-sleeping-with-my-daughter relationship.

When Wren nodded, not pausing in either her monosyllabic responses to her mother or her pencil-twirling, he put her bag and keys on the counter and hung her coat up alongside his in the closet, then disappeared down the hallway.

Either the bathroom, or her office, she guessed. Sergei had been away from the office all day, and while he was getting better at letting his assistant, that kiss-ass weasel Lowell, handle things, he still liked to have a hand on the spoon if things were actively cooking. Which was a terrible metaphor, but she was distracted, damn it.

"Wait a minute, he did what?" Wren put her pen down, to-do list half-made, and listened more carefully to her mother's story. Family politics were as intricate as *Cosa* politics, but far more entertaining....

Down the hall, Sergei sat down at Wren's computer and booted it up. Her voice carried down the hallway, and the sound of laughter lightened his own dark mood considerably.

There had been very little laughter in this apartment, lately. Too much tragedy, tension, trauma, and all sorts of words beginning with *T.* Very little laughter in their lives, overall, actually. Since... Since Lee died, probably. Before then, even when things were making them crazy, even when Wren was injured and he was losing his mind over keeping her safe, and they didn't know when—or if—the next job would come in, there had still been laughter. Strained, sometimes; but laughter. When had it gone wrong?

Sergei knew when: the moment he had negotiated that deal with his former employers, abandoning ten years of hard-won independence on his part in order to make sure Wren was protected from the Council. And for what? The Silence had their own issues, and that agreement put him—and Wren—smack-dab in the middle of those issues, exactly where they couldn't afford to be.

He had put them there; it was his responsibility to get them out. But it was as delicate a process as the original deal had been, and small steps that took forever. He didn't tell Wren everything; she didn't need to know. But she knew he wasn't telling her everything, and that was adding to the tension between them.

He had begun to wonder if he'd imagined the flashing brightness of her smile, or the liquid sound of her giggle, it had been so long since he'd encountered either.

Then a peal of delighted laughter came down the hallway, and he smiled. No, he hadn't imagined it.

The computer's Talent-proof, safety-rigged-seven-ways-from-Sunday system finally powered up and he logged on, surfed to the gallery's site and checked his e-mail, humming softly under his breath as he did so.

It wasn't a lot, that one surge of laughter. It was barely anything.

To him, it was everything.

And he would do whatever it took to keep things that way.

To: a_felhim@shhhh.info
We need to settle this. Call me.
—S.

He hit Send, and waited.

Across and far uptown, there was considerably less humor. The building could have been deserted, for all the noise that filtered down into the lower levels, where a coded key was needed to call the elevator, and a simultaneous retinal scan and biometric scan were needed to choose a floor destination. The technology used was on par, or in some cases excelled anything the government had, mainly because this organization could afford to pay for it—and had no need to justify to anyone where the money went.

Two figures emerged from the elevator doors, walking with an unconscious unison of movement down the hall-way, so much so that it was difficult to see who was mir-roring whom. Both wore wool slacks, button-down shirts of lightly starched white cotton, and expensive shoes. An educated consumer might note that the younger man was more fashionably dressed, but the older man's shoes were the more expensive, and better maintained.

A female figure with a dark blue lab coat over her street clothes moved past them in the other direction, barely ac-knowledging them with a preoccupied nod.

"Denise Vargha. One of our better people. She's in charge of the seventh team." The speaker—the younger man—was clearly aware that he wasn't telling his companion anything that his superior didn't already know, but felt the need to say something to fill the space.

"Indeed." The older man's voice was modulated for extreme politeness, bordering on boredom, with just a hint of "don't annoy me." As director, he signed off on all of the forms for R&D; he knew all the players, down to the laboratory's off-hour sanitation crew.

The subordinate took the hint, and went back to silence for the rest of their walk, until they came to the end of the hallway and went through another set of security measures to gain entrance to the rooms beyond that doorway.

"Director." The human element of the security partition didn't quite salute, but his spine did straighten noticeably. The guard nodded to the other man. "Doctor Hackins."

"You've made some improvements since I was here last," the older man said, looking around at the cold-tiled walls and cement floor with drains set at two-foot intervals. This time, a hint of approval colored his words; a carefully calculated effect, negated by his adding, "No more fire starters?"

"No, sir." The reprimand stung, but Hackins—as manager of the project—had already taken responsibility for that incident; it was over and there was no need to apologize. Apologies were a weakness worse than the original mistake.

The two men were passed through the security buffer and into the main lab, the reason for the entire building. Two more doors, each one a simple steel slab which could be opened only by a triple-checked thumbprint of a verified team member, or the director's personal override.

The room they were in now, after the second door, was capital-C clean; white walls, tiled floor, and stainless fixtures. A man in a white lab coat over his shirtsleeves was seated in front of a glass window, while the subject he was working with rested in an elongated, dentist-type chair on the other side. The chair might have been comfortable if it weren't for the leads affixed to her scalp and pulse points, and the leather restraints around her ankles, wrists, and neck. She was a slender, freckle-faced blonde, who looked as though she should have been running through a meadow with Disney-style animals leaping at her heels, not tied down inside an underground laboratory.

"Bethany. One of our more valued resources. I will admit to resisting putting her to this use; however, it does seem—"

"Gareth. To the point."

"Ah. Yes." Gareth Hackins didn't do anything as clichéd as tug nervously at his collar, but had he been less well trained he would have wanted to. "This is the third team's pet project, as was detailed in the yearly report."

He paused, and when there was no response, he continued as though given an enthusiastic go-ahead.

"It is a variant of conditioning response we have been working on for the past few years. Ideally, we will create a reaction *against* using magic except under direct command. Specifically, our command. Past attempts to accomplish this have used more traditional brainwashing procedures, with variable results. The effects would not last long enough for the subject to remain useful, and most of the projects, as you saw in the report, had to be terminated. A waste, really. With this approach, we are using their own abilities to create a loop, so that the more they use their magic, the more they tie themselves to the structure we create, emotionally."

"And how is that coming along?"

Hackins gave a faint, almost unobservable shrug. "Putting their magic under restraint is simple enough. They are already predisposed to take orders from the basic training all of our operatives go through. However, the next step has proven to be slightly more...problematic. Seven of the subjects have responded by shutting down all access to what is commonly referred to as 'current,' in effect lobotomizing themselves. One other—subject nine—accepts commands, but only of the most passive sort. Bethany, subject eight, seems to have the most potential to work on an active level. However, she has been resisting the final breakdown."

The director leaned in to look at the subject. "Touch her again."

The technician tapped a key, and the girl in the padded chair convulsed once, and then lay still. Her brown eyes were open wide, staring at the pale cream-tiled ceiling, and sweat trickled down the side of her face, dripping into her tangled hair and onto the padding of the couch.

"Response?"

"None."

"Move it up."

The tech used his thumb to slide the lever up, and then went to tap the key again. A slight hesitation, a glimpse backward at his boss, and he touched the key.

"Fffffuck you," the girl managed around her clenched jaw. Her gaze flickered off to the side, taking in the two newcomers, then went back to her direct tormenter.

"Interesting," Hackins said. "Most of them have broken by now. She's, yes, most interesting. The higher level of Talent seems to indicate a higher level of stubbornness, as well." He turned to the tech and checked the readouts the man was monitoring. "There's been no push back along the leads?"

"We had to replace the first two sets," the tech replied, "but once she realized that we'd insulated the main boards, she stopped wasting her time. Bethy's a smart one, she is."

"Yes. Very smart." Hackins looked through the glass at the subject, thoughtfully. "Interesting."

"This insulation allows you to stop their magic?" the director asked the technician.

"Sir. Not exactly, sir. It merely routes it through several layers, slowing it down with each turn. If she really wanted to do damage, she could, but we suspect that it would burn her out to generate that much energy."

"You suspect?" The man's face went still, and the tech and Dr. Hackins both felt the temperature of the room drop significantly with his disapproval.

"Despite our resources, there is still a great deal about these Talent that we do not understand," Hackins said. "That is why the work is progressing more slowly than anticipated. A wrong step, a push too hard, and we burn them out before the desired result is accomplished. But if this new procedure works, we should be ready for the next level quite quickly."

"She will not balk at commands?"

"She would be incapable of distinguishing between our wishes and her own," Hackins assured him.

"Excellent. On with your work, then. Gareth, you said that you had the remains of the other subjects on storage? I would like to see the results of the autopsies."

"Of course. This way, please."

The two men exited out the door at the other end of the control room, abandoning tech and subject without a backward glance.

Left alone with his work, the tech's shoulders sagged slightly in relief. He was very good at his job, but the ratio of failures in this project had been higher than anticipated, and the Boss was not a man you wanted to disappoint. Ever. Especially not when you were in his direct line of sight. The head of R&D was a fair man, nobody ever said he wasn't, and a good man to work for, if you pleased him, but he had no tolerance for anything he considered sub-par effort.

A tapping noise drew his attention to the other side of the glass. "Loosah," the girl managed, her face stretching into something that might have been a snicker, as though she had read his mind. "Sssssuckbutt."

Snarling in response, the tech tapped the button again, and electricity surged through the electrodes attached to her skin, rocketing through the nerve endings—and the extra channels that made her a Talent, overloading her core into painful quivers that wasn't *quite* what her kind called overrush, when the core exploded into the rest of the body, but close enough to give her a taste of what it might feel like.

Her body arched off the padded chair, her upper torso shaking in a scream that didn't escape her throat. Muscles in her arms corded against the restraints, trying to break free, and the monitors in front of him red-flagged as her current reached out, trying to find him, destroy him.

"Don't struggle so much, Bethy," the tech advised in a mock-sympathetic voice, watching as the monitors subsided out of red into yellow. "Like we've been telling you all along, it doesn't hurt if you don't resist it." He paused, then pushed a lever up a notch. "Unless of course I *make* it hurt."

The girl shuddered again, but the monitors stayed within the yellow range. Her lips pulled back again, this time clearly in a grimace, but she refused to give him the satisfaction he craved. She could clearly feel the things they were doing to her brain, was aware of the insinuations, the subtle suggestions they were whispering to her, feeding into her through every pulse of current around her. But Bethany was more than stubborn. She might have taken employment, against her mentor's advice, with the men who had betrayed her, strapped her into this chair and tried to use her for their own purposes. But she was Talent. She was *Cosa*. She would not break.

She would not betray her family.

four

Wren stared up at the ceiling and wondered what idiot had first decided that sheep were a soothing image. Sheep did not, in her mind, equal sleep.

The dark paint on the walls and the heavy curtains on the window were usually comforting, making her bedroom a restful hideaway, conducive to sleep, sleep, and more sleep. Tonight, the combination made the room feel like a coffin. Wren stared at the ceiling where dark shadows rested and tried to understand why.

It was too quiet, she finally concluded. That sounded like a cliché but it was true: Wren was so used to the constant rumble of traffic coming down the avenues, the hum of news copters and Coasties off the river, the thud-boom of construction, and the ever-present counterpoint of horns...even at night, there was enough motion to justify the city's claim to never sleep. But the recent snowfall was also muffling the usual nighttime sounds. And without it, *she* couldn't sleep.

Unfortunately, her other option: wake Sergei up and make him suffer with her, would require actually waking him up. And that, she was discovering, had been easier when it involved a phone call rather than rolling over and poking him. Not because he would be annoyed with her, but because he was just so damn cute when he slept. The stern features that worked so well in his Business-guy persona relaxed and softened, and his ruthlessly groomed hair fell into his face, rising and falling with the exhalation of his breath.

She watched him for a few moments, as best she could in the dim light. It was rare to see him this relaxed: the past few months had both of them all tied up in knots, between the Council's power games, the vigilantes, and the threat of some shadowy power behind that bigoted organization, directing and arming them….

And now, the added stress of the three-way negotiation between lonejacks, fatae, and Council was making her stomach ache, and putting new lines between Sergei's eyes.

The next round of that particular joyride was this afternoon, and she needed to be well rested, on the top of her game, not exhausted and fretful. And staring at the ceiling, listening to Sergei snore, wasn't going to get her there.

Wren slid out of bed, shivering as her feet hit the carpeting, and grabbed her robe, wrapping it around herself before turning back to tuck the quilt around her partner's still-sleeping form.

When in doubt, act. When outnumbered, run. When insomniac, obsess. It was a simple creed, but one that worked for her. Without turning on any lights despite the 2 a.m. darkness, she padded down the hallway to the kitchen, pulled out a can of diet Sprite and a half-eaten package of Oreos cookies, and padded back down the hallway to her office. Once the door was closed behind her, she flicked the overhead light on, blinking at the sudden illumination. "Ow." Another flick, and the hum of her computer started up. Sitting in the chair, the soda placed carefully away from the mess of wires and electronics, she reached in and grabbed a cookie, crunching down with gastronomic satisfaction. There was nothing better than the gritty-and-creamy combination of crisp cookie and sludge filling.

Her computer came alive, running through screens until the familiar icons appeared. She pulled up the tabbed files for Old Sally, and started reading through the last known sightings, both verified and alleged, for the bad-news-bearing bansidhe. There hadn't been anything to add to the file in almost three months, but it was entirely possible that her sleep-deprived state would see something, or make some connection she hadn't before.

It would be nice if her job was all adrenaline and action, but, regrettably, more and more it seemed to be all about the paperwork. Wren didn't know if it was because Sergei was giving her more to do on that side, or she was just getting jobs that required more than a blueprint and a prayer—or if it was the fact that she was so frustrated all the time that was making her *feel* like the job wasn't fun anymore.

"Probably the last," she said out loud. There had always been workups and research. She just used to enjoy it more.

"Oh, screw this." She closed the file, and stared at the screen, then reached over and made a few keystrokes. It had been a while since she'd had the time or energy to just sit and chat. The moment she logged into her IM account, however, she was pounced on—

<ohsobloodytalented> Hey figgie!

Figgie, short for 'figment of your imagination.' Wren found herself smiling as she typed a response.

<downtowntalent> hey. de-figged.
<ohsobloodytalented> Been worried. How goes?

Wren had no idea who was behind the screen name, other than the fact that she was a member of the *Cosa*, female, and lived in the Southern hemisphere. And, based on their last conversation, was a member of the Council down there. Wren had asked her—delicately, as it wasn't really a topic for casual conversation—about Wren's then-fear that the Council had been involved in the attacks on the fatae, as well as trying to intimidate the lonejacks into coming under their protection. The Australian Talent had denied the possibility of both actions—denied it so strongly that she had fried the system with her current-powered outrage.

<ohsobloodytalented> I owe you an apology.
<downtowntalent> s'okay, my system was fine.

<ohsobloodytalented> *whew* But no, not that, well, yes that but I meant, about how I reacted, not just how I reacted. Or, why I reacted...

Wren waited. The other Talent wasn't normally a ditherer, but the situation had been, well, embarrassing. Losing control of your current and frying electronics happened on a regular basis, even with the best control, but you always felt like an idiot, after.

<ohsobloodytalented> I asked around. Listened. Gossip's the only thing faster than current and the minute I put an ear to the ground I heard more than I wanted to. Blessed Goddess, woman!
<downtowntalent> um...

She honestly didn't know how to react. It was bad enough to find that her reputation had spread via gossip to Italy, but to literally go halfway around the globe...

Don't assume, Valere. You don't know what *she heard. You don't even now that she knows who you* are, *just a New York-area lonejack....*

<downtowntalent> so....what're They saying?
<ohsobloodytalented> Council's gone wrong up there. Bad-wrong.

Oh. Not anything about her, then. That was good. Except Wren would rather it had been about her; her own behavior she could get some control over. If the situation within the

New York Council was so bad even Council members in another *continent* were talking about it...

<ohsobloodytalented> They're a disgrace.

Wren couldn't imagine what it had taken the other Talent to type those words; the first rule of Council membership was unity, the second rule was line up neat and narrow behind your local Council, and the third rule was don't screw with the first two rules. To gossip inside was one thing, and nobody doubted there was a lot of that. But to admit it to not only an outsider, but lonejack and a doubter?

<downtowntalent> I'm sorry.

She risked the electronics to send a pulse of regret along the connection, to give her words more weight.

<ohsobloodytalented> Oh for fuck's sake...don't apologize! You guys have your hands full and then again, even if half of what we're hearing is true.

A pulse back, of gentle exasperation and a hint of concern.

<ohsobloodytalented> Are *you* okay?

Wren blinked, then smiled a little, and typed back:

<downtowntalent> yeah. mostly. it's...complicated up here, but we're managing. you?

There was a question in that one word that Wren wasn't able to elaborate on. The one thing she and the rest of the Quad were afraid of—so afraid that they hadn't been able to do more than dance around the possibility out loud—was the threat of KimAnn's attitude spreading; of Council turning against lonejacks, trying to force them into lock-step, across the country and elsewhere.

<ohsobloodytalented> Yeah. We're okay. And…we're watching.

Words hidden inside words. No promises, but a promise, nonetheless. Whatever was going on here, it would not be allowed to take root down under, not while this woman and her friends were on guard.

<downtowntalent> good.

So why did she have the feeling that neither of them actually felt so good?

<ohsobloodytalented> Time for me to log off. Take care, downtown.
<downtowntalent> you too.

Wren stared at the screen for a few minutes after the other account signed off.

It's not growing. But people are paying attention. Whatever we do, people are going to notice. We're setting precedent. And if we lose…

Her stomach ache suddenly got worse, and the Oreo cookies weren't so appealing any more.

"I need coffee."

Three hours later Wren blew on her fingers, trying to keep them warm enough to stay nimble, even as her ass threatened to turn into paired ice cubes through the heavy denim and silk underwear. The small storefront she was studying across the street was dark and closed, the iron grating pulled down over the windows. She could feel the electrical shimmer of the alarm system running through the store. Door and windows, plus a motion detector.

As pawnshops went it wasn't anything out of the ordinary, but there was an object there she intended to Retrieve before the night was over. Nothing special: a gold locket that had been pawned a week before. A small locket with nothing but emotional significance. Nothing inside except one faded picture of a man long-gone.

"Why couldn't we stay inside, where it was warm?"

"You could have stayed there."

The demon huffed in response. His mistake, showing up at dawn looking for breakfast and companionship. He had been twiddling his claws as even more snow fell for the umpteenth storm of the winter, and he had known, somehow, that Wren would be awake. And she was right, he could have stayed in with Sergei, drinking coffee and reading the newspaper, or gone home to stare at the TV, instead. He had, in fact, just decided to do the latter when Wren announced that she wanted to "take a walk." Wren never just took a walk.

He and the sleepy-eyed human male had exchanged glances, doing a quick mental paper-rock-scissors. P.B. still wasn't sure if he'd won or lost.

"Stay here. Hold this."

She handed him a plastic stopwatch, and took the small black bag he was holding from him, closing it up. When he would have asked another question, she stood up, stretching her legs out as she did so. The snow coating the sidewalk was soft and slippery, and her boots made a faint crunching noise as she strode forward.

"Valere…"

"Stay there. Run the clock."

He stayed, looking more like his nick-namesake, the polar bear, than he ever had before, surrounded by snowdrifts taller than he was.

"Piece of cake," she muttered, stepping through the slush of the street and up onto the curb on the other side. She was the best Retriever in the area, probably the best Retriever on the entire damned continent. This was easy. This was almost too easy.

The electrical current of the burglar alarm was thicker than an ordinary alarm; the strands were woven with magical current, as well. The owner was a member of the *Cosa Nostradamus,* the magical community, just as she and P.B. were. He knew all the ways that a fellow Talent could break in, and protected against them.

She was the best. She could do this in her sleep.

Closing her eyes, Wren let the cold night air seep into her skin, feeling the contrast between the cold and the warmth of current inside her. A deep well, where neon-flashed snakes slithered and coiled around each other, sparking in anticipation as she slid into a light fugue state.

"Easy. Easy…"

She wasn't sure who she was talking to: the live current within her, the alarm in front of her, or herself. Maybe all three. They all listened; her breathing slowed, her hand steadied, the current inside her slipped along the pattern she created, and the two types of current touched, her own magic slipping into the shopkeeper's system and convincing it that she was an extension of the system, an accepted guest, not an intruder.

It was simple, but it sure as hell wasn't easy. Even in the cold air, Wren felt sweat drip under the wool cap, down the side of her face. Using current burned a huge amount of calories.

In contrast, the door really was easy: a turn and a bump, and the lock gave way.

Inside the store, the air was thick and dark. A few faint red lights indicated emergency exits, while a white glow illuminated the glass cases behind the wooden counter. The locket was in one of those cases.

Wren was a Retriever; she was hired to take items belonging to her client, and nothing more. Even on a training run like this, you kept discipline. But there were so many pretties sparkling there, abandoned by their owners, just waiting to find new homes….

Watch it, she thought sternly. *That's how people end up with Bad Things following them home.*

Selecting one thin thread of current, she shaped it with a picture of the locket, and released it like a butterfly into the store.

The current was blue and yellow, like a butterfly itself, and the strength of her visual made it move like one as well, flittering from one glass case to another before finally alighting on one in the far corner.

"Gotcha" she whispered. The butterfly broke into tiny sparkles, fading into the air as Wren approached the case. Keeping her tool bag balanced on her leg—you never, ever put your kit down on the floor, for fear of leaving a trace—she withdrew the thin pick P.B. had been looking at earlier and made short work of the sliding lock.

She picked the locket up off the small acrylic stand without touching anything else, and slipped it into her pocket.

And that was that.

"Seven minutes thirty-two seconds," P.B. said, checking the stopwatch as she came back across the street, having carefully closed the door behind her, and allowed the alarm system to reconnect without a tremor.

Wren shook her head in disgust. "That's just…sad."

"You get distracted in there?"

"No. Okay, a little. But not more than ten seconds' worth. Simple job, no problems, I should have been in and out in six minutes, tops. Damn."

"Yeah, obviously you're getting old and sloppy, and the hot new Talent's gonna come up behind you and take all your jobs." He handed her the stopwatch and dusted snow off his backside. "Watching you train is about as exciting as watching snow fall. I expected at least something blowing up. Can we grab breakfast, now?"

Wren looked up at the sky, as though expecting to see the sun—or an answer of sorts—appear from behind the clouds.

"Valere?" He looked up, as well, then up at her face.

"Something's building. And we're not even close to being ready."

The demon shrugged. "One thing I've learned? Nobody's ever ready, cause what happens is either worse or better than what we were expecting, and never exactly what we planned for."

She reached into her pocket and touched the locket again. The cool metal filled her with a sense of calm, but no voice came out of her memory to advise her. "So what do you do?"

P.B. scratched his muzzle, and shrugged again. "Burn that bridge when you get to it?"

Wren laughed, the way he meant her to. She let the locket fall back into the depths of her pocket, and she pulled her gloves back on. "Right. Let's go make Sergei make us pancakes."

five

The minor adrenaline rush of her training run had worn off completely by the time lunch came around, and Wren was struggling with the desire to chew her leg off, if it would give her a way to escape.

She had once joked with Sergei about the terrifying prospect of an organized *Cosa*. Sitting in the now overly familiar meeting room, she had proof to back up her own incredulous laughter at the joke; a week of discussions and negotiations and yelling at each other, and maybe an hour's worth of progress had been made. If that.

She looked around now, taking in the room the way she might a Retrieval site, half out of boredom, half just to keep in the habit. The remains of a platter of sandwiches and flaccid pickles, the notepads and pens, paper coffee cups and soda cans littering the table. The scene could have been any conference room anywhere, in any office. Or maybe, she thought, the better analogy was a teacher's staff room. Less tech, more opinions.

And a considerably wider range of species than in your average boardroom *or* school.

The Truce Board—a boring but practical name someone had come up with—now officially met in an empty apartment of a building belonging to one of the Council members. Wren had scoped the place out when she came in, the never-ending habit of a renter in Manhattan, and decided that—even with the upgraded facilities and parquet flooring, she'd rather keep her own place. But the apartment had a large main room that, when filled with a long table and a bunch of faux leather padded folding chairs, could hold everyone who was required to be there. And the kitchen had not one but two coffee machines running. She approved.

Turning her head slightly to the left, she let her gaze touch on the players: the four lonejack representatives, Jordan and another Council member she didn't know, and four fatae: Beyl the griffin, a piskie named Einnie, a solid, square-faced trauco with the unlikely name of Reynaldi, and a strange, frail, lovely young woman dressed in veils, whose back was hollow like a dead tree. She wasn't introduced, and nobody seemed to pay much heed to her, which made Wren pay careful attention to everything she did.

Between the delegates and the advisors each of them had brought along, like reluctant seconds to a mob-scene duel, it was controlled chaos. The voices were loud, but involved, not angry, and there were more arms waving in emphasis than she'd thought could be attached to the number of bodies in the room. Everyone had an opinion about how to implement the Patrols, and enforce the Truce, and nobody wanted to hear anyone else's points or rebuttals, and at least once the trauco threatened one of the older Council gentlemen with bodily harm for the crime of being—direct quote—a dweeb.

Bored. Yes. She was very, very bored. And there wasn't anything worth stealing here, even for the practice value. The owner had made damn sure of that before offering it up.

Wren leaned back in her chair, feeling it creak dangerously as she balanced on two legs. "Looks like everything's under control, here."

The gnome sitting next to her—Beyl's assistant—snorted, sounding enough like P.B. that Wren did a double take at it. Demon were a created breed: was it possible that there were gnome bloodlines involved? The height was close…

And when she started contemplating the genetic makeup of the fatae breeds, it was time and past for her to get the hell out of there. Three hours of waiting around for someone to say something she could contribute to, and all she'd gotten was a bad case of numb-butt. Her time was worth more than this.

Wren put the chair back on all fours and got up, moving through the bodies until she got to the one she needed to speak to.

"And if you think that we're going to allow—"

"Bart."

"I'm busy here, Valere." The NYC representative was

brusque even when he was in a good mood, which he decidedly was not, right now.

"Yeah, I can see that. I can also see you guys have got everything under control, and I hate fiddling my thumbs. When you need me, call."

"Or you'll wipe yourself out of my line of sight anyway?" he asked.

Ooops. Nailed.

"Go," he said in dismissal, and went back into his argument without missing a beat. He hadn't even turned his head to look at her.

Wren slipped out of the room without anyone noting her pass by, without having to actively invoke her no-see-me. Boredom apparently brought it forward naturally. That explained why she'd never gotten caught when she cut English class, back in junior high. Odd, that she'd never made the connection before. Then again, she wasn't often bored, either. She—and Sergei—spent much of their waking time ensuring that.

The kitchen was busy—someone was refilling one coffee machine, so there was a line at the other. Wren didn't even bother to queue up, but grabbed her coat and hat from the indecently large hall closet, and went down the elevator and out of the building into the cold morning air.

She found a working pay phone on the corner, and—after asking someone passing on the street what time it was—placed a quick call.

You've reached my cell. Try to speak clearly and repeat your number twice.

"Me. It's a little before two, and I'm fleeing the scene of the crime for some window shopping. If you can get away, I'll meet you at Rock Center, at the rink."

She hung up the phone, and checked how much cash she had in her wallet.

"'Tis the season to overindulge and splurge," she said with satisfaction, and stepped off the curb to catch a cab discharging a fare.

Forty minutes and two stores later, she found her partner leaning against the window of one of the high-end stores that flanked the skating rink at Rockefeller Center. Sergei was watching the crowds of warmly dressed tourists milling about, splitting their attention between the garishly lit tree and the skaters frolicking on the rink directly below.

She tucked the small shopping bag into her shoulder bag, and came up alongside him.

"Hey. Been here long?"

He turned to smile down at her. "Not much, no. I picked up your message and escaped as quickly as I could. Gallery's been a madhouse this morning. Everyone's doing their usual 'oh dear god it's the holiday I must buy something that shows I spent a lot' dash."

"You are a bad and cynical man."

"I am not. I'm observant. The people who love art, the ones who are buying for someone who loves art, they did their shopping months ago, most of them. It's already been bought and paid for, and is waiting on delivery. These people…" He shook his head.

She flushed, guiltily, at her own last-minute purchase. "Are they at least buying?"

"Enough to pay to stay open," he said. "And it's good training for Lowell. It makes him happy to help them load up their credit cards with debt. So why did you want to meet here? I thought you hated crowds. No, I *know* you hate crowds."

She brushed away his comments with an air wave of her hand. "This is different. It's the Tree! Plus, it's too cold to stay out here for long. Just enough to soak it in, and then we can go get hot chocolate."

Sergei didn't understand the appeal of standing in the cold and staring up at a garishly lit, oversized tree that definitely had looked better standing in its original field, covered with bird shit and squirrel nests, but then, he didn't have much holiday spirit at the best of times. Or so he'd been told. Christmas was midnight mass, and presents exchanged in the morning, and then you went back to work. But Wren's childhood, as far as he'd been able to determine, had been about scrimping and saving and making festive with whatever they had. He'd rather get frostbite than cut into her enjoyment of the season, as much as she let herself indulge in. Especially this year.

"I wonder how many volts it takes to run those lights," she said now, her eyes dangerously dreamy. "Do you think Christmas lights have a different flavor than regular lights?"

"What, you never shorted out your own Christmas tree, as a teenager?"

"My mother would have *killed* me," she said. "Anyway,

we usually had one of those tabletop dealies. Night-lights used more voltage than those."

She stared up at the tree, and he could almost see the moment she went away from him, sliding into what she called the fugue state, where she could draw most easily on the core of current within her. As best he could understand, it was a little like meditation, and a little like orgasm, and the smile on her face made him more than a little nervous.

"Wren, I really don't want to be trapped inside a crowd of thousands of pissed-off tourists a week before Christmas, when you put the Rockefeller Center Christmas Tree out of commission."

"Spoilsport." But she shook the fugue off, and came back to him. "Come on. Buy me a massive hot chocolate. No, a peppermint mocha. Two shots. With extra whipped cream, and one of those cookie straws."

"Because a sugar high combined with a caffeine rush is just so what you need right now," he grumbled, but slid his arm into hers, and escorted her away from the crowd, down the stairs into the lower level of Rock Center.

It was a maze down there, filled with hallways and stores and subway entrances, but they both knew where they were headed: there was a food court off to one side, with a Starbucks. The line was as long as expected, so Wren went to find them a table while Sergei stood to place their order. One tall tea, one grande peppermint mocha with extra whipped cream. They weren't serving those crunchy cookie-straws here, so he grabbed her a chocolate-dipped biscotti instead. It wasn't the same, but it was the thought that counted. Plus the chocolate-dipped part.

"Ooo, Santa," she joked when he sat down at the little table next to her, and handed her the drink and the biscuit. "I guess I've been very, very good this year, huh?"

He merely smiled, thinking of the gift already wrapped and hidden in her apartment—she might search his place, but never think to look in her own space. He hoped. They'd agreed, early-on in their partnership, that one gift each for Christmas was a reasonable limit. But this year he'd gone on a little splurge, as she would say. This year was special: being *partners* as well as partners required something... more. Difficult as it was to buy presents for a woman who didn't wear much jewelry, couldn't use personal electronics, and had a deep-set habit of stealing whatever she liked, he thought he'd done well.

"I take it that the meeting this morning did not require your taking minutes?"

"Hah." She sipped at the mocha, making a happy little contented noise as it hit her taste buds. "They're going along gangbusters, yowling and screaming and waving arms and generally accomplishing absolutely nothing."

Sergei's experience with meetings was more along the lines of small groups being told what to do; he almost wished that he had been able to sit in on this one, simply to see how the *Cosa* did it. Then again, considering the *Cosa* members he already knew, he suspected that her description was, if anything, underplaying the chaos.

"In the end, though...?"

"Oh, in the end, they'll hammer the details out. Bart and Beyl won't let anyone out of the door until they do. But they didn't need me there to get to that point. And, honestly? Being in the room with that many people was starting to make me itch. Nobody had a damn thing worth lifting except Ayexi's wallet, and if I asked him he'd just hand it over to me. What's the fun in that?"

Sergei drank his tea rather than answer. While he understood and appreciated his partner's need to keep her hand in, as it were, he sometimes understood her mentor's reported exasperation with her light-fingered tendencies. For Wren, Retrieval wasn't just something she did—it was what she *was*. And if she wasn't either working on a job, or recovering from a job, she was wondering where the next job was going to be. Time to find something for her to do.

"At the risk of being rude, I gotta go pee." She grinned at the expression on his face. "Sorry—I have to use the facilities to relieve my dainty female form, how's that?"

"Worse," he said.

"Don't drink the last of my mocha," she warned, and grabbed the last chunk of the biscotti to nibble on as she walked, as though not willing to trust him with it while she was gone. It was amazing, the calories she managed to put away. Current burned a lot of energy, even in passive mode, but she used to at least moderate her intake. The past few months…

The past few months she's been using current almost continuously, between the Cosa and the jobs, and the general chaos…and you. She didn't touch him with current every time they had sex, but often enough that he was starting to feel the cumulative effect internally—and he knew that it had to be draining her, too. He tried not to ask for a jolt, but it was like putting a chocoholic into a fudge factory and handing them one of those little plastic knives; you were just asking for something to snap.

Thankfully, Wren was well trained; he had never met Neezer, but even by the time Wren was a teenager, she had some of the best emotional and physical control he had ever seen, and her mental control—as befitted an almost-Pure Talent—was even more developed. As she often said, current was power, and skill was all about controlling that power.

And yes, he admitted, he got off on that, too. Like a high-level sports car, knowing that there was so much horsepower under the attractive frame. You didn't have to be in the driver's seat to appreciate the surge of speed.

He thought about getting her another biscotti, but to do so he'd have to get up and stand in line, and then they'd lose the table to one of the groups cruising the food court, looking for an empty space. He watched a few of them; people-watching was something he didn't do very often, but it was always interesting. His gaze moved past the gaggle of teenaged girls exclaiming over something one of them had bought, paused on two overbulked teenage males long enough to rate them not a threat, then lingered for an enjoyable moment on an attractive woman with skin the color of Wren's mocha, wearing a bright red shirt and skirt. She was moving with the long stride of someone who only had so long to do something before she had to be back upstairs in her office, and he felt a moment's smug superiority before something else snagged his attention.

A single bright green sheet, tucked under a plate on the now-empty table next to him. He didn't know why it attracted his attention, but he knew better than to ignore that kind of mental hijacking. As nonchalantly as he could, Sergei leaned forward and snagged it from the abandoned tray.

> *Tired of coming home to unwanted visitations? Concerned about the infestation of your building? Your neighborhood? Call us. We can clean things up for you.*

The company was Midtown Pest Control Services, and there were two phone numbers and a Web site listed at the bottom of the page. A plain sheet, black type against the green paper: impossible *not* to read, once your eye found it.

Scanning the food court, aware now, Sergei could see half a dozen of the lime-green sheets and a packet more of them on one counter, in a plastic dispenser. *Son of a…*

He crumpled the sheet in his fist, and tossed it into the nearest trash can, taking grim satisfaction at making the shot. Could he grab all the sheets and the dispenser, too, before Wren got back? Or would she come back and see him, and see the ads, and make everything worse?

He decided to risk it. If this was an innocent bug-disposal company, he'd feel guilty later. But the wording they used was exactly the same as the ads Wren had gotten, the ads the vigilantes used to spread their "services" back when this all began. And that was a coincidence he wasn't willing to ignore. Not if they were advertising again, soliciting "business." Recruiting new bigots to the cause. Building their troops against the coming confrontation. Or even just spreading their own brand of intolerance and filth into a city that already had enough, thanks.

Sergei wasn't unaware of the irony; he had once been deeply uncomfortable in the presence of any fatae, even before he knew how many were out there, passing as human. Even now, the thought of them occasionally made his skin crawl in a way he didn't care to investigate. But these people… They were targeting not only the fatae, but anything magical.

And that included Wren.

Keeping one eye on their table, with the coats draped over chairs to indicate it was still in use, Sergei snagged four of the sheets and shredded them methodically into strips before dumping them in the trash can. He moved back to the table just in time to prevent three office workers from sitting down, despite the coats, and glared at them until they backed away.

There probably wasn't any way to get the pile of flyers off that counter, without attracting someone's—

"Sergei. What a surprise."

All thoughts of the flyers got tucked away for later, as he turned to face the speaker.

Andre Felhim, dapper as ever in a charcoal-gray suit and a burgundy tie that emphasized the dark mahogany of his skin. He was followed a step behind by a taller blond-haired, pale-skinned man: Poul Jorgenmunder, his second-in-command.

Sergei used to stand just that way, at Andre's elbow. For about two years, before they started to disagree on almost everything. He didn't envy Poul his spot, although Poul was clearly jealous of Sergei's history with Andre.

Relationships were the most confusing of all human inventions. That was a quote from somewhere, but Sergei couldn't remember who had said it.

"Andre." He didn't acknowledge the other man. It was petty, but satisfying.

The two men had laminated ID tags around their necks, with Visitor stamped on them in large red letters. That explained what they were doing here, then, although Sergei wondered what company in this complex had cause to call on the Silence. He hoped it wasn't NBC, although their fall lineup had certainly been a crime of inhuman proportions….

"Here alone? How…unusual for you, these days." Poul looked around, obviously looking for something. "No, no obvious freaks here, unless they're hiding."

Lonejacks weren't the only ones who knew how to control their emotions. Poul's baiting was too obvious; what was he really trying to get at?

"I received your letter. And your e-mail," Andre said quietly, ignoring Jorgenmunder.

"And filed them appropriately, since you declined to respond?"

His former boss spread tapered, manicured fingers in an openhanded gesture. "I wish that you would reconsider…"

"You know I can't. And won't." They had been over this ground in previous meetings, before he sent the letter.

That letter had merely been a formal breaking of their contract, the devil's bargain that had tied Wren to the Silence, in return for a monthly retainer. Effective next month, January 1, the deal was null and void. *If* he could get Andre to sign off on it.

Sergei went on, quoting the letter almost verbatim. "The situation has changed on both sides, making the agreement impossible. If you try to fight it—"

"The Silence will not contest your right to end the agreement," Andre said. He looked older, more tired than even the last time Sergei had seen him. The difference between this man and the man who had recruited him out of college, trained him, was striking; far more than could be accounted for simply by the passing of years. "I made the offer in good faith and yet, as you rightly pointed out, we have not followed suit."

The weight of guilt settled again on Sergei's shoulders. It wasn't Andre's fault, entirely. He, Sergei, should never have gotten Wren tied up with them, no matter how much they thought they had needed the Silence's help.

Once he had called himself an Operative with pride. Even when he left, it was burnout from the cost of the job, not dissatisfaction with what they did. Now… Now, he was afraid that the Silence was the greater threat than the Council; their motives less clear, their end purposes more shadowed. The organization he had once sworn his life to no longer existed; he was unsure what stood in its place, now.

He did know that he would mortgage the gallery rather than allow Wren to take any more of their money, and risk her life for their ends.

"I really don't have anything more to say to you," he said to the older man. "Andre, I'm sorry, I have to go."

"Afraid someone will see you talking to us?" Poul asked, still looking for a place to push the verbal needle.

"No," Sergei said, turning to look at him full-on for the first time. "You merely bore me."

Sergei picked up the coats off the chair, snagged Wren's mocha in his free hand, and walked away. With perfect timing, he intercepted Wren at the hallway leading from the food court to the bathrooms.

"Hey," she said, surprised. "Sorry, there was a line like you wouldn't believe… You have to get back to the gallery?"

He grabbed at the excuse, which had the virtue of not being a lie. "Yes, I'm sorry. If I'd time I'd take you out for lunch, but…"

"S'okay, I'm not hungry, anyway. I've got some more errands to run, as long as I'm in midtown. And then I suppose I should go back and see if our fearless leaders have a new assignment for me, or if they're still wrangling over how to arrange the patrols." She rolled her eyes, and he chuckled: he had more faith in the *Cosa* than most of the *Cosa* did.

"Maybe I'll get you a new job."

"That would be nice. Something—"

"Without hellhounds. Yes, I remember."

She laughed. "Catch you later tonight?"

"Absolutely. I'll pick up dinner on my way home."

He helped her into her coat, gave her the mocha and kissed her, lingering a little more than he usually did, in public.

"Stay safe, Zhenchenka."

"They won't even see me going," she replied, and he smiled; it was what she used to say, when he sent her off on a job, back in their early days.

When had she stopped saying that? He didn't remember. Probably around the time he stopped sending her off personally, every job. He thought he might start doing that, again.

"Stay safe," he said again. But she had disappeared into the crowd, and even he couldn't find her.

Wren hadn't actually gone anywhere, using the crowd to backtrack to the food court. From there, she watched two men sitting at a table, one of them drinking a coffee, the other flicking an unlit cigarillo between elegant dark-skinned fingers. She had seen that restless motion before; Sergei, with his thin-rolled cigarettes. She had never seen him actually light one, never known him to inhale anything other than the aroma of a good wine. But he would roll a cigarette between his fingers like a magician with a coin, whenever he was deep in thought. Or nervous.

Now she knew where he had learned it.

"Idiot man." If she'd come back and surprised the three

of them together, she would have known by Sergei's reaction what was up, end of story. He could pull the poker face only so far on her, these days. She thought, anyway. But the way he rushed her off...

It didn't matter. Much. Keeping her and his Excellency Andre Felhim far apart was an excellent idea, no matter the circumstances. Someday she really was going to forget what manners Neezer had taught her, and give that arrogant, supercilious know-little a good shocking-to.

So. Sergei probably had the very best of intentions. *Let it go, Valere.* She really did have errands to run, of a sort, and this was as good a place as any to do them.

She found a quiet place to sit, on the edge of an indoor planter, with weird frondy things that almost hid her from sight. Closing her eyes and letting the clatter around her fade into white noise, she grounded and centered, reached inside and stroked one thin snake of current inside her. Prepared, she sent out a flurry of pings, directed mental knocks, to half a dozen Talent that she knew worked or lived in the immediate area.

Then she sat back to wait. It took exactly six and a half minutes for the first response to come in.

Wren lifted the lid of her gingerbread latte and inhaled the aroma as though it were oxygen, and she hyperventilating.

"Are you going to drink that, or have sex with it?"

"I can't do both?"

There were three of them around the small, round table: Wren, in jeans and sweater dressed for warmth and comfort, an older man with a smooth-shaven head and dark blue eyes, wearing a white shirt over dark cords, and a woman with a thick black ponytail setting off her red sweaterdress. She looked like a college student compared to their crisp professionalism.

The man watched while she took a deep sip, tracking the liquid as it slid down her throat.

"You must be a hell of a co—"

"Michael!" The woman in the dress slapped his arm before he could finish the thought.

Michael's eyes twinkled innocently, and Wren managed to swallow before laughing.

"Seriously," he went on. "You called. We're here. What do you want from us?"

Wren put her drink down on the table, needing to take a moment to collect her thoughts. The last time she had tried to canvass for information, half the *Cosa* had crossed the street rather than talk to her, and the ones who couldn't get away balked at every question. Now, all she had to do was ping a Talent, and they showed up. *And* paid for the coffee. All it took was a rumor that you were responsible for lifting the darkness of the summer heat wave, even if nobody was quite sure what the darkness had been or how it ended; of being the lonejack who faced down the Council; of being...all things she wished she'd never become. But today, it was useful. So she'd use it.

"Is this about the meetings they've been having?"

"What have you heard about it?" Michael was a lonejack and Seta was Council, but neither of them worked with their Talent: he was a lawyer, she taught history at a charter school in midtown. They were about as close as you could get to the *Cosa's* middle class, if such a thing existed.

"Not much." Michael took a sip of his coffee. "That there were meetings going on, high-level stuff, the Council coming down among the unwashed masses, more fatae seen in town than anyone can remember... Is it true, that someone's hunting them?"

Seta sighed. "You are so painfully out of touch.... Didn't you hear about the Moot Massacre?"

Wren blinked. All right, she had missed that particular nickname for the attack....

"I figured it had been exaggerated, or something." Michael didn't seem too abashed.

"Lonejacks," Wren said with a long-suffering sigh. "They just don't *care*."

"Damn straight," Michael agreed.

"Well, you have to care, now," she said, suddenly serious. "Because it's true, all of it. True and serious and in your face, right here, right now."

Wren suddenly felt a tingle on the back of her neck, as though someone was staring at her. But when she glanced casually around the Starbucks, everyone seemed intent on their own business. She looked out the glass window, thinking it might have come from out there. For once, there was no snow actively falling, but the streets were slushy, and the curbs and sidewalks were still coated with a dingy gray-white mix of slush and ice that caused pedestrians to walk with particular care or risk going down on their backsides. Preoccupied with staying upright, none of them were looking in at her.

Wren shook her head, telling herself that it was probably just someone's fur coat against the gray of sky and street that had flickered in the corner of her eye.

Whatever it was, it was gone now.

"Yo, you with us?" Michael asked, peering at her intently. "You zoned for a moment."

"Did you…" She shook her head, dropping the unasked question. "Yeah. I'm here. So, now you know the deal. My question is—would you join a patrol if they were organized, all three groups together? Keep an eye on things, report back, be willing to be part of a multipronged, *organized* approach to what's going down?"

Michael nodded once, firmly, without having to consider the question very long.

Wren added, because she had to know: "Even if the Council voted against it?"

Seta looked like she'd just felt the rough brick of a wall come up against her back, hard. "Voted…" She sighed, and stared down into her cup. "Look, if the Council says no, we—Council members—jump no. You *know* that. But if they don't say anything specifically that is shaped like a no and sounds like a no and smells like a no…"

"Then it's not actually a no."

"Not actually, no."

Wren nodded. It wasn't good enough, but it was the best she was going to get. And there were others she needed to meet with before she could call it a day. No rest for the weary…

six

Sergei walked into the main room and came to a full stop, staring at the disaster that greeted him. "Merry Christmas?"

Wren made a face, glaring at the pile of cards she still had to sign, stamp, and mail out. She'd conned Sergei into printing up her address lists on his computer at the office the month before, so all she had to do was peel off the labels and stick them on. Her mother would be horrified— "holiday cards should always be handwritten, Genevieve"—but she figured the Miss Manners points she'd lose she'd make up in ego-points with her fellow lonejacks, who would know that she'd somehow managed to use not only a computer, but a printer, as well.

That time-saver hadn't managed to keep her piles of envelopes, cards, and colored pens in any semblance of order, however. Nor had it gotten her ass in gear any earlier, despite everything being ready and waiting for weeks now.

In her own defense, she *had* been a little busy. And, damn. Tea. The urge to make it arrived, a little late.

Sergei was going to have to make his own this time.

Sergei closed the door, unwound the muffler from his neck, took off his coat, and hung them both in the closet. The snow was falling again outside, based on the dampness of his shoulders and hair. Normally snow on Christmas Eve would be a thing to delight in. This year, it was just cause for sighing and shrugging. The weatherfolk were reporting a record seven feet of the cold stuff so far for the winter, coming up on the record from 2001, and there were still two months of the season to go.

She'd gotten too used to Sergei being here, maybe, for the old early warning tea-urge to kick in.

Wren had all the curtains drawn across the windows, and in the corner, instead of a tree, there was a metal candelabra in the shape of a Christmas tree with thirteen green candles burning. She saw her partner studying it, and knew that he was seeing Lee's work in the turn of the metal branches, and the solid but somehow delicate design of the base. It hurt, still, to look at it, but it was a good kind of a hurt, now. It was a remembering kind of a hurt, as well as a missing hurt.

For a borderline klepto, she didn't have many belongings—she'd take something she liked, and then discard it when she got bored—but this, and the fabric painting Shin had sent her all the way from Japan, were more than things. They were *gifts*.

She looked up at her partner, now, indicating the piles

of holiday cards in front of her. "Why do I send these things out, anyway?"

"I have no idea."

If you sent them out early, they were an unwelcome reminder that the holidays were coming and you still had too many things to do. If they arrived during the holidays, they were just tossed with the rest of the cards in some sort of display that just meant another thing to clean up after. And if you sent them too late, you looked like a slacker. You just couldn't win. But this year at least it gave her hands something to do, and occupied a portion of her brain so that she wasn't always circling around back to the thing she couldn't actually do anything about.

Sergei slipped off his shoes and sat down on the floor next to her, wincing as his expensive slacks came into contact with the floor. "Been cleaning again, have you?"

Wren sniffed, smelling the wood oil she had used on the floor. "I couldn't sleep," she said. "And it was on my to-do list."

"You've never had a to-do list in your entire life." She wrote things down, but for memory-jogs and references, not to keep things orderly or organized.

"In my head. My head is stuffed full of to-do lists." A whole list of things to keep her hands busy. "Here," and she pushed a small pile of invites across the floor to him. "As long as you're here, be useful and stuff these in the envelopes."

He obligingly started placing the cards inside the addressed envelopes, and tabbed the stamps on them without being asked.

"I miss licking stamps."

She shook her head; her hair, still wet from the shower she had taken once the bathroom was spotless, slid pleasantly on the back of her neck. She had taken extra care with her appearance tonight: a long velvet skirt and sleeveless top in a deep purple the exact shade of shadows. She had even used eyeliner to give herself what she thought was a slightly exotic look. But her hair was merely combed through and left to dry by itself. There was only so much fuss she was willing to go through, even for Sergei. "You're a sick, sick man."

"True. But I brought dinner, so I'm forgiven."

She had heard him messing about in the kitchen just after he entered the apartment, even before he took his coat off. "Yeah? And do we have a Christmas goose resting in the oven?"

She looked up at him again as she said it, and did a classic double take at the crestfallen look of "surprise ruined" on his face.

"A goose?" She did not squeal—she *never* squealed—but the noise was apparently enough to restore some of Sergei's self-satisfaction, even as she launched herself onto him in an exuberant hug. "Goose!"

The world, apparently, could go to hell in a snow-covered hand basket, so long as one had goose for dinner.

"I invited some people over for dessert, later," she said, letting him up after appropriate thanks had been offered and accepted.

"Oh?" They had never actually spent Christmas Eve together before, so he couldn't know if this was normal or not.

"Well, Bonnie. And P.B."

"You had to actually invite him? I expected him to appear the moment the refrigerator door was opened."

"Hush. Yes, for dessert. Also a couple of Bonnie's friends, a bunch of PUPs"—the rather grandiosely named Private Unaffiliated Paranormal Investigators—"and P.B. said he would bring some 'cousins' he wanted me to meet."

"So this is more of a working get-together, then."

Wren twisted her mouth as though tasting something sour. "I like Bonnie, and she is a neighbor. And it's never a bad thing to be on good terms with PUPs. And although most of the fatae don't seem to have any religion as such, I have yet to meet one who didn't love sweets."

"Then I'd best get dinner warmed up, or we might not have a chance to finish before the sugar-craving hordes descend." He leaned forward to kiss her again, and then got up off the floor, more slowly than he'd sat down.

"I'm getting too old for this," he said, stretching out his back. "Would you mind terribly actually buying some comfortable chairs, at some point?"

A year ago, he would have insisted that they go to his apartment, or just said nothing and kept his discomfort to himself, aware of how touchy Wren could be about her personal space. She supposed that this was progress, that he felt comfortable enough to make suggestions—and that he was phrasing it so delicately.

"I had been thinking about getting a few beanbag chairs—they're all popular again, you know?"

Sergei just groaned and went off to the kitchenette, her laughter following him.

She had just finished off the last of the cards when a series of mouthwatering smells tickled her nose and made her salivate. She gathered up the cards and went in search of her dinner.

"Where's that table you bought?" he asked as she poked her nose into the kitchenette.

"Office." She had bought it in order to have a place to meet with a client, but had decided after that it didn't fit in the main room.

"Get it. I'm not eating Christmas dinner either at the counter, or on the floor."

Grinning, she went in search of the table and chairs. She added a white cotton tablecloth, draping it over the inexpensive wood, then stood back to admire the effect.

"Much better."

Somewhere, she was pretty sure that she had napkins, too....

Going back into the office, she pulled open the dresser drawers and rummaged through the fabrics stored there, coming up—much to her surprise—with a set of dark burgundy napkins, and a narrow runner to match. She couldn't remember buying those, or stealing them....

"Mother," she said with a sigh, taking them out and closing the drawer with her hip. Someday, her mother would accept the fact that her only daughter had all the social graces and homemaking skills of a stick. Until then, these sort of secreted-away "gifts" would continue.

Still, she was using these. So maybe there was hope for her yet.

They had barely cleared the dishes when a white form appeared at the kitchen window, black nose pressed to the glass like an urchin in a Charles Dickens novel. Then he scratched on the glass with his claws, and Wren amended that reference to something out of a Stephen King novel.

"Should I let the little moocher in?" her partner asked.

"Might as well, or he'll freeze there, and I won't get rid of him until Spring."

Sergei pushed up the window, and P.B. came in, followed by a form draped in a heavy dark cloth. They shook the snow off themselves, letting it fall to the tile floor, and then P.B. helped his companion out of the cloak, revealing not one but two fatae.

"Oh!"

Wren couldn't help it; the sound escaped her without thought. Sergei muttered something in Russian that was probably turning the air blue, but she didn't have time to slip into fugue state and check.

The first fatae was delicate as a reed, with skin like mother-of-pearl and a face that could have launched a thousand alien sighting reports. And on that pearlized skin, from oversized eye to pointed chin, was a clear and unmistakable bruise in the shape of a human handprint. The bruise was, undoubtedly, what had caused Sergei to swear—the fatae itself caused Wren's exclamation. She quickly averted her eyes, as much to give it privacy as for her own recovery.

The second fatae was a gnome—short and sturdy, only the leathery gray skin set it apart, at first glance, from a slightly overweight toddler. It removed the watch cap from its skull, and ran its knobby fingers through the coarse gray hair, trying without luck to fluff it up.

"Ma'am," he said, bowing to Wren, cap held at his waist. "Many thanks for your invite. I'm far from my family and welcome the chance to not be alone on Christmas Eve."

All right, so much for my assumption that the fatae don't celebrate Christmas…

"You're quite welcome. Please, join us—P.B.!" Her voice sharpened slightly. "Stop shaking your fur! Go get a towel, if you need one. Not like you stand on ceremony around here."

By now she had her emotions under control, and was able to turn and meet the fairy, as well.

"And welcome, as well, to our home."

The fairy inclined its head, as regal as a swan, and those huge eyes blinked once, and then looked around itself in fascination. The fairies were one of the oldest, purest breeds, and now that she had experienced her delight in encountering one, the thought of someone—a human—lifting a hand to one outraged her at the deepest level of her core. If there was any breed that ought to be sacrosanct, a hill-fairy was it.

P.B came back with a towel, rubbing it briskly over his fur, bringing the moment back into the realms of the ordinary. "So, Valere, where's the chocolate?"

"Oh, did I say there would be chocolate?" she asked him innocently, making a moue of surprise.

He didn't even bother to respond to that, but opened the fridge and started poking around.

"There are too many bodies in this kitchen," she announced. "Sergei, could you please show our guests to the living room," *and bring in some chairs* she suggested mentally, already running through the seating available. As much as she loved her apartment, right now she would have traded it for Sergei's to-die-for sofas, and the gourmet kitchen, and…

"Valere." She jumped, looking down at her friend, who was staring at her with unaccustomed gentleness. "They're here for *you*, not fancy surroundings or snooty service. Cookies and milk are the traditional gifting, and half the time they're left on the hearth, anyway. You ever try to eat a soot- or dust-covered cookie? Bleargh."

She laughed, the way he meant her to, and reached over his head to pull down the bakery box from on top of the refrigerator. "There's a platter in the cabinet behind you, on the bottom shelf. Get it for me?"

By the time Bonnie thudded up the stairs to join them, the main room had been turned into a surprisingly comfy gathering space. The one bit of real furniture in the room, an overstuffed armchair, had been taken by Sergei, while the gnome was comfortably ensconced on the small matching footstool Wren had almost forgotten she owned. P.B., Wren and the fatae were sprawled on her dark green velvet quilt, stolen off her bed and folded twice, and surprisingly comfortable. The tray of miniature pastries was on the floor between them, and several glasses in various stages of fullness were scattered among the seats.

"How many of your kind have been reported missing?" the gnome was asking, sipping his cider with surprising delicacy.

Wren got up to answer the knuckled rat-tat-tat at the door, and so missed Sergei's reply. Bonnie came in the moment the door was unlocked, a bottle of spiced wine in hand and a gangly male with straw-red hair and a crooked smile at her heels.

"Hi. Sorry we're late. I couldn't get rid of my folks." She was wearing a black lace sweater over a knee-length black leather skirt and black hiking boots, laced with red and green laces. "Here, a present." She gestured with the bottle. "Alphie couldn't make it. Got stuck on-call tonight, poor bastard. Who's—wow."

Bonnie, like Wren, simply stopped and stared at Aloise. Her companion—more traditionally dressed in dark brown cords and a sweater with a cross-eyed reindeer on it—took the bottle out of her hands before she could drop it, and handed it to Sergei, who carried it off into the kitchen.

"Hi. I'm Bonnie. You're amazing."

Aloise laughed soundlessly, and her eyes sparkled. Wren didn't know if all fairies were silent, if Aloise was unusual or—God forbid—the attack on her had rendered her voiceless—but she seemed perfectly able to communicate without vocal cords. She seemed to find Bonnie just as fascinating.

"You already know P.B.," Wren said, making the introductions around. "And Sergei, who absconded with the wine. This is Aloise, and Gorry."

"I'm Nick," the redhead said, reaching around the still-fay-struck Bonnie to shake Gorry's hand. "I'm Bonnie's partner."

"Oh?" Wren started to reconsider the vibes she had been getting from Bonnie.

"Work partner," he clarified. "Although if she'd have me, I'd fall at her feet in an instant."

"You would not," Bonnie said, shaking herself free of Aloise's spell. "You like 'em blond and busty."

"Come on, sit down," Wren said, laughing. "Although you're last to arrive, so you get the nonslouching chairs...."

"Hah. You, girl, need to come furniture shopping. There's stuff at ABC that's absolutely calling your name." She turned to Nick and put one fist on her hip. "Bring up the moose, willya?"

Nick rolled his eyes, but sketched a bow at her command, then looked at Wren. "Where do you want it?"

"Anywhere you think it will fit," Wren said.

Nick nodded, and closed his eyes, his lips moving in a silent cantrip. He opened his surprisingly dark green eyes, and focused on a spot across the room from the easy chair. An instant later, the tingle of current heralded the arrival from Bonnie's apartment downstairs of the moose—a huge, scarred brown leather ottoman that could easily seat two moderate-sized people.

"So why shop?" Wren said to Bonnie. "I'll just borrow your stuff the three times a year I have people over!"

Sergei came back with the opened bottle, and placed it on the table next to the already-opened one, and the bottles of soda.

"You're both puppies?" P.B. asked, reaching across Wren's legs to grab another éclair. "How many of you are there, now?"

"Depends," Nick said, sitting cross-legged next to the demon with depressing ease. Bonnie claimed the moose, while Wren sank less easily down onto the blanket again. "Actual working field agents? About… eleven?" He looked at Bonnie, who nodded. "Another seven people in the office, such as it is, and maybe a dozen who're in training. Probably only half of those'll make it."

"How much work are you getting from Council members?" Wren asked, grabbing another cookie for herself. "We were just talking about the missing lonejacks… have any Council folk disappeared, that you're tracing?"

The two humans looked at each other, as though trying to decide what to say, and then Bonnie took the lead. "Not many, no. But we've had a couple of calls… y'know, there's a whole population pool that's totally unaffiliated? I mean, even more than we are? They're from Council or lonejack families, but they've sort of walked away from the whole thing, don't identify with any particular culture. Even more gypsy than the gypsies. They don't even really consider themselves part of the *Cosa*. Not really."

"And some of them have gone missing?" Sergei leaned forward, his wine glass cupped between his hands as though he were going to warm the wine by his own body heat.

"Yeah. Some. The first instance we know about was before anything started with the Council, by almost a year. But the most recent one was just last week. Her folks came to us, when she didn't come home for the weekend like she'd planned."

Wren looked at Sergei, who had an expression on his face that she really, really didn't like. But when he didn't follow up on the question, she let the conversation roll on to the more pressing gossip about the brand-new Truce, and what everyone thought about it. That, of course, was why she'd invited everyone over in the first place. Letting the conversation move on, Wren let herself fade just enough that nobody would remember that she reported directly back to the Quad. Not that she thought these individuals would care, overmuch—and there wasn't anything she could do about Sergei's presence—but being in the background allowed her to watch the body language, which often told more than words ever would.

The first two bottles of wine were consumed, and another one opened, before the last crumbs of cookies were devoured and the last, somewhat tipsy celebrant was kicked out the door—Wren refused to let P.B. use the fire escape as usual, citing the ice on the rungs as cause.

"Oh God. No wonder I never have people over. It's damned *exhausting*." Wren collapsed into the chair. Flicking a tiny strand of current, she turned the stereo on, and the soothing sounds of something with an alto sax came out of the speakers. The receiver had scorch marks and scratches marring the silver-tone surface, and the plastic dial had warped from current years before, but for some reason it still worked, even when she abused it like that. She'd often wondered if they had a testing lab filled with cranky Talent, putting their equipment through the wringer before letting it into the market. There had been rumors, a friend of Neezer's had told her once, that Detroit did that with their cars, back in the 1960s.

"But at least we know something useful. No, two things. One, that there are more Talent missing than we thought, and two, that no fatae are missing—they're either present and accounted for, or known dead, by known means." She sighed. "The fatae take better care of each other than we do."

"Or they have no concept whatsoever of privacy."

Knowing P.B., Wren was forced to acknowledge the probability of that. No fatae had ever, as far as she knew, displayed any concept of personal space. Not even the ones who didn't have a herd or pack system in place.

"But what does it all mean? That's the real question. We have all this information now. I feel like I'm collecting sticks, but don't know how to build a fire."

"I think the fire's going to light itself," Sergei said. He pulled the ottoman over so that he could sit down near her.

She waited. Either he would tell her what he was thinking, or he wasn't ready to yet. Either way, asking wouldn't do a damn bit of good.

"Those Talent who've gone missing, the ones the PUPs

are investigating? I think they might have been working for the Silence."

Wren closed her eyes, and counted to ten. Then: "Tell me about them."

She could see him, even with her eyes closed; the nose just a shade too sharp, the jawline maybe a bit too square, the hair beginning—all right, well on its way to—silvering at the temples and sides. And his eyes, that odd, inviting pale brown shade that made her not notice the lines and shadows that crept in, long night after long night. His voice painted the picture of who he was; if he were current, he would be a solid steady silver coil, ropey with power but quiet in it, too.

"There's not much I can tell you. You know about the FoCAs, the Talents the Silence hired."

"You told me a little…that they were low-res, mostly. The Silence used them for the jobs that involved out-of-the-ordinary stuff, probably of fatae or old magic origins?"

"Yes, although the Silence didn't know any of that, just the results." They didn't know—until he told them. Part of his deal, to win his freedom, to keep Wren free of their grip. *That worked real well, didn't it?*

He shook that thought off, went on. "Mostly they were kids, same as you were when we met. Bored with their lives, wanting something bigger, more important to do." Like he had been, when Andre recruited him. The Silence specialized in that.

"One of the things Andre let slip, during one of our conversations a while ago, was that some of their operatives have gone missing, too. Talented operatives."

Wren started to say something, then held her words, indicating that he should continue.

"It started almost…no, more than a year ago, now. They just disappeared, didn't report to work. At first, they—Andre—thought that they were caught up in what was going down between the Council and lonejacks, or that they had just gotten bored and backed off, or some normal…

"But it's too much of a coincidence. I dislike coincidences."

"It's slim," she said, opening her eyes and looking, not at him, but at the candles still flickering on Lee's candelabra. She focused, and one by one each tiny flame went out, a thin trail of smoke rising from each wick. "Slim, but you're right, the timing is ugly. You'll find out more?"

"How much am I allowed to give them, in return?"

She did look at him then. "Nothing."

He sighed, but wasn't surprised. "I'll do what I can."

And with that, she stood up, reached down to take his hand in her own, and tugged him to his feet, down the hallway, and into bed. A minute later, he went back down the hall to pick up the coverlet from the floor, shake pastry crumbs off it, and return to the bedroom.

When he came in, she was already naked, pulling something from the dresser drawer. A small something, tied with tasteful silver-and-white wrapping paper, and a single strand of silver ribbon around it.

"Merry Christmas," she said, holding it out to him.

He raised an eyebrow in the way he knew she loved, and

took it from her. It was surprisingly heavy, for a box barely the size of his open palm. Sitting on the side of the bed he merely said, "Look under the bed."

She blinked, and then swung headfirst over the bed, like a five-year-old looking for a friendly bed-monster. All right, a rather grown-up, naked, highly appealing-in-that-position… and she didn't look five years old at all, no.

Chuckling, he carefully undid the wrapping on his present.

"Oh. Wrenlet."

She swung back upright onto the bed, her cheeks flushed with the effort of hanging upside down, her hair mussed and her eyes bright. "You like?"

He held up the figurine, admiring the way the light washed over the harsh cuts and soft curves. "I like. Very much." It was an owl in flight, carved out of reddish-brown pipestone, the wings so well formed that you could almost make out each feather, the head so finely crafted that you could swear that at any moment it would turn sideways to blink those eyes at you.

"There's a gallery in midtown, they were having a display of Native American carvings, and I thought you'd like one. I know you like owls."

"They're called fetishes," he said, closing his fingers around the owl. "And yes, I like this very much."

He placed the figure down gently on the nightstand, and looked at his partner. "And now, yours."

She grinned, and reached over the side of the bed to pull out her gift. "I can't believe…how long has this been here?

Did you…okay, I don't want to think about what that says about my housekeeping skills."

Her gift was considerably larger, and much lighter. Laying the rectangular box across her lap, Wren unwrapped the paper almost as neatly as he had—they were both like that, which pleased him. No anxious tearing into gifts, but instead a slow enjoyment of the process.

"Serg. Da-yum. You went on a splurge, partner."

She ran her fingers over the fabric almost as though she was afraid she might damage it.

"I suspect we both did. Go on, take a look."

She lifted the fabric from the box as gently as she might have handled one of her Retrievals. The hand-painted silk fluttered like butterfly kisses as it rose and then settled in the air rising from the radiator. Shades of purple, red, blue, silver, green, and gold danced and merged, then separated out again.

"All the colors of current," she said softly. "All my current." She had described it to him, over and over again; cyber-snakes and whiplash lighting; trust him to find a way to translate it into silk and shimmer. Into art.

"I think I need to make love to you until neither one of us can breathe, now."

He had no objection to that, at all.

In the last minutes before she did fall asleep, sweat slick on her skin and a pleasant if slightly uh-oh ache in her thighs, Wren listened to Sergei snoring lightly beside her, stared at the faint flickering of the streetlight reflected off snow and onto her ceiling, and counted down the days.

Seven days between Christmas and New Year's. Seven days until the Truce was supposed to take effect. Seven days before they could possibly get the Patrols formed up and running.

Seven days. Seven days for everything to totally fall apart.

Think positive, she told herself, finally closing her eyes and giving in to sleep. *It's entirely possible everything will fall apart on January second, too.*

seven

"Dude! Get over here!"

Sergei swam through the crowd, moving to where the arm was waving wildly at him. He was accustomed to gliding smoothly through crowds, to the point where a long-ago female companion had once accused him of being coated with Teflon, but tonight, he found himself stopped at every turn, to shake hands or clink glasses or receive an exuberant kiss on one or both cheeks, or in one memorable case, square on the lips.

"He likes you," his partner said, her eyes sparkling.

"He's not my type," he said, resisting the urge to scrub at his lips.

"Happy new year!" Their latest accoster had clearly started celebrating early, from the flush on her cheeks. Rosie hugged Wren, then lifted her glass and toasted Sergei, who raised his own glass in return. It wasn't actually New

Year's yet, there being three hours yet to go, but the holiday cheer was in full bloom. He wasn't sure if everyone in the room was a Talent, except for him—surely some of them had to be dates, significant others, spouses, or random wander-ins—but the jukebox had been turned off and the neon lights over the bar were on half power, so clearly the owners were expecting a significant percentage to be shit-faced before the clock stuck midnight.

Sergei had seen firsthand what could happen when Talents got drunk, in Italy over the summer, and that had been two half-trained teenagers. What a bunch of adult, trained Talents, all on edge from the past few weeks—hell, *months*—and sheets to the wind, might do? He didn't want to be around for that, no.

But Wren had promised him that, alcohol and nerves or no, the Manhattan lonejack community had things under control. They might get soused, but there would still be Control. So no rowdy Talent-drunks here tonight. Hope-fully.

And hopefully no last-minute hiccups in the Truce that was set to take effect on the stroke of twelve. Wren had spent the past week wandering from one coffee shop to the next, hitting every single greasy spoon in the city, trying to catch what was being said, and feeding it back to the double-Quad.

He looked around the room one more time, automati-cally noting the nearest emergency exits, just in case, and then let his gaze rest on his partner, animatedly talking to the other Talents at the bar. Wren looked lovely tonight, even more than she had on Christmas Eve. She so rarely had cause to dress up, it was a surprise every time, and he couldn't understand why someone else, someone Talented, hadn't stolen her years ago. Rhinestones glittered along the neckline of her scoop-neck sweater, brilliant against the black wool, and her skirt—short, flirty and gold lamé—should have been eye-catchingly bright, but on her just looked fabulous. If she were a painting, he would have placed her by the door, so that people saw her just as they were leaving, and would stop and stay a while longer.

He didn't think she would take that quite as the compliment he meant it to be, so kept the thought to himself.

They were down in the East Village, in a noisy, garish local bar that had surprisingly decent beer on tap, mediocre booze at top-shelf prices, and bartenders who knew their shit. Sergei approved. Not a place he would ever go to on his own—his taste ran more to good wine and quiet chatter—but tonight, for this one night, it was kind of... Fun.

Rosie grabbed one of the bartenders and gestured in some obscure sign language that all three of them needed refills. Beer for Wren, bourbon for him, some strange blue fizzing—yes, it was fizzing—drink for Rosie.

"Hell of a year, huh?" she said, after downing half the fizzy stuff in one long swallow.

"You could say that," Wren allowed.

"Dude. I just *did*."

Sergei laughed, helpless in the face of the Talent's drunken indignant response. Rosie wasn't much of a powerhouse in terms of current, but she was one of Wren's best sources of gossip, and entertaining as hell, drunk or sober.

"So, heard you were seen coffee-cozying with some Tall Black and Dapper type last week."

Sergei was suddenly, totally Unamused with Rosie.

Wren, on the other hand, sprouted several new ears. "Really?" She drawled out the word, ending on a rising note of fascinated inquiry.

"That's the talk," Rosie said, gulping down half her fizzing blue thing. "That, and the fact that a certain member of the Troika went missing couple-two months ago, and nobody's talking, and nobody's missing her all that much, either." Rosie blinked up at Wren, fascination in her gaze. "Did you really splatter her guts all over a diner?"

Stephanie, the Representative for Connecticut lonejacks. Stephanie, who had been selling them out to KimAnn's Council.

"It was a joint action. I was only acting in an advisory capacity." Although in this instance, by "advisory" she meant that it had been her hand guiding the joined current of everyone at the table, taking down the rogue lonejack—and wasn't *that* a redundancy—with perhaps a bit more force than was absolutely necessary. But they had all been in accord on the need to act.

"Well, it's gotten some folk all sorts of interested…."

"And upset?" The use of force had been sudden and unsanctioned, mainly because the lonejacks had never thought about the need to have a sanctioning process before.

Rosie considered the question. "Not so much, no. It

needed to be done, clearly, if she was acting against us. I mean, that's the point, right? We're protecting ourselves? If someone inside's hurting us, we stop them, same as someone outside. And overkill? Beats not getting the job done the first time."

Sergei was of the same mind. But he knew that Wren didn't believe it.

Rosie finished off her drink, and patted Wren on the shoulder. "Anyway, I wouldn't worry about it. Chatter's positive, people like the thought of the patrols, although nobody thinks this so-called winter truce is going to last worth a damn. And no, your name's not getting mentioned as such, just a vague sort of optimism having to do with the guy brokering all this, which, to folk as can remember, means you. So enjoy the night, and stop looking so frownie around the eyes. Give you wrinkles, and make you look old."

With those words of wisdom, she left her glass on the bartop, and slipped off into the crowd.

"So," Wren said. Sergei braced himself. "Tall, Black, and dapper, huh?"

Andre Felhim.

"We met, yeah. To discuss breaking the contract." The agreement that bound Wren to the Silence, for a monthly retainer and the promise of their resources as she needed them, to be on-call as they needed her. Only the Silence was in disarray, internal politics and policies making that contract a danger rather than a safety. It had been a totally private meeting…unless they were talking about bumping into Andre and Jorgenmunder at Rockefeller Center? Damn it, he'd barely run into the man, in a purely public place!

Fortunately, Wren had gotten distracted. "Money still landed in my account, first of the month. Do I have to give it back?"

Bless her for the mercenary she was. "No. If we can make it through the next few hours without them calling you, it's yours, no strings. They're already in breach of contract, by not giving us all the information we needed to accomplish the Nescanni situation; they're not going to push it." He hoped.

"Sergei… All this was fascinating. Really. But you were supposed to be getting rid of the damn contract, not schmoozing with Andre over money. Especially money I'd feel dirty about having in my account."

She heard what she said, and then backtracked quickly. "Not that I was going to return it, or anything…"

"It takes steps," Sergei was saying. "Andre—"

"Andre wants you by his side, fighting his battles. I can understand that. But—"

"Andre knows I've made my choice."

"Do you?"

"What?"

"Do you know you've made your choice? Because it's sounding a lot like you're still heeling to Andre's command. Or you could have just had a nice little conversation with him last week, and let me tell him to go take a hike, instead of hustling me away like the girlfriend as wasn't supposed to meet the wife."

It was a low blow. They both knew it was a low blow. Wren had the decency to look ashamed the moment the words left her mouth.

"I've told him no, Wren. But if we can slip out of the contract—and out of any dealing with him at all—without him losing face, you get to keep the money we were just discussing. So what's the problem?"

He didn't think she was annoyed simply because he was seeing the old man. Although, in some way, that would make sense that she found it threatening. The lonejack way was a mentoring system. To her eyes, Andre was his mentor. Mentor trumped everything except birth parents, and sometimes even them.

In any case except this, she would have been right. But heart trumped everything, for him. *Everything.*

"I told him no and I meant it. I'm not getting involved in his battles. Not while we have our own to fight. And not after, either."

"Sergei." The crowd in the bar was too loud to impart the full level of amusement and resignation she clearly felt, but he could see it on her face. "You can tell him no until the cows come home and go back out again. He won't believe it. And neither will you."

"I made my decision. Do you think—" He was starting to get annoyed.

She put her hand on the crook of his elbow, her fingers curling into the cloth of his jacket, pressing the flesh underneath. Her touch, as always, both soothed and tingled, his skin practically twitching in anticipation of current hitting it.

"I think you're loving, and loyal, and smart, and all those other qualities that make you a great partner, on both the business and personal side. And I think—I know—that Andre had you first, and had you when you were still young and malleable, and you're never going to be able to cut through all the hooks he has in your psyche."

Sergei had no comeback for that.

"Partner." That was a low blow, there. It was more intimate than "lover," or "sweetheart," even when she said it in that exasperated tone. Maybe even especially then. "You're the one always telling me to finish the job. And you're not finished with Andre. Not yet."

All that got her was an exasperated sigh, more sensed than heard in the noise of the party. Wren had no idea why she was playing Devil's Advocate—she wanted out of this contract as badly—more!—as Sergei did. But something about it made her feel awkward, and it wasn't simply giving up the stipend they had been paying her. Although that was part of it, yeah. The Worth-Rosen job was going to keep her healthy for a while longer, and the current situation—pun unavoidable—had given the Council more important fish to fry than her ownself, but…

"The money has blood on it," he said.

Wren couldn't argue with that. Lee's blood. Sergei's blood. The unknown Silence operative struck down in a suspicious accident before she could meet with them in Milan. The people who suffered from the Nescanni parchment here in Manhattan, because Silence infighting prevented them from getting access to all the data. Blood everywhere.

"Does that mean it won't pay the rent, the utilities, and the grocery bills? The repair work my slicks—" the light-absorbing bodysuit she wore on night jobs "—so desperately need?"

"No. I thought you'd maybe have trouble with it. I guess I was wrong."

"Pragmatism first. I won't do something I think is wrong. I haven't done anything for the money that either of us thinks is wrong. Right?"

Sergei said his former employers were Good Guys, all for righting wrongs and helping the helpless. And she had no beef with the kind of cases they took on, based on the little she'd seen. Bad stuff happened, and you needed to clean it up. Protect the innocent, or even just the oblivious. But…

"But I don't want to get tied up in their infighting, especially if Andre's going to want us to fight his battles, not the stuff we signed up for. There wasn't any rider on the contract for that.

"This is where I've chosen to be." He said it with such firmness she finally believed him. More, she believed that, if he said it that way to Andre, the old man would believe it, too, finally.

"I know. So you do what you can," she said, sliding her hand down his arm, fingertips touching the back of his hand lightly, feeling the tendons tighten under contact, as quickly as they'd tensed at her first touch. "Do what you can and I'll take care of what's left." His gaze met hers, pale brown eyes meeting darker ones, and she smiled before taking her beer and mingling with the crowd.

Much as she'd love to blow off this party and take her

partner back to the nearest apartment, there would be time enough to celebrate the New Year with him. For now, she was on another kind of job.

"Hi. Hey there. Hey." Unlike her partner tonight, Wren was able to slip through the crowd tonight as though she were greased. People moved aside for her without seeing her, and the words went unheard into the white noise she seemed to generate; a side-effect of whatever it was that made her an effective Retriever. Someday she ought to volunteer for some kind of study or something, except the only people likely to make it worth her while would be the military, and thanks, but no thanks.

"Hey. Hi. Oh." A snippet of conversation caught her attention and she went into full listening mode, like a hound scenting game.

"You really think they can pull this off?"

"Not a chance. But at least we'll go down fighting."

"I sent my kids to their mom's."

"You hate that bitch."

"Yeah. But she loves the little brats. She'll keep 'em safe."

The voices rose out of the happy din, less pessimistic than casually resigned.

"I've been working on a new cantrip. Protective, but with a hook, gets triggered when I die, takes my killer with me."

"Nasty."

"Yeah. Made me feel slimy, making it. You want a copy?"

A long pause, then— "No. I'm just… call me a wuss, but if I'm gonna die, fine. I don't want to take anyone with me."

Wren made note of the two speakers, and moved on. That spell might be something of interest, if not to her— she was more the mind of the second speaker—then to the Troika.

"Hey, *bébé!*" A drunken reveler swung Wren around in a tipsy do-si-do, and then staggered off into the crowd. Wren laughed, shaking her head. She had no idea who that woman had been, and suspected the woman had no idea who she was, either. Just a drunken grope in a crowded bar.

Well, at least she'd been cute, in a sort of boozed-up way.

A voice came from another corner of the bar. "Okay, so you tell me what Howe is up to. Because Christ knows we're not getting the full story from our so-called leaders."

The voice was the next step beyond exhausted, and Wren naturally gravitated toward it, trying to see who it was speaking. If she knew them, that would be of interest. If she didn't—also of interest, but for a different reason.

"Valere!"

Fuck.

The heavy hand on her shoulder kept her from engaging full "disappear into crowd" mode, anchoring her in place. She *could* disappear, if she wanted to, but it would be obvious now, and considerably rude.

"Yes?" She looked pointedly at the hand on her, noting the thick silver ring on the index finger, the black stone drawing the eye directly to it. On principle, Wren looked away. Anything that drew the eye that overtly was either a. nothing you wanted to look into or b. trying to distract you from something you should be trying to see.

"John Merrian."

The name meant nothing to her. She wasn't sure if it was supposed to or not.

"Just wanted to say, nice job at the Moot. You told us, and told us good."

John Merrian was a heavyset man, thick fingers leading to a thick arm, leading to a total lack of neck and a wide, rounded-jaw face topped by a brush-cut head of black hair. But his face was surprisingly kind, and the lines around his mouth were more from smiles than frowns.

"Keep it up. Getting our asses kicked is a good thing, no matter what the grumps say."

He released her, and moved back into the crowd. Caught in some sort of invisible stasis, Wren stared after him for a long instant, unable to move. "That was…strange," she mumbled to herself finally. *Sergei said there would be changes, people who would insist on seeing me, now, no matter what I did. I didn't believe him.*

Mentally giving herself a shake, Wren kept moving, having to duck under the arm of a rather elongated Talent waving his beer around as he led a group in a rendition of "Auld Lang Syne" several hours early—for an instant, Wren felt the pang that came whenever something or someone reminded her of Lee, whose "Tree-taller" nickname was come by honestly.

Happy New Year, my friend, she thought. *I hope, wherever you are, you're having a good laugh at what you started….*

"Excuse me… hi, Happy New Year, yeah." A circuit around the bar, and she found herself in the corner, by the windows looking out onto the street, perched on a short wooden stool with a new beer in her hand and absolutely no idea who had bought it for her.

"Oh no doubt." A woman, off to her left. "If you place two spells, layered over each other, you don't double it, you increase the toxicity exponentially."

All right, that was interesting. And totally not what she was here to overhear, worse luck. Still, worth noting, since that was the second time she'd heard people discussing actual Talent-work. If one of the side effects of all this teamwork and playing-well-together was that Stuff got shared horizontally, among peers, and not just from mentor to student, the way things always had been done...

That could be as much a change to the *Cosa* as KimAnn's own personal ambitions regarding the Councils. For good or ill, Wren had no idea.

Time enough for that to come out in the wash, or whatever. Assuming there's a wash to do, when all this is done.

"Night, Wren. Happy New Year. Happy Truce." The voice broke into her semifugue working state, and she looked up in time to see a hand raised in passing, someone shoving their arms into a coat and pulling a hat down over their head, exiting before she could react, or even determine who the speaker was and if she knew them.

That was the fourth time it had happened, tonight. Four times more than usual. No, five times more, because they were not only seeing her, they were reacting to her, and acting as though it was totally normal.

The question she found herself wondering was, did these

people see her because they were now looking for her—or were they looking *out* for her? Was she really a positive, or did her newest, bestest friends have a guilty conscience prompting this new hyperawareness?

No way to tell. Not right now, anyway. So she noted down everyone who looked at her, rather than slipping past her—and made special note of those who looked at-and-then-past her. If that wasn't guilt, it was fear, and she was going to have those individuals looked closely at, first thing in the New Year.

"Time, gentlemen, ladies, lonejacks. Time!"

Someone was standing on the bar, clanging on something loud enough and discordant enough to cut through the noise and clamor.

"Time!"

Wren glanced around, but there was no clock on the wall, and in a crowd full of Talents there were no wristwatches to glimpse at, either, not even a cheap one you might not mind having totally destroyed by current-contact.

"Say goodbye to the old year's shit, and in with the—"

"New shit!" someone yelled, to mixed laughter and boos.

"You're all a bunch of heathens and do not deserve this lovely toast I am about to make."

Wren placed the speaker now: Menachim. One of the few Pure Talents who was able to function past his fiftieth birthday without even—as far as anyone had been able to tell—a hint of wizzing. Pures were the total opposite of Nulls; they had nothing in their system that impaired current, which made them the most susceptible of all the *Cosa* to wizzing, or being overwhelmed by the current they used to the point of insanity.

"To my brothers, my sisters, my cousins, my loves, and those of you I can't stand."

By the time Menachim had gotten three words into his speech, the entire bar was silent. They could all feel the current rising, outside and within, triggered by the Pure's words and intent.

"To my brothers, my sisters, my cousins, my fellow warriors in the battle to come.

I give you courage. I give you faith. I give you strength. And I give you pride."

Almost unwilling, Wren felt all those things surge inside her, swelling her veins like current-fire, burning out the doubts, the hesitations, the what-ifs and why-nots. Even knowing what he was doing, technically, she was still swept up by it. By the expressions of the faces around her, she wasn't alone.

"We are the *Cosa Nostradamus*. We are the Weird-bloods. We are the protectors of our fatae cousins, and their students, as well. The world does not dance to our tune, but gives us music that we might dance with it.

"So dance, my brothers, my sisters, my beloveds. Dance. For tomorrow… we will have hangovers that could kill a horse!"

To that, Wren could and did raise her glass. As she did so, there was the sound of heavy thudding bursts starting outside, as people let off firecrackers a few minutes ahead of the yearly fireworks display over the East River. Madmen, everyone out there, crushing together in the cold, just to see some sparklies. All right, they were lovely, impressive, totally unmagical sparklies that often rivaled Gandalf's much-vaunted fireworks, but the crowd was too much for her. She preferred seeing in the New Year indoors, a good drink and good cheer and… She scanned the room, and spotted her partner, coats over one arm, coming toward her with intent written all over his face.

Suddenly, the desire to bring in the New Year properly, overran any thought of sticking around to do any more eavesdropping.

Sergei rolled over onto his back, staring up at the ceiling and waiting for the haze to clear from his eyes.

He heard the drawer of her nightstand open, and then the cool weight of a tube of Bactine landed on his open chest.

"You didn't burn me," he said mildly. *Not,* he added to himself, *anywhere the Bactine could reach.* He didn't have to go to a doctor to know that his internal organs were taking a beating every time they had sex. It was the same thing that happened whenever she grounded excess current in him, used him to store power until she needed it. Only here, now, he didn't have the excuse of her safety, her effectiveness, to justify it.

His fault, purely his fault, for encouraging her to let go

entirely. She was already starting to pull back, and he couldn't blame her, even as his body craved the touch of her current.

The problem was, his orgasm, never mild, was three times as intense when the surge of current that accompanied her own climax "leaked" into him.

She rolled onto her side, and cuddled against him, arms folded, her head resting on his chest so that she could feel him breathing. He wasn't much for postcoital cuddling, but his skin prickled, anticipating any leftover current.

"And even if I did, you couldn't stop, could you?"

"I…" *I don't know*. And he couldn't lie to her.

"Fuck. All right. That's it."

"No more sex?" He knew he sounded like a kicked puppy, and they both let out nervous laughter at the tone.

"Never been a fan of cutting off my nose to spite my face. I'm a Talent. I can control this. And you don't tell me any more ever to let go. Not ever."

She was so fierce, so strong, that he could only smile. Her mentor had nicknamed her "wren" because she was as innocuous, as inconspicuous as that tiny brown bird, but Sergei saw her as a tiger, tawny-striped in the grass and fierce as any great cat could be.

"Don't you smile at me, mister," she warned, but he could tell from her voice that she was about to fall into her usual postcoital snooze so he merely pressed a kiss to the top of her head, rearranged them both so that she wasn't resting on his current-battered kidneys, and let himself drift off into sleep with her. He couldn't help it: sex made him sleepy. It was a good thing his Wrenlet wasn't one for company after sex, either. At least not the awake kind. She fell asleep before he did, half the time. Compatibility was a wonderful thing.

There would be an entire city filled with problems for them to face tomorrow, with the dawn of a New Year. For tonight, this morning, it was just them, and a warm bed, and the sweat of fabulous sex drying on their bodies.

He couldn't think of anything more he might want.

Wren felt her partner's breathing even out, his heartbeat slow into the deep patterns that meant he was totally, absolutely relaxed. She liked to believe that she was the only one to ever see him like this, that no one else who had ever shared his bed was privileged to be so trusted.

Trust.

Such a simple word. Such a harsh sticking point. She loved him, she trusted him…but she wasn't as sure as he was that all the ties had been cut with the Silence. Not after his bum's rush at Rock Center. She knew him, knew the deep pockets and hidden doors of his personality, even if she wasn't entirely sure what lurked behind them. She knew him, maybe even better than he was willing to know himself. But how do you accuse the man you love of keeping secrets in his brain, even from himself? Especially since she already worried about the damage *she* was doing to him, simply by being close to him.

She could control herself during sex. She had to. Because she no longer trusted him to be able to say stop, if there was overrush.

Overrush. When current overflowed, overrode the ability

of a Talent to control it. In small doses over long periods of time, it drove Talents to wizzing, madness. Fast, furious… It killed.

And it would kill a Null even faster, leaving nothing behind.

It was a long time before Wren was able to sleep.

Dawn was breaking across the glass-and-brick buildings when the last stragglers left the bar, less drunk than punchy with exhaustion. And one figure wasn't drunk at all, although the stagger and sway was picture-perfect, blending in with the others without hesitation.

As soon as they turned the block and separated for different subway lines, that one figure held back, ostentatiously looking up and down the street for something.

"You wanna join us?" one of her companions offered. "Gonna grab breakfast at J.P.'s."

The petite redhead shook her head. "Nah, gotta find a working pay phone, check in with the boss, make sure there's no emergency he needed me to sit on."

"Hell of a way to start the New Year."

"Yeah, well, work waits for no hangover." The others laughed, and went on their way. A phone booth spotted, she jogged across the street, hoping against hope that the phone would actually be intact and working.

Luck was with her; unlike most of the pay phones in Manhattan, this one was still being serviced on a regular enough basis to be working, not vandalized. Feeding coins and punching ten numbers in, she waited until the phone rang three times, then hung up.

A minute later, the phone rang, and she picked it up.

"One hundred seven people, estimated ninety-four lone-jack. No Council. No fatae that I was able to discern, although some might have been passing, in the crowd. Limited use of current, save for an end-of-year blessing and at least one observed instance of water being turned into cheap wine… No sir, that is not a joke. Well, it is a joke, a sort of parlor trick. It makes a mediocre white zinfandel-like wine, that's all… No sir. Not amusing at all, sir."

She actually thought it was funny as hell. Would be more impressive if they could turn it into bourbon, though.

"Was solicited four times for my opinion on the situation, lectured twice on the evils of the Double-Quad's plans and saw one argument over the situation break into physical conflict, which was ended by the waitress dumping a beer down the back of one participant. Overall, the mood is tense, but anticipatory. Estimated eighty-three percent think that they have a fighting chance to run the vigilantes out of town. Seventy-four percent are willing to settle for a truce. Somewhere between twenty-five and forty percent still think that the vigilantes aren't the real problem, but a smoke screen, and that the Council is what needs to be addressed, first."

She listened to the voice on the other end of the phone, and dipped her head in acceptance, even though the speaker couldn't see her.

"Yes, sir. I have noted the names…. Yes sir… No sir, I did not… Yes sir."

Her hand trembled on the receiver, and she, noting it, stilled it through sheer force of will. The current whispered in her brain, reassuring her. There was no cause for fear. There was no cause for concern. She worked for the greater good, for the betterment of all, and her master would not allow her to come to harm in the commission of these duties.

The fluttering protest died, smothered under her conditioning, and she hung up the receiver, suddenly exhausted and wanting only to go home, and go to bed.

eight

On the first business day of the New Year, Sergei stood outside his baby, looking at it with the eyes of a proud, if somewhat still-astonished, parent.

He'd found it almost by accident, walking home one evening, thirteen years and seven months before. Then, the street had teetered on the border between seedy and smart. He'd paid too much money for what it was, cheap for what it would become.

The neighborhood was originally cheek-by-jowl warehouses, solid sturdy buildings of red brick; classic New Amsterdam architecture. Over the decades gentrification had crept in, updating old spaces into trendy boutiques and sidewalk cafés with overpriced wine lists. Bad for rents, good for luring high-ticket browsers.

He had replaced the original clear glass front with a stained glass design. The deep blues, reds and greens looked like abstract art from a distance, but if you came closer, they gave the effect of an underseascape. He had commissioned the piece from one of the first artists he had showcased, a young man who had gone on to larger showings. It cut down on his ability to display works, but gave him the advantage of individuality.

Between the window and metal double doors left over from the building's original purpose, a small bronze plaque announced that this was the home of The Didier Gallery.

It had been his dream, during his last year with the Silence, the thing that kept him going, made him save his pennies and make his contacts, putting a longtime love of art and a passion for negotiating into a career that had nothing to do with blood, or pain, or danger....

With a sigh that was equal parts disgust and amusement at the complications that comprised his life, Sergei unlocked the metal door, and turned off the security system. Even now, with all the tsuris his life contained, the simple act of walking in the door soothed his ragged nerves.

Twelve years to the day, after major renovations and agita, he had turned the sign in the door over to Open.

"Happy birthday, baby," he said into the cool dark space.

The space was split into three portions: the gallery, which included a galley space connected to the main floor by a spiraling metal staircase, a back office, including his own private space, and the storage and delivery spaces below, connected by an old freight elevator that Wren refused to get into. There were crates in the storage area he needed to go through and double-check against inventory lists, before anything was brought upstairs. Not that he didn't trust his assistant, Lowell, to have done it properly, but…

It was his name on the door. His name on the authorizations. Most important, his name on the bill of sale.

This was what he loved: not the paperwork but the handling of artwork, finding the perfect place to display it in order to bring the right piece together with the right buyer. Getting the right price to support the artist and encourage him or her to create more, and starting the process all over again. It was a part of him nobody else shared, not his immigrant, politically minded parents or his aesthetically pragmatic partner.

The closest he had ever come to a soul mate in this had been Lee, the lonejack artist whose work he had exhibited twice before the man's unfortunate death during the Nescanni situation. The man's death hadn't hit him as hard as it had his partner—he hadn't known Lee nearly as well, and hadn't felt the misplaced guilt that still rode Wren's shoulders over it—but he did miss their conversations. Even before Lee held his first exhibit at the gallery, the lanky lonejack Wren called "Tree-taller" would stop by, and they would spend an hour or so talking about light, shadow, texture, and viewer interpretation of the artistic intent.

Wren, bless her, would have fallen asleep midsentence, even if she'd wanted to be included.

"You need to mingle more," he told himself. And it was true; he used to go to all the openings, have drinks with the agents, the scene-makers….

"As soon as everything's settled," he told the gleaming

aluminum sculpture that was showcased in the current installation. "As soon as I know there's going to be an art scene to worry about."

Survival before soul.

Security lights made the rest of the installation into indistinct shadows, blue and red. The front lights would stay off until Lowell showed up at nine. Going through the sliding panel door that led to his private office, Sergei touched the small metal bird perched on a narrow pedestal right inside the door. Lee's work—the lonejack had said it was an emu, but Sergei just knew that the quizzical look on the avian face made him smile, even on very bad days.

The gallery itself was designed to showcase the wildly varied types of artwork he sponsored: clean lines and subdued cream walls. His office, on the other hand, was designed around him; his preferences, his indulgences. The desk was huge, a wide flat surface that held both a flat-screen monitor, and enough room to open a paper file and work without bumping elbows into anything. His chair was a tall leather swivel, and there was a matching leather sofa against the far wall, under a striking black-and-white photograph of Manhattan in the 1940s. Everything else was the work of an artist he had promoted, from Lee's metal bird to a handblown glass sphere that swirled dozens of colors from the same woman who made his front window, to a tall pearlescent raku vase that arched like the neck of a swan, or a lily petal.

He sat down at the desk, feeling the chair creak familiarly under him, and touched the base of the desk lamp, bringing a faint yellow illumination to the office. He had a folder of invoices that needed signing off on, and the layout of a new installation to approve, and a host of other details that only he could deal with. But the light on the "other" answering machine was blinking, and everything Sergei had planned to do got pushed back a bit. Like the bat signal, messages left at that phone number, which went to no phone at all, were given priority.

An hour later, Sergei put down the phone a final time, pulled a sheet out of the fax machine behind him, and put it into the third of three piles, then pushed back in his chair, steepled his fingers, and stared over them, contemplating air.

Three piles: three possibilities. One of them would be their first job of the year, and he tried to begin as he meant them to go on. So. One would pay obscenely well. Really, really, obscenely well. The other two were at the normal going rates, but might be of more interest to Wren, more of a challenge. And right now, keeping her interested and involved—all right, *distracted*—might be more useful than cash, even hard untraceable get-out-of-town-fast kind of cash.

Not that Wren would be willing to leave town. Her, and P.B., both of them turning into *Cosa* activists under his disbelieving eye.

And where Wren stayed, he stayed. No matter how doomed he thought it all was, facing down an enemy they could only see iceberg-glimpses of. Not that he would ever tell her that. Not either one of them; not that he would stay, although they knew that, and not that their entire mad, well-meaning alliance was doomed. Although he suspected that they knew that, as well.

Not that they couldn't win; he rather thought that they could. Bigotry couldn't be erased—that was human nature, to fear what was outside your understanding, and to hate what you feared. But you could stop those who acted on their bigotry, and make others consider the cost too high to act on their hatred. And, if you did that often enough, with enough force, it became habit, and habit often became a stand-in for understanding, which would reduce the fear, which in turn would reduce the hate.

Sometimes.

Sergei had been in enough battles to know that you couldn't fight what they were fighting, couldn't fight that kind of all-out war, and then go back to where and what you were, before.

He shook off those thoughts as useless: life was change. The only stillness was in dying, and none of them were ready to be still.

And if they were going to live, then pragmatism and practicality had to be served. The maintenance fees in Wren's apartment building had just hiked up, probably a result of the blast from this summer, or maybe just the general age of the building. Plus, he'd been thinking about expanding his business, maybe using his contact with Shig, the Japanese Retriever-fatae they had met over the summer, to establish the gallery's name in an overseas market....

He sighed, pulled himself back to his desk, and touched

pile number one, almost a caress, before pushing the well-paying bid away. His hand then hovered over the remaining two sheets, coming down gently on the one to the left, purely out of instinct.

Was this how Wren took that job, the one she took without him, without involving him? They had never actually talked about that, whatever it was that had driven her to meet with a potential client herself rather than pass it along to him, the way they had been doing for the entire length of their partnership, since the very first job. He was the one who researched, who interviewed, who…decidedly did not pick jobs on whim, or turn down better-paying jobs because they seemed boring or…

Sergei bit back another sigh and drew the chosen slip closer toward him, to read it again, just in case there was something in there that he, maybe, might have missed.

"Hello, sailors!"

Sergei's head lifted at the sound of his partner's voice coming over the intercom that connected his office to the main desk. They left it in the on position as a safety measure; if someone were to come in and try to rob the gallery, Sergei would be able to call the police without being seen. Normally he could tune out the quiet conversations of customers, and the occasional phones ringing, but Wren's voice caught his attention every time.

"He's in the office."

Lowell, who in every other way was the ultimate of professionalism, hated Wren the way only one cat could hate another, with delicate hissing and slitting of eyes. Wren returned the dislike, fighting back with a breezy obnoxiousness that was designed to irritate him even more.

Sergei fluctuated between being amused, and feeling like a chew toy. He'd let Lowell know, as carefully as he could, that in an out-and-out battle he would side with his partner, not his employee, no matter how valued, and told Wren flat-out that she was not to force the issue, that if Lowell quit, it would make their lives—and their jobs—more difficult. And he monitored their interactions carefully, especially when he wasn't there to quell them in person.

"What are you doing here?"

"Sergei called, wanted me to meet him here."

"He's in back," was all Lowell said, but his tone clearly conveyed the message "go away, don't break anything, don't scare any of the well-heeled customers, don't touch anything, leave me alone."

Sergei looked at his watch, and winced. No wonder his back ached; he had been hunched over these invoices for three hours.

He had just put the folder off to the side, and tossed the white take-out container holding the remains of his lunch into the trash, when she breezed in through the sliding door.

"It's snowing again," she announced, as though the white flakes melting on the wool of her ski cap and the shoulders of her black coat didn't offer enough evidence. Her grin was manic; Sergei could relate. At this point, they'd already gotten twice last year's snowfall, and it was only January: there were two more months of winter yet to go. He'd grown up in the Midwest's Snowbelt, son of a Russian parent, and *he* was beginning to think that the weather was a bit overdone, this year.

"I've got the means to take us somewhere warm," was all he said.

"A job?" She wasn't as hyped as usual, although her face made all the right expressions of attentive interest.

That was the problem; he had seen her becoming more and more obsessed with the situation with the *Cosa,* more involved with the plight of the fatae, even as she protested that she wasn't a joiner, that she didn't play well with others. He had been there once, himself, when he worked for the Silence. Even when you realize that you can't change the world, once you get caught up in trying, a part of you had to go that last inch of that last mile, just in case that was the bit that made the difference.

He had gotten burned out: the Silence had taken him in, chewed him up, and would have digested him whole if he hadn't escaped. She knew that, although not the entire story, and reminding her of it wouldn't do anything except start a fight neither of them wanted. Instead, he merely waved the folder of the job he'd decided she should take under her nose, as though wafting perfume.

She took it, flipping through his carefully annotated information with her usual casual eye, trusting him to have done all the detail work. Her foray into soliciting jobs had shown that she could do the prep work as well as he did— she just chose not to.

"So, it's what, snatch-and-grab?" she said, closing the file and looking up at him. She'd absorb what he said faster and more completely than she would from reading what he'd written.

"Basically. Private citizen this time. Well, semiprivate. A local councilperson has had materials taken from his home safe that he wants returned."

"Ooo. Blackmail worthy?" He could almost see the wheels in her head turning, as though her forehead was made of glass, sorting and discarding what it would take to make her actually use such material, rather than Retrieve and return it. Then, as he knew she would, she sighed and let those fantasies go.

"I had been assuming the worst," Sergei admitted. He had a sudden craving for a cup of tea, but that would require getting up and going to the kitchenette in the back of the gallery space, and he didn't want the tea that badly, to interrupt the briefing. "But no, the guy seems surprisingly decent, for a politician."

"Damning with very faint praise."

"Indeed. He was stupid enough to keep copies of things he shouldn't have had, and now someone knows about it— that someone being not unwilling to use the copies, either on our client or the original owner."

"But it is dirt? We're not stealing back something that's going to be used against us, or anything, are we?" He wasn't taking her queries as her not trusting his research skills, but just natural caution after the Nescanni disaster, and her own recent toe-dip into the client-management side of things. They'd been played too many times, lately.

"Oh, it's dirty," he assured her. "This guy may be council, not Council—" and Sergei stopped, bemused by how stupid that sounded "—I mean, he's a borough councilperson, not a *Cosa* Council member, but that doesn't make him lily-white pure and clean."

And that would be enough for her to play with for a little while; figuring the best way to approach this job being the best possible nonlethal distraction from setting up the patrols, or keeping people reminded that they were under truce, or her fallback obsession, that damned horse she pulled out and worried at whenever things weren't moving on other fronts. God, how he wished he'd never accepted that job for her. The one thing she hadn't been able to settle, one way or another, in her entire career, and he was beginning to think it was sent to haunt *them*, not its actual owners, for all eternity…

"You're fussing."

"I am not." It was an automatic retort. "I'm being thorough. I was being thorough. Now it's all yours."

He had done everything he needed to do: taken the queries, sorted, evaluated, brokered the deal, done the client background research. That was as far as he could go. Everything going forward required his partner's specialized skills.

Wren didn't seem convinced, but took the materials from him and, sitting down on the sofa, one leg curled under her in her usual pose, began to sort through the information.

Sergei was pretty sure he wasn't fussing. But he would, deep down and quietly, admit to himself that he was a bit…overanxious. And not all of it had to do with his concern for Wren's state of mind. He really didn't want to leave her alone, not now, but there was a trip on his schedule that had been set up almost six months ago, and…

"Sergei." Wren was looking at him, sensing something.

He forced a smile. "I'm okay. Going to go make some tea. You want any?"

"Ugh." She shook her head, and went back to the papers, reassured.

He slipped out of the office, a quick once-over of the gallery space reassuring him that everything was running smoothly: Lowell was speaking with a customer who was clearly just killing time, looking at a watercolor that showed a dove overlaid over the Manhattan skyline. It was exquisitely done, but lacked the sense of soul that would have gotten it off the wall and into someone's collection. The artist showed real potential, though, and someone would buy it to say they had something of his, when he hit his stride and the quality work skyrocketed in price.

The kitchenette barely deserved the name, but there was a sink and a minifridge, and enough room for his electric kettle and Lowell's four-cup coffeemaker. Running the water until it was cold enough to go into the teakettle, Sergei stared at the tiled backsplash, willing himself to stop thinking. His willpower, however, wasn't up to the level of even a tyro Talent, and his thoughts kept circling around to his own justifications. If he didn't get his head straight, he was going to be no use to anyone.

Why are you pushing her so much?

Because he was trying to prove to himself that he *did* have a role to play in Wren's life, still. Between her reluctant move into becoming a major Player in the *Cosa*, even if she hadn't realized it yet, and the fact that she absorbed—like a sponge—almost everything she needed to know about the basics of running a freelance business like theirs, he was painfully aware that she didn't really need him as the "front" anymore. The original need for obscurity, for cutouts between her and the clients, was ironically being reduced as her reputation increased: people might try to kill her, but nobody would turn her in or double-cross her.

So?

So…he had to do more. Be more…something. Because going back to "only" being a businessman, no matter how emotionally engrossing he found the art world? That didn't appeal to him.

It was laughable, really. He'd thought, when he left the Silence, that it was all he wanted: an ordinary, common-place, *not* life-or-death world. But obviously not, since he kept getting involved in life-and-death things every single damned day. And night. And…

And that led to the real problem, didn't it?

You're a junkie. You've always been a junkie. If it wasn't the Silence, it was the thrill of the Retrieval secondhand through Wren, and now this damned thing with the Council, and the fatae, and every damned magical creature on the entire damned coast, apparently.

"Nothing wrong with the adrenaline kick, every now and again. It's not like I'm jumping out of planes. Exactly."

Sure, and it's better than getting hooked on drugs, better than alcohol, but it's still a jones, your need to meddle and fix and be in the thick of things. You're not even an adrenaline junkie. No: you're a responsibility *junkie.*

Fine. Accept it, own it, move on. Why is it becoming a problem now?

That was something he had the answer to, already. It hadn't been a real problem, before, because he could focus all of his attention, his need, on Wren. It had been just the two of them, and she needed him as much as he needed her, so it was…what was the phrase? A closed loop.

She wasn't so deeply tied with the *Cosa*—hell, the *Cosa* wasn't deeply tied with the *Cosa*—before this, so they hadn't impacted him. Now, however…it wasn't competition or jealousy he was feeling. Then what? He touched at it like a sore tooth; probing, testing.

You're not Cosa, *no. But you* are *connected. Through Wren, through the friendships you've made.* Lee, yes. But more than that, the fatae he had encountered: P.B., unbelievably, undeniably loyal. Shig, with his desert-dry sense of humor. Rorani, the dryad Wren so adored. Creatures that used to make him uneasy, and now were associated with laughter, and companionship.

It wasn't the bond they had first agreed to, Wren and himself. Everything had changed, even beyond the physical aspects of it. He wasn't the man he used to be.

So, who was? You changed, you rolled with the changes.

This is your world now; you need to find where, exactly, you fit in.

And how you can keep that spot, keep her and keep the

world you've gotten to want, without everyone around you getting killed.

"Duncan."

"Andre."

It was almost polite, if you didn't listen for the undercurrents. Once, not so long ago, Duncan had been one of several up-and-comers within the Silence's hierarchy, a part of the machine that served their motto: To Defend and Protect Against the World's Darkness. Once, long ago, he and Andre had been—not friends, but coworkers. Comrades.

Now, Andre walked carefully around the man, while Duncan moved in far more rarified circles, answerable only to the full Board of Directors, so far up in the rarified levels that Andre did not know anyone who claimed higher access. Duncan came down from his offices seldom, preferring to move people like chess pieces around him, setting the board to his own satisfaction. Duncan was cold, methodical; damned good at his job and covertly hungry for more, even as he amassed more power than anyone was comfortable speculating about. It was purely Andre's imagination that the faintest whiff of sulfur and smoke followed the other man whenever he appeared. Probably.

There was no one above Duncan you could go to for assistance. You could only work with him…or fall by the wayside.

The hallway bustled with activity, the daily hum of the Silence: at any given moment teams were being sent out to deal with situations, and each team had its own support system to back them up with information and resources.

Ideally, that was. In recent days, the information had been faulty, and the resources scarce. At least, for Andre's teams.

Duncan was the director of Research & Dissemination. Information came from him. Information—the lifeblood of the Silence—being choked off by Duncan's hand on the controls.

Andre needed to know why. But he needed to be careful. The hand on the controls could oh so very easily become a hand around his neck.

The memory of Sergei's face guided him. His former protégé, his former right-hand man. The Silence had played him, used him. They would use him again, if the need arose. That was the way the game was played.

But Andre had been a game-runner for too long to let himself be passively played in turn, even by such a master as Duncan had proven to be.

"Might you have a moment?"

Duncan turned to one of his underlings, an intense-eyed young woman with exquisite bone structure and the warily coiled presence of a cobra. "Melissa, please take everyone on up to the room and start the meeting. I'll join you later."

"Of course," Melissa said, not even glancing at Andre and yet managing to project resentment at this outsider who was taking her boss away from this meeting.

Cadre, Andre thought. Duncan had gone beyond team, and created a cadre.

"Now," Duncan said, his narrow, aesthetic-looking face more at home over a cassock than a two-thousand-dollar suit. "What can I do for you?"

This would have been better done behind closed doors. He was not being given that courtesy. Fine. Andre was not without skill of his own, and one of the sharpest had always been to know when to go for the jugular.

"I want in. Whatever it takes to get my people what they need to get the job done, I'll do it."

Only the slightest twitch of the corner of one eye gave it away, but Andre felt a deeply hidden flicker of satisfaction at the tell. He had succeeded in the impossible. He had surprised Duncan. Now all he had to do was stay alive long enough to use that fact.

nine

The night was quiet, the way only a major city can be, after all the clubs and bars had closed down, and the sober and the drunk alike made it to bed, and before the morning workers started their shifts. Into that silence there was a sudden sharp noise that could have been a thunder crack, or a transformer blowing, or a flash of scentless gunpowder.

"You catch that?" a voice piped up from beside Nahir's ear.

The slight, Sikh man in a dark red snowsuit and a traditional turban looked at the sky and frowned. "Could be anything." But he was already increasing his pace, walking in the direction his companion indicated, fast enough that the foot-high piskie had to cling to his ear to keep from falling off her shoulder perch.

For the sins only Allah knew about, the two of them had drawn the sixth corner quadrant for their patrol: not much except run-down concrete housing complexes and a hand-

ful of good-intentioned parks gone to hell, rounded out by
the never-ending noise of the highway running alongside
the East River.

At four in the morning on a cold, snow-blown Friday, the
only ones who should have been out were drunk twenty-
somethings, an occasional stubborn—and frozen—homeless person, and a pair or three of weary, frost-hardened
cops. Nahir didn't expect to find any of them at the heart
of this disturbance, and he wasn't surprised.

Static was discharging off the blacktop of the old bas-
ketball court. Tar not being the most naturally current-pro-
ducing of surfaces, Twinkletoes was right to point it out.
Something was up.

Under the corona of current, five middle-aged men faced
off against each other. Three of them were down to slacks
and shirtsleeves, showing either a total lack of common
sense or an impressive level of macho in the face of the weather. Or, more likely, they were using a significant level of
current in order to keep themselves warm. Conspicuous
consumption, *Cosa*-style. The other two had more practical jackets and gloves on, one a Polartec squall jacket over
his jeans, the other wearing a long black wool overcoat and
a brimmed wool hat, to keep the snow off.

Those two were the ones Nahir approached. Anyone
willing to look like a weak-wuss in what was clearly a pissing contest was either completely clueless, and thus a
danger to themselves and everyone else in the area, or justifiably cocky, and a danger, period.

The other three were probably just arrogant assholes,

secure in superior numbers—and might already be at their limits. They could wait.

"Gentlemen." That was probably giving them far too much credit. "Stand down."

Another bolt of current sizzled underground, shaking the blacktop and giving Nahir a bad case of hotfoot. One of the assholes—#3 on the left—jumped and swore as the bolt struck home, right through his soles. Sneakers, which meant rubber soles, Nahir noted. That was some seriously directed current. Also, must be tough to multitask enough to stay warm, maintain a defense, and plan a counterattack.

"Gentlemen, stand *down*," he warned them again.

"You want I should buzz them?" Twinkletoes asked, sotto voce in his ear. He could hear the anticipation hum in her voice, without even turning his head to look at her. Piskies; Allah bless them for the mischief-makers they were. And this one, still a teenager, and so worse than most.

"No," he said firmly, then, "not yet, anyway."

"Back off, boy," Overcoat said. "This is a private matter."

"Tolja they should have issued us uniforms," Twinkle-toes said. "A badge, at least. I'd love to flip 'em a…badge."

Nahir choked back a totally inappropriate laugh, and sent a quick ping back to Patrol leader, a mental snapshot of the moment, giving them a face and a voice to work from. That was his skill-strength, and why he had been chosen for Patrol: the combination of memory and strong mind-to-mind contact, the latter being an unusual gift. Contrary to popular wishes, telepathy wasn't in the top ten of uses current could be put to.

It only took a minute for the Patrol captain to relay his information to the brains at Truce Central, for them to check records, and ping back the relay with a name to go with the face.

Unfortunately, that minute had been enough to let the assholes regroup, and go back on the offensive. Blue current wove through the air, looking like ribbons his daughter tied in her hair on special days. Only these ribbons were three inches wide, and had teeth on either edge, looking for skin to latch onto.

"*Mister* St. Meyers. Stand *down,* you and your friends. In the name of the *Cosa* and the Quad, I order you to stand down and cease breaking the Truce with unauthorized use of current against fellow members."

"Stupid speech," the piskie said.

"Shut up." He knew it was stupid, yes. And useless, too, as Overcoat struggled under hungry current, and Polartec sent out a nasty stream of purple-flecked static to cut the ribbons, with mixed success. Defensive stuff, that, totally within the scope of the Truce—but only by very careful interpretation.

"Twinkletoes, now would be a good time to do that flutterby-bye thing...."

She extended her wings, then paused. "You okay on your own?"

"You going to be any particular help if I'm not?"

Piskies were great as distractions in a fight, especially if your opponent wasn't used to being buzzed by Tinkerbell's punk cousin, but there was little they could do against a prepared, current-wielding opponent more than twenty times their body mass.

"Right. Off to fetch the cavalry. Give 'em hell, turban-boy."

She lifted off, and Nahir reached down to grab a chunk of his own current from his core. He wasn't great shakes as Talent went, but he'd meditated and recharged before coming out on patrol, and so he would be able to distract them, at least.

He only needed to do that. The nearest Patrol pair was only a dozen blocks away, and somebody at the HQ had to be half-decent at Translocation, to get troops here quickly if needed. He hoped so, anyway. That hadn't been covered in their briefings.

Before he could decide how to stage his distraction, Asshole #2 staggered and fell to his knees, bleeding from the nostrils, the blood shiny black under the flickering street lamps overhead. One core-depleted, and down for the count. But rather than evening the odds and making the assholes rethink their position, it just seemed to get them more riled up. Any blood in the water, even if it was their own.

"Stand down!" Nahir snapped again, aiming his words at St. Meyers, as the name he knew and the only guy who seemed to have brought brains to the party. "Back off and go home."

"Those asswipes called us out!"

Ego would get you every time. Nahir had tangled with a neighborhood gang, back when he was a teenager, new to this country. He had gotten a gutful of what ego could push you to, then; enough to last him all this life and into the next. None of the players here were teenagers. They had no excuses.

"Back off, or this is just going to escalate. Do you want to go down in history as the schmuck who killed an entire city?"

"Fuck off," Polartec snarled.

"I can't do that, my friend. *I* don't want to go down in history as the schmuck who let you go down in history."

Right now, he had the advantage, however slight. Backup was coming. All he had to do was distract them. Keep them from attacking each other, because someone dying was the exact thing that would break apart the Truce, send each faction into a frenzy of finger-pointing and paranoid self-defense, and that was exactly what he was there to prevent.

Asshole #1 was about to say something, and Nahir made a judgment call not to wait and see if it was a comeback, abuse, or a spell. He struck.

"I speak for the Truce-Board.

The Truce-Board speaks in me.

Hold, you five

For disciplining."

As poetry went, even Nahir knew that it stank on ice. As a cantrip, designed to put oomph into the blow of current he delivered, it was a thing of beauty. He felt the waves of current rise up in him, met by four strains of power washing through him, from outside: the Quad picking up on and working with the spell, exactly the way they'd promised when it was taught to all the Talent taking part in the Patrols. Next thing he knew, he was on his knees, weaker than a runt puppy, and the five troublemakers were laid out on the ground, bound with shackles of current at hands and feet, wads of the stuff shimmering to mage-sight in their mouths, stifling any counterattack they might have tried to speak.

You *could* direct current without verbalizing, but it was a lot more difficult unless you were top-tier. And top-tier didn't scuffle in common playgrounds.

"Nice work."

From the voice, coming somewhere over his left ear, Twinkletoes was back.

"Thanks," he managed, watching as shadowy figures moved in from behind him and started carting the idiots off, presumably to be seen to by the Truce Board. Good riddance, and not his headache any longer.

Speaking of which…

"I need coffee. And a Tylenol."

A human hand helped him up off the ground and offered him a flask. Nahir hesitated, then swigged it anyway. He felt a burn start in his throat and down to his gut that was harsher than any diner coffee, and twice as effective as Tylenol.

"Good work," the district Patrol leader was saying to him. "We'll cover the rest of your shift—you go home. Fairy-juice only lasts so long, and you're going to crash, hard, after that for at least forty-eight hours. Report for debriefing when you wake up."

Fairy juice, huh? "Right," Nahir said, and—with Twinkletoes giggling in his ear—staggered off for home, and bed.

Truce Headquarters was the grandiose name they had
given to the back room of a local Portuguese bakery. The
apartment they had met in previously was still being used
for meetings, but a bakery could handle a better flow of foot
traffic without raising eyebrows, as Patrol leaders reported
in, and new Patrols went out. The split locales were useful
for another reason: there had been a quick and unanimous
consensus not to leave all their players in the same location,
just in case they were sold out again. The *Cosa* could, occasionally, learn from their own disasters.

As with the apartment, the bakery was *Cosa*-owned: the
family was from a long line of Talents who had been in Manhattan since the Dutch were still clearing the land above
Canal Street, the youngest of the line a teenage daughter
who was studying with Michaela's old mentor. Lines and
lines of family. They didn't call it the *Cosa* only as a joke.

The long worktable had been cleared of flour and was
now covered with papers and half-empty take-away coffee
cups. Most of the Truce-Board—the Double Quad, plus the
Council additions—were at the other building, but Bart, the
Council Rep, and a handful of various Talents pressed into
reluctant duty had been huddled around the table, hanging
over a map of Manhattan; placing, moving and removing
markers as updates came in and plans changed.

"Quadrants one, five, and nine are quiet, or at least reasonably not badly behaved. Two, three, seven, and eight had

minor scuffles, mostly one-on-ones that were broken up without fuss. Mostly it's cabin fever and the resulting hijinks. If we'd just get a thaw, let people stretch their legs, maybe see some sunshine..."

Despite, or perhaps because of the willpower required for successful long-term current-working, most Talent either lost their sense of humor early on, or channeled it into mischief-making and pranking. Wren had been in the middle of a few of those pranks herself, before one went south and she lost her taste for them. Pranking could be—mostly was—harmless, but when you kept Talents locked down and deprived them of the usual social outlets because of the snow, add in a touch of nerves and paranoia—she was only surprised that the pranks so far hadn't gotten ugly.

The fatae currently reporting wasn't a breed she recognized. Not unusual, but it still surprised her, every time she came face-to-face with a new breed. It—she couldn't tell a gender—looked too frail to be let out alone, but the scarring on one of its gossamer wings and the wary but confident way it stood told a careful observer that it might not break as easily as it seemed.

Wren was sitting in a corner, well out of the general fuss and bustle in the room. The only other person who was still was Colleen, the Council representative—or as Bart had unfairly but not unjustly tagged her, the Council Mouthpiece. A slender young woman with brunette hair perfectly shaped into a 1940s-style chignon, Colleen was reportedly KimAnn Howe's own student. That rumor might or might not have been true—unlike most, Madame Howe kept her mentorships hidden from public view—but the Double-Quad was careful to say nothing within her hearing that was not fit to be heard by the woman in charge of the Council, and Colleen was careful to return the favor.

The Truce might be holding, but it was an uneasy bridge, and not one you wanted to dance on.

That said, Colleen was undeniably capable, competent, and irritatingly smart. Wren didn't like her, particularly, but she'd want the girl at her back for as long as the Truce held, and not one instant longer.

"Yo."

Wren was broken from her thoughts by the entry of a new player to the hum and flow of the reporting room. The man looked familiar. Not a lonejack, not even *Cosa*. She rummaged through the mental filing cabinets and came up with a reference: the Retrieval in November, between the chaos of the Council facedown and Sergei's cutting ties with his old mentor, Andre, and the psi-bomb attack, and...well, it had been a busy month, but she remembered the face. The movers who had been moving the mark, Melanie Worth-Rosen, out of her apartment. The older one, who had gone to help the Japanese fatae-Retriever, Shig, when Sergei had "roughed him up" as part of their planned distraction.

Not *Cosa*, not Talent, although he was—in her limited experience—a pretty good guy. So, who was he, and why was he here?

"Morgan." Colleen greeted him, almost casually, as she looked up from her notes.

And the Council Mouthpiece knew him. Curiouser and curiouser. He nodded to her in return, but looked to the fatae Quad to report. *Innnteresting, yes. Have to remember that not all Council are assholes, and not all Nulls are bigots....*

"We had some trouble over in quadrant six, East Side," he was saying. Hands loose by his thighs, shoulders straight but not tensed, face tired, yeah, but his gaze was alert and his body language overall spoke of unwired, unstressed, active...activeness?

So not a word. I'm full of not-words, these days. I need about twelve hours of sleep, and a little less coffee.

"Five respectable citizens of the testosterone-fueled sort got into a school yard shoving match. The Patrol in that area took them down, when reasoned discussion proved less than effective." His tone was matter-of-fact, not even a hint of irony or sarcasm.

"Who was the aggressor, Council or lonejack? Were there any fatae involved? Any non-*Cosa*?" The questions were thrown at him from every side of the table.

Morgan shrugged, a "don't know, don't give a damn" sort of shrug. Wren admired it, with a pained sort of nostalgia. She used to be able to do that. "The Patrol didn't stop to ask, I'm guessing, and you all look alike to me."

Beyl's gnome assistant giggled at that, and the griffin swatted him gently with a forepaw. Tacky to laugh, even if it *was* funny. Particularly with the comment coming from a Null.

Wren tagged Bart, the closest Quad member, with a ping-query pointed at the man, Morgan.

Martial arts expert, he sent back. *The drakneef*—a sense of recognition to the name: the delicate-looking fate reporting earlier—*hired him to teach them basic self-defense, when the vigilantes became a real problem.*

He was the one who gave that fatae the quiet confidence she'd sensed? Wren was impressed. But why was he here? Who was paying him, now?

He showed up when the Patrols were being organized, volunteered to help. Got voted to quadrant captain a week later, and not just 'cause nobody else wanted the job.

The fatae trust him?

Bart snorted, causing the person standing next to him to glance at him curiously. *Ask me, he's the only one they do trust. 'Case you missed it, not a lot of lovey-dovey touchy-feely good vibes going around, for all that the Truce is holding.*

Trust Bart to get to the meat of the matter. He was the Manhattan representative for a reason, and it wasn't his adorable personality. "No-bullshit Bart" was his nickname in the construction business, he'd told her more than once, with real pride.

"So long as nobody's getting killed," she said out loud. "Trust is overrated, anyway."

"Trust will come." Colleen said, moving closer to Wren.

Wren ignored the response to her words. Nobody asked the Mouthpiece into what had been a private conversation, but there she was, anyway.

"Those on the front lines, the lonejack and the Council, the fatae and human. They are learning to rely on each other, guard each other's blind spots, use the network and support we provide, to keep the city safe." Colleen smiled, a practiced, peaceful, "we're all drinking the same Kool-Aid together" smile that made Wren's scalp itch. "It is a good thing that we are building, out of troubled times."

Bart looked at the Mouthpiece, and Wren could see the same thought in his mind as was rising in hers, even without benefit of tagging. Smooth and pretty words, trying to whitewash over her boss's previous bad behavior, as though to make all the ugliness not have happened because *now* they were all on-board with the peace, love and friendship? Someone should remind Miss Priss that the Council had wanted as little as possible to do with the fatae, even now.

And even if you left the fatae out of the equation, and pretended that the Mouthpiece was only talking about the humans…it still made Wren deeply uneasy. Not that she had ever been a die-hard adherent of What Had Been, Must Be, but what was the nature of a lonejack—the stubborn, separatist, individualist pain-in-the-ass maverick—once each individual became part of the collective, no matter how quickly gummed together? And, if this went on for very long—would there be any way back? Or would Madame Howe have won through the back door of good intentions where coercion and threats failed?

Wren didn't have a clue. And that was definitely making her twitchy, even when the news seemed good.

Not your problem. You're only here in an advisory position, and when the shit hits the fan and fingers start pointing, you're not the face the pointers were going to reach for. She hoped.

Her instinct was to run, hide, get while the getting was still good. *Well, screwed that but good, didn't ya? You may not be front and center, but you're a long way from the nearest exit, now.*

"Maybe so," was all she said now in response to the Councilwoman's words, "maybe so. And maybe not." She rose from her chair with what she hoped was casual grace. "If you'll excuse me, I have a few things to take care of, elsewhere."

Time to start listening to her instincts again. Let politics and policing occupy others, for a while. Bart and the rest of the Quad were better suited to those sorts of mind games, anyway, and Bart certainly would enjoy it more. She wanted the ground firmly under her feet and a solid result in her hand. And money to pay the rent, yeah. Time to go to work: thanks to Sergei, she had a new Retrieval to plan.

"Valere, we need you here." Bart was cranky as only a foul-tempered New Yorker could get running on coffee fumes and two hours of sleep, and Wren didn't want to deal with it.

"No, you don't."

"Ms. Valere, I really think that—" the Mouthpiece started to stay, and suddenly Wren had. Had. Enough. Enough of the leash they were trying to slip around her neck, enough of the careful wording and the tiptoeing, and the way everyone seemed to think that she would be oh so happy to do this one more thing for them.

She wasn't, and she wouldn't, and there wasn't any way any of them could make her.

A dip into her core, a twist, hardly even thinking about

it, and she went no-see-em. Another twist, and even a
Talent looking for her couldn't see her. A third twist, like
slipping down a familiar waterslide, and the other woman
forgot she had even been speaking to her. Bart shook his
head, puzzled, then turned away back to the rest of the
room.

This was more than no-see-me. She had disappeared
from their recent memories, as well.

She shoved her hands into her pocket, and touched the
locket, still resting there.

"That's rude, Jenny-Wren."

*She was sixteen, sitting very quietly in the back of the class-
room. He had been working at his desk when she came in,
wrapped in layers of no-see-em, holding back the giggles at the
thought of sneaking one past her mentor, literally.*

*She should have known he would have sensed her. No matter
how good she was, he always knew.*

"How…?"

*"You smell of that godawful gum you're always chewing. You
sound like a cow chewing its cud."*

*Wren took the gum out of her mouth and looked at it, then
put it back in her mouth.*

*"You're very Talented. You could probably have slipped past
me if you'd thought about covering all the senses, not just
sight. But it's rude," Neezer said again, then closed the essay
book he was grading and looked up in her general direction.
"So don't do it just because you can. That's rude, too."*

Wren stopped just outside the door of the bakery,
looking down at the slice of almond cake she had lifted

out of the display counter. Habit. Habit to take what appealed. Habit to slip into no-see-em when she didn't want to be bothered anymore.

"That's rude, Jenny-Wren."

She was losing the memory. Sharp at the center, but fading and fraying at the edges, his voice fading in and out. Every year, Neezer faded more and more. Even touching the locket, his picture, his sense inside, couldn't hold back the inevitable.

It ached, that loss; if she let them come, the tears would be bitter in her stomach. She didn't let them come anymore.

She tossed the pastry into a nearby trash bin and wiped her hands on her coat, then pulled her gloves on, wrapped the scarf around her lower face, and headed home, determined to drop all political shell games the same way she'd dropped that cake.

She didn't like being rude. But sometimes, you did what it took in order to survive. To escape.

Being polite hadn't gotten Neezer anywhere. He had still wizzed. Still left her.

That thought gnawed at her brain until she forcibly locked it down and put it away. Only that allowed all the other thoughts to rush her, fighting for space and attention. Sergei. Job. Weather. Her mother. Money. The Truce-Board. Lee. The fatae, who were, for some reason, counting on her.

Easy to say you're going to let go of the entire business. Tougher to actually do. The thoughts followed her from Truce Central, for the length of the 6 train and the crosstown bus, jolting forward and back with the movement of street traffic. She scored a seat by the window, with nobody squished in beside her, but not even that victory distracted her. Not even the unaccustomed sight of a clear blue sky and distant winter sunshine could shake it from her brain, like a terrier fixated on one particular doggy bone. She picked at a scab on the back of her hand, a scar still healing from that scuffle with the hellhound, and let her mind run over the things she had seen and heard. Nothing settled into place; it was a mosaic of broken bits. Broken truces. Broken promises. Broken bridges falling down. She frowned. No, that wasn't the way the old kid's song went. Not broken, London. "London Bridge Is Falling Down."

The bus came around the corner, and she signaled for a stop. Getting off the bus, she pulled her gloves back on—it might be bright, but it was still cold—and started walking to her apartment, still chewing over what she had seen and heard.

There were enough clues, she knew it. But she wasn't a detective. She was a thief. What did she know about solving things like this? What right did she have to stick her finger in and stir it up?

What are we becoming? What have we done? Did I advise them to do something really, really stupid?

"Of course, you're assuming we're going to survive the winter...."

"Jesus, Danny!" Wren didn't, as far as she knew, have a history of heart attacks in her family, but she almost started a new chapter, then and there. "How the hell—"

"You were practically broadcasting, darlin'." Danny

looked human, from ankles to ears. Only the ever-present cowboy boots hid his maternal inheritance, distinctly fatae hooves, which had moved him from the NYPD to private practice when the force started cracking down on yearly physicals.

Bullshit. Wren was too tightly closed down, naturally and by personal inclination, to send anything without intent. Even assuming someone could "find" her current-signature to eavesdrop on, which was almost as masked as her physical presence, even when she wasn't working. You had to ping with intent to find her, not just open your psychic ears. Unlike some, who never seemed to hush.

The Mouthpiece had picked up on her conversation with Bart, too. Maybe she was leaking, just a little. That was a disturbing thought, and she didn't want to be thinking it.

"You were stalking with intent," she accused him, trying to distract herself.

"Technically, 'stalking' implies intent. So that's redundant."

Wren bit the inside of her cheek to keep from making a response. Only thing worse than a cop was a former cop.

"So. Want to tell an old friend how things're going?" he asked.

"No."

Danny had the most efficient information highway in the city: his former fellow cops, snitches, respectable citizens, and some not-quite-legit characters all went through the Danny-toll at one point or another. If he had to come to her to get Intel, that meant the Truce-Board was, miracle-of-miracles, leak-free.

Be damned if *she* was going to become the weakest link, loose lip, leaky pipe, whatever cliché rocked your world. She might not lead, but she sure as hell didn't squeal.

"C'mon, Valere…" Danny didn't wheedle. But he walked a fine line next to it. "I've always shared with you…."

He had, too. When it suited him to. Although he had been first-on-the-spot when someone set off a psi-bomb next to her office, he hadn't actually told her anything useful, and certainly nothing she couldn't have discovered on her own. On the other hand, he had saved her a little work, then. More, he had cared enough to use the excuse of investigating the blast to check in on her. There weren't so many people in her life who would do that, that she couldn't just diss them.

"The Truce is holding," she said, not looking at him as they walked. She could just have been talking out loud to herself, something she was known to do. "Council is sharing their resources, whatever they know about the attacks on the fatae. Which, by the way, isn't much."

"So they really weren't behind the attacks on us?"

Wren would have shrugged, if she weren't suddenly so dog tired it was more effort than the effect was worth. Too many days sitting in rooms, waiting for the infrequent moments she could say something useful, listening to everyone and their sister play verbal games with each other, sifting and evaluating, processing everything she saw and heard the way she would on a Retrieval, and none of the adrenaline rush or payoff she actually got during a real Retrieval.

She was brain dead, physically bored, and craving a bowl of sweet-and-sour and a month-long nap, neither of which was going to happen, for various reasons.

"It may be the vigilante movement was nothing more than badly timed bigotry," she said. "Not exactly unheard of. Sometimes, Occam's Conspiracy of Razors is just para-noia. You know?"

"You believe that?" It was clear from his voice that Danny didn't. "Valere, these bigots aren't long-term thinkers. Someone had to be directing them. Or using them."

"Hell, Danny, I don't know. I'm not being paid to believe anything. I'm being paid to watch and advise." And she wasn't being paid anything even close to enough. "And you're not the one doing the paying, so you don't get the advice."

"Sheesh. Who taught you to play almost-hardball?"

Sergei, actually. And her partner thought she didn't listen to him…

"How 'bout I buy you lunch, bribe you with a bowl of Jimmy's best?"

The mention of her favorite addiction sent a cold chill down Wren's spine, and she increased her pace as though to escape the words. "Thanks, but no thanks." She hadn't ordered from Noodles in over a month, long enough for P.B. to notice, and probably Sergei, too, although he hadn't said anything. She was in Chinese food withdrawal, bad. But she wasn't going back there. Not while all this—and by "this" she meant her entire life, right now—was still such a disaster.

It was simple, if not logical: going to Noodles meant getting fortune cookies. Getting fortune cookies from Noodles mean getting a fortune written by his Seer. His Seer was one of the most terrifyingly accurate in the city, maybe in the state. Wren didn't want to know. She really, *really* didn't want to know. And once you got the fortune, you Knew. That was way worse than suspecting.

She wasn't sure if that made any sense. She was way too tired to be philosophical right now, and if she was leaking, anyone with any sense would be backing away from her right now.

"Dan. Buddy. Pal. I really don't want company right now. Job calling, you know? Real job, as pays the rent, feeds the tummy, shoes the feet? So go pester someone higher on the food chain, okay?"

They weren't friends, her and Danny, but close enough that he took the blow-off with decent grace. Someday he'd dig his hooves in and get stubborn—but today wasn't it.

"Keep your light under that bushel of yours, Valere," was all he said in parting. "And eat something. Sergei's a Russki, he likes some meat on his women."

He's from Chicago, she thought reflexively, silently, not giving the fatae the pleasure of eavesdropping on her response.

They parted ways at a huge snow pile on the corner, Wren having to step carefully to get around it, while her companion simply clomped through it. Physical memory, and Danny's offer almost made her turn north instead of continuing east, and she checked the inclination ruthlessly.

If she wanted soup that badly, she could go somewhere else. Noodles wasn't the only Chinese restaurant in town. It wasn't the cheapest, it wasn't even the closest, anymore. Never mind that eating anyone's Chinese but Jimmy's felt like ethnic adultery, or something.

"Change out the brain, Valere," she warned herself. Pick up one of the other thoughts still shoving for front space. Sergei had dropped off the client's dossier last night, but she hadn't taken the time to even flip through it, knowing she had to be at Truce-table at oh-fuck-early. Bad of her. Worse, it was lazy. Normally she didn't much care one way or the other when she had to work—dawn, dusk, noon and midnight all had their useful points. What she hated, beyond all else, was having to get out of bed. Didn't matter what time the wake-up call came, even if it came with a soft-voiced partner bearing a mug of coffee.

What all that meant was that she didn't have anything more than Sergei's preliminary briefing on the client in her head, which meant that she was in dead space, mentally. Wren worked best on her feet, pacing as she thought. Wasting the blocks until her apartment because she didn't have anything new to work on was…annoying.

"All right, what *do* you know? Get it rolling. Null, the client, yeah." So was her last—nothing unusual in that. If she relied on the *Cosa* for her jobs, she'd be living in a studio in Queens, not her relatively spacious Village walk-up. "Not a crook, or a creep, or a lost cause, according to Sergei's quickie evaluation." Which was usually pretty accurate.

"Retrieval's papers. Nothing currential about them."

Currentical was her new favorite nonword: it meant anything touched by, dealing with, or likely to contain current. She'd coined it during an argument with Bart, and he hated it so much she just *had* to keep using it, even when he wasn't around to be annoyed.

A guy scraping ice off the walkway stopped to stare at her, then went back to work. The only difference between a crazy street person and a CEO these days seemed to be the level of tech carried around. Most street people didn't have earpieces, for one: they really were talking to themselves.

Besides, she had taken a shower that morning, and homeless people didn't usually smell of sage and lavender soap. Usually. She hoped. She'd paid too much for that soap to be eau de vagabond.

"Problem's going to be finding the guy as took him. Client's political, even if unscummy, he's going to have pissed people off. Need to get Sergei running down recent public and private scuffles, if he's not already, and generate a list of possible suspects. Once I have that, I can scry for cause."

Wren was so preoccupied with her muttered thoughts, she didn't notice the figure behind her, out of the other pedestrians passing her by on the street, until the gnarled fingers closed around her upper arm.

Then she yelped, like a pooch whose tail got trod on. Current boiled up, reflexively, and she swung around to blast whoever it was that was attacking her.

"For you. I look for you, find you. You take."

Total confusion reigned, as Wren struggled between the instinct to defend herself, awareness that the being, rather than a threat, was so hunched over and wizened that Wren couldn't tell the species, much less the gender, and the fact that he—she, it?—seemed less intent on causing harm than inducing her to take whatever it was it was trying to hand her.

Normally, she was invisible to panhandlers, pushers, and religious glad-handers, same as she was to regular citizens. From the look in the tiny, but very bright black eyes almost lost in the wrinkled face staring at her, this being had zoomed in on her like it was fitted with a Wren-scope. What had it said, that it had been looking for her? Great.

"Take! You take!"

She took, almost a reflex. The moment her fingers closed around the small object, feeling the too-familiar folds and ridges even through her glove, she groaned and tried to shove it back.

"No, no! Yours, for you! You take. No more delay."

Wren looked down at the fortune cookie starting to crumble in her hand, then looked up again. The figure had disappeared faster than it had appeared.

"Sweet Jesus…." Figured. Seers. They just didn't know— or care—when they were being avoided.

Hounded into a figurative corner, Wren gave in gracelessly, and pulled her fortune out of the cookie, then popped the remains into her mouth and crunched, loudly.

Jimmy's Seer was the best around. Maybe even the best, period. But his cookies weren't bad, either. She didn't look at the fortune, though, shoving the crumpled scrap of paper into her coat pocket. You couldn't put it off forever, not once the damn fortune found you, but she was going to need nourishment first. And a chance to put her feet up, and maybe take another shower, and…

One bright glimmer broke through her sulk. And now she had no excuse not to go get sweet-and-sour soup.

When she walked in the door of her apartment, Sergei was already there, lounging in the one comfy chair in the main room, drinking a mug of tea and listening to some weird-ass tech-sounding music.

"You like?" he asked.

"I hate," she said. She was surprised to see him there, then realized that the overcast day had fooled her; it was already after five, and the gallery wasn't open on Tuesday nights.

He turned off the stereo with a snap of the remote, and looked at the bag in her hand. "Noodles?"

"Nope. Wan Moon's." A distant second place in the Chinese food sweepstakes, but she was still pissed at Jimmy and his back-room Seer. Besides, it was easy in, easy out, on her way home. And as far as she knew, they bought their fortune cookies in bulk from the local fortune cookie factory. No personalization. Or none that had bitten her on the ass—yet.

"What ended the embargo?" He had gotten up and followed her into the kitchen, all of four steps away.

"I got delivery service." She put the soup down on the kitchen counter, and dug the fortune out of her pocket, handing it to him while she got down to the important business of feeding her addiction.

"A hungry man might as well cook his soup off a burning bridge as a campfire."

Sergei placed the slip of paper down on the table and shook his head. "Nice to see that Jimmy's Seer hasn't lost his touch." They were always obscure, that was what was so frustrating about them. They were all true, and really important to what you were about to do, but you never knew what they were talking about until you were already in it. Useless.

"Her touch. I'm pretty sure she was female. Although when you get that old, does it make a difference anymore?"

"How old do you think she was?"

Wren shrugged. "Cricket-old, probably." Her partner was always curious about those things. She wasn't, except as it impacted her life. And the damage was already done.

"Bitch came *after* me." She wasn't letting go of that any time soon. This was the second time a Seer had sought her out, specifically. That wasn't good. That wasn't good at all. It meant she was being all piviot-ish and important to the ordering and occurring of things, and Wren wanted to be very much not pivoting, thanks all the same.

"Weren't you the one who told me that you can run but not hide from a Seer once they have you in their Sight?" her partner asked, watching her carefully, with a sort of wary sympathy.

"Yeah, but if you dodge long enough…" She sighed and gave up. "Damage done, and since I can't understand it, I'm going to go the time-honored route of ignoring it." Had the Seer actually been useful— "Avoid gatherings on a full moon" or "stay out of the councils of crazy people," then she could do something about it. Cooking? Not her thing, over a stove or a campfire, or any kind of open flame.

She finished the container of soup, scraping her spoon around the bottom for the last drop, then got up to toss it into the garbage. No more reason to procrastinate. To it, Valere.

"So. List?"

He indicated the manila folder on the counter by her change-and-keys bowl. "Our client's been a busy boy."

"So haven't we all," she grumbled, taking the file and wandering down the hallway to her office, flipping it open and scanning the typed list as she went. Oh yeah, lots of folk the client might have ticked off. Bless her partner, it was annotated and color coded, cross-referenced, and all those things he did so well.

"Right then, I'll leave you to it" she heard her partner say, before he—and everything else—faded from her aware-ness. She had a job in-hand. She could already feel her mood starting to improve.

ten

"Wren."

She could smell coffee, as she surfaced. That was nice. But the pillow was nicer.

"Wren, come on, I know you're awake." The voice was cajoling, deep, and just on the edge of laughter.

"N'mnot," she mumbled into the pillow.

The laughter won out, thick and rich and familiar. Nicer than the pillow, if only just. "I made you coffee. It's here, on the dresser." A pause. "I have to go."

"Mrrrmmph."

Slowly, the sense of what the voice was saying got though, and she opened one eye enough to locate the mug of coffee steaming just within reach.

Once she had ingested enough to feel human, she pried open both eyes enough to see her partner lounging in the doorway, backlit by the hall light. He was already showered and dressed, even though it was still dark outside.

"Go?" Her mind was slow moving and foggy.

"Yeah. I told you about this, last week. I have to go to a meeting in St. Louis. New artist, the one who works in pewter and leather? I want to get him in before the trend-makers discover him. Could get me splashed in a couple of magazines…" He trailed off, aware that she really wasn't interested, and wouldn't have been even if she'd been awake.

"Oh." She didn't remember. She figured she had been a little busy when he was telling her about it. There was a lot going on. *Understatement,* she could almost hear him say, as though she had voiced her comment. Still, this was his job, his *other* job, and the least she could do was try to pay better attention. *Bad Wren.*

She stretched, toes digging into the sheets, wishing they were both still asleep and neither of them had any jobs to worry about. "You'll dazzle 'em. You always do." He did. He had that way about him; artists responded to it. Lee had said it was because he understood art, the way artists did. Wren thought it was just the way he got enthusiastic about it all, made 'em feel like they were the only artist he'd ever gotten the hots for.

"I'll be back tomorrow." He sounded as though he were considering canceling the trip, then and there.

Wren shook her head, trying to clear more of the fog. Not good. Oh, she wanted him here, yeah, but he needed to do this. She used to joke that the gallery was his real lover; truth was that he *needed* it, the same way she needed current: it was what made him whole. That was why he was so good at it.

And she wanted him gone, too. Not forever, just a little while. Last night's sex had been amazing, and comforting, and all that, but she'd felt it, the moment when he'd wanted to ask her to ground in him, and had held off…but only just.

Current-intensified sex; there was a reason why the old-time sex magic was so popular, even now when there were smarter, more effective ways to renew current. But it wasn't smart. It wasn't safe. And she couldn't fix the damage it was doing to him, and she wasn't strong enough, right now, to tell him no.

A little time apart would be good for them both. She hoped.

"You'll go and do the job, take as long as it takes. And then you come home, yes."

He hesitated. "You'll be careful?"

"Didier, you're going away for what, twenty-four hours? I'll be fine."

He waited, staring at her. "I'm always careful." He knew that. "And I got Bonnie downstairs." Bonnie, the other Talent in the building. A paranormal forensic investigator, one of the new young hot-shit careers for eager and curious Talent, Bonnie was a good kid—more, she came with a covey of coworkers who were all also good, hot-shit kids, and seemed fascinated by her upstairs neighbor Wren, but drew the line at poking too closely at the details of what Wren actually did for a living. If there was sudden, urgent need for help, Wren need only yelp. Which there wouldn't be, so she needn't, but Sergei did worry.

"P.B. should be coming by today, anyway," she told her partner. "I sent him off to pick me up something in Albany. A friend of a friend had some materials I needed for the job."

Like most demon-breed, P.B. was a courier, trusted with all sorts of private or dangerous information. Partially that was because demon had no loyalties other than to their employers—they did not form social groups with their own kind, or even seem to *like* their own kind very much. Mainly P.B. was a courier because very few people, *Cosa* or otherwise, wanted to tangle with a four-foot-tall fireplug of fur and muscle and claw. He was also a fierce friend, and for all that Sergei had some lingering knee-jerk humancentric reactions to the fatae, she knew that he trusted P.B., maybe more than he trusted anyone else in the world, at least when it came to keeping her safe and steady.

Not that she needed the help. But she always felt better when the demon was around, too.

"All right." But he stood there, not moving.

"You called a cab?"

"Yeah. He's outside."

"You're letting the meter run?"

"I didn't want to wake you until I had to."

She got out of bed, then, stark naked and shivering in the cool morning air, to go wrap herself around him. "Go safe, do well, come home soon."

His arms came around her as though he wasn't ever going to let go. "You're going to freeze to death. Go back to bed."

"Oh sure, wake me up, give me coffee, then tell me to go back to bed." She was awake now, and no help for it. "Sadist."

"Which would make you a masochist."

She smiled, the way he knew she would. "Go already, if you're going, before your fare hits triple digits."

By the time she had wrapped herself in her robe and reclaimed the coffee, he was already down on the street, folding himself into the waiting cab. He didn't look up to see if she was watching, but she knew that he knew she was.

As though on cue, the moment the cab pulled away, the clouds overhead darkened, and small snowflakes began to fall.

"Great," Wren said in disgust. "More snow." At least the last batch had—mostly—melted and been cleared away. But she had been looking forward to unobstructed street corners for a few days longer.

"Lord, please. If you love me? No more accumulation, okay?"

There was no response, and Wren shrugged, let the curtain drop back to cover the window, and went to take her shower. Snow or not, there was more job-planning to be done. If the materials P.B. was bringing were going to be useful, she had to have everything else lined up first.

"Yo. You order a buncha documents, lady?"

Wren looked up from the sink full of dishes to see a white-furred, snow-dusted face grinning at her from the small kitchen window. "That was the worst Cagney impersonation I've ever heard," she told the demon, reaching over with a sudsy hand to open the window enough to allow him in, wincing as that let a blast of snow-flecked cold air in, as well.

"Oh good Lord." She looked out the window for the first time since that morning, and sighed. "So much for God listening to prayers. Or the hope of cleared streets." She gave a passing thought to Sergei's flight, but then mentally shrugged it away. If flights were being cancelled, he'd be in full rearrangement mode, and would call her later. If he was already in the air, then hopefully he was out of the worst of it already.

"Oh, it's snowing like a small mother out there," P.B. agreed cheerfully, dropping the courier bag—thickly stuffed—onto the counter and brushing snow off his fur. Since that fur was thick and white to begin with, the overall visual was that of the Abominable Snowman, miniaturized, coming in out of the cold. Only the dark slouch-brim fedora on his head ruined the image.

"Where's the scarf I gave you?" she asked. "It doesn't do you much good if you don't wear it."

The demon gave her a Look. "Valere, my neck does *not* get cold. Yours gets cold, *you* wear a scarf. Anyway, orange isn't my color."

"What, it clashes?"

He ignored her, moving sideways to get at the fridge. "Ooo, someone hasn't been shopping again. What are we going to have for dinner? Why don't you just give in and order online like everyone else?"

"Because I get frustrated with the interface being slow and wonky, and I'm tired of trying to explain why I'm plagued with brownouts to the Dell service guys, who barely speak English enough to go off-script, anyway."

"You need to get some therapy for those frustration issues, babe."

"You need to get out of my fridge, boy."

The demon shut the fridge. "Let's order Chinese." He took a look at her face, and backtracked. "Pizza? Ribs? Let's get ribs!"

She was exhausted, but amused. "Do you ever eat anywhere other than my apartment?"

"No. Dial. I'm starved."

Some things were as predictable as sunrise. "You dial. I'm busy. Get me an order of chicken, burned, and extrasalty fries."

If she was lucky, he'd eat and leave, and she'd be able to get some work done, because while P.B. was an entertaining companion, a good friend, and a solid presence in a fight, he was king of the short attention span when it came to sitting around watching someone else work. Although she did feel more relaxed—less wound up—when he was there. Somehow, she was able to focus, rather than jumping from thoughts of one crisis to another.

"Money's in the usual spot. Take out enough for dinner, too." She opened the courier case and pulled out the manila folder that had the sigil he used for her orders on it, then left him still staring into the fridge as she took it back to the office.

By the time the ribs came, the snow was six inches

deep on the cars outside, and she tipped the delivery guy an extra fiver because he'd actually got the food there still warm.

When she came back into the apartment, the phone started ringing. She handed the bag off to P.B., who opened it and started unloading white cartons onto the counter, and picked up the receiver.

"Hello?"

It was Sergei.

"Hey. What's up? How's St. Louis? Oh." She listened a few minutes more, her hand curling in the telephone cord. "Damn."

P.B. looked up, and she waved him down.

"Okay. No, nothing you can do. Might as well make the most of it. Yeah, P.B.'s here." The demon paused midmunch on a baby back rib bone to wave one greasy paw hello. "He says hello. Yeah. Okay. No, we're good. Yes, I have candles, you *know* I have candles." She grinned, and a flush started at the base of her neck, turning her pale skin a gentle red as he said something low and rude.

"Don't even start, not while you're there and I'm here. Yeah, you, too. Sleep well. I'll talk to you tomorrow." She hung up the phone, untangling the cord with exaggerated care, and stared at it as though there was some answer just waiting to leap out at her.

"He's in St. Louis?" P.B. asked, not even pretending not to have eavesdropped.

"Yeah. Business trip. He was supposed to come home tomorrow morning, only he doesn't think he'll make it.

Storm's slamming everyone. They were one of the last flights out of JFK, and one of the last to land in St. Louis. They're shutting down there, too, he says. Snow's supposed to last all night, most of tomorrow, maybe even through the night again, here. If the weather guys aren't shitting us."

The demon shook his head, waving the rib bone like a pointer. "We pissed off momma nature but good, this year, seems like."

"Yeah." She turned to look at P.B., a long, considering kind of look.

"What?" He got nervous suddenly.

She didn't want to do it, wanted to have her apartment all to herself, tonight, but... "You should stay here tonight. If it's that bad out, I don't want you trying to walk through it, maybe get hit by a bridge-and-tunnel driver who can't tell you from a mobile snowbank."

"Sweet, but—"

"Wasn't a request. You eat my food, you have to indulge my whims. You're crashing here tonight." She played her trump card early, not wanting to argue. "I've got fixings for French toast for breakfast."

He showed her white fangs, showcased by black-rimmed lips smeared with barbecue sauce. "Sold." A pause, purely for effect. "Can I have the feather pillows?"

There was concern, and then there was no way. "Not a chance in hell. Hey! How did you know I have down pillows? If you've been snooping in my bedroom, you half-sized excuse of a..."

"Jesus, Valere, mellow. I was on sick-Wren watch, remember? You on sleep-cure, me fetching and carrying soup and coffee?"

After the Frants case, when she'd drained her core almost to empty, trying to save her worthless client from a revenge-crazed ghost. God, it felt like years ago, lifetimes ago.

"Everything was different then, wasn't it?" P.B. sounded wistful.

"Yeah." The Council had been a gnat-shaped annoyance, she had never even heard of the Silence, and the vigilante attacks were just a dark rumor even among the fatae. On the plus side, she and Sergei had been dancing around their feelings for each other like the protagonists in a bad Lifetime movie, leaving them both wordlessly frustrated without knowing why. They still had a ways to go on the relationship stuff, but frustration? Not a problem anymore. Well, sexually, anyway. In the sense of itches getting scritched. There were still problems in the bedroom, but she wasn't going to worry about that tonight, not while she had a houseguest.

"I'll give you one pillow," she said. "And the air mattress, if you promise to keep those claws of yours under control."

"And the green quilt. I like that quilt."

"Quilt. Right. So you can shed all over it again? Why don't you go make up your own damn bed. I'm going back to work."

If she was lucky, the snow would stop by morning, the forecasters would apologize for jumping the gun, and she could get on with everything that needed doing.

It didn't quite work out that way, though.

eleven

"It's started again."

Wren couldn't get warm. Her skin was flushed, like she had a fever, but her fingers and toes felt snow-bitten; painfully numb and strangely thick. She had put on a heavy sweater, one that Sergei had left behind one evening, over her turtleneck and jeans. It still smelled of him, but even that wasn't working its usual magic.

Her blood was ice. Her core was molten. It wasn't a good combination.

She wrapped her hand around the phone cord, and *focused*. Control. She had to stay in control.

"You there?"

"Yes, Wrenlet, I'm here. What happened?"

Sergei's voice was crackly and staticky over the phone, and Wren didn't think it was just from the distance between them. The entire *Cosa* was twitching, and it was a wonder the phone lines were even working, right now. Three sub-way lines were down for the count; two counties in Jersey were in brownout due to a generator blowing rather spec-tacularly. Things were... tense.

"Someone strung up an angel. Left him to bleed out and die."

"I got that part. How did the vigilantes get close enough? I thought everyone was on guard?"

His voice was thin, even over the phone line. "It wasn't them." His tension was affecting her, stretching her already worn nerves. She turned the control up a notch, until her ribs ached from the effort, just to stay calm.

Her words took an instant to sink into his awareness, then that flat voice rounded and deepened in shock. "What? How—and who? How do you know?"

She took a deep breath, feeling her fingers cramp on the phone. *Control...* "The PUPs. They said... there were traces of current all over his body."

"Cosa?" Sergei's tone was clearly disbelieving, even through the static. "Who? And why break the Truce? Do you think it's the—"

She cut him off before he could speak specifics. "I don't know, I don't know, and I don't know. It might be anyone. Anything." Her voice cracked, and she felt the slithers of current reach up her spine, trying to break free and do dam-age. She needed to ground, badly, but there wasn't any room: everyone was so locked down that all of Manhattan's bedrock had toe-marks in it. "Look, I gotta go. Board's meeting." She didn't refer to it as the Truce Board anymore. Both of them noted it. Neither of them commented on it.

"Valere." Michaela came to the door. Her face was marked by a lack of sleep and sunshine, tension holding her eyes tight and making her mouth a narrow line. "Everyone's here."

She nodded once roughly. "I'll call you later," she told Sergei.

"You do that." The line went dead, and Wren followed Michaela inside, to a conference room filled with enough nervous tension to run all mass transit in the city for a month, assuming it didn't short the system out first. Fatae stayed down the bottom half of the room, humans at the upper end. Nobody was actually sitting at the table. Not good. Not good at all.

Twelve hours since she and P.B. had found the angel. Twelve hours, and she couldn't remember much of it; a blur of movement, wrapped in snow that didn't seem as white as it should, anymore. Shadows and snow, and flames flickering in between, threatening to take the entire city down with it.

"Back to the beginning," she said, almost under her breath. The first fatae death she observed had been one of the angeli, too. That one had been taken down and beaten with bats, or metal bars; a less dramatic but equally fatal end.

Who would do this? Current ruled out the vigilantes, the exterminators; no one with an ounce of current would be involved with them, not even the most radically Human-first extremist. Not after they started going after Talents, too. But for a Talent to go after an angel…

They were among the most obnoxious, annoying of all the breeds, God knows that's the truth. But killing one like that is more than annoyed-off-the-deep-end. That was hatred, and fear, and making a point with a capital P.

Beyl made her way to the table, her wings unfurling just enough to get everyone to look at her. Those within wing-span moved away, just in case she decided to go full-mast. A griffin's wings might look pretty, but they were all muscle and bone; instruments of fighting as much as flying. "We don't know who did this…" she started to say, and was immediately shouted down.

"Of course we do!"

"They broke the Truce!"

"Humans will be the death of us all!"

"Council's behind this, you know they are!"

There was a less vocal outburst from the human side of the room, mostly protesting the claims of the fatae, or denying responsibility for the murder. It was an obvious conclusion, one that Sergei had leaped to, almost immediately, and not entirely beyond the Council…but it was out of character, even under Madame Howe's leadership. KimAnn Howe broke rules, yes, but only when it benefited her, and her plans. This…she was the one who had brought the Council to the table in the first place. Unless something had drastically changed, this made no sense. Wren was suspicious of any assumption that required a traditional, hide-bound organization like the Council to act out of character simply because the result would fit the prevailing theory.

But it *was* possible.

The majority of humans here today were lonejack; Wren saw maybe a dozen faces she knew were Council, including Jordan and Ayexi, who were staying very still and quiet, taking in the tenor of the room. Ayexi was a strong enough Talent to protect himself; she had to assume Jordan was at least as good. If things got ugly, they were on their own.

Michaela tried to inject some calm into the scene. "Nobody knows for certain who did this, why, or even when it happened! You came to the Truce Table in good faith— let us investigate likewise in good faith! I give you my solemn oath, there will be a full inquiry, and no lead will be overlooked or refused. On wing and tail, heart and head."

There were still catcalls and jeers, but some of the outbursts were silenced by her words. The oath she had given was one the fatae used, not humans. Wren was impressed; she didn't think Michaela knew it.

"This murder has many of the same aspects of attacks we know the antifatae humans, the so-called vigilantes, made. The PUPs are still working the scene. But the snow is making things difficult, as are the sheer number of individuals trying to get a look."

Some of the fatae, and not a few humans, looked abashed by that.

"So please, people. You've all watched enough crime dramas to know that the PUPs need their space to work, and crowding in to watch is only going to make their work harder. Not to mention the fact that you might, accidentally, destroy a clue they need."

Someone in the fatae-side crowd made a rude noise. "The PUPs are—"

Beyl spread her wings a little wider, the feathers lifting as though air was circulating under them, and let the light glint off her four-inch-long claws. The voice cut off midword, as though someone had put the speaker in a chokehold.

She clacked her beak together in grim amusement, then went on. "The PUPs are ego-driven, not agenda-driven. We can trust them to come up with the truth, because to do anything else would be an insult to their training and their abilities. I trust we can all understand and appreciate the ego?"

The fatae weren't entirely appeased, but Wren spotted a few reluctant smiles among the humans. Yes, the *Cosa* knew about ego, all right.

Colleen and Michaela were standing next to Beyl now, each under her wing. The symbolism wasn't lost on any but the most obtuse. For a moment, it seemed almost as though sanity would prevail.

But this was the *Cosa*. Nothing was ever easy.

"Why should we trust anything the humans say or do?" a small, clay-colored figure asked from up near the ceiling where it was perched. "There are no fatae among these so-called puppies, only humans, and humans are who kill our kind."

"Humans, but not Talent," a piskie retorted, hovering up near a window with several others of its kind. Of all the fatae, piskies lived the most closely with humans; they understood the difference between Null and Talent that some others might miss. Mainly, for a piskie, that a Null would never be able to catch them when they pranked, while a Talent would and did. In the strange logic of piskies, that made Talent worthy of respect. More specifically, it made the lonejacks worthy of respect: the Council had shown itself less willing to take a prank in good humor, even when it came from a human; piskie pranks were insults.

"How do we know that? There was current! How could a mere human kill one of the angeli?"

"Angeli are difficult to kill," other voices agreed. "Tough bastards, too mean to die easy."

A human Wren didn't know raised his voice from the other end of the table. "In both cases we know of, the angel was left to bleed out. If you have blood, and you lose too much, you die. This is pretty basic stuff. And even the most Null of humans can kill the most powerful of fatae, if they have numbers and weapons on their side. Or did the recent Moot show you nothing at all?"

"What about the current-trace?" another voice demanded. A human voice, interestingly enough.

Bart answered that one. "The PUPs have not yet determined that the current is linked to the murderer, merely that current was used near the body at some point. It may even have been long before the attack occurred."

"May have," someone snorted; from the wetness of the snort it was probably one of the muzzle-bearing fatae. "Because the angeli were so known for letting humans near them."

Wren, remembering the angeli youth she had seen being threatened on the subway, might have argued that point, but she had learned her lesson the hard way: her job wasn't to get into things, but to observe, sift, and report back to the Quad.

At this point, though, she wasn't sure what she'd be able to tell them that they hadn't figured out for themselves. Some of the *Cosa* were willing to listen. Too many had already decided, one way or another, who the guilty ones were, and what should be done about it. The room broke up into clamor again, some of it involving dangerous-looking hand-waving and jaw-flapping.

Wren had only the faintest whiff of precog, too whiffy to be useful, but she could feel, deep in her core, things begin to crack and fail. *Burning bridges. Cracking and falling into the river. Was that what the Seer meant? How did you cook a meal on something like this?*

"Lonejack maybe not, but the Council's always been johnnie-come-reluctant. They've never made any bones about thinking we're less than they are, barely *Cosa* at all. And they were behind the disappearances of lonejacks, too, last year, weren't they? If there's current involved, I say look at them!"

Wren stiffened, trying to spot who that shout had come from. She didn't believe it. She *wouldn't* believe it, not without some reason, some proof. But it was possible, and— given the history—plausible. And for someone to voice all that, in this crowd…match to kindling, and kindling someone had presoaked in lighter fluid, at that.

Beyl and Jordan exchanged glances across the length of the table, but said nothing. Bart looked as though he wanted to step forward, but didn't. The tension built until Wren was ready to scream, just to push it into breaking. And then, creating an almost physical wave of shock, Rick slammed an open palm down on the table, causing everyone to shut up and stare.

Rick looked like every suburban matron's worst nightmare of a biker dude, down to his wildman hair and leather gear, but the South Jersey-Philly-area lonejack representative was the one member of the Quad Wren was honestly fond of. And the fact that he'd let her ride his bike once had nothing to do with that.

"Once, we were threatened, and we turned on each other. We pointed fingers, and deflected official attention from us onto others, and be damned the cost. History has a name for that time, they call it the Salem Witch Hunts. Do we remember what the *Cosa* calls it? Does anyone here remember?"

He didn't wait for anyone to actually answer.

"It's called The Shame. Shame on them for doing such a thing. Shame on us for allowing it to happen. Shame enough to go around and cover us all with the stink of it. Shame that lingers to this day, and turns us into cowards the moment we again feel threatened.

"Nulls can kill fatae. Fatae can kill humans—if we have our own Shame, they have generations of history of that, as well. The myths and legends came from a justified fear of things that went bump in the night. These so-called vigilantes act not from nothing—they have the same racial memory we humans all hold, of children dead in the dusk, of loved ones gone missing in the bogs, of spirits unquiet in the night. We all hold within us the destruction of the other, and all that keeps us from it is one thing, and one thing alone.

"Trust."

His gaze felt like boiling water on Wren's skin as it passed over her, and from the silent shifting of the crowd, she suspected she wasn't alone in the sensation.

"Can you turn to the person next to you, and trust them? Just one step further? Trust that they want what you want— to live, to love, to pursue happiness, without fear?"

And he was doing it all, Wren realized suddenly, without resorting to current at all. Just sheer personal willpower. Dark green jealousy rose in her throat, and she let it, then let it go.

Rick shook himself, like a shaggy dog shaking off water, and the hold he had on the group was broken.

Jordan came forward then, the jacket of his seven-hundred-dollar suit off and his custom-made shirt open at the collar under his tie. Wren thought it looked like he was getting ready for a presidential photo-op.

"All right, folk, we've got the PUPs on the scene, and they'll give the Board a report and we'll pass it along as soon as it's in. Other than that, all we can do is stay calm and keep ourselves alert. Go home, now."

It was deeply anticlimactic after Rick's speech, but it did the trick. The meeting didn't so much break up as it siphoned off, dabs of people moving off into smaller groups, with a steady stream heading outside into the cold in order to have a cigarette. Some, but very few, of the fatae present lingered to speak to a few humans Wren recognized as fellow lonejacks, but the moment a Council member approached, the conversation ended. Rick might call for trust and tolerance, but the fatae had made up their mind: the Council was not to be trusted.

Wren could certainly empathize. But the look on Ayexi's face: a sad, worn-down hound look, tore grooves into her heart, and she found herself by his side, reaching out to take him in a consoling and totally unexpected hug, without being aware that she was moving at all.

He returned the embrace, briefly, then they both stepped back, and he walked away, joining the other Council representatives huddled in a heated, isolated conversation.

"Goodbye, Ayexi," she said softly. Feeling suddenly and totally useless, Wren got gone; if anything came up, the Quad knew damn well where to find her. The sky had stopped cranking out the snow, and she paused for a moment to take a deep lungful of the air, sharply crackling in her mouth and throat and sparking her mind into new wakefulness.

The busses were running, but she didn't feel like sharing space with anyone right now. It would be a long walk, but a pretty one. And she hadn't been to the gym in too long, anyway.

Pulling a warm wool watch cap down over her head, and wrapping the matching scarf around her neck, Wren set off down the street, her gaze firmly on the icy sidewalk, but all other senses scanning the area around her. The unreliable sense Sergei had dubbed "Mage-dar" was in full flare, making her hypersensitive to any Talent or fatae who passed by. From the glances she received in turn, everyone else was on the same kind of high alert.

But they're not who the danger's coming from. Are they?

Where once there had been certainty, now was doubt. What if the whisperers were right? What if the danger, the funding for the vigilante attacks, had not been from some distant, unknown, surprisingly observant human bigots, but from within the *Cosa?* Wren believed the Council, as much as she could, when they'd said that they were not officially behind the attacks. Harassing lonejacks, yes, but it made no sense to murder fatae. State the obvious: If there was one thing about the Council that was consistent and countable-on, it was that there was an end to every means they went through, and the ends always profited them.

This brought them no profit, no end-result plus. Maintaining the Truce benefited them, too. Specifically, it benefited Madame Howe, at the moment. Breaking it…

The walk took longer than expected, in part because she stopped at a Starbucks to pick up a grande mocha, but by the time she got to her street, Wren had determined to her own satisfaction that the Council was no more scummy than historically established.

This didn't mean that the bad guys weren't family. Because yeah, once a sufficient number of Nulls might be able to take down an angel. But twice was unlikely. Forewarned was pissy and dangerous, two things the angeli excelled at. While alone the angel she had seen threatened had been vulnerable, the moment he was able to call on his brothers, the two human toughs had been toast.

A Talent, though…or another fatae, who could get in close because the angeli would never expect an attack from one of the "underling" nonhumans—that was a distinct and unlovely possibility. It might even be a probability.

She got to her building, and could practically feel some of the tension slip off her shoulders. Home wasn't where the heart was, or where you hung your hat, or even where they had to take you in. Home was where you wanted to be, at the end of a lousy day. Or even midday in what was shaping up as a doozy of a lousy day.

"Valere."

Bonnie sidled in the entry door just behind her, her usual redheaded goth princess look muted by the royal blue down coat covering her from chin to knee.

"Hey." Wren was too tired to muster a more polite greeting. "You come from the dog-and-pony show?"

"Nah, I'm too junior to merit that." Bonnie had been the first PUPI Wren had ever met, on assignment to track down the men who had assaulted P.B. in her apartment. That attack had been ordered by Madame Howe, and been swept under the rug of the Truce. P.B. didn't seem to hold a grudge, but Wren did. Even if she was able to work with them, she didn't forget, and she didn't let go of people hurting people she cared about.

Bonnie, on the other hand, seemed to work on the "discover the facts, move on" mode—she had never once referenced the case once her input had been filed, even once she and Wren became building-mates and, slowly, friends.

Then again, that was the whole point of the PUPs—to

not let it become personal. Rick had mentioned the Shame, but that hadn't been the only time that Talents had turned on each other. Even the most functional of families had bad decades: even the inter-*Cosa* relations in Italy had been strained for generations after WWI, for all that they spoke well of each other in public; fatae had little to do with humans, and Council made pronouncements and the unaffiliateds ignored them as best they could.

PUPs were impartial; they didn't take the side of anything excerpt the determined and verified facts. But they were still new, and not everyone believed impartiality was possible.

"I'm starved. You want some lunch?"

Wren had already learned not to pass up Bonnie's home-cooking; her Talents were matched by her talent with a skillet and whatever odds and ends were in her fridge. How P.B. hadn't glommed onto her as a mooch-source, Wren didn't know.

"Anyway, no, not part of the show, but I did come straight from the autopsy." Bonnie unlocked her second-floor apartment door, shed her coat, and dropped it; the coat disappeared before it hit the floor. Probably Transloc'd right into the closet. Show-off.

"The angeli allowed an autopsy?"

Wren's own coat had to be hung up the old-fashioned way, by opening the closet door and taking out a hanger. Sure enough, there was Bonnie's down jacket, neatly stored.

"We didn't ask them."

PUPs were also becoming known for their arrogance.

Justified arrogance was still arrogance, to Wren. But Bonnie managed to make it look cute.

That must have been a pretty after-the-fact confrontation. Wren was glad she hadn't been around for it. "And?"

"And the angel died from exsanguination."

Wren put her hands, fisted, on her hips, and stared at the PUPI, an exasperated puff of breath making the tendrils of hair along her face rise and settle like Beyl's wings. "We already knew that."

Bonnie shrugged, a helpless-looking move rather than one of indifference. "You didn't know that the vic was incapacitated before being cut—by a rather massive dose of current."

Wren's blood temperature dropped ten degrees, easy, despite the heat blasting through the radiators.

"Current?"

"Of one kind or another—we're not certain, yet. Which is why that bit of information is not for widespread release? In fact, the boss is telling the Double-Quad, and that's it."

"And you're telling me."

She blinked. "Am I? Ooops." Cute *and* innocent-looking. Bonnie was dangerous.

"Wait a minute." Wren's mind was already chewing on this new information. "Of one kind or another? You can't tell?"

Current, in *Cosa* parlance, was magic; Talent was the inner ability in some humans to channel it through their body and turn it into something useful. Current was also, in more common terms, electricity.

"Nope." Bonnie went into the kitchen, which was twice the size of Wren's. The apartment only had one bedroom, though; Bonnie didn't work out of her home and so didn't need the space. She pulled down the Skillet of Doom, a huge cast-iron monstrosity that was at least as old as she was and almost the same weight, and thunked it down on the stovetop.

Wren didn't move, thinking over what Bonnie had said. Mage-current was madly individual, practically a living entity in and of itself. The fact that *Current* ran alongside electrical current, using it as the path of least resistance, was merely a fluke of nature and design…wasn't it? But then, elementals lived in electricity as happily as current; maybe they couldn't tell the difference, either? Or they didn't care?

Wren's brain was beginning to hurt. She had never cared about the whys and hows of her skills, only the practical application of it.

"Savory or sweet?" Bonnie called from the kitchen.

"Savory," Wren replied, following the redhead into the kitchen and perching herself on the opposite counter to watch the show.

"In fact," Bonnie went on, grabbing a head of garlic and tossing it to Wren for peeling, "realistically speaking, you can't absolutely determine that there's a real difference between current and, oh, a nasty lightning strike as a cause of death. In both cases, there's a red mark, sort of like a leaf pattern, where current hits or exits. Ditto for lightning. Most people don't die from the hit, or related burns, you know that? It's the heart that kills them. Shock stops it, *bam*, just like that. Like the opposite of a jumper cable, or defibrillator. Current does the same thing. The stuff that's in us allows us to channel it. Kills everyone else, 'cause their cells just collapse under the rise in internal energy."

Wren had just slammed the garlic on the counter to loosen the skin when what Bonnie said filtered through her already-hurting brain. "You're saying that Talent is just insulation?"

That stopped Bonnie for an instant, and made her laugh. "Yeah, I guess so, aren't I?"

She rinsed her hands at the sink, then went to the fridge and pulled out a packet of salmon, a couple of stalks of celery, and a head of something dark green and leafy, but too small to be lettuce. Taking it all to the counter, she dumped it into a small pile, then started slicing the salmon into strips. "Anyway, that's all academic, because that's not what I was talking about."

Wren stopped peeling garlic, totally confused. "What wasn't?"

"Lightning. This wasn't lighting. Or man-made power. It was current. But we don't know whose." Fish dealt with, she shoved it to one side of the cutting board, and went to the sink to rinse her hands again, then started in on the vegetables.

"No signature?" That was Wren's greatest concern about PUPs, and why she tended to keep her usage low to nil around Bonnie: the fear that the girl would, even accidentally, someday be in a position to match a current signature to a Retrieval investigation, assuming anyone ever called a PUP in for something like that, and recognize Wren's particular "fingerprint."

"Oh, if we had a database or something, if the user was in the database, we could match it, sure. But it wouldn't be even close to bona fide evidence—current isn't DNA, it's more like, oh, a mug shot. More important to the situation, you can't tell anything about the user, in a vacuum. Like, oh… Council or lonejack. There's no damn difference between the current itself. " She turned the heat on under the skillet and then paused. "Well, actually, there is, but it's totally subjective. It *feels* different, but there's no way to point to something objective. Which isn't a problem normally, because we know what we know. Except…"

"Except you can't use what you know to change the mind of someone who's convinced otherwise." Not that there was a court of law, as such, in the *Cosa Nostradamus,* but you still had to be able to argue the evidence to get a majority view to…what? To convict? To sentence? Wren had never thought that far ahead. She didn't have to; that was the Quad's job. Like the technical details of current, it just didn't interest her.

All the lectures and rants she'd ever been subjected to about being a good citizen and taking part in the system started to flutter in the back of her memory. This wasn't American Civics 101—she didn't have time to get into philosophical discussions with herself about the privileges and demands of society. She focused instead on what Bonnie was saying.

The PUP had finished with the prep, and was going to

the fridge in order to pull out something in an opaque Tup-
perware container. "Exactly. So we're effectively useless at
saying who actually committed the attack."

"Except they were Talent." Was an inside job, in other
words.

"Or were able to mock it up, yeah. And before you ask,
no I don't know of anyone who can imitate current...but I
don't know that they can't, either."

In short, the more they learned, the less they were able
to narrow it down. The fatae was killed by basic, brutal vigi-
lante-style methods...but he was incapacitated by *Cosa*-
specific means. The implications of that were ugly: not
only was the angel killed in a brutal manner, and staged to
make a maximum, can't-hush-it-up scene, but that it could
have been done by a *Cosa* member specifically to break the
truce and scatter whatever solidarity the *Cosa* had managed
to build.

Wren should have totally lost her appetite by this time.
But when Bonnie made a gesture indicating that it was time
to hand over the garlic, she discovered she was, mordantly
enough, starving.

Crisis, like everything else, burned calories. Replace 'em,
or fall over.

Wren was damned if she was going to fall over.

She finished the jobs—they didn't finish her.

twelve

It was almost midnight when Wren made it up the stairs to her apartment, replete with excellent food, new information about the nature of current, and a surprisingly entertaining amount of gossip. Bonnie had perfected the art of scandal without cruelty, mainly because she so clearly loved knowing to *know*, not to use that information in any way. Wren supposed that was what made her so good at her job, that sense of information as an end within itself. Let others put what she knew to whatever use they wanted; it was enough that Bonnie got there first.

Wren made a mental note to buy the PUP flowers, or something. She hadn't given the Retriever anything of specific use tonight…but you never knew when something might come around.

There was a flat manila packet propped up against her apartment door. Wren stooped to pick it up, checking—as had become habit—for any disturbance in the elementals she had left clustered around the entrance. They were mostly mindless creatures, satisfied to bask in any pooling of current they could find, but there was enough coherent thought in a mass of them to make semireliable watch-dogs, as needed. And they worked cheap; all she had to do was siphon off a bit of power and leave it there for them.

They were still there, like old ladies clustered around the bingo table, chatting to each other about nothing at all. She stroked her way past them, and went inside.

After the warm cheeriness of Bonnie's apartment, Wren's own place seemed depressingly bare. Even the lovely, deli-cate Japanese silk-painting hanging on the hallway wall outside her bedroom just served to point up the fact that, despite best intentions, she still hadn't managed to do any sort of significant decorating at all.

"I'm just not the nesting sort," she told the empty apart-ment. "And there's nothing wrong with that. At all."

She dumped a plastic bag filled with fresh-baked dinner rolls on the counter, stored her baked salmon leftovers—in a container marked Poison For Demon—in the fridge, and opened the manila packet.

Inside was a series of clippings she had requested, in-volving her client: the guest list of every gathering—social or otherwise—he had held in his Forest Hills apartment in the past year. If this had been a theft of opportunity, as so many blackmail-related thefts were, that person had access to the client's belongings at some point, probably more than once.

"Hrmmm." Her brain clicked over, almost an audible sound, from *Cosa* to Retrieval mode.

Blackmail was always ugly, no matter what the cause or cost. Although it was odd that the man hadn't received a blackmail demand yet, for the return of those papers, no? Might there be another reason—maybe the material stolen had more going for it than they'd been told? It wouldn't be the first time a client had lied to them, God knew. Sergei had provided a list of proposals that would be coming up for vote in the next few months...she'd have to double-check that list against this one, see of any names jumped out at her.

Dropping the lists off on her desk, she switched on the computer. As she did every time, Wren held her breath and sent up a quick prayer to whatever saint watched over fool-hardy Talent who owned computers that the machine would boot up without problems. Cell phones and PDAs, being carried on the body, were more subject to current fluctuations, but computers were notoriously unreliable, and the longer you owned it, the more so they became; she'd had this desktop for almost two years now, and every moment she expected it to go up in a flare of sparks and put-upon indignation.

Even more so, considering it had survived—barely—a drop-in visit from a wizzart not so long ago. Wren paused to wonder where Max was these days, if he was still func-tional, or if the damage had finally taken him over the cliff. He had been mad, bad, and definitely dangerous to be around, but she hoped he was okay.

This time, the computer behaved itself, and she was able

to log onto the Internet and check her e-mail without too much difficulty. There hadn't been time to do that for almost a week, and there was more than the usual number of list mails and spam to go through, plus a couple of personal e-mails, all of which were sorted into the proper folders, to be ignored until she had time and energy to deal with them. Most of her lists were on digest, these days: she missed the mostly friendly exchanges, but simply couldn't deal with them right now. Someday, maybe, things would go back to normal, if she could even recognize it by then.

When she was done, there were three e-mails that looked to require immediate dealing. One was a follow-up to a previous case: a curator at the Meadows Museum wanted her help in evaluating a proposed new security system. The e-mail had been sent to Sergei, and he had forwarded it to her, with a question mark.

"Sure," she typed back, amused. The museum in question was one she'd hit numerous times, so much so that she'd suggested, gently, to the curator that they just give her a key and be done with it. It sounded like they were finally giving in to the inevitable and making use of it; use a thief to keep out other thieves—especially since the other thieves were the ones who would likely do more financial damage.

She assumed the fiscal offer was enough to warrant Sergei even forwarding it on to her, although she'd do it for free, just for the fun factor. Her life was sadly lacking in fun, these days.

The second e-mail was from her friend Katie in California, announcing the arrival of labor pains. She had sent the e-mail via her cell phone in the back of a taxi on the way to the hospital. Wren looked at the time stamp, and—based on Katie's previous pregnancies, made a mental note to check back tomorrow to see if they were allowing texting from the delivery room.

The third e-mail was probably useless, but the header—"sidhe sighting"—was guaranteed to pique her interest.

Sure enough, the e-mail was in response to a query she'd placed on an electronic bulletin board a few months ago, about the stuffed horse she'd been chasing since forever. Her mind clicked over again, switching between jobs.

Saw what I think you're looking for, two nights running. Greengrove, Connecticut. Nothing dire's happened yet, but I'm keeping an eye out.

Two nights. Traditionally, the bansidhe showed for three nights, and then disaster struck. And here she was, snow-bound, stuck....

Or not. It all depended on how badly she wanted to track down this horse. Wren made a face, then sent a quick ping downstairs to see if Bonnie was still awake.

Six hours later, Wren was knee-deep in snow, puking her guts up. Even with Bonnie's help, Translocation still made her insides try to turn into outsides, with nasty results. Finally, the retching subsided, and Wren used a handful of clean snow to cool down her face and rehydrate her parched throat, then pulled one of Bonnie's dinner rolls from her pocket and used a bite of it to clean the taste out of her mouth, shoving the remains back into the pocket. Only then was she able to look around, and get her bearings.

Greengrove, Connecticut was more rural than she'd expected, this close to Boston. Not that she knew anything about Connecticut, or Massachusetts, for that matter, but she'd always assumed it was cities surrounded by acres of suburbia. The field she was in seemed to be attached to a house some distance away, and its neighbors were even more distant, all in the "don't mind me and I won't mind you" way that had long since given up the ghost to McMansions and high-rise condos everywhere else.

Despite growing up in the suburbs, Wren was a city girl, bone and marrow. This much open space, without the reassuring sound of traffic in the near distance, was unnerving. The snow had stopped, but the sky was still a leaden gray shading to dirty white where dawn touched the tree line, and she could taste the metallic glint of bad weather coming in the back of her throat. Whatever she was going to do, she needed to do it quickly.

Pity she didn't have a clue what that whatever was.

"All right, there's the barn." She hoped. It looked like the barn the e-mail had described, and Bonnie was pretty good with the map-scrying which had sent her here, but how the hell did you tell one barn from another, anyway? They were all the same color, and they didn't have numbers painted on them, and every single one was the same barn-shape….

She yelped, and jumped a little, as current zinged from deep inside the bedrock and raced up through the soles of her boots, into her veins, and shot directly into her core, shocking the relatively somnolent current-serpents into a hissing pile.

"Jesus wept," she swore, reaching down to calm them back under control, while one part of her tracked the source of the current. It hadn't felt directed, like a tag, or like a widespread attack, the way a psi-bomb did. This was more...like Mother Nature twitching.

Something prickled on the back of her neck, and Wren spun in place, in time to see a green shimmering glow appear in the distance, just in front of the barn. A green, shimmering, horse-shaped glow.

"There you are at last, you annoying stuffed beast." Over the years she'd started to wonder if someone wasn't having the longest-running prank on her; it wasn't beyond the capability of several Talent she knew, but even the most dedicated prankster couldn't generate something like what was in front of her, not unless they were so crazy-wizzed they'd risk pulling out current from the magma itself, and no wizzart would be able to hold a prank together that long.

Which meant that it was real. She had finally done it, finally finished the damn job. She was looking at one of the rarest and least pleasing manifestations in the supernatural world: a bansidhe, a harbinger of misfortune.

Why this particular one had chosen to manifest inside the sawdust-stuffed remains of a moth-eaten war mount was one mystery; why it had, several years back, decided to go a-wandering out of its ancestral glass-cased housing was another. Wren wasn't being paid to solve those mysteries. Just to get it back to the family the warhorse belonged to.

Problem was, she had absolutely no idea how to do that. All of her energy until now had been spent on *finding* the damn thing; tracking it down before it moved on to the next disaster announcement. Wren had never actually come up with a plan to capture it, mainly because she had no idea of the form, power or intelligence level of the thing. Now she knew two of the three, at least...

As far as she had been able to determine, like most supernatural entities the bansidhe had no magical abilities of its own, neither old style nor currential. That was a plus: it couldn't actively negate anything she tried. It was also a negative: current was unlikely to be able to impact it significantly. But what the hell; try the most obvious, first.

She moved, slowly and cautiously, closer to the beast, stopping when she was about ten feet away. The snow between them was untouched, covered with a thin crust that wouldn't support the weight of a sparrow.

She stared at it, trying to come up with the right words to match the visual in her head: a circle of power, glowing around it, rising up to form a corral of sorts, as best she could recreate one from too infrequent viewing of Westerns on TV.

"Equine form of doom
Long I've been searching for you;
Stay put where you are."

The bansidhe tossed its head and stared across the distance: Wren could almost see the derision in its glowing eyes as it deliberately moved several paces sideways. Across the line of current.

"Bitch." The body it was occupying was that of a stallion, but the bansidhe were traditionally female. Why a woman always got stuck handing out bad news, Wren didn't know— probably all the male bansidhe refused to get involved, leaving the dirty work to the females.

But this indicated a certain level of intelligence, to understand what was being done, and a definite stubborn will, to override the current. More information to add to the equation.

So. Current was out, at least of the passive sort. Wren supposed a lasso of current wouldn't work any better, even if she thought she could "toss" it with enough accuracy to get anywhere near the beastie.

"What now? 'Here, horsie horsie horsie?' It's not a damned horse!"

Although…

It's been in horse-shape for a long time. Stuffed with sawdust, yeah, but with the hide and hooves of a horse. Intelligent, but maybe that intelligence is limited to what a horse might have?

The problem was, Wren knew damn-all about horses, other than you fed one end, saddled the middle, and avoided the backside. *Carrots. Horses like carrots.* She had no carrots. She hated them with a passion, in fact. *Grass…* Would be a good idea, if everything wasn't covered under a foot of snow. Even if she dug some up, it would be dead and probably not all that appealing to either a horse or a bansidhe, no matter how hungry.

And the damn thing's stuffed with sawdust. What makes you think it's going to be hungry, anyway?

Instinct. Just hope there was a horsey instinct in there, somewhere…

Any food might do the trick in that case. Horses were herbivores, herd animals, grazers. The body the bansidhe was inhabiting had been a warhorse, trained to respond to its rider's signals without hesitation. Maybe it would react to other human body language, too.

"Hey there, bitch. Lookie what I got for you." She dug in her pocket, then held out her fist with the half-eaten roll in it. It was whole wheat; maybe that would be close enough to oats to appeal. "I was going to finish it myself, for breakfast, but if you come here and let me get hold of you, I'll share." She thought of horse-slobber on the roll, and changed her mind. "I'll let you have all of it, even."

Old Sally made a noise that sounded like the horsey version of a laugh—or a snicker—and tossed her head, looking away.

"Don't play hard to get, darling. You've already proven you're hard to get—your reputation's secured. Just come here and eat the damn roll, and let me get hold of you…."

And do what? If she could Translocate, no worries. But even with Bonnie's help, that was a bad idea. Alone? She could do it, but it wouldn't be pretty. And there wouldn't be any guarantees they'd all come out in the right place, or intact, or…

Another, better idea, then.

Maybe… She had been playing with an idea that had

grown out of all the cages she'd been making lately, for various Artifacts she kept falling over: rather than the restraining spell she had tried before, maybe a variant on the self-reinforcing, self-containing lockdown she had made for the damned parchment, something that built on the object's own power, set on a constant loop so every time it tried to get out, it fed the spell, not itself.

That required a certain intelligence level for it to work—useless on most inanimate, unaware objects. Maybe, maybe…

But to use that spell, she needed to actually lay hands on the object. This led her back to the immediate, non-magical problem.

"C'mere, c'mere. There's a good horse. You're a wise horse, an old horse, and your job here's done. It's time to come in, out of the cold, yes, no more racing around you've earned your rest, haven't you…"

After a few words she had no idea what she was actually saying; her tone was the important thing: projecting all the calming, coaxing, reassuring notes into it she could manage, talking both to the bansidhe, who had been working endlessly for so many generations, and the valiant, gallant horse-body which housed it.

Amazingly, it seemed to be working.

The bansidhe rolled an eye at her, but didn't move when she stepped forward, the bread outstretched in her palm.

"There's a good girl, good horse, good horse. Yah, stay right there, Jesus wept what am I doing? Stay there, good horse, good horse."

She deliberately soothed the coils of current roiling in her core, *not* drawing on it for fear of spooking the bansidhe out of its equine instincts. When the time came, she would have to move quickly, but she couldn't worry about it now.

"There you go. Here I come. Steady now, steady..."

Her hand trembled, and she stilled it. Horse instincts: they were pack animals, weren't they, so if she got spooked, it would probably get spooked, and then she'd be screwed, but good.

"There you are. There you are, oh such a good horse, good horse..."

Quiet voice, hand with the bread held palm up, fingers flat. Huge flat white teeth were revealed under thick horse lips, making her start to sweat even in the cold air. The great head reached forward, lowering slightly, and taking the bread from her with a surprisingly delicate touch.

"Hi there." She placed her free hand against the thick neck, just under the mane, which was cut like a Marine's, standing up in thick bristles. The hide was cool, not warm, but surprisingly supple, and she could almost, *almost* imagine the beat of blood pumping underneath.

She had been right—the bansidhe had inhabited the body long enough for horse-memories to bind with sidhe-memories.

Horse, horse, horse, she thought quickly, reinforcing the instincts, even as she reached down into herself and grabbed quickly at the nearest snake of current, pulling it up with such speed that her conscious mind couldn't catch up and alert the creature in front of her.

The current sprang into being, crackling in cold, dry air around them.

"Into existence;
Bind the creature before me
With its own power."

The current flowed downward, into the horse-frame, and Wren could sense it shedding her own signature and taking on the bansidhe's own flavor and structure. As it did so, it also formed the "sense" of a glass case around it, similar in appearance to pictures of the glass case Old Sally had been stored in, before it decided to go a-wandering. There were details to it, however, that Wren had never seen or imagined, and she sighed in relief—the bansidhe was adding to it from its own memories, recreating the place it felt was "home," where it felt safe and secure.

Like any animal, when threatened, it just wanted to go somewhere enclosed and protected.

At the last minute, just when Wren was starting to feel that she'd nailed the job, the bansidhe woke. Thankfully, there was still enough horse-memory in control that, rather than use its own magic to escape, it merely curved around and kicked out with its powerfully muscled hind legs. Sawdust or no, the damn thing packed a nasty blow. Wren felt the impact in her side, and went down hard on her ass. Snow cushioned her landing, and went down her jacket, front and back.

It happened so fast, there was seemingly no transition between being upright, and being horizontal.

The horse snickered; she swore she heard it snicker, but the current-built case held, and it stayed put.

"Yay, me," she said from her prone position, even the cold snow not dimming the sense of accomplishment she felt. Finally. Fin-bloody-ly, she could put this case in the Closed drawer. After she figured out how to transport the damn thing back to the owners, that was, but even that thought didn't dim her satisfaction.

The thought that followed hard on the heels of that, however, did.

Technically speaking, she hadn't found the bansidhe. Sure, she'd been told where to look, but there was no reason the creature had to return to that spot, for the third, final appearance just when she was there. There hadn't been anyone around to announce its message of disaster incoming, no witness to its presence. Except her.

Looking at it one way, it was coincidence, maybe bad timing on the bansidhe's part, to not have an audience. Or it could be considered good Retrieval, arriving before witnesses hit the scene.

Looked at another way…she didn't know who had sent her that e-mail. Pure luck she had looked then, been able to react as fast as she had. Except luck was sometimes someone's hand, offstage, stirring the pot.

Either way, it was as easy to say that, instead of her finding it, *it* had found *her.* Which meant that its historically accurate "warning of great and dire portent" could, reasonably, be assigned…to her.

Wren let her head fall back into the snow, staring up at the now-black sky.

"Oh boy."

thirteen

Something was bothering him. It took an hour of letting it nag at the back of his head, and two cups of execrable coffee, before the vague something crystallized into a determinable fact: the office was too quiet.

Andre Felhim was used to being in and out at odd times; the benefit and cost of being middle management; the work never ended, but you had your own office to settle in with it. But this quiet wasn't the sort that you got early morning or late at night, when everyone was either gone or buried under work. It was the quiet of people trying very, very hard not to be noticed.

And yes, the irony of an organization nicknamed The Silence being too quiet was not lost on him. He did have a sense of humor, despite what many thought.

That humor was absent from his face today, however. The silence was a worry, but not the most pressing of them.

His primary source of all information, researcher par excellence Darcy sat in front of him, her tiny frame radiating concern. From anyone else, he might have questioned the findings she had delivered to him. You did not question Darcy; she was that good. She was better than *that* good, actually.

"So. Where are they?"

"I don't know."

Darcy knew everything, or knew where to look to find it, and she never gave up until she tracked it down and understood it. For her to come up here, to make a report, and to say that…

"People do not simply go missing," Andre told her.

They did, of course. All the time. But not *their* people.

She didn't bother to contradict him, merely restated her data. "Seventeen, to date. All FocAs." FocAs—Silence slang for Focused Actives, field agents who were also Talent. Once, there were only half a dozen within the Silence. In the past decade, that number had more than quadrupled, and then doubled again. Seventeen of those nearly fifty were now missing in action. And no reports had been filed to that effect. Nobody had noticed they were gone. Nobody had cared.

Or nobody had dared to care.

They had been the first to note something was coming, Andre suddenly remembered. Almost a year ago, the rumblings had begun. Darcy had been the one to warn him about it, a merest muttering she had overheard, a scrap of discontent, the whisper of a rift, a schism….

He had been distracted then. He had asked her to follow up on it, but never followed up himself on what she had discovered. You couldn't cover every base, every time. Things slipped, especially in the press of more urgent, more immediate disasters. But even if these individuals hadn't been under his direct management, they deserved better than to be filed and forgotten.

He touched the intercom button on his phone. "Bren. You got a minute?"

"No. But I'll be there in two."

Bren, the office manager, dogsbody, and all-around dragon. If he trusted Darcy to give him every detail in existence, he trusted Bren to guard his back. She was an Amazon, in more ways than her build, and totally without fear.

"Three of their Handlers have taken a leave of absence in the past six months. Their FocAs were assigned to others." Darcy's voice had gotten flat, the way it did when she was reciting facts she personally did not enjoy knowing. If he hadn't worked with her for years, he wouldn't have been aware of that.

The detail about the Handlers was an interesting fact. A very interesting fact. Handlers were usually possessive unto death of their Operatives, and would rather work with a life-threatening injury than trust someone else with the running of the Op—especially a FoCAs, with their temperamental personalities and quirks and the not-totally-unsubstantiated feeling that nobody at Headquarters understood those personalities and quirks.

Sergei had been an excellent Handler; still was, if you

extended the job description to include his work with Wren Valere. But he had been terrible at every other aspect of the job, limiting his usefulness.

Sergei's successor, on the other hand, had lacked that particular directed empathy, and moved over to the administrative side with obvious relief. Andre sometimes wished that he had been able to merge the two, Didier and Jorgenmunder, into one perfect second-in-command. Although, the way the dice rolled, he would likely have ended with all of their negative traits rather than the desired ones....

"Have you been able to contact those individuals?" he asked Darcy while they waited for Bren to arrive.

"One. She checked in for a rest cure at a rather exclusive detox facility. The Silence is picking up the tab."

"Of course."

Andre steepled his long dark fingers in front of him, and stared at his fingertips. They were perfectly manicured, as was everything about him. Appearance was everything, even in the middle of a crisis. Never let them see you sweat, or otherwise indicate anything out of order. He had cut his hair short, to keep himself from tugging at it once he became aware of that habit, and even now that he trusted himself to manage stress better, it remained short. Nobody should ever know it was anything other than a stylistic choice.

Bren appeared in the doorway, clearly mentally juggling a number of things but equally ready to drop them at Andre's request. He wasn't the only manager she reported to, but he knew damn well that he was the most interesting.

"Has anyone seen Poul in the past week?" The question

was casually worded, but the fact that he was asking spoke volumes. Poul Jorgenmunder was his protégée, his successor-in-training, and should have been at his side constantly, in times like this.

Bren frowned, shook her head. "Not since last Tuesday, when he came in to pick up an expense check."

Darcy looked at Andre's fingertips, and said nothing. Andre noted that, as he knew that she knew he would.

So. The wind blew that direction. Hardly surprising, although it was of course disappointing. Still, Poul was a grown man, and had the right to choose and discard his own alliances.

"Bren, take this list of Operatives, find out if they're still drawing salaries, benefits, anything. Quietly." The last word wasn't needed, but he said it anyway.

She nodded, holding her hand out for the paper. No questions why, no reasons needed.

"Darcy. I need to know what's happened with our AWOL children. Whatever favors you have to promise, whatever money or goods has to change hands, do it."

He didn't tell her to hurry. He didn't need to. They both knew, through Sergei, what was happening in the city around them. It wasn't a good time for a Talent, any Talent, to be missing.

And these were *their* people, when all was said and done. The Silence took care of their own.

Sergei walked in the back door of the gallery, not wanting to frighten any potential customers with his unshaven, jet-lagged self. It had been a hellish couple of days, and not even the fact that he'd gotten signatures on an agreement, and dates set for the Fall, was enough to cushion the eventual crash he was going to have. Adapting from an overnight trip to a three-day enforced exile—even in a comfortable hotel— shouldn't have taken that much out of him. He just wasn't as young as he used to think he was, and no getting around it.

Still. He was home. He could drop the papers off for Lowell to deal with, make sure nothing had blown up in his absence, go take a shower and shave, get some fresh clothes, and find out what the hell was happening with the *Cosa.* It worried him that Wren hadn't called back, but he took some comfort from the fact that if things had really gone into the proverbial handbasket, he would have heard.

He thought he would have. Now that he considered it, he wondered…would P.B. think to contact him, if something went wrong? Would P.B. even know *how* to reach him, if he wasn't at home or at the gallery?

That brought him to a full halt. "You aren't seriously thinking about giving him your mobile number, are you?" he asked himself out loud. The question bounced against the narrow walls, mocking him. Of course, the demon had called him once before, when they were in Italy. Technically, Lee had called, but P.B. had been part of that. So odds were that yes, the demon already had his cell number. And yes, he would have called if anything had gone wrong. Even if Wren had told him not to call. Probably *especially* if Wren had told him not to call.

Reassured, he strode forward again. The rear of the

building was where deliveries were made; it opened up into the lower level, where the storage rooms were. The floors were concrete, the lighting was bare and harsh, and his steps echoed against the pale green walls and bounced down the corridor in front of him like a herald to announce his return.

"You're not supposed to be down here."

Lowell. Why was Lowell down here, and not upstairs schmoozing clientele? Sergei adjusted the strap of his carry-on more securely on his shoulder, and sped up to the room where the voice came from, already knowing fairly well whom his assistant was speaking to. Lowell only ever got that tone in his voice when he was dealing with Wren.

Sure enough, when he got to the main installation storage room—a grand name for a cinder-block-lined space, even if it was large enough to qualify as an apartment by New York standards—Lowell was in full bristle mode, hands on his hips, carefully styled blond hair quivering with outrage, pretty-boy blue eyes full of righteous indignation.

Wren was standing in front of a wooden crate about the size of an SUV, which filled half the available space, forcing her closer to Lowell than she usually cared to get. In contrast to Lowell, she looked less indignant—or even evilly amused, her usual reaction to his assistant's temper tantrums—than...he looked closer. She looked like shit, actually. Wrung out and worn-out and several shades paler than even she should be. Her hair hung down her back in lackluster strands, rather than being pinned up as usual, and the lines of her body—so familiar to him now—were too tense for such a common thing as a showdown with Lowell. Usually Wren treated that like catnip, not a cause for stress. Was it just that he'd been away, that he was seeing this, suddenly? Had she been so worn before he left? Or had something happened while he was away?

"What's going on here?"

He didn't mean to use his Dad-voice. Just like Lowell's tone, it always seemed to slip out when confronted by the two of them hissing and spitting like cats.

"Your…friend seems to think that she can waltz in here and use the gallery instead of renting a storage room like everyone else."

Lowell knew better than to diss Wren to Sergei's face, but he'd never been able to refer to her as his partner, even after they started being obvious about it. It wasn't a sexual jealousy, thank God—his life was already complicated enough, thank you—but pure possessiveness.

"I didn't have a choice." Wren wasn't apologizing, not exactly, but the look on her face said "please understand, I can't go into it now."

In other words, it was *Cosa*—and possibly Retrieval-related. *Please God, do not let it have anything to do with the murdered angel, or anything smelling of violence. Not here, in this one sanctuary…* "Lowell, do we need this space for any incoming installations?"

His assistant didn't have to go upstairs to check the database. "No." Grudging, but honest. "The current exhibit is almost entirely sold. The new owners will be taking possession in the next ten days." Sergei Didier Gallery did not let things go as they were sold—they were there to highlight the artist as much as sell the works, and so nothing left until the exhibit's run was over. "The new exhibit's already in Storage D. We won't need this space until March. But—"

"You'll have this out before then?" he asked his partner.

'Well before then," she said, a hint of desperation under her words that made him madly curious as to what was as in there. But first things first.

"That's settled, then. In the future, please try to check with us before you have anything delivered, all right? And Lowell, did you close the gallery, or are people waltzing in and out with our livelihood under their arms, unpaid for?"

His assistant had the grace to look abashed. "I put the Back in Ten sign up when I heard someone down here."

"It's been ten. Go back upstairs. I'll take care of this."

Lowell nodded, shooting another look at Wren. No, not at Wren: at the crate behind her. And the look was less annoyance than…a step below fear, but above discomfort. Interesting.

"Go."

Lowell went.

"All right. What is that, and why is it freaking my assistant out?" And him, too, now that he thought about it. He was more on edge than he had been when he walked in the door, when he should have been more relaxed. And it couldn't just be chalked up to their spat—lord knows he was used to it by now.

She mumbled something, he couldn't quite make out.

"What was that?"

"It'soldsally."

"Again?"

"It's. Old. Sally."

"Sal… The bansidhe?"

"Yeah." Wren looked up, and behind the desperation there was pride. "Got her."

His first reaction was one of pleasure—he knew how hard she had worked on this job, and how much it bothered her to leave it open. Having it off her to-do list would be one less thing for her to stress over, and he would be able to say with absolute honesty and no dancing in semantics, that The Wren always got the job done, rather than the "never walked away from a job" he had been using.

Hard on the heels of that thought, however, came a wave of more negative reactions. The damned thing was a harbinger of bad tidings, a warning of doom and disaster imminent, and while Sergei wasn't particularly superstitious, he had noted over the years that bad news tended to attract more of the same. Not something they needed in their life, right now, and certainly not *here*. Especially if *Lowell* was picking up on it.

"And this…thing is in my gallery…why?" The moment he asked, he had a bad—worse—feeling about the answer.

Wren shrugged, that pale and worn look back on her face. "Because I can't leave it unprotected. Here, I can put in extra wards, and know nobody's going to stumble over it by accident."

The reference, even unsaid, was clear. Stumble over it

like unfortunates had stumbled over the Nescanni Parchment; stumbled upon it, and been eaten by it, mind and soul as well as body, before they—Wren—were able to box the damned thing up and drop it somewhere deep.

She was worried, too. Only she was worrying about everyone except them.

"That's not just a crate, is it?" he asked warily.

"Umm." If she were the type, she would have dragged one toe in the dust. "It's not a crate at all, actually. It just looks like one, 'cause... You really want to hear all the details?"

Sergei could feel a headache coming in on top of the one he had already. "No. I don't think I do. You'll get it out of here pronto?"

"As soon as I can arrange a pickup," she promised.

It wasn't specific enough to satisfy him, but he had to settle for it. "And next time? Ask me before you bring *Cosa* business here, all right? Not that I mind, as such, but I like to know what's going on under my nose, if at all possible."

The look in Wren's eye's changed, and his uh-oh alert kicked into high gear. She only ever got that look when she was about to, in brutal terms, get out the pointy-toed kicking boots.

"Yeah." The way she drawled the word out made him start to worry about himself, rather than her, or Lowell, or the gallery. "About that whole 'in the know' thing." She paused, and he couldn't tell if it was for effect, or merely to gather her thoughts for the most devastating attack. "I stopped by your place before I came here. Needed to get the keys—didn't think you'd want me futzing with the alarms to break in."

"I appreciate that." He waited, warily, wondering...there hadn't been anything even remotely incriminating at the apartment—he didn't *have* anything incriminating that she didn't know about, anymore.

"The phone rang. I answered it."

He waited, the headache splintering off and having devil-babies that kicked at the inside of his skull, screaming bloody murder.

"Your doctor is a very ethical man. Even though I was clearly in your apartment, he refused to give me any of the details of the test results."

Oh chyort. He hadn't expected the office to get back to him for at least another week.

"You didn't break into his office to get them?"

"That would have been rude. I figured I'd give you a chance to explain, first. Then, if you balked, that would be next."

Of course. Not that he would have expected anything else, from her.

"I love you, Zhenchenka, but there are some things you're not going to be privy to." Not until he'd had a chance to talk to his doctor, first, at the very least. But Jesus, he wasn't ready to deal with this.

"Fine." Said in that tone of voice, it was completely and emphatically not fine. "I can understand that. I can respect that. We had the whole 'keeping important things secret' fight already, not going to rehash that, so anything you'd keep from me would be minor and totally unimportant and not caused or relating to anything I might have done, right?"

"Right."

"Pee much blood, lately?"

"Don't do this, Wren. Not right now."

"When, then? Because you keep telling me it's nothing, and it's *not* nothing. Not if you've got the doctor running tests you're not telling me about."

Wren could hear her voice getting thin with anger, and hated herself for it. She had sworn, all the way over here, that she wouldn't do this. That she would respect his decision to keep this away from her, that she wouldn't assume the worst, that she would give him room and time to come clean of his own accord.

The damned horse had her on edge; that was all. It affected everyone that way—that was why she'd decided to hide it here, where its effect on the general public would be limited. She had reason to know that these storage rooms could be remarkably well insulated, magically. What went into them, stayed in them. And she could warn Sergei…

Well. That had been the theory, anyway.

"So tell me. How much damage have I been doing to you? And how much of it can't they fix?"

He looked as bad as she felt. How much of that was normal travel-crap, and how much of it was stuff that had been going on, stuff she had been too immersed in her own trauma, her own selfishness, to notice? His chest was rising and falling faster than normal, but his breathing sounded shallow. She tried to focus in on it, using current like a stethoscope, an MRI, to look under the skin, past the flesh and blood, down into the internal organs that took the brunt of every single shot of current he had ever taken, every time she had ever grounded in him, or dragged him into a case, put him in the line of fire.

"Wren, it's okay." He was trying for Reasonable Adult, but it came out all wrong. "There's been some impact, yes. But it's under control. We already discussed this. I'm an adult. I can deal with this."

"No, you're not. Adult, that is. You're a hormonal idiot in an adult's body." She could feel her hands clenching into fists, and forced them, slowly, to unclench. What she *wanted* to do was hug him, snuggle into his embrace and let him tell her she was the best at what she did, how impressed he was that she'd managed to finally close the one case even he had given up on, and pretend the rest of this wasn't happening. But she couldn't give him that out; couldn't pretend she wasn't angry, wasn't hurt, wasn't scared out of her mind.

He didn't seem to understand, didn't seem to *care* what she was doing to him. Didn't seem to care that if they weren't careful—if *she* wasn't careful, she could lose him.

Yes, she had abandonment issues, a little. Her dad was a one-night stand, her mentor had walked out when he started to wiz—Sergei, of all people, should understand that she had issues. He was the one who made her take the psych courses, in college.

No more Sergei. Yawning black pit under her feet, when

she tried to think about that. So she didn't think about it. Better to be angry. Angry at the assholes who thought that killing was the way to deal with anything that was different, and scary. Angry at the idiots who saw threats under every rock and behind every street lamp. And angry at her clueless, oblivious, stubborn partner, who couldn't understand that losing him, that being the thing that killed him, might kill her, too.

Angry that the bansidhe might have appeared to warn her of exactly that happening.

"Jesus, Wren. You were the one who told me that you could control your current. And I'm telling you that I can control my…kink. So what's the problem?"

"Because I don't believe either one of us."

There was a long heavy silence, standing like a third person between them, then Sergei picked up the carry-on bag he had dropped when he came in, and shook his head. "Then that's your problem, isn't it? I suggest you deal with it."

And then he walked out.

fourteen

It was snowing. Again. At this point, it wasn't novel, it wasn't pretty, it wasn't keeping anyone safe at all, it wasn't anything but a damned annoyance, and Wren was heartily sick and tired of winter and cold and the bleak barren nothingness of the city.

On the way home from the gallery, she stopped at a specialty food market to pick up precooked ribs and a bottle of diet Sprite, plus a box of hot cocoa. Her hand hesitated over the box of Double Stuf Oreo cookies, and a pint of Ben & Jerry's, but she decided that that would be pushing the stereotype a bit too far. This wasn't a breakup; she wasn't going to dive headfirst into breakup foods.

She had to believe that. Had to. Nothing else was acceptable; therefore nothing else was going to happen.

That is not logic as we mortals know it.

Neezer's voice, faint and almost forgotten. Her mentor

had been a damned good role model for facing up to the facts of the situation: when he screwed up, he dealt with it, by himself and on his own, the way a lonejack should. You didn't drag anyone else into your own mess, and they returned the favor. A lonejack was strong. A lonejack took care of herself.

And a lonejack took care of her family. She had gotten her mother out of the line of fire. P.B. was in it, thick as she was, but it was his mess, too. Sergei...

Sergei is an adult, and tougher than you are by a magnitude. Her own voice this time, with maybe a touch of her mother in the tone. *You insulted him, by telling him otherwise. Just because he puts out this urbane man-about-town thing, don't ever forget he's got as much macho in him as the next guy.*

"Oh, shut up. He doesn't understand." Yes, he'd seen firsthand what current could do to someone, both physically and mentally. But Wren *lived* it, every minute of every day. She had seen her mentor go insane, watched as people were burned alive from inside by overrush, had shared the thoughts of mages fighting against madness to get out one more rational thought before sinking back into the morass. Any of it could happen to her, at any point. And none of that scared her as much as the thought that she might be damaging her partner. That she, herself, might be bad for him. Dangerous to him.

He didn't know how often she grounded in him, without asking. Without thinking. It wasn't just the sex; it was the pattern of their partnership. She needed, he gave. The fact that he got off on what she gave made it all right, to him. It wasn't all right. It was *worse*.

She stopped in front of her apartment building, and looked up. Her apartment was dark. Bonnie's apartment was dark. She didn't want to go home. She didn't want to be alone.

She didn't have anywhere else to go.

Unbidden, a memory rose from deep inside, from a place she never went, wasn't even sure actually existed. The recent sense of another presence within her, heavy and solid and secure: like bedrock, only warm, living.

Without conscious thought, Wren turned away from her apartment and started walking, following that memory, the sense of completeness, of never-ending support and stability at once familiar and totally alien.

The snow stopped falling at some point during her walk, and she looked around, blinking, to discover that she had covered a quarter of the City without noticing it. Admittedly, Manhattan itself was only about 13 miles long and 2 miles wide, but it was still impressive, even discounting the weather.

She was downtown, all the way downtown, near the financial district. It was closed up tight for the evening: storefronts shuttered and lights dimmed. But the whitewashed brick building in front of her had one small light in the window in the basement, and it was there that she found herself heading.

The sidewalk-level door was battered—and unlocked. She pushed through, and went down a narrow staircase. It was grim, but clean, which was better than expected. The door at the bottom of the stairs was open, as though she had been expected. She didn't even think to be alarmed by that—alarm had no place here.

The main room was small, but cozy; a comfortable-looking love seat covered in some nubby, velvet-looking blue fabric, and a low table that looked old enough to either be junk or a valuable antique. The walls were painted a warm deep rose color that should have been fussy but instead came across as being intrinsically masculine, complementing the assortment of black-and-white and sepia-toned photographs placed on shelves, among a scattering of books and knick-knacks.

It had the flavor, she decided, of royalty in exile. Poor but dignified.

The white noise she'd been vaguely aware of in the background stopped, and only then did she recognize it for the sound of running water. A door across the room opened, and P.B. walked out, briskly rubbing a towel over his furry back.

"Was wondering when you'd show up."

Wren had always thought "jaw-dropping surprise" was a silly phrase, until she felt her own jaw do it. "How…okay, I'm confused now."

The demon grinned, and for the first time in years the sight of his gleaming white teeth under black gums left her uneasy rather than reassured.

"Relax, Valere. For such a hotshot Talent, you really don't know anything, do you?"

Apparently not.

* * *

An hour later, Wren was still confused. But now it was from too much information, not too little.

"So." They were seated on the love seat, Wren with her legs curled up under her, a mug of strong, black coffee in her hands and a plate of thin and disgustingly, sweetly addictive waffle-cookies on the table in front of her. "I grounded in you, when I was fighting the thing in the Parchment, and that created a bond between us, which I used—subconsciously—to find you tonight. That about sum it up?"

The demon nodded his head. "Simplistic, but yeah. Grounding in anyone creates a bond, Valere. You did know that, yes?"

"No, actually." It seemed like there was a lot she didn't know. A lot Neezer hadn't known. Had Ayexi, Neezer's mentor, known? Or was this yet another example of the drawbacks of the mentorship system, where one slip in one generation meant information was lost to an entire line?

"So Sergei and me..." *Oh God.* The thought chilled her deeper than the weather could reach.

P.B. shook his head. "No. Trust me, Valere. You two...that's electricity, not just current."

She took a sip of her coffee, waiting for it to warm her insides. "How do I know? I grounded, and he..." She stopped, unable to actually share that bit with the demon.

"He...?" When she showed no sign of continuing, he went on. "I've been around a long time, Valere. I've known a lot of humans. He loves you. You love him. Everything else…it comes from that, not the other way around. It's not even close to being current-made." The demon sounded certain of that, at least. Wren wasn't so sure.

"Anyway," he said, not quite changing the subject, "you think it's easy to ground in another human, especially a Null, the way you say you've done?"

"No. Neezer always said it couldn't be done, not successfully. But…"

"But you did it. More than once. Let that be your guide. He let you in, all the way in, and gave back. Anything he gets from you…fair trade, no?"

Back to the crux of the matter. "Not if it's hurting him."

And with that, the floodgates opened, and all her fears, her *terrors,* poured out. Poured, hell. She babbled. Wren suspected it wasn't making any sense, but P.B. sat there, listening intently, occasionally nodding his head or rubbing the side of his muzzle in thought, and that was more reassuring than any well-meant sympathy.

Finally, the words slowed, and she leaned back, drained. "Even if I can get him to…not do it, not let me use him like that when it's not an emergency…if he really does love me, the way you say—he says he does, then he won't stop. Not if the alternative is me being distracted or overloaded when it could be dangerous. Not even if he's risking himself, because he'll say that's a risk that he's willing to take."

P.B. had no answer for that.

She snuggled back into the sofa, which was as warm and comfortable as it looked, and let the demon refill her coffee mug. The window, at ground level, had snow shoved up against it, and the lights were dimmed, giving the entire room the feeling of a hobbit-hole.

The cookies were gone, although she didn't remember eating any. Her stomach didn't feel overloaded, so maybe P.B. had eaten his share.

"Too many decisions, P.B. Too many...too many *things* depending on me. How the hell did I get in so deep? I swear, I just didn't say no once, and...

"I can't do this anymore," she said, finally. "This... Quad-advising-leadership thing. I'm not a damned hero. I'm not a leader. I'm a damned lonejack thief who is in way over her head."

"We all are," P.B. said, and whatever pity had been in his voice before was gone now. "Over our heads, anyway. You think anyone knows what's going on? You think anyone's got a clue?"

She sighed, having wanted—but not expected—him to say something soothing and comforting again. "More benefit of your years of experience?"

"Decades, Valere. Decades and decades. And every one of them I see the same thing. People getting thrown into the deep end of the pool and learning how to swim. Or they drown. You have no idea how to drown, so you're gonna swim."

She almost cracked a smile at that. "How old are you, P.B.?"

For a moment, she didn't think that he was going to answer. "Old. Older than I want to be."

That opened up a whole bunch of questions, all shoving for space, but one of them was more important than the others. One she should have asked months ago, but had never found the right time or place.

"So how come I can ground so easily in you?"

P.B. stared into his own mug, the low light making his white fur appear tinged with blue, and his dark red eyes almost black.

"Because it's what I was created for," he said, finally. "And no, I don't want to talk about it. Just…accept the fact that you can ground in me, without injuring me, if you need to."

Something, less in the words he said than how he said them, set Wren's nerves on edge all over again.

"Never without asking," she said. "Asking, and your permission."

She wasn't sure, in the bad lighting, but she thought his shoulder relaxed a little, as though he had been braced against the wind, and come into shelter unexpectedly.

Someone hurt him. Someone used him. Oh, P.B.… But she knew any expression of sympathy would shut down the moment, so they sat and drank their coffee, each sunk in their own thoughts and wrapped in the comfort of the room, until a screech cut through the night.

She was on her feet before he was, but P.B. pinpointed the source first. "Outside."

He made as though to go outside, but she grabbed at him, her fingers digging into his fur, into the muscle beneath. "Look before you leap."

"Right. Caution. I used to know that." Instead of the door, P.B. shoved open the window and, disregarding the snow that came in and dusted the floor, stuck his head out to see what was going on. The window was large enough for Wren to get in beside him, pressed up hard against his body. The demon's fur had a surprisingly spicy smell she had noted before, but for the first time she wondered if it was natural, or some sort of cologne.

Then what was happening on the street drove all other thoughts out of her head. Two humans, and a snarling dog on a heavy chain, had cornered a little girl dressed in a white coat and cap against the wall of the building across the street. The street lamp overhead cast everything into bare relief against the snow, black-and-white and painfully sharp to Wren's eyes.

Her first thought was horror—someone was attacking a child!—and then she realized that no child of that age would be out wandering at night in a snowstorm, and second, no child of any age would be likely to make that kind of sharp, keening noise which was definitely coming from the creature in white.

She didn't know every fatae breed in the city, although her knowledge was expanding daily, but she knew one when she heard it.

The dog lunged, and was pulled back by the human holding the chain; not to keep it from attacking, but to prolong the fatae's terror. Wren felt her muscles tensing, readying to go to the child—the fatae's—aid. Next to her, P.B. was doing the same. But they stayed put, watching it play out in front of them.

Almost without realizing it, Wren brought a coil of current up, a slender copper-red thread.

I have a claim in the Truce
I call on that claim
I place—

"Damn it!" P.B.'s voice shook her out of her cantrip, the first time that had happened since she was sixteen. She tried to grab at the current, and it turned on her, sizzling viciously enough to make her entire core shudder in response, like a hundred geese walking over her grave.

"You're in the wrong part of town, Thingy," one of the attackers said, his voice clearly audible in the night air between them, distracting her from the current-burn. "Only humans allowed here."

"You think so, do you?" P.B. growled in response, a low, menacing noise like a freight train. Wren's hand on his arm tightened, as much to keep herself upright as him from getting involved. The white-coated fatae—no, not a coat, she suddenly realized, but down sheltering the body—shuddered and tensed, as though about to make a break for it.

"Go on, run," one of the humans taunted the fatae. "Run. Ripper here needs the exercise."

"Yes, run," she urged the fatae in a whisper, then louder "Run over here!" If the two of them could hear the humans, maybe the fatae could hear them, as well. If it could make it to the apartment, she would be able to protect them all…

The fatae, rather than running, let out another squeal, twin to the one that had alerted them. Run, or stay, it could not defend itself three-to-one, and the attackers started to move in for the kill.

"Screw this!" P.B. was halfway to the apartment door when Wren caught him by the arm and pulled him back. "Don't," she said urgently.

"What, you don't think I can handle them?"

"I know you can," she said. He had already dispatched one of these bigots' dogs, and she never wanted to know the details of how. But there were two humans, as well, and she was a shit fighter, even at her best. She wasn't going to let him get killed, not when there was another way. "Let the patrols handle it. That's what they're here for."

"Truce's broken, Valere. Nobody's going to come."

"Maybe. Maybe not." She had seen the Patrols reporting in. The Council Mouthpiece had been right, if annoying: there was more going on there, on the front lines, than following orders. If there was anything of what they had tried to build, it would last beyond petty politicking. She hoped. Oh how she hoped…

"There. Did you feel that?" A vibration, starting in the hollow behind her earlobe, only deeper in, sliding down her neck like a caress. Her call had gone through, after all. Or someone's had, anyway. She doubted they were the only ones looking out their windows. Hopefully if anyone actually called the NYPD, the right people had gotten the call and forwarded it on.

"Nuh-uh." P.B. was still straining against her hold, but not seriously: if he'd wanted to, he could have broken the grip—and her hand into the bargain. "Valere, I've got to, we've got to stop that."

"It's okay. She's been heard. Let them do it."

"Them" was the pair walking up the snow-coated street,

an easy lope that seemed as though they had all the time in the world, even as they covered the ground in no time at all. Wren couldn't help but expect to hear the soundtrack from an old Western start to play in the background, the shussshing of the snow substituting for the blowing of tumbleweeds.

With the newcomers' backs to them, Wren and P.B. couldn't hear what was being said, but the body language was clear. The two Patrollers, one with a long, slender tail twitching underneath the ankle-length coat, confronted the attackers. The dog snarled and lurched at the one with the tail, and his companion reacted with a flash of current that set the dog back on its haunches, looking up at its owner as though to ask "what the *hell* was that?"

"Not the dog's fault," Wren murmured, to which P.B. gave an eloquent and disagreeing snort. He wasn't fond of dogs on a good day; she had never asked why.

Tail-guy turned out to have claws P.B. might have envied, and he used them well, springing into action without any warning whatsoever. Wren had no idea what breed he was, either, but she knew that she never wanted to meet him in a dark alley. Or a well-lit one, for that matter.

His companion, the Talent, seemed content to hang back and let the fatae do his thing. Once he was convinced that things were well in-hand, er, claw, he turned to the would-be victim and, hand held out in what was meant to be a soothing manner, seemed to be asking permission to approach.

The streetlight fell on him as he moved into the direct glow, and Wren was able to make out a secondary armband under the Patrol one. White, with crossed red stripes through it. A medic. Smart—she didn't think the Double-Quad had come up with that, it was something that the Patrols had thought of on their own. A symbol everyone recognized, in one form or another: if not "I come in peace" then "I come with bandages."

"It's okay. They've got it under control," she said to P.B., who was still quivering with the need to get into the scrum. "Look." One of the vigilantes was on the ground, not moving. The dog was nowhere to be seen; Wren just hoped it had run off, and not gone down someone's gullet as an after-dinner snack. The other human was backing up, slowly, limping a little, as the tailed fatae advanced on him; a two-step pushing the human up off the street, onto the sidewalk.

The medic turned from his patient and made an impatient gesture toward his partner, telling him to stop playing with the human-toy and get over there. The fatae hesitated, clearly wanting to finish what it had started, and the medic made the gesture again. The fatae's tail lashed once, angrily, but backed down from the human, going to his partner's side.

The human, freed from direct threat, ran, disappearing into the white-frosted shadows, and the falling snow quickly filled in his footsteps. Meanwhile, the medic was picking up the smaller fatae, cradling her—him? It?—in his arms as they headed back down the street, presumably to better medical facilities. Wren thought, only then, to call them inside, where it was warm. But they were halfway down the street, and she didn't know what kind of supplies P.B. had in here, anyway. Better to let them take the victim somewhere they were set up to treat her, and hopefully get useful information out of the report.

"We should—"

"We are *not* going after them."

P.B. snarled at her, black gums pulled away from gleaming white teeth, and Wren snarled right back at him.

They pulled themselves back into the apartment, shaking snow off fur and hair, and P.B. shut the window with a firm slam, probably more than was needed. "Maybe you're right," the demon said in bloodthirsty satisfaction. "That human excuse for garbage will go back and tell the rest of them we're not to be messed with."

"Yeah," Wren said, but more in sadness than agreement. She sat back down on the sofa and drew her feet up underneath her, resting her chin on her hands and staring out the window, even though there was nothing out there anymore except snow. "It will teach them that we're dangerous. We're deadly. We're even more to be feared than the animals they already thought we were." Even without the Truce Board to back them up and direct them.

"That's a bad thing?" P.B. clearly didn't think so. Rather than sitting down, he paced the perimeter of the room, restlessly touching objects, as though reassuring himself. His paws, rather than being clumsy, were remarkably agile, and Wren thought, not for the first time, that whoever had first created the demon breed had made certain they would be tool-using creatures.

"Bad?" she said in response. "No. Not bad. They saved lives here, now, by being deadly." She had nothing against violence, as a tool. "But where does it stop? Where do we draw the line, and go home?"

"When they're all gone." P.B. was definite on that. Wren wished she could be so sure. Working with Sergei had taught her that you had to look at the smaller picture within the larger one; always calculate the repercussions before you acted. Otherwise, one simple ripple could come back as a tsunami.

Nothing was simple. Especially the things that, on the surface, *looked* simple.

"It's not enough to stop them." She tilted her head back to watch him. "They're like ants, these bigots. We need to find their source, their funding. That's what the Truce was supposed to do."

"Truce is broken." He gave up on wandering, to the relief of her aching neck, and sat on the love seat opposite her.

"Yeah. But who broke it?"

He didn't know. She didn't know. But she knew someone who might have the resources to find out. Only problem was, she'd thrown away her right to call on them for anything.

fifteen

"No, no, you did the right thing. The Patrol handled it."

It was probably the first time Wren had ever heard Bart being consoling. It was…*unnerving,* was the best word for it, she decided. He was far better at being bracingly abrasive. Even the fact that he was supporting her take on the situation didn't make it sound any better.

Wren wasn't sure if P.B. really resented not being able to get a claw into the fight, or if he was feeling guilty that he hadn't really wanted to get involved and so was talking loud to get over it. He could have shaken her off, easy—but in the process might have broken her arm. More guilt, if he did that. Some days she really did feel sorry for the demon. He just couldn't win.

They were sitting in Bart's apartment, huddled over mugs of coffee so strong Wren was surprised her hair hadn't spontaneously curled. The Manhattan representative looked like crap: his beard was unshaven, his eyes heavy-lidded and red-lined, and his posture more like a question mark. In short, he looked like a stretch of bad road after an ugly storm, and she would have guessed a wild round of drinking with sailors on leave, if she didn't know for a fact that he had been doing damage control up at Truce Central until daybreak.

Jesus wept, and wept again. Was it really only four days since the angel was killed? She blinked, calculated the hours. It was.

P.B. was still arguing. "I thought the point was to get involved?"

"If the Patrol hadn't been there, you would have been. That's involved. But letting them handle it...gives them purpose. Shows the rest of the *Cosa* that even if the Truce has been unofficially broken, we're still working together."

Wren raised an eyebrow at that. "Unofficially?"

Bart sighed, leaning back on the overstuffed plaid sofa and resting his arms along the back in a pose that might have been relaxed except for the tension practically humming off his sinews. "Yah. The Council swears that they had nothing to do with the angel's death, that they have not, in fact, had any contact of any sort with any non-*Cosa* group since the Truce went into effect, and that they are as outraged and sickened as we are. That's a direct quote, by the way. Makes me wonder if spinmeistering's an undocumented Talent."

"Just a Human one," Wren said.

P.B. came out of his funk long enough to riposte. "Don't

overestimate your species. If it breathes, it Spins. Except demons."

She was never able to resist the lure. 'What, you're more noble?"

"No, just fewer and a lot less involved. We stopped caring what other species thought a couple-three generations ago." He shrugged, dismissing the entire discussion. "Tough to spin the truth when everyone was either there, or doesn't care, anyway."

In the past twenty-four hours, Wren had learned more about demon than she'd ever known before. She might now, in fact, be the reigning expert in the *Cosa* on the subject. Pity there was no real call for an expert on the topic. Not exactly the sort of thing that popped up on Jeopardy or Trivial Pursuit, either.

Her brain felt like it had been rolled in sand and left to bake on the beach for too long, and her eyes were just as gritty. *I'm not thinking straight anymore.*

She and P.B. had spent the entire night—after giving up on any thoughts of sleep—sitting in an all-night coffee shop, replacing adrenaline shakes with caffeine ones, trying to trace back everything they had done, seen, and said, since the very beginning of all this, starting when P.B. first encountered the vigilantes on the street, and Wren called the "pest exterminators" number on the flyer she had been given.

"Do you think we caused this?" Wren had asked at one point, coming to the thing that was digging at her. "By not ignoring it? Because that's what we've always done—put our heads down and worked around it, and eventually they give up and go away or something else distracts them, or…"

"Or a lot of Talent die under stones, or in fire, or by gunshot or drowning or gassing…"

"Right. I guess ostriching's not so effective."

"It can be." P.B.'s dark red eyes got even darker for a moment, as though shadows were moving behind them. "You said it yourself. A lot of times the threat gets bored and goes away. Victims aren't fun when they stop squealing, or don't have anything more to give…."

Wren blinked at him, her too-tired brain latching onto his words in a way they wouldn't have if she'd been thinking clearly.

"That's an angle we haven't looked at, have we?"

"What, squealing?"

"No…advantage. It's been all about bigotry and intolerance and yadda yadda discrimination against us, woe is us. But what if it's even more basic than that?"

"*Cui bono?*"

"Huh?"

"Who will profit?" he clarified.

"Right. Who comes out ahead, if we're gone, or torn apart?"

"The Council." Then P.B. stopped, frowned, and said the same thing that Wren had been thinking. "Except they wouldn't, because suspicion would naturally fall on them, because it's so obvious…everything about this has obviously pointed to them, even the fact of one of the angeli being killed to break the Truce, because only a Talent could do that, right? We've been trained from the first steps to be suspicious of them, and them of us."

"So."

"So," he echoed.

At that point, they had paid their bill, and hotfooted it over to Bart's. Not only was he the closest in terms of location—Wren wasn't even sure where the other Quad representatives lived, actually—but he was good at poking holes in other people's theories.

"So," Bart said to them now, living up to her expectations. "It's an interesting theory, and I'm as much a fan of a good conspiracy theory as anyone—but it's sort of limited by the fact that there isn't anyone out there who would really profit by us eating each other, as it were."

"The government?" It was the first thing she could think of.

Bart almost laughed. "The government doesn't care, one way or the other, about us. They never have, not the Democrats, the Republicans, the Socialists, the Fascists... we're neither thorns to pluck or shit with which to fertilize."

"Nice image," P.B. said, wrinkling his muzzle in disgust.

Bart shrugged. "Talents have been useful to the government at various points, but it's always been on an individual basis, and as far as anyone's been able to determine the Powers that Be have no clue that we have anything even remotely like organization. As far as they're concerned, their Talents are random sports within the general population. They like thinking that, so they're going to continue thinking that."

"They'd not be so blasé about the fatae. If they knew."

"If they knew, you'd all be lumped under illegal immigrants, not contributing to the economy, Homeland Security's problem," Bart said in agreement. "Has any brownshirt approached you?"

P.B. showed teeth in a way that was surprisingly comforting. "If they had, they wouldn't be doing it again." He caught sight of Wren's grimace, and shook his head. "You said I could do what I wanted to people, so long as I didn't eat any more dogs."

"That's *not* what I said!" Wren exhaled like someone had sucker punched her, swiveling in her chair to look at him in outrage.

"Children. Back to the topic at hand, please?"

The two of them glared at each other, the demon stuck his dark blue tongue out at the lonejack, and she responded by giving him the finger. It was almost, for a moment, like easier, kinder days.

Bart seemed reluctant to break it up, but did so anyway. "Children? On your own time, please, not mine."

"Right." The moment past, Wren was all business again. "So in order to make this work, we need someone who a. knows that there is a *Cosa* to be manipulated, b. knows *how* to manipulate us, and c. has something to gain from doing so."

"It does all scream Council," P.B. said. He tipped an invisible hat in Wren's direction. "Despite what you said, before."

"Uh-huh." Wren had a bad itchy feeling at the back of her scalp that had nothing to do with not having had a chance to take a shower that morning.

"What?" Bart looked at her as though expecting something.

"I dunno. You have a phone?" There were times—days at a stretch—when she didn't mind not being able to carry a cell phone like the rest of the known, Null population. But sometimes it really would be useful.

Bart looked at her as though she'd suddenly turned green and sparkly and dangerous. "In the study. Down the hall."

"Thanks." She forgot, sometimes, that not everyone turned electronics into quivering masses of uselessness just by standing near them. It was a matter of pride, mostly; the stronger your core was, the purer your connection to current, the less time you could spend in contact with electronics before they went kablooey. Wren was strong; she'd killed three of Sergei's cell phones just by stroking her current, much less using it. Bart wasn't at the same level. It wasn't a breach of manners to remind another lonejack of that; one-upmanship was more highly regarded than manners anyway, especially by someone like Bart. But her innocent question could also have been seen as a put-down, or some kind of power play. Rather than try to explain herself, she went down the hallway to make the phone call.

His apartment was like hers: sparse, and mostly undecorated. She stared at the phone, a plain beige plastic number the kind they sold in discount stores for $9.99. He had basic protections hooked up to it, but nothing like her own. And no answering machine—although he might have a service, which someone with money and sense would have, just to keep electronics to a minimum. Although there was no computer, either, even if this was clearly his office area. Computers were almost as vulnerable as PDAs to current, no matter how many ways you safeguarded it. Either his control wasn't all that hot, or he did most of his business in person. Or both.

Calm. Controlled. Centered. Grounded. She felt her core, and was reassured that it was smooth and unworried, despite the bad feeling in her scalp, and her own distaste for what she was about to do. Picking up the phone, she dialed a number she had, reluctantly, under protest, memorized.

The phone rang at the other end. And rang. And rang some more, until the click of a voice mail system came on.

"You have the number, you know who this is. Tell me what you want."

Despite herself, she had to grin. Nice message. She had one in return.

"Andre. It's Valere. Time to pay the debt. I need an answer from you."

It was a simple enough question. She only hoped he was willing to answer it.

She could have called Sergei, had him get the answer for her. Even with him not in the city, it would have been easier. Faster. Probably smarter. But something made her shy away from the idea, and instead deal directly with the devil himself.

Hanging up the phone, she touched her core again, just

for reassurance. Losing control of that tendril had shaken her; she hadn't done that since she was a kid, not without a lot more cause.

It was all getting to be too much. Too much effort. Too much responsibility. But there wasn't any way out; not now, not then, not ever since this had all started. Wren had always refused Fate, denied karma, but… But she had the particular skills and—in this case—contacts the *Cosa* needed, and no matter how dirty it made her feel, it had been the right thing to do.

She envisioned the current stored and renewed within her as snakes, coiling and slithering around each other in the warmth of her core, the dry papery sound of scales their endless song. It soothed her. She wondered, briefly, how Bart saw his current.

Gah. She needed more coffee.

By the time she got back to the main room, P.B. had already left. She was somewhat taken aback that the fur pile hadn't said goodbye, but considering how often they'd been seeing each other recently, and how soon they'd probably be in the same room again, it did feel a little silly. He'd never been much on goodbyes, anyway.

"I have a call in to someone who might be willing to help us," she said, sitting down on the sofa again.

Bart made a "go on" gesture, but Wren shook her head. She was uncomfortable enough calling on Andre, without letting people know she was calling on him. Or, more specifically: the resources of the Silence, which had, after all, failed her rather spectacularly before.

So why are you trusting him now?

Because we're out of options, she told herself.

Bart got a look on his face that indicated a game of mental tag in process, probably with the other members of the Quad. Wren waited. They conferred, came to a conclusion: "I don't suppose you want to go back with me to do some more damage control?"

Wren didn't. At all. But that was exactly what she had signed up for: guiding them through the nasty little dance steps of working with the fatae and the Council, and all the other players that most lonejacks had the basic common sense to stay away from. The Truce was broken, but the talks were still going on. So long as that was true, Lee's legacy was on hold, and her guilt alone would keep her at the table.

So she sighed, and grabbed her coat from the brown leather armchair it had been tossed over. "Let's go."

"You don't need your coat," he said, and Wren only had time to feel her gut seize up before the Translocation hit.

I fuckin' hate *this,* she thought, even as her stomach twisted on itself and she reappeared in the Truce headquarters, trying very hard—and failing—not to throw up.

"Next time," she heard a voice say in disgust as she was falling to her knees, "we let her take the subway, okay?"

There was a hard knock at the Quad-commandeered apartment's door, breaking into the irregular rhythm of the ongoing arguments.

"Is she here?" a voice demanded from outside.

"Yeah." The person on door-duty didn't seem inclined to let the first speaker in, despite the affirmative answer, and at Beyl's signal her gnome-assistant, who still hadn't been introduced by name, was sent off to expedite matters.

Sergei came into the dining room/meeting area, shedding his coat and looking like a two-legged thunderbolt. The seven humans at the table variously braced themselves, and Beyl's top feathers fluttered as though catching a faint breeze. The only one looking unruffled was the folletto, a tall, almost translucent fatae who was currently serving as lieutenant-reporter to the Patrol sectors.

Wren braced herself. "What couldn't wait?" Her tone was cool, meant to remind him that he was allowed in here only on sufferance. That he was a Null, and not a part of these deliberations. *He walked away. He wouldn't take your concerns seriously. If he won't protect himself, then you have to do it for him. But it was hard. God, it hurt.*

"I got a phone call that was of probable interest." He looked at her, directly, without any emotion showing at all. For the first time in years, she couldn't read him.

"A call from…" Colleen prompted.

"A mutual friend," Sergei replied, still staring at Wren.

Andre. The rat bastard had gone to Sergei, instead of getting back to her directly. Bastard. Cowardly little… Ignoring the fact that she had told him off in a significant fashion the last time he had tried to come to her with anything.

"Did he have anything useful to share?"

"Not particularly, no." But the carefully controlled look on his face suggested otherwise; she could tell that much, still.

"But the things he did have to say were…interesting. The situation with the missing operatives is possibly deeper than we knew." He brought himself up hard, then gave in, a little. Not an apology, but a sidestep: this was, like her calling Andre in the first place, too important to let their personal emotions interfere. "He's being stonewalled, even beyond previous miscommunications and delays, and that's made him curious. He's going to put his best people on following up on your suggestion. His best person, actually. If it's knowable, Darcy either knows it, knows someone who doesn't know they know it and knows how to get it out of them, or can put together pieces and be the first person who knows it."

Wren actually followed that sentence. "And she'll bring it to our mutual friend?"

"Without doubt."

"All right." She turned back to listening in on the conversation they had been having when Sergei came in, semi-absently pushing an empty chair next to her out for him to take. Not quite the "welcome home" she'd like to give him, if things were different, but it would have to do for now.

"Even with that—" Beyl tried to pick up where the argument had been interrupted "—we still need to establish some sort of public face…."

They didn't say anything to each other the rest of the meeting, sitting side by side with the distance growing between them with every word they didn't say. Finally, as the afternoon wore into evening, she felt a touch on the back of her hand, under the table. She didn't look at him, didn't react, but slowly turned her hand over, so that his fingers rested across her palm. And there it rested, until Bart finally decided that further discussions were just going to send them shrieking into corners, at this point. "Get some sleep, we'll come back tomorrow."

Wren wasn't going back tomorrow. At this point, they didn't need her, they needed Henry Kissinger. On steroids.

They picked up their coats from the sofa where they had been piled, and left the building together, still not speaking to each other directly. Colleen had offered to Translocate them home, but they both had declined, not particularly gracefully. Wren threw up no matter who was doing the Transloc, never a pleasant experience, and once a day was once more than she really wanted to subject herself to. She'd rather brave the weather, the mass transit, and the inevitable damage both were going to do to her shoes.

Finally, after a few minutes of walking through the slushy streets, Sergei broke the silence. "For those of us who came in late, how go the desperate measures, really?" His words were flippant, but his tone wasn't. "Because I got the feeling that the conversation was way too polite, once I got there."

"Badly," she said, not denying his observation. "The Council's still at the table, you saw that, they're taking part in the Truce, technically…but they're not listening. It's totally for show, although I can't convince Rick or Susan of that."

"Bart, on the other hand, is convinced *everyone's* lying to him," Sergei said wryly.

"You know our boy. And Beyl and Michaela are both trying to hold on to hope, outwardly, but it's uphill both ways in the snow. Literally. Is it ever going to stop snowing?"

Sergei had his arm around her, less for support, although the streets were difficult to walk on, and more as though to reassure himself that she was there, that she wasn't about to slip away into the soft curtain of white around them. If she was smart, she'd do just that.

She didn't.

The subway was a block away, but a bus was coming up to the corner as they approached, and Sergei tugged her into line, coming up with a metro card before she had a chance to reach into her pockets. And he said that *she* was the magician?

The bus was crowded, so he found a handhold to grab on to, and she stayed next to him, this time actually needing the support.

"So what did Andre really have to say?" The question had to be broached, even though she was leery of going anywhere near anything even remotely personal, and this took a whopping big step there.

"When we get home." And that was all he said. She took her cue, leaning against his side as they rode the bus, halting and jerking into motion again with each stop, the snow coating the windows outside and the moisture from people's breath gathering on the windows inside, until it seemed as though they were riding through blackness with no landmarks to tell them when or where.

But the gift of a regular bus rider—something Wren was,

if not her partner—was an inner knowledge of when your stop was coming up. So two streets before, she came alert, and began easing their way through the crowd of evening rush hour commuters to get to the rear exit in time.

They were still two blocks from her apartment, but the snow was light enough now to see through, and the streetlights had come on. For a moment Wren could forget how thoroughly tired she was of winter, and look at the white-and-black shadows without seeing, like an afterimage, the ghastly splash of angel's blood dripping onto it.

The apartment was quiet, except for the hum of the heat rising through the ancient radiators. There was no traffic on the street below, and the sounds from the avenue a block over were muffled. Wren walked in the door and, for the first time in months, felt the once-familiar soothing presence of her home drape itself over her.

"It worked," she said in tired satisfaction.

"Huh?" Sergei stopped midway through unwinding the dark blue scarf from his neck, and looked at her.

"Last night, I remembered a cantrip Neezer used to do, before exams. He'd cast it over the classroom, so everyone would come in and stop stressing so much and just remember the stuff they'd been studying."

"Isn't that cheating?" He had never met her mentor, but the man's innate honesty was one of the few things that had stood between a perfect student-mentor relationship, according to Wren.

"Nah. If they had cast it, or if it had actually done anything to their memory, or heightened their smarts…all it did was relax them, like incense only without the smell or smoke."

"And you did that here."

"A version of it, yeah. I don't know why I didn't think of it earlier."

Pointing out that she'd been under a considerable amount of stress lately, which was inevitably screwing with her logical thought processes, was probably not the wisest thing he could say, so Sergei didn't say anything. Love didn't *have* to make you stupid, although you apparently couldn't prove it by either of them.

"Wren."

"Yeah?"

"I love you."

She blinked at him, and exhaled. "I know." It might have been the cantrip she cast, that made the muscles between his shoulder blades suddenly relax, but he didn't think so. She took her coat off, and held out a hand for his. "You hungry?"

"Sure." She put both coats away in the closet, and he leaned against the hallway wall, watching her. "You back on the Noodles kick now?"

She gave him a grin that suddenly made him nervous. "I got food in the fridge."

He mimed falling over dead from the shock, and she laughed. "Yeah, I know. P.B. got fed up and did an online grocery store order thing for me. So now I have no excuse— and he gets to pick out what he thinks I should eat."

"God save us all."

"Yeah. But there's chicken in there, and fresh vegetables, and Christ knows what else…"

That was all the excuse he needed. Shoving her gently into the chair, Sergei opened the fridge in her tiny kitchen and set to work.

"So. Andre," she promoted.

"Called me."

"I got that part."

Sergei rinsed the chicken breasts and patted them dry with paper towels, aware that he was using delaying tactics. He was also aware that he had no reason to be annoyed: Wren had, in his absence, gone directly to a potentially useful source. She hadn't bypassed him, merely not waited. Except she had gone to a source that she had made—delete that. That he had chosen to give up, to show his allegiance and support for her, for her side of things, her safety and well-being.

And to maintain that well-being, of her and her side of things, she used Andre. Isn't that what you've always done? All to support and protect and maintain her, and the partnership? So why are you so bent out of shape?

Because he had been the one to walk away from her. And she let him come back…because he came with information. If he hadn't…would that door have been opened as easily?

He had always assumed that he would be the senior partner, the one with the contacts, the information, the upper hand, even with her skill set. Even once their partnership evened out, he felt, somehow, that she would always look to him, always need him.

Instead, she was growing away from him. Refusing him. And that stung. Ego, and emotions, and everything in between.

He set the chicken breasts on the cutting board, still not answering her. He wasn't delaying, he was processing. Logic, for him, was the great mellower. He couldn't stay angry, even at himself, once the flaws in his logic had been driven home and dealt with.

"Andre says, as I reported, that he has no information about the attack. And that he will put Darcy on the job." He paused, taking down a knife from the board and testing the sharpness against the chicken flesh. Satisfied, he started to slice the breast into pan-ready fillets. "Darcy's his researcher, which is sort of like saying you're a decent housebreaker. If there's any information anywhere in the Silence about the angel's death, and who might have had a hand in it, she'll find out."

He could see Wren processing that, and could almost see the connection being made between the existence of Darcy and his seemingly inexhaustible storehouse of knowledge. He regretted, in a small, petty way, giving up that secret, but only for an instant. She still didn't know all his magic tricks.

"Do you think…"

"That the Silence had anything to do with it? That they were the ones who broke the Truce?" He didn't stop with the knife work. "It's possible. You followed the same logic trail: who knew about the *Cosa*? Thanks to me—" and his bitterness seeped through the words, despite his best effort "—they do. Would they profit from the *Cosa* being fractured?" He shook his head. "I can't see how, or why. It would make no sense. Even with the infighting that's going on now, they're the good guys, Zhenchenka. High-handed, yeah, and arrogant and know-it-all beyond belief, but the entire reason for their existence is to protect the innocent, the helpless. To fix wrongs, not create them." He had spent almost as long with them as working with her. He spoke with solid authority on that aspect.

"And you don't think an organization like that can be… what's the word I'm looking for? Subsomething-or-other."

"Subverted?"

"Yeah."

He'd had cause to wonder, in his last days, when the burnout and exhaustion almost killed him. "I think it would be highly unlikely. It's easy to corrupt one man, one individual. It's almost as easy—maybe easier—to corrupt a small governing board, like the Council. A bureaucracy? Not impossible. But damned difficult. And a bureaucracy with as much power in different levels, as many checks and balances as the Silence tends to have, with each department operating on their own?"

"Uh-huh." Wren had that Tone in her voice, the one he suspected her mother had used on her a lot. "The words are good ones. But you're not resounding with the ring of certainty there, partner."

She was right, and he hated it.

"There's only one way it could happen. If Duncan made it happen."

"Duncan?"

He had never mentioned Duncan to her? Of course not.

You didn't even mention Duncan to yourself. "The Power that Be, near the top of the food chain. And I mean the very, very top. This is a guy who makes the Council's Madame Howe look like a schoolgirl."

Sergei wasn't kidding. He wasn't even exaggerating in the slightest. Duncan was legend in the Silence, in a community that didn't believe in legends or myths or anything else that couldn't be dealt with by a practical application of know-how, elbow grease, cash, and weaponry as needed.

The steel weight of the knife in his hand felt solid and flimsy at the same time, compared to the reassuring mass of a pistol, and he could almost hear his palm ask for the blued steel weight against it. A knife would be enough, with his training. But it didn't have the distance, didn't have the range of his pistol, tucked into the safe in his apartment, halfway across town.

I would die to protect you, he told her silently as he sliced the chicken. *But I'm no use to you if you won't let me in. If you don't trust me.*

Honesty forced him to add: And I'm no use to you after I'm dead, either. And if Duncan is involved… I will be dead. The moment he determines that it's needful.

He couldn't linger on that. Any one of them, all of them, might be dead tomorrow, anyway. All he said out loud was "Did P.B. happen to order any fresh garlic?"

sixteen

Having someone make dinner for you didn't quite wipe the slate clean of all the gone-befores. But it *did* make you more charitably inclined toward them. Wren's stomach let out a distinctly ungraceful noise, and she giggled into her pillow.

"You're such a delicate creature," Sergei said, heavy on the irony.

She turned her face to the side in order to speak. "I never claimed to be delicate. Or demure. Or any of the words that describe women who don't eat, or at least don't have audible digestive systems. Besides, mister, I seem to remember someone emitting a stench that could send skunks into raptures not so many months ago, after indulging in a huuuge damn plate of ziti alfredo I warned you about."

It was silly, but silly was what she needed, right now.

Sergei clearly felt the same way. "Hey. The honeymoon

phase is now officially over, if we're making fun of each other's bodily functions."

"You started it! Anyway, I've never been much for pretending they don't exist. Seems silly."

In addition to the forgiveness thing, there was something about having someone else cook a meal that just guaranteed she'd end up in bed. Not that Sergei had to worry on that account, mostly; she was pretty willing to drag him off—or be dragged off—on the slightest pretext, these days. And it was only just sex—good sex, fabulous sex, but no current use—abuse—no anything she had to feel guilty about. Feel-good sex, physically and mentally.

If she could, she would have stayed there, physically and emotionally, the rest of her life; or at least a month. But there was still work to deal with. The plus was that now they could do it naked and postcoital sweaty, too.

The dark green-and-gold quilt was thrown over them, in addition to a blanket she had pulled out of storage when winter started; it had gotten kicked to the bottom of the bed at one point, but she had reached down to pull it back once the sweat started to cool. The room was filled with night-shadows, but they had an odd sheen to them, as though dawn was trying to seep through the walls, and the blackout curtain in the window. "Time's it?" she asked.

Sergei twisted to look at the clock on her nightstand, and she ran one cold finger along the exposed length of torso as he did so, just to see his skin shudder under her touch.

"Three-thirty. Damn it, woman, you have the fingers of

a corpse. Give me those and let me warm them up before you touch me again."

He grabbed her fingers and held them under his chin, folding them in his larger hands. "How can someone with so much current be so cold?"

"Dunno. Nobody's ever done a study of the effects of current on circulatory systems. I don't think they have, anyway. Nobody asked me to participate, if they did."

It was too early to even think about getting up, too late to expect much in the way of sleep. Wren was trying to remember if she had any of that high-test coffee still in the freezer, the stuff that made her hair curl.

"You guys should have your own wing at St. Vincent's," Sergei said. "And a research facility at…"

"You think we don't?"

That gave him pause for about half a second. "No, because if you did, it would be funded with Council money, and none of you would trust it enough to go there, anyway."

That made her laugh, mainly because it was true.

"I wish you did have doctors, though. You don't, do you?"

"Not many." She let her hands rest under his, enjoying the contact as much as the warmth, lying there in the late-night darkness of her bedroom. They were talking now. That was good. "You can survive the training, maybe, but working in a hospital…too much stress, too many things that can go pfffft, too many people going to get hurt when the wrong thing goes pffft. So Talent with the healing itch tend to go for traditional healer routes and nontraditional certification. Mostly, we self-heal, best we can—" he had seen her do that, with minor external injuries, and she'd tried it a time or three on others with worse damage inside, with mixed results. "—and there are only a couple-five doctors I know of, total, who're familiar with the stuffing of your average lonejack enough not to be freaked by it."

"Is it that dissimilar?"

Wren felt the comfort level shift, tense up. He knew that they could handle levels of electricity that would kill a Null, knew it firsthand, but she'd never given him the details. Never saw the need, before. Enough that he knew *he* didn't have it. Not that those particular facts seem to stick with him. He was treading dangerous ground, here; she wondered if he knew it.

She hesitated, thinking about moving the conversation onto another topic, then answered him. "According to Bonnie, our internal organs are lined with something that insulates us. It's icky and mucus-y and I really don't like to think about it, thanks. Evolutionary whatchamacallit, keeps us from dying before we can reproduce."

"Nice." He bent forward to kiss the top of her head. "Pity it can't be harvested and sold…" He stopped, clearly considering the actual probable market for such a thing, and they both shuddered at the same moment. "Right. Forget I ever thought of that."

"Totally forgotten."

"Anyway—" and she stretched out along his body intending to make him lose track of what she was saying "—I'm less worried about my medical situation and more worried about yours. Thought about it a lot, while you were out of town."

"Did you now." He was totally focused on her words. Damn. So much for distracting tactics. But it had to be said, before she lost the nerve.

"Yeah." She rolled onto her side, facing him, but hiding her face under her hair, which was a bad combination of winter-dry and sweat-damp. He brushed it away to see her face. She let him, which would have been a warning sign, if he'd been paying attention to the right things. Wren never let him fuss with her hair like that unless she was either injured, or trying to avoid a fight.

He was going to expect her to bring up the current-sex. Which is why she wasn't going to.

"This…don't take this the wrong way, which you're going to, because I *know* you, but angels are tough to kill and someone's managed it twice already, and that Kirin, did you hear about the Kirin? They didn't even take the horn, just left it there to decay. Abandoned a thousand-dollar profit because they didn't know, or didn't care, or were making a point…and I want you to get out of town. Take another business trip. Visit your relatives. Something. Just until…" She didn't know until what. The storm was building, and she didn't want him here when it broke.

He was clearly taken aback. "It's all been fatae, Wren. No humans. Not even Talents. Not in singled-out attacks like that."

She went still in his arms. "That's going to change."

"You know that for a fact?" He wasn't doubting her, just questioning the certainty of her tone.

"If you ever trusted my instincts, Sergei. If ever you

trusted me, now's the time. Yes, it's going to change. And I don't want you anywhere near their sights. It's not enough that my mom be out of range, I—"

She ran out of words, or hit a brick wall, or something that made her just *stop*.

He tried to keep his tone mild, even as she could feel him tense up. "We've had this...discussion, before. In all the years you've known me, you never once even implied that I was a liability to you, that I could not keep my side up in a fight. Now, suddenly... at the risk of sounding like the girl in this, why does sex suddenly give you any right to say what I can and can't do?"

She pushed against him, just enough to create a small space between them. "It doesn't, and that's not...it gives me the right to worry out loud, rather than biting it back because I didn't have the right. Except I always did because you're my partner, damn it, and if I know something's coming that's meaner and nastier than you are, and fights with things other than fists and guns, I have to say so."

"Except they *do* fight with fists and guns," he pointed out. "And baseball bats and knives. All things I have more experience with than you do."

"Stop being logical! This isn't about logic, damn it!" she cried out, frustrated, and then collapsed against him, shaking.

He knew her well enough to know, instantly, that the shakes were from giggles, not tears. Slightly hysterical, perhaps, but her innate sense of the absurd was reasserting itself, rather than letting drama take over.

"You're an idiot," he said.

"So're you." The words were muffled, but understandable.

He smiled into the sweaty tangle of her hair. "So let's be idiots together, as the saying goes."

That, apparently, was the right thing to say. Her hands weren't cold anymore, he discovered, as she reached down his torso, this time raising shivers of an entirely different sort. Faint flickers of current trailed in her wake, dancing on the surface of his skin, carefully not sinking into the flesh. He could only imagine the concentration it took, to keep control of the current even after it left her, while still focusing on other parts of his body. Or was she even aware of it? He wondered, sometimes, how clear the delineation was between Wren and the current she carried within her.

Then she shifted, and took him into her mouth, and he didn't much care how she did it, or why, only that she kept on exactly whatever it was she was doing. He didn't know which felt better, the current on his belly, or her tongue flicking at the head of his cock, or when she slid…*all right,* he thought, *definitely, that feels best of all.*

She played him like that, back and forth, shifting him through the sensations magical and merely physical, until he felt like a twist-tied rubber band in dire need of release. He would have agreed to anything she asked of him, at that point, and loved her all the more for knowing that—and not asking anything of him at all.

And even so, something inside, some devil of the purely human sort, niggled at his brain and twitched his nerve endings.

Don't do it.

Angeli were bastards. You could ignore what the angel on your shoulder warned. Right?

You're an idiot.

It wasn't idiocy. It was okay. She had been grounding in him for a decade, and he was a little battered, but okay. And she grounded in P.B., when the Toscanni creature was trying to eat him, during the summer, and P.B. was okay....

He didn't like the thought of her grounding in P.B., not even to save his, Sergei's life and soul, and so pushed that thought down quickly.

No, this was between the two of them. She needed to use current; it was what she did. What she was. It was part of her. And he wanted to know that part, know everything. Just a little bit more of her, just a bit...she was in control. He trusted her to keep control. He just wanted...a little bit more....

Idiot, and then the angel was gone.

"Wrenlet...more. Let go just a little more...."

She tensed, and his fingers dug into her shoulders, massaging the knot forming there, encouraging her to go on. Letting her know that it was okay, he was okay.

She said she trusted him. He trusted her. It was all about the trust, wasn't it? He could take anything she gave. He *wanted* it. He was her partner, not that half-sized fur-toy. Something so much a part of Wren, so essential...he would be the one to ground her, not him.

You're an idiot, even the devil said, then faded, as well, as his vocal cords took over.

"Wren. Please. Just a little more, you're making me crazy, finish me off…"

At any other moment, under other conditions, he would never have asked. Under other conditions, she would have—and had—read him the riot act just for asking.

He knew his partner. Knew that, once committed, she didn't back down. Not during a Retrieval, not during…anything.

"Wren, please…"

She heard him, he knew she did. The pressure of her hands on his thighs lessened, then increased again, her efforts redoubled in order to drive the thought out of his larger head.

"Ah, Wrenlet, you're killing me…."

The wrong thing to say. Completely the wrong thing to say. Her fingers dug into his flesh in response, nails probably leaving nasty little marks. But even as he realized it, and backtracked mentally if not verbally, the current dancing on his skin sizzled and sank into his flesh, shocking his nerve endings in a way that was *almost* enough. Then her mouth covered him one last time, and everything from his toes to his heart clenched, as though he had been gut-punched, only in a good way. Sergei wasn't one for talking when he came, but he let out a heavy, labored sigh that could have been her name, could have been a swearword, but probably wasn't any language at all except satisfaction.

And then his entire body went cold as she was out of bed, a pale white blur in the darkness, backing away from him with the uncertain steps of someone reeling from a deathblow.

"Wren?"

"You... I didn't mean to do that."

He started to tell her that it was okay, that he was okay, when what she was saying clarified in his head. Her letting go of the current, allowing it to go beyond the borders of his skin, hadn't been a result of his somewhat incoherent pleas, or even an instinctive response to what he needed.

She had done the one thing she—and every lonejack—feared the most. She had lost control.

"Wren..."

But she was gone, a sudden, totally unexpected zap of current taking her elsewhere, and leaving everything in the room—including himself—quivering in the aftermath.

"Oh, fuck."

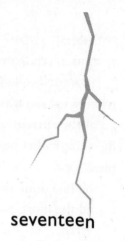

seventeen

In retrospect, P.B. thought later, it was probably a good thing he had decided to put off clipping his nails until another, even more boring evening. Otherwise, when the naked human female appeared in his living area, he might have lost a toe. And even for demon, toes were tough to regrow.

"Hemeltjelief!" A beat, then: "Jesus—Valere!" Something Didier had said once, tugged at the back of P.B.'s head. He remembered it the same instant that the woman fell forward onto her hands and knees, and began puking all over his rug.

She's not very good at Translocating. Screws her system up seven ways from Sunday.

He grabbed the blanket off the back of the sofa he'd been sitting on, and threw it over her shoulders. Not so much to cover her nudity—it didn't do anything for him, and he was pretty sure Wren wasn't much on modesty—but because it was brass-nuts cold outside, and not much warmer in the apartment. When you have fur, you tend not to worry so much about if the furnace is working or not.

"Okay, okay, it's okay." She kept retching, so it wasn't okay, but he didn't know what else you said to naked lonejacks who appeared and then poured their dinner out over your floor. It wasn't covered in *anything* Emily Post had ever written.

"Oh God."

"No, just me." It was a feeble joke, but all he had at the moment. "Come on, come on, Valere, come with me." He led her, like a child, into the bathroom. She stood there in the middle of the dingy white tiles while he pushed aside the shower curtain and turned the water on, as hot as he could make it. He remembered that, from taking care of her after the Frants case: she liked her showers hot.

"Get in."

She stood there, still huddled in the blanket, but at least not throwing up anymore.

"Valere. Tub. In. Get."

Her shoulders hunched, she swallowed once, hard, but otherwise might as well have been made out of mannequin-plastic, she was so unresponsive. He finally gave in and hauled her, unresisting, into the tub. The twelve inches or so difference in their height made it awkward, but he only *looked* cute and cuddly—demon were, by design, solid muscle and bone.

The blanket came off a second too late, and landed, already waterlogged, in the tub.

"Needed to wash that, anyway," he said, then drew the

curtain and sat down on the toilet seat to wait. He'd give her privacy to recover from whatever it was that sent her here—there was no blood, no damage that he could see, so he wasn't going to freak out just yet—but she was clearly in some kind of shock, so he wasn't going to be more than a paw's grab away. Just in case.

He'd told her once that she could always count on him, that she could ground in him; that was what he'd been made for.

Looked like part of her, at least, had heard and believed him. And remembered, when she needed to remember.

Wren didn't remember anything. Her first, last, and only memory was standing under a heavy fall of hot rain, surrounded by the smell of something musky, and…baby shampoo?

"No More Tears?" she guessed, her voice, to her ears, too high-pitched and squeaky to actually *be* hers.

"I get tangles, all right?" P.B.'s voice was reassuringly grumpy, from the other side of the waterfall.

She opened her eyes, and saw white tile, and a green-and-black striped shower curtain. At her feet, tangled, was the waterlogged weight of a blanket of some sort, now totally ruined.

"Where am I?"

"My apartment. Specifically, my shower."

"How did I get here?"

"Damned good question, Valere."

And then she remembered…

"Don't you dare throw up again!" P.B. warned, when she made a noise somewhere between a choke and a scream, caught midpoint in her throat.

Translocating made her toss her guts. Always and every time, whether someone else sent her, or she went under her own dubious power.

She had done this to herself; Wren was pretty sure about that. There was comfort, and afterglow, then the sickening thud of realizing something—*Sergei! I hurt Sergei!*—followed hard on the heels by a memory of him lying there, looking at her, all right, unhurt, at least as far as she could tell.

"I lost control. I said I would control it, and I didn't." But she said it quietly, letting the water keep the admission to itself, not letting the demon on the other side hear her secret.

"Everybody loses control, Valere."

Damn demon hearing. She kept forgetting that, because he was so good about—usually—not hearing what he wasn't mean to hear. She tried to work up the energy to get mad, then supposed, considering the circumstances, she'd waived the right to privacy.

"Is anyone dead?"

A fair enough question. She considered it. "No."

"Then there's nothing that can't be dealt with. Come on, Wren. You're going to drown."

She waited a moment, as though weighing the possibilities of drowning, then reached forward and shut the taps off. The water went away abruptly, and the cold air hit her skin and made her shake with the realization that she was a. naked and b. freezing.

"Here." A towel appeared around the edge of the shower curtain. It was huge, blue, and thick enough to hide in.

"Thanks."

"There's stuff here that might fit you. I'm putting soup on."

She wasn't hungry, but the thought of something warm and salty to get rid of the taste in her mouth—and replenish the electrolytes she had undoubtedly lost—was appealing. Plus, you didn't refuse hospitality, when offered, from the being who wasn't making you clean up after yourself. He might just change his mind and hand her a mop.

The "stuff" was a pair of sweatpants that, when cuffed three times and the string tie pulled in to a ridiculous degree, stayed on her hips and didn't trip her when she walked. They were thick, and fleecy, and bright red, and Wren didn't want to know whose they had been, originally, or how they'd ended up in P.B.'s possession. The sweater was an easier guess—it had been a gag gift to him from her, Christmas the year before: the Coca-Cola polar bears wearing Santa hats and cavorting with penguins.

It really *was* impossible to look at penguins, and not feel better.

P.B. didn't have a kitchen, not even the walkthrough-and-turnaround she laid claim to, but the corner stove was more than adequate for heating a couple of cans of soup and serving them up into clunky white bowls. They sat on the sofa—the rug mysteriously rolled up and sent away while she was drying herself off—and lifted spoons until she started to feel the warmth come back into her bones.

"Want to talk about it?"

"No."

"Right. You appear in my home, bare-assed like the day you were born, shocky as hell, like a soldier that's been gassed, and ruin a rug I've had for years—okay, it was a crap rug, it was still mine—and you don't want to tell me why?"

"No."

"Okay."

The sound of spoons scraping stoneware filled the room, accompanied by human and demon slurps and swallows. It was a rude, homey noise, and Wren started to feel like she might not shatter if she moved too suddenly.

"You think maybe you could call me a cab?"

"Poof, you're a cab."

She looked sharply at the demon, and he met her gaze evenly, his dark red eyes unblinking. Most of the time she could forget he wasn't, well, human. Suddenly, tonight, she was completely aware of his alien-ness…and it didn't matter in the slightest. The only thing in those eyes was a compassion and concern on a level she had only ever seen once before: in her mother's eyes. *Grounding.*

"Whatever it was you were doing, you were somewhere comfortable enough to get comfy. That means you were home…or at Sergei's. If you were at home and something spooked you, spooked you enough to use current to get the hell out of there, it's fifty-fifty where you would have ended up." He reconsidered. "All right, seventy-five-twenty-five. But there was still a chance that you would have gone there, not here.

"But you weren't surprised to be here. You haven't asked me to contact Sergei. You haven't worried about him at all."

He blinked, then, and she could almost hear the cogs turning, slipping into a new configuration.

"Did he do this to you?"

If she said yes, Sergei would be dead. Wren understood that, in a flash like understanding current, like knowing how to call lightning down from the skies, power from power lines. One word.

"God, no!"

The demon blinked again, and he was P.B. Her friend. Her companion.

Her demon.

It was another thing she understood, now, without knowing how.

"I want to go home. It's okay, now." She knew that, too. "I'll call a cab."

The ride home was silent; P.B. had, somehow, somewhere, found a livery driver who not only didn't want to talk, but didn't blare his radio, either. The sedan was clean, the driver sane, and the ride uneventful. It was a gift from the gods.

She didn't have her keys. She didn't have anything—thick moose-hide slippers on her feet, sweats on her body, and her hair scraped back into a short braid and tied up with a rubber band.

She pressed her own buzzer first, on the off chance…

Nothing.

She pressed Bonnie's buzzer.

"Wren?"

"Yeah."

The buzzer sounded and Wren stumbled inside, out of the cold night air. Bonnie met her on the stairwell.

"Oh my God. Are you okay?"

"I need to go to bed. Alone. For a day. Maybe two."

"You want me to make you some soup or something? For lunch?"

It was almost dawn. Wren couldn't bear to even think about daylight, right now, much less food.

"I'll stop by later," Bonnie said. "Go. Sleep."

Wren climbed the last two flights, each step adding a pound of lead to her feet. She dimly remembered, once, creating a cantrip that allowed her to move up the stairs with less weight, even in her exhaustion. It was too much effort, now, to try to remember what she had said, how she had done it. Too much effort to even poke at current, much less… Control it.

She wanted nothing to do with her current. *Nothing.*

The apartment was empty, which wasn't a surprise. She shed the now-filthy slippers at the door and headed for the bathroom, where she snagged her robe off the hook and changed it for her borrowed sweats. Although technically less warming, the robe felt better: her own clothing, it *smelled* right.

It smelled of Sergei, actually, but she didn't linger on that thought. She was still not thinking about that at all.

Which was why she didn't read the note he had left tacked to the coffee machine. She didn't throw it away, either; she just plucked it off the plastic casing and put it aside.

She hit the replay on the answering machine, without thinking.

"Hi." A long pause. "Right. Either you're going to call me, or you're not. Or you're going to show up on my doorstep and we can have this out like ranting, screaming, emotionally overcharged adults. Look, I—"

She hit Stop. She didn't press the delete button.

She'd listen. She'd read. But…not right now. She wasn't ready to deal with him.

It wasn't his fault. It was mine. Totally, completely mea culpa. I knew what he wanted, and I had the ego to think that I could still be in control, control myself, and control him.

Worse, something inside her kept asking—if he needed that feel of current badly enough, so badly that he was willing to risk his own personal safety, and her own hard-won control…

She went back into the kitchen and started dumping coffee into the machine, making it stronger than usual.

She didn't want to think about that. She didn't want to have the answers that came bubbling up through the sewers of her too-active mind.

He loved her. He left the Silence, told Andre off, all for her. He would never do anything to hurt her, even if he was too stupid to know when she was trying to protect *him*.

It was insane. It was impossible. But once suspicion was planted, it was mental kudzu, growing over everything you threw in its path. Sergei was an addict, or on his way to becoming one. And addicts weren't masters of their own fate. Not if someone else knew about their needs. Now, it was only her current. But she couldn't give it to him, not like that. And if the need grew...

Or if the need had existed, before, and she was just the newest provider, the easiest? He had worked with Talent before, in the Silence. Had Handled them. If he'd gotten current-buzz before...did anyone else know?

Consider the time frame: Sergei left the Silence, formed a partnership with her, and slid into the world of the lone-jacks. As she got to know other Talent in the area, so did he. When she got dragged into *Cosa* politics, he threw himself in with the *Cosa*, and their fate, as well. Why? For love? Sergei was, first and foremost, a businessman. He always but always had his eye on the profit. It was one of the things she counted on, without even thinking about it, when they were working.

That was the question everyone was asking: where was the profit?

No.

But the thought, once allowed into the light, had to be dealt with. The Silence had Talented operatives, used them. They had something going on. What was Sergei's angle? Was it all a show, that declaration of independence, to get someone inside the Quad?

Was he, in fact, still working for the Silence? Was he their tool?

No other Null knew as much about the *Cosa* as he did.

Nobody was as trusted. And the Silence, she was coming to realize, took the long view, and looked at the big picture, valued it more than the individual's well-being. Sergei…was his addiction something that started before he met her? It would not be impossible or even improbable that the Silence had planted him in her life that long decade ago…arranged for the entire situation with the Council exactly so that she would be vulnerable when the Silence came calling….

"Oh, Jesus wept, *stop it!*" The coffee was done, but her hand was shaking so much, she didn't trust herself to pour it. She was losing her mind. That was all. She was…. Losing it.

Her entire body was shaking, so much that she had no choice but to sit down. Only her body wasn't working quite right, and she fell, instead. There wasn't room to sprawl in the small kitchen space, so instead she huddled on the floor, arms around her shoulders, quivering like someone was shaking her.

"Sergei…oh, Sergei…"

After a while, the shakes were replaced by a numbness that had nothing to do with the cold, inside or out. She simply couldn't handle it anymore, so she didn't. Wren could almost hear doors slamming and locks locking, as portions of her life shut themselves off into tiny little rooms, one by one, until she didn't have to look at them anymore, didn't have to deal with them.

A cool veneer, like the frost on her windows, settled over her, through her. Her thinking was so sharp, her brain was bleeding a little. The Wren was back in control.

Getting to her feet, she tightened the tie of the robe, got down a mug, and poured herself a coffee. It was thick and harsh, and needed three spoonfuls of sugar to make it palatable. But the warm bitterness, like a Turkish kick in the pants, was enough to get her into the office and gather up all the materials on the Retrieval, then cart them all back into her bedroom. She put the mug down on her nightstand and crawled under the covers—the bed was fully made, with fresh flannel sheets—and threw all the pillows behind her back, to support her as she read.

Blueprints of the target's office and home were in the file, with small, precise writing in the margins noting specific problems or opportunities. Sergei had suborned someone in the department of buildings, to get this much detail. Hopefully it didn't cost too much. Not that the costs weren't built into the invoice Sergei submitted at the end of every job, and she wasn't supposed to think about money when she was working, damn it.

"All right. If I were a sneaky someone who had pinched off with something very, very naughty, and I didn't know yet how I was going to use it, where would I put those naughty bits? Somewhere safe, yes, but not obvious. Not with anything someone in my family might need, or look for…"

By the time the coffee worked its way through her system, Wren had a pretty good idea of what needed to be done. The question now was timing: when to move. Plus, she needed to do something special for this job. It wasn't enough to get the material back. She also needed to do it in a way that left a distinctive calling card, so the target would know that he'd been smoked.

She didn't always do that; in fact, she hardly ever did that, preferring to leave as clean an exit as possible. But politics were pissing her off, right now, and she wanted someone to learn a lesson, in all of this.

And you might as well wish for cave dragons and piskies to play well together, she thought wryly. Her back twinged, and she stretched her arms over her head, hearing things crack back into place. Gym. She definitely needed to get back to the gym at some point. The last real exercise she'd had—other than toss-the-covers with Sergei—had been that aborted snowball fight with P.B. Not good.

Wren looked over at the clock, and blinked. No wonder her back was bitching at her. She had worked through the entire day; it was dinnertime.

She consulted her stomach, decided that no, she wasn't hungry. Better to sleep now, on an empty stomach, and eat when she got up. Tomorrow was going to be a seriously busy day.

Decision made, she shoved the materials over the side of the bed, turned the light off, slid deeper under the covers, and went to sleep.

And if she dreamed of Sergei, of dead ends and dragons, and blood on cobblestones, she didn't let herself remember the details in the morning.

eighteen

For the most part, traditionally, Council business was conducted in hotel suites or private function spaces, the room chosen on the day of the meeting, and carefully guarded until the moment. It wasn't that Council members were paranoid; they were merely quite...cautious.

KimAnn Howe broke with tradition, as she had broken with almost everything else her predecessors on the North-eastern Council had done. She met with people anywhere she damn well chose to, at her convenience, and they would accept it, or refuse the meeting.

It did not pay to refuse a meeting with Madame Howe.

She was not, at first glance, a figure of terror: older, edging on elder; a slender figure, with carefully coiffed white hair coiled at her neck and graceful fingers tracing the rim of her china teacup. Mussolini, however, might have recoiled from the expression on her face this afternoon.

Not many lonejack had ever had the pleasure of seeing her, in any form. Sergei had met with Madame Howe once, standing in for Wren at a gathering of the Council entire. Wren had encountered her a few times, once most notably when the Council leader appeared at Wren's own apartment, to confront what she saw as the opposition leaders. KimAnn had been wearing her Public Face both times. She wasn't, now.

In fact, since the revelation that she had made a deal with the San Diego Council, had gone against generations of tradition in creating a joint Council under her own control, Madame Howe had not appeared in public. Wren and the Troika had kept what they knew quiet in order to ensure that the Council joined with the rest of the *Cosa* in dealing with the vigilantes and their mysterious backers, but they all knew that it was merely a temporary alliance. The Council wanted control, order, assimilation: three things that lonejacks were typically dead set against. It was a long-standing tradition, and another one KimAnn was determined to break.

"Madame?"

The young woman offered her more tea, which KimAnn accepted with a nod. The liquid was gently scented with jasmine, and rose into the air on warm waves, complementing the faint perfume of deep purple roses from the vase on the table. The younger Talent replaced the teapot and sat down in the upholstered chair, not showing any sign of how uncomfortable the Edwardian-era piece must have been. She was a credible assistant, with the perfect recall KimAnn demanded of all her assistants. KimAnn missed the active mind of her usual attendant, who would always have interesting views afterward, but this was a discussion that Colleen, since she was assigned to the Truce discussions, was best off not hearing.

She fixed the other two occupants of the room with a gaze that showed every bit of the powerful current in her core. "You are suggesting that we tuck our tails between our hindquarters, and run away?"

Mussolini would definitely have quailed from the icy disdain in her voice. The man directly facing her across the low coffee table, here in the heart of her own home, did not even blink.

"I believe that a strategic marshaling of our forces, without the accompanying scrutiny, is best for our long-term plans. And that we cannot do any such thing while taking part in this...little squabble."

He was brash, independent, a maverick. All qualities that had appealed to KimAnn when she was looking for the first link in her eventual chain of power. And he was smart, as well. Unpolished, and more than a little too rash, but smart. What he said had solid political merit.

"You were the one who put me squarely in the middle of all this. What *possessed* you to meet with a representative of those...Null vigilantes?"

Sebastian Bailey, the leader of the San Diego Council, barely tightened his grip on the china, but KimAnn noticed it, and he knew she had noticed it. "They contacted me. I tend not to dismiss potential allies before I've assessed them."

"You should have spoken to me before you did anything in my city."

"You weren't holding my leash, then." It clearly burned him to admit, even in the privacy of that room, that he was her dog.

She smiled and leaned back. Having made her point, she was willing to be gracious.

"Perhaps there is a way that this can yet benefit us. Heather." The girl looked up alertly. "Pass the word. No Council member is to offer succor to lonejack or fatae, except as it directly impacts their own safety."

"Madame…" Heather was no Colleen, no, but she had spine, KimAnn would give her that. Good girl.

"Yes?"

"We have committed to the alliance. If we withdraw from the Patrols."

"The treaty has been broken. If any Council member wishes, of their own, to continue crawling the streets at night, putting themselves at risk, then they of course are to feel free to do so. But we will not sanction it, nor will we support them should injury occur." In other words, they would be paying their own medical bills—and any other costs they might incur—rather than the Council's usual safety net helping them out.

KimAnn pursed her delicately colored lips thoughtfully, following a thought that occurred to her. "This organization, the Silence. They have the Retriever Valere on their payroll, as well as other Talents?"

"Yes." Heather had all that information at the ready, as KimAnn knew she would.

"Who speaks for them?"

"Madame…we don't know."

"I beg your pardon?" One silvered eyebrow rose.

Heather held her ground, nervously. "We know through Colleen's reports of them, and of the Double-Quad's concerns that they are somehow set against the *Cosa*. Members who work for them have been...they have drifted from their families, or disappeared entirely. In fact, some of those who went missing were laid at our doorstep."

"We had nothing to do with those?"

"No, Madame."

"An oversight. Find the head of their organization. I want to meet with him or her, immediately." She wasn't sure what she might say to this individual, but anyone who was a power in this town—anyone who had any influence whatsoever over the *Cosa*, as they clearly did—was someone she needed to know, to judge. To use, if possible, and placate if dangerous.

"It may be that they are the key we need. First to prove we are not the—what is the phrase the children use these days? The Big Bad? And second, to create a more terrifying danger." KimAnn laughed, a noise that managed to be both delicate and robust at the same time. "And to think that we were creating a straw tiger, when all the while not one but two already lurked in the bushes!"

Heather did not protest further, and the meeting was adjourned without further comment. Only then did the fourth person in the room stir from her silence.

"You go too far, Kimmie."

If there was anyone else in the world that KimAnn Howe would accept that nickname from, it was a deeply buried secret. Perhaps her husband; if so, he had never taken that liberty in front of witnesses.

"You've been manipulated, the same way you've manipulated others for years. I'd say turnabout was fair play, but none of this has been about fairness."

"Make your point, Elizabeth."

The speaker was a tiny little woman, barely four feet and totally engulfed by the chair she sat in. Wizened and worn, she looked like she might have been a dryad from a particularly ancient tree, but she was completely human, if very very old; old enough to remember when KimAnn had been a promising, brash young Talent.

"My point has already been made. You go too far in your fear."

"I am not afraid!" That stung, badly.

"Only fear makes a woman into a tyrant. And that is what you have become."

"Now, you argue my tactics? You, who taught me how to marshal power, to control others with their own needs?"

"Power makes a dictator, and dictators may be benevolent, even in their most extreme control. A tyrant is nothing but abuse in action." Her short, age-spotted fingers moved restlessly over the blanket on her lap, the small needles she was using to knit up the edge stuck into the ball of yarn by her side.

"I am as I was made," KimAnn said. "Powerful." Her voice softened, as it only did when speaking with her husband, and her mentor. "I'm doing what's best for the Talent—*all* Talent. You agreed with me, once."

"I still agree with you," Elizabeth responded, sharp-voiced. "The lonejacks were always a mistake; I have maintained that since before you were born. I am merely cautioning you against hubris. You go too far, messing with those outside the *Cosa*. It will not end well, not for any of us."

Wren adjusted the collar of her blazer, twitching the strands of hair out of the way. Every summer she was glad for the length, for the ease of getting it up off her neck, but in the winter it was always an itchy, uncomfortable mess under her hat and collar. Someday she was going to break down and chop it *all* off to her ears. Or maybe a buzz cut.

Her slicks were still unusable, but this job wasn't anything she needed them for. The target was a private citizen, one without the property or reputation to require major security, and the papers she had been hired to Retrieve were being kept in his personal home.

Piece a cake. Or it would be, if Wren believed any such thing existed. She had seen too many easy jobs turn to shit in the execution, and jobs that should have taxed even her skills slide like silk.

You planned as much as you could, then you tap-danced like mad.

She squared her shoulders, set her jaw, and walked briskly up the stairs, her blazer and short pleated skirt almost crackling with starch, the white cotton turtleneck underneath making her want to scream. In deference to the weather, she was wearing a stylish but not too eye-catching down jacket that went to her knees, and ankle-high snow boots instead of the shoes that normally would finish off the schoolgirl look.

She was a decade past the usual age for this outfit, but her Retrievers' no-see-me worked as usual—people looking at her saw only the outfit and thought she was the daughter of the house, home a little early but not unusually so.

Up the steps and to the door. The alarm system wasn't on; it would be turned on at night, probably. They were careless, in daylight. A slim leather case held in her left hand opened, and she withdrew a small metal hook pick with her right hand. It took the average cat burglar less than fifteen seconds to open the average household door, if they were so inclined. Wren wasn't average; it took her closer to ten. If anyone were to look closely, though, it would seem that she was merely having trouble turning her key in the lock.

The lock was high quality, an SFIC cylinder, and Wren finally resorted to sending a tendril of current down the tool, melting it to fit the pin stacks. It was humbling, and annoying: Wren was very proud of her lock-picking skills. But you did what was needed to get the job done.

The entry hall was gorgeous, and about the size of her entire apartment. Politics must pay better than crime.

"Upstairs. In the master suite's office," she reminded herself, forcing her attention away from the sleek statue of a dancing girl stretching one leg above her head, and up the gleaming hardwood staircase.

"One maid, one cook. Maid's running errands, cook is

deaf and tends not to leave her domain." She was reminding herself of stuff she had already memorized, which wasn't like her.

But it beat the hell out of letting her mind wander, which was what it kept wanting to do. Wondering what was happening with the Quad. Wondering where Sergei was. Wondering how she was going to deal with all the things she had to deal with.

Focus. It's all about the focus.

She went up the stairs, remembering to run up it like a teenager might, carelessly, and with way more energy than she had in her, naturally.

She felt the focus slip, and grabbed at it with mental hands, shoving it back into place. The way her luck was running, she'd crash headfirst into the cook, or worse yet, the target, home unexpectedly.

But she made it upstairs and down the hallway without incident. Bypassing the suite, she went directly for the bathroom where the wall safe was. She should be in and gone within the twenty-nine-minute window that she had set up for herself. Go her— "Oh. Oh, oh, oh."

She lifted her feet gently over the ankle-height laser alarm, tsking under her breath. "Tricky, my children, very tricky. I approve."

The alarm was a minor inconvenience, but it was also one that could be set up by the home owner, and therefore did not appear on any of the reports Sergei had collected and collated. Like those window alarms that they sold in all the houseware stores, it flew under the radar.

The safe was time-sealed: it could only be opened once a day. Wren grinned, a distinctly feral grin. The only thing they'd overlooked was the fact that the sealing was dependent on an internal mechanism that was—oooo, shiny!—run on electric batteries. She had no problem whatsoever using current, here. She whispered,

"Ticktock. Pretty lock.
Time of day, come 'round again;
Let me in the door."

The safe's lock, convinced that it was the right time of day, was amenable to Wren spinning the code. Seven tries, the little clock in the back of her head ticking off the seconds, and she had it. Most people, even the smart ones, used a secure code that they could remember. Not a kid's birthday, no—even the idiots knew better than that, mostly—but if you knew something about their life, you could probably guess their security codes. In this case, the target used the same five numbers and two letters he used for pretty much everything, according to the files she had assembled, only scrambled differently. It was a good thing she wasn't after his bank accounts.

Wren gave thanks to the god of laziness, slipped the safe open, and reached inside—

And jerked her hand back as though she had picked up a live wire.

"The hell?"

She looked inside, and swore under her breath. There

were the papers she had been sent to get, just like advertised. And on top of the packet there was a short branch tied in on itself in a circle, festive with bright white flowers and red berries. Freeze-dried, at the moment of absolute potency. Rowan. Witch-bane.

Old magic: a warding spell, specifically to keep witches away. Witches—or Talents. Rowan was said to keep lightning from striking. Lightning...or current.

"They're getting smarter," she muttered to herself, glaring at the wreath. "Life was easier when people scoffed at stories about witches and mages and magic."

The thing about Old Magic was that it was unpredictable as hell. Current was a science, in a lot of ways: you did A, and B followed. Assuming, that was, you could channel the current in the first place.

Old Magic was more random, and a lot sluttier. Anyone who wasn't a total Null could train themselves to sense the power, no matter what you called it, and there were a lot of shortcuts—like rowan, or bribing elementals—that allowed humans to fuck around with that power. But they were dipping their wands into stuff they had no understanding of, trusting to gods or luck or charms to protect them.

It was a wonder any Talents had survived long enough to figure out what was what, much less develop into the *Cosa*.

But the hedge-witches and alchemists and sorcerers weren't entirely wrong, either. Rowan *would* keep her from using current on the safe.

However, it wouldn't keep her from reaching in, purely

physical, nothing magical, and taking the papers by hand. It stung, but she was prepared for it this time, and the faint burn she could feel starting on the backs of her fingers where they had brushed the rowan's leaves were nothing that would hold up as evidence in the court of law.

The temptation to look at the papers passed through her, but she merely tucked them into the inner pocket of her blazer and—after placing a small feather on top of the remaining papers—closed the safe. The lock cycled shut, the time lock kicking in again. Nobody would even know the insides had been disturbed until 7:27 pm rolled around and the first person to check would find a wren's pinfeather where the purloined materials had been.

That sucker had been surprisingly hard to find. She hoped it would be effective. Maybe he'd know what had happened. Maybe he wouldn't. But either way, he'd known he'd been blown. And maybe he'd behave himself from now on.

An honest politician would be a wonderful thing.

Going downstairs, Wren detoured through the kitchen, risking the cook's appearance long enough to grab an apple from the bowl on the table. Walking out into the sunny, snow-white day, she crunched down into the white flesh, and felt pretty damn good about herself.

nineteen

Bren was never late for work. Ever. She had things to do, people to do for, and getting in before any of them was a matter both of pride and practicality. So when she realized that she was almost seven minutes off schedule, she lengthened her already impressive stride, and be damned any black ice foolish enough to get under her feet. The building that housed the Silence had no signs over its door, no indication that it was anything other than a nondescript office building on a nondescript side street; except for the fact that it was so very, intentionally, obviously nondescript. For years she had thought, to herself, that they would be better served putting a sign of some sort up there, merely to distract from its obvious anonymity, but nobody asked office managers about such things.

The usual cart at the corner of the street was missing. She wasn't going to take time to get a coffee this morning, anyway, but it was enough to make her frown. Micha was *always* there. Foul weather or blazing heat, through garbage strikes and Blue Flu, the jockey-sized Israeli was always pouring coffee and slathering bagels with more cream cheese than any one being could consume, always with brusque but friendly efficiency that Bren appreciated.

The cart was missing.

Under the full-length cashmere overcoat, underneath the silk knit sweater and the wool trousers, Bren shivered from what another, more superstitious person might have said was someone walking over her grave.

"Call the police! Someone, call the police!"

She had her cell phone out of her bag and was dialing before she'd gotten close enough to see what the cry was about.

Her steps faltered, and strong, capable fingers almost crushed the phone before she was able to answer the voice at the other end of the line.

"There are…two bodies. Murdered."

She gave the address, and hung up while the dispatcher was still speaking. Afraid to look, she moved closer. One body lay facedown on the stairs; the other was sprawled faceup. Both had thick lengths of what looked like wire wrapped round their necks, like grotesque scarves.

She didn't know either one of them.

By the time the police and the ambulances came, Bren had gone inside. Bodies or no bodies, there was still work to be done. She went through the security dance, rode the elevator up to her floor, and settled into her cubicle, slipping off her sneakers in exchange for a pair of comfortable shoes. With her height, heels were fun but not practical when dealing with men who might or might not decide to take offense at being towered over. And her legs looked good in flats, too.

She booted up her computer and started scanning the e-mail that had accumulated in her in-box overnight, putting the bodies out of her mind. There was nothing more she could do for them; let the professionals handle it.

"So…" a voice behind her said, quietly, and thoughtfully.

And Darcy would let her know what there was to know, as soon as there was anything to know. She didn't bother to turn around, confident that the tiny Researcher was making herself comfortable on one of the filing cabinets, perched like a hummingbird, and just as filled with energy. She didn't like the other woman, but she didn't dislike her, either. And she did respect her, possibly more than anyone else within the organization: it took cojones of steel to say no to the head of R & D, which Darcy reportedly had, to continue working in Ops with their mutual boss, Andre Felhim.

The two women weren't friends, no, but they had worked together long enough to forge bonds that neither of them questioned. And that included keeping each other alert to things that might impact them—or Andre.

"The bodies? They were human."

In any other context that statement would have seemed ridiculous, but both women knew about the fatae, and how many of the species could and did "pass" on a regular basis.

"Ours?" Bren had finished with her e-mail, and was now

typing up the week's agenda for the managers she dealt with; each of them had a master schedule and individual sidebars, and they all had to be completed and double-checked against each other before going out.

"Not that anyone's claiming." That meant nothing. They could have been R & D; Duncan's people answered to no one save Duncan, and even Darcy couldn't always get the low-down on what was happening up on the seventh floor. She wasn't even sure that she knew all the inhabitants of the offices, they kept things that closely buttoned.

"There was a note."

"On one of the bodies?"

"On both of them. Half on one, half on the other." She paused, less for effect than to ensure she had the details absolutely correct. "In their skin. Someone had branded it across their stomachs."

Bren didn't flinch, but she did hesitate for a longer second than usual before hitting the enter key when she came to the end of the paragraph she was typing. She didn't ask what the note said: Darcy would tell her if it was something she was free to share. And if it wasn't, then Bren didn't need to know.

"'Blood is paid in blood; different flesh this time for the burning.' Burning was capitalized, like it was an event."

"You don't know what it's referring to?"

"Not yet," she said. "But I will."

Bren believed her.

"Ladies."

This time, Bren did tense up, but she didn't stop typing.

"Poul." She liked the Operative—he was smart, sharp and efficient, and didn't waste time on bullshit, the way so many of the street players did when they got into the office. But unlike Darcy's quiet ways, he always gave the impression of trying too hard to sneak up on you, so when he managed it, it was as though you'd lost points in a game you didn't even know that you were playing.

"Is Himself in yet?"

"Not yet."

"Not like him, being late. Especially with all the excitement outside."

"I wouldn't call that exciting," Darcy said, and Bren paused her proofreading of the schedules long enough to slide a look at the other woman. Darcy's face was still set in its usual serene lines; like the pocket-sized know-it-all she was. But her eyes, rather than sparkling from newly acquired knowledge, were flat and hard when she looked at Poul.

Interesting. Bren didn't know what that meant, and she might not have Darcy's way with ferreting out details, but she knew when something was important.

And she also knew enough not to draw attention to it.

"Himself will want my full report," was all the Researcher said, slipping off the counter and making oblique farewells. "Bren, Poul."

The two of them nodded, then Bren went back to her typing. Poul, taking the message, went on down the hallway and into the office next to Andre's. It was currently empty, so Bren assumed he was going to do some work while waiting for the old man to come in. None of her business, so long as he wasn't hanging over her shoulder getting mixed up in *hers*.

"Did you do it?"

"Excuse me?" Sergei paused with his tea halfway raised to his lips. Andre had barged into the gallery just before they opened, taking Lowell by surprise as he set up the day's brochures and business cards on the front desk, and gone directly to the hidden sliding door of Sergei's office. The simple fact that the old man knew where the office was slowed Lowell's reaction down, and by the time he got to the doorway himself, Sergei waved him off.

"It's all right," he said to his assistant. "You deal with the front."

Lowell wasn't happy, but he didn't argue.

"Did you do it?" Andre asked again. He had always been graying, from the first day Sergei met him, but now the close-cropped black hair was more gray than black, and the wrinkles in his ebony skin were deep-set creases around eyes and mouth. And none of them came from laughter.

"Do *what?*" There were a great many things that he had done over the years, but he wasn't going to cop to anything until and unless he knew what the old man was talking about.

Andre stared at his former protégé, sitting calmly behind the desk, eyebrow raised in query, his steaming cup of tea placed back carefully on a coaster next to the computer screen.

"Might I have a cup of that?" he asked, letting his shoulders settle back into a more relaxed position, the angle of his elbows softening, his face becoming at once both more serene, and sadder.

"Of course." He spoke into the intercom. "Lowell? If you would be so kind as to fix our guest a cup of tea? The Black Rose, with milk, no sugar." Sergei then indicated the leather sofa. "Please. Sit."

Andre slipped off his heavy overcoat and hung it on the brass coat tree, then sat without any of his usual grace. He wasn't wearing his usual suit and jacket, instead a dark blue sweater over a black shirt, and black wool trousers. He looked as though he had come from a library filled with leather-bound books, where he had dandled a grandchild on one knee, and a picture book held open on the other.

"Two of our people were murdered this morning."

Sergei absorbed the information without outward emotion. "Unfortunate, but not exactly unusual. The life of a Silence member is a risky one, we all know that before we sign on."

He wasn't as cold as he sounded; he probably hadn't known the victims—Andre would have used that on him already—but he might have. He had worked there for a very long time, long ago and far away. The last time he had gone into the Silence building, he had run into too many old friends among the Handlers, the men and women who worked directly with the field operatives. The last time he had ventured into their territory, he had lost some of those, as well.

He gave a moment's thought to Michael. The old man—old when Sergei had first joined the Silence—had refused to speak to him. In fact, he had *begged* Sergei not to speak to him.

At the time, Sergei had thought it was a reflection on his, Sergei's status within the Silence—the rogue who got away, the insider-turned-outsider. Now, he had to wonder if there had been something going on among Handlers even then. Some unease that had nothing to do with him, and everything to do with internal politics...

Andre leaned back against the comforting leather embrace of the sofa. "They were murdered at the same time, in the same way, and dumped on our front steps."

"All right, that's a little more unusual." Sergei also leaned backward in his chair, palms flat on the desk, in plain view. If Andre was jumpy, best give him no cause to jump. But poke. Prod. Get as much out of him as possible, without giving anything in return. Those were the rules to play by. "And your first thought was to come here and ask if I had anything to do with it? Because the Silence doesn't have any real enemies?"

He badly wanted to ask if the bodies were anyone he had worked with. If it had been Michael, or Adam, or Jordana, or Leslie or... Better not to ask, not to know. Stick to the attack. Never show any chink Andre might exploit later, because you knew damn well that he would.

Andre smoothed the fabric of his slacks, in a move that could have been fastidiousness, nerves or a delaying action.

"Andre?"

"They were strangled and left on our steps with a warning about a 'Burning' to come."

Sergei waited for further details. "And this means…?"

"The Burning, my boy, is a term that has some resonance among your *Cosa*. It refers to the persecution of witches and those who use magic."

"A persecution the Silence has been known to take a hand in," Sergei said calmly. Not often, and never without perceived cause, but hands washed in blood, nonetheless. Another secret he'd kept from Wren. "So it may be that someone in the *Cosa* has a specific grudge. Why come to me, accuse me?"

"They laid these bodies on our doorstep, Sergei Kassianovich. I am not being entirely metaphoric here. They were discovered this morning by the cleaning crew, the warning burned into their skin."

Oh. The Silence's building was one of the best-kept secrets, maintained since the plot of land was first purchased in the 1950s. A great deal of money had been spent to keep it more off-the-radar than even Wren could manage.

Two murders, a *Cosa*-specific reference, plus an implied we-know-where-you-are threat against the larger organization. Yes, he could understand why gazes might turn in his direction—or Wren's, although anyone who knew her at all would know how unlikely violence was from her.

Him, though? The Silence had *trained* him, *praised* him for violence in the greater cause.

"It wasn't me, Andre."

It was all he could do or say; either his former boss believed him, or he didn't. If he did, it might or might not carry through to the rest of the Silence, who would never forgive him for taking up with a lonejack, anyway. If Andre *didn't* believe him… Well, that would be too bad for the old man, wouldn't it?

"And Miss Valere?"

There was a chime outside, and Sergei hit the remote that opened the door. Lowell brought the tea in, a full silver tray service with cream, sugar and narrow Italian butter cookies the bakery down the street specialized in. Lowell had many skills, and the ability to smell money on a potential customer was one of his best, second only to his ability to make those potential customers feel deeply valued, if not outright cherished.

"Thank you, son," Andre said, accepting a steaming cup from the tray. Sergei accepted a refill from the teapot, then nodded at Lowell to indicate that he should leave the tray on the desk.

The conversation did not resume until after the door had closed behind his assistant.

"Wren has no love for the Silence." In fact, Wren had great hate for the Silence, on several levels, and almost all of them totally justified. "But can you see her killing someone, marking their bodies with a message, and then dumping them on your stairs? She'd be far more likely to get into your bedroom at night and leave a rude message written with a Sharpie on your still-breathing body."

That almost got a flicker of a smile from Andre. Wren didn't like him, but he liked her.

"It doesn't matter if you did or did not do it. You are the most likely—in fact, the only reasonable suspect, in the eyes of those who will take action."

"You've lost that much power, that you can't do anything? Or…" Sergei looked at his former boss with knowing eyes. "You *won't* do anything. Because if Duncan acts against me, and it's proven—if *I* prove that it was someone else, then Duncan will have been shown as fallible, not only in not being able to protect the Silence, but also incapable of striking back against those who would harm the organization. His information will have been shown, publicly and irrevocably, to be flawed."

Information was the lifeblood of the Silence; it was what they traded in; who did what to whom, and the means to set it right. Or, Sergei amended to himself, with a tired, low-level bitterness, to set according to what *they* deemed right.

"You're a bastard, Andre Felhim."

"I do what I need to." He put his teacup down on the small table that was placed next to the sofa for just that purpose, and leaned forward, engaging Sergei's attention completely. "I had to know if you were involved in this, in any way. And I wanted to warn you. If that makes me a bastard, then so be it."

He stood, adjusting his sweater with a tug, and reclaiming his overcoat from the coat tree.

"Do what you need to do, Sergei Kassianovich." For the first time Sergei could remember, the patronymic did not set his teeth on edge. "Do as I trained you to do."

twenty

Sergei had waited all of ten minutes after Andre left before doing anything. Ten minutes spent sitting, quietly, his hands folded in front of him.

Was Andre playing him?

Yes.

Was Andre lying to him?

No. Probably not. Most likely not.

Had Andre told him everything?

Assuredly not.

Did that change what he needed to do?

No.

A full ten minutes, until his tea had turned cold and bitter, and he shut off his workstation, turned off the lamp, and took his own coat off the rack and left the gallery.

"I won't be in tomorrow," he told Lowell, scooping up a

mint out of the bowl on the counter before pulling on his gloves and tucking his scarf more firmly under his chin.

"We're supposed to get a delivery tomorrow—"

"You can handle it," he said, and was gratified, in a distant way, to see Lowell's already perfect posture straighten and broaden even more.

Lowell was good. He had to tell the kid that, more often. It was just tough to remember, most days.

The streets were cleared, for the moment. A few cars were parked on the side of the road, coated with ice on the windows, a dusting of snow on the hoods and roofs. He hoped to hell the owners had quality lock deicers, otherwise they weren't going to be getting into the cars any time soon.

He stood in the cold air and debated with himself. Go home, and wait for Wren to get in touch with him? Go to her place, and hope that she was there, that she would let him in? Stop in at Truce Central, even though there was no more truce, and see if anyone would give him the time of day? He didn't know, without her, where he stood with the supernatural community. He was the reason the Silence knew about them—did they know that? They must, by now. On the other hand, he was also the reason many of them were alive. And he was still Wren's partner. He thought. He hoped.

"You Didier? Of course you're Didier, who else would you be?"

He turned in the direction of the voice, and blinked at the sight of the creature standing in front of him.

"You're…"

"Yeah, I know, I hear it all the time. Notoriety's a bitch." To the passerby, he was merely a particularly grotesque old man, wizened and bent, with a face liked a dried apple and drool threatening to appear at the corner of its pale-skinned lips. Only the creature's dark red eyes gave its species away: demon. Wren had told him that demon all looked different, except the eyes; she hadn't said that one of them looked like Koshschey. Koshschey the Invulnerable. Koshschey the Damned. Koshschey the Murderer.

"You are Didier, right?"

кузен Аракона. I mean, right, yes, I am." The sight had shocked him back into Russian, as though he were a six-year-old terrified by his father's stories, all over again.

"Good, because if I had the wrong street again I was going to hand in my courier's badge and go hibernate for another decade or seven. I hate this city."

Of *course* it spoke Russian. Sergei had trouble keeping up, mentally translating in his head and stumbling over a few words. "You have a message for me?"

"Yeah. You're supposed to meet Herself at Dante's. Half an hour. Was more time but these damn streets twist and turn on one another, I swear to god Kana'ti couldn't find its way through this without a compass."

The demon turned and walked away, its message delivered. Sergei stared after it, trying to parse what he'd just been told. She hadn't come to get him herself, had sent a courier, a demon to fetch him like an errant schoolboy.

And yet, could he blame her? At least she was still calling

for him, for whatever reason. Maybe she couldn't get away, or she was around too many lonejacks to use a phone safely—or all that were available were mobile phones, and those crapped out if she so much as looked at one, these days. There were a dozen reasons why she wouldn't have come to the gallery herself, and only half were because she was still angry, or upset....

Only when it had passed a couple of students and disappeared around the corner did he realize that he had no idea where Dante's was.

It turned out the place was in Manhattan, although the Javits Center was not an area he typically thought of for food above the grease-cart level. He walked in and a waiter—an overweight, bald-pated man in traditional black pants and white shirt, and a drooping mustache—rushed over and directed him to the right table. They were seated, he noted, out of the direct line of sight of the doorway, in an alcove without windows, with an emergency exit off to the side. He approved, then wondered who had chosen it, and why; he wanted Wren thinking smart, but there was a fine, scary line between planning for a fast exit, and anticipating a gunfight.

"Where the hell have you been?" The object of his thoughts looked up from the table, lines forming between her eyes as she frowned at him. Her hair was pulled back into a tight braid, and she was wearing all black. Retriever-mode, even if the black was jeans and a turtleneck rather than her slicks, or the less expensive, more easily explained sweats she sometimes used.

She was working, even if she didn't know it, consciously. He wasn't going to start a fight, not here or now, but—"Next time, send directions with your invite, okay?"

Wren had the grace to look abashed, but only for a moment. In point of fact, if he hadn't been able to call an old friend in the restaurant business and ask for help, he would never have gotten here at all. From the outside, the place looked like a warehouse: an abandoned warehouse, specifically. He'd almost told the cab driver to forget it, and take him home. But the smells that hit his nose the moment the door opened made him willing to forgive any cosmetic default, so long as someone put a plate of something in front of him.

"You guys are taking this whole '*Cosa*' thing a little too seriously, don't you think?"

From the looks he got, Sergei suspected that he wasn't the first to make the joke, and it hadn't been funny the first dozen times, either. He reached over and tore off a chunk of garlic bread, and closed his eyes in ecstasy as the warm bread, butter and garlic did terrible, wanton things with his taste buds.

All right, so there were real benefits to having crisis meetings in downscale Italian restaurants, yes.

It was back down to the lonejack's Quad, Wren, and a man with long orange-red hair that Sergei didn't recognize but seemed to be leading the meeting. After so many months of having fatae at elbow and heel, it felt strange to be surrounded only by humans.

"The local police department is also working on the case."

The man resumed speaking, once Sergei had settled in. "Our connections there are keeping tabs on anything that may come up. So far, their findings echo that of my PUPs—the bodies are normal, in all ways except the manner of their death."

"You are referring to the remnants of current found on them?" one of the unknown faces asked. "Their manner of death was strangulation. Cruel, but normal, as these things go."

"Yes. My apologies."

Sergei was willing to bet that this guy had never misspoken himself a day in his life. He knew who he was now—Ian Stosser, the co-founder of the PUPIs, or private unaffiliated paranormal investigators, the *Cosa's* answer to the metro CSI labs. Sergei made a point of knowing the identity of as many movers and shakers as he could, no matter what they were moving or shaking. You never knew when you might need someone.

"Do we even have names? Affiliations?" Michaela, tapping a pen against the side of her place; uncharacteristically jumpy. "Are these souls innocent scapegoats, or do they have some connection with what has been going on?"

"Again, we don't know just yet."

"Does it really matter? They were Null, yes?"

"Yes." He hesitated. "I should say, that as far as we know, they were not members of the *Cosa*, neither Council nor lonejack. That much we got from the Council, before they slammed the doors shut."

"What?" Sergei hadn't heard about that.

Michaela filled him in. "KimAnn has decided that, with the Truce broken, and these murders, she has no obligation to do anything other than protect her own. They've called their members off patrol, and are not offering any more information."

It didn't surprise Sergei at all; the Council had come to the Truce-table for their own reasons, which involved KimAnn trying to keep control of her organization in the aftermath of a rather spectacular power grab. With humans—Nulls—being killed, and Talents suspected of the murders, she could use that as a justification for her actions and as a reason to close the borders, as it were, as well.

"We keep acting as though the murders were in retaliation for the angel's death. Why?"

"Because I don't believe in coincidences," Bart said grimly.

"Nor do I," Stosser said. "But sometimes, what look like coincidences are simply things happening within the same geographic and chronographic areas."

"I almost understood that," Wren muttered, but Sergei suspected only he heard her. The past few months she had been making an effort to stand out, shaking off her natural tendency to meld into the background noise in order to be heard and seen by the rest of the *Cosa*. But since the angel was killed, she had faded a little, and he wasn't even sure she was aware of it.

He didn't mind, at all. He'd never been comfortable with her taking such a front-and-center position, even as he understood the need for it. It might be parochial, or sexist, or just overbearing of him, but he wanted her out of the spotlight—and therefore out of the sights of whomever was gunning for Talents.

He knew better—barely—than to say any of that. He was still in the doghouse with her for recent events: she might not have brought it up, and he wasn't going to say anything, either, but he knew. If he ended up sleeping alone tonight, it was his own damn fault. She had warned him, and he had pushed anyway.

The waiter came by with a menu, and he waved it away, asking only for a glass of the house red. The way his stomach was tied up in knots, suddenly, he didn't think food was such a good idea after all.

After the meeting broke up, and the plates were cleared away, Wren stayed at the table while everyone else stood up and said their goodbyes. Sergei pushed his chair back, but didn't stand up. Bart swirled the dregs of his wine in his glass, thoughtfully, and didn't look at either one of them.

Bart was an opinionated, arrogant jerk, who never hesitated to say what was on his mind and damn the fallout. Recent events hadn't put any diplomatic polish on him, either. But he was smart, and he was a survivor, and Wren had every intention of listening to whatever it was he was about to say.

"They're idiots." Bart's sideways glance at his departing fellow Quad members made it clear who he was talking about. "Well-meaning, and good people, don't get me wrong, but they're idiots. All this discussion about who and why and what can we do about it…they're missing the point, and I don't know if it's intentionally because they're scared, or they honestly are too dumb to see it. But either way, it makes them idiots."

"And what do you see?" Sergei asked.

"That we're being played."

Well, duh. Wren was suddenly less impressed with Bart.

"Okay, yeah, you figured that out already. You're not an idiot, either of you. At least not when you're out of bed."

"Excu—" He steamrolled right over her.

"But the question everyone's been asking is the wrong one. They're asking *why*."

"And you know why?"

Bart scowled. "You ever play war games? No, of course you didn't. You probably never even played Risk, did you?"

Wren looked at Sergei. He was the strategic one, the chess player. Her partner was still sitting back in his chair, carefully not showing anything on his face. That meant he was listening, and listening intently. She hadn't wanted to bring him in on this, not with her suspicions, her fears. But she needed him, damn it. *They* needed him, and his brain, and his knowledge. She would keep her fears locked in their boxes, for now. Until there was proof, one way or the other.

"You have an enemy. A big, bad enemy, with powers you don't have, powers you don't understand. What do you do?"

"Find their enemy and make him or her your ally?"

"Not bad, and that's part of it. But—"

"Divide and conquer," Sergei said. "Find the enemy's soft spot, and cut there, deprive them of their support, *their* allies."

"Better. What do you use for a knife?"

Sergei tapped the table with his forefinger, his eyes going clouded, like he was looking a million miles away. Wren felt a surge of glee at being half a step ahead of him. "You use something of theirs, something they'd never think to question. Like, oh, paranoia or extreme reluctance to trust anyone."

"So we have someone or several someones who know the *Cosa* well enough to use their own weaknesses to take them down. That's the how. You said you knew the why."

"I just told you. Someone who is afraid of us, of what we are."

Wren frowned. "List's small, there."

"The government knows about us, somewhere, in some office or another. Enough of us have been useful over the years, in various wars and wartime scenarios, there have to be records. How many people *believe* it is another question, though."

"I shall hereby refrain from the obligatory Mulder and Scully joke," Sergei said with grave dignity.

"If you make reference, it counts as the obligatory joke," Bart said.

"It does not."

"Yeah, it does."

"All right, focus, gentlemen." Was she the only person in the entire world who hadn't liked that show?

"No need to. I know who did it."

"What?" She had missed something, somewhere. Not an uncommon occurrence when Sergei started seriously cranking on something.

"Not what. Why." Sergei blinked, frowned, and pushed away from the table. "I need to take a walk."

There were few things scarier than Sergei's mind on that full-forward push, Wren decided. He had his head down and smoke practically pouring out of his ears, and you got the feeling that if you were to step in front of him you'd wake up a week later with tire tracks across your head, or something, and he wouldn't even have noticed. But was he thinking *for* them…or was he trying to decide who to betray now?

Stop it, Valere!

They had left Bart back at the restaurant, and were presently walking down Eighth Avenue toward the nearest subway station, dodging icy patches and piles of shoveled snow as they went. Not that she minded the fast pace, exactly; she was dressed for the weather, but the wind kept sliding under her turtleneck and sending shivers up and down her skin.

So do something about it, you idiot. She shook her head; God save her, she really was an idiot sometimes. Or maybe her brain was so focused on the big problems, it forgot how to solve the little ones.

Crooking a mental finger at a small strand of current in her core, she coaxed it up and out of the pile. Just a bit, enough to do the job and no more.

"Winter's chill
Is boring to me:
Warm my flesh."

Sergei checked his pace half a step. "Did you say something?

She looked at her partner, already feeling the spell take effect as tingles touched the epidermal nerve endings like reverse goose bumps. "Nope."

It was petty, she knew. But he could just make do with his expensive jacket and cashmere scarf. She wasn't going to give him any more current until he admitted that he had a problem, damn it. And not after then, either. God, she had to retrain herself, too. She wasn't going to be able to work current on him, either, no matter what...like not cooking with wine around an alcoholic...fuck. *Okay, focus on the problem at hand. If you all die tomorrow, it won't matter worth a damn. If you both survive, then you can have a major-ass Intervention and force him to deal with this.*

And what if he won't? she asked herself. What *will* you do then?

She didn't know. She'd already tried being the strong one, the one in control, and that didn't work; she wasn't going to compound the failure by being stupid and pretending it would work if she just tried a little harder, put in a little more effort. She'd tried walking away, and that was just as abject a failure; she'd been bouncing her brain off his for too many years now to go cold turkey, especially in the middle of this mess.

"Talk to me," she said instead. "You said you knew who…why," she corrected herself."

"It's my fault. I was afraid of it, and now I'm…not entirely certain, but pretty damn near sure certain."

"Your fault? How…" She stopped, stared at the point between his shoulder blades as he kept walking. *No. No, oh no…*

She gave him the opening she didn't want answered. "The Silence. You think it was the Silence—but why? You said you knew *why*."

"I have to talk to Andre again."

He stopped at the stairs leading down to the 1/9 train, and looked down at Wren. For the first time in months, she was reminded how much taller he was than she; so many of their conversations recently had been held horizontally.

"If you don't want to come…"

"Am I going to want to kick him when he answers your questions?"

That got a faint smile out of him. "At the very least."

"Lead on, Macduff."

They weren't back on. They weren't even getting onto getting back on. But they were on the same train heading for the same goal—literally—and Wren would work with that, for now.

Especially if she got to kick Andre Felhim in the ass. Hard.

The subway wasn't crowded, and they each got a seat. Wren was inwardly relieved and disappointed that the car was just crowded enough that those seats weren't together.

She wasn't sure being pushed up against him was where she was ready to be, just yet. Although it still beat being pushed up against the rather large woman next to her...while winter subway riding was better in some ways than the summer—the smells were better, for one—the fact was that the same number of people wearing winter coats made space tighter than it should be. At least they were done with both the preholiday buying frenzy and the post-New Year's sales buying frenzy; overloaded shopping bags on mass transit should be considered deadly weapons. Especially when carried by little old ladies with attitudes.

Across the car from her, Sergei looked like he was sleeping; eyes closed, posture slightly slumped but still alert enough to warn off potential muggers. She took the opportunity to study him, comparing the visual to the image she still carried in her head from the first time ever they met:

The car slammed to a halt, the crunch of metal and plastic echoing across the park. Instinctive, what she had done: using current to cushion the impact, kept the impact from being far worse, suppressing any sparks that might have ignited the fuel tank. Genevieve slowed to let Joe go by first—he was a cop, he'd know what to do. He tossed her his phone, yelled for her to call the accident in. She dialed the number, speaking to the dispatcher, even as her eyes scanned the scene in front of her. And then the driver got out, staggering even under the helping hands, and looked up and stared at her, through all the people and chaos.... And she knew he knew who she was. What she was. *What she had done.*

And he very clearly, very carefully, mouthed "thank you" to her.

Sergei Didier then had been wearing a suit that cost more than her mother paid in rent on their place. His hair had been darker, more stylishly cut, and the lines on his face had been, ironically enough, deeper-cut than they were now. He had looked like what he was: a burned-out businessman facing a crisis.

Now…he dressed more casually, even on his most client-heavy days, even in his choice of suits and ties. His hair was touched with the first hints of silver, and the lines around his eyes and lips creased upward in laugh lines as much as with tension.

You've been good for him. Even with all the bad, the worries, the stupid things you do to each other, the stupid things he does to himself, he's better now than he was before.

Before, when the Silence had him. When the man they were going to see now was his boss.

He had warned her, back when the Silence came in to save the day, and her bank account, that there was a price to pay for dealing with them. She had listened…but she hadn't remembered.

The Silence held secrets, and used their people to bear the weight. They played close to the vest with all their cards, and they'd hide the ones in the river, if they could. What secrets was Sergei still carrying? Was it possible to escape? And what did they have to do with the *Cosa*'s enemies today?

Think. What do you know about the Silence, Valere?

They were a watchdog organization, according to her partner. Their mission statement was to protect the innocent against larger, darker forces.

Their funding came from a bunch of Dead White Guys with an overdeveloped guilt complex, back in a previous century.

They were set up like a corporation in a lot of ways; one branch not always knowing what another was doing, and a lot of infighting and turf battles, based on what was happening with Andre, and Sergei's mention of this guy named Duncan.

And that was about it, sum and total of her knowledge. She hadn't bothered to look, even when she signed on with them, trusting Sergei to deal with all of that. Even when Silence operatives burned them on the Nescanni job, she'd left it to Sergei to deal with the particulars, limiting her involvement to snarking at Andre.

You can't do that anymore she thought to herself as the train pulled into their stop. *You've been letting him take too much, stuff you should be handling—like current,* the guilty voice in her head said, like she needed reminding—*and that's not good for either of you. Especially 'cause he's never going to say no...and you can't say no to him, either.*

One was personal, and one was business, and once they'd been separate things. Or, at least, they'd managed a halfway decent firewall between the two. Now...

Wren needed to relearn that wall. For both their sakes.

Wren had never actually been to the Silence's headquarters before. She hadn't even known it was in the city, although that made sense, considering Sergei had been based here, when they met. She was expecting something suitably Gothic, or maybe ultramodern.

She wasn't expecting him to lead her to a small, somewhat dingy coffee shop in SoHo. Hopes of a secret password, maybe a shady-eyed waitress and a sliding door in the back, were dashed when instead they got into a booth, the vinyl upholstery squeaky but surprisingly well-padded, and were handed oversized menus by a waitress who looked like she came right out of Don't Give a Damn Central Casting.

"We meeting someone here?"

"Maybe." He was shut down, even to her. Fine. She'd been surprised he'd even let her tag along—*face it, as little as you wanted to get involved with the Silence, he wanted you involved even less. So, okay, why is he letting you in, now?*

"Why'd you let me come along?"

"Because you scare him."

Wren felt both her eyebrows go up in surprise at that. She did? Most excellent…

"Also, you need to hear this directly. Because I might not tell you."

"Huh?"

But the waitress came back before she could push for clarification. Sergei ordered a cup of tea, hot, and the chicken-fried chicken. Wren, having had a real meal at the restaurant during the meeting, just asked for a diet Sprite and a plate of fries.

"Craving salt and grease. That time of month?"

"Do guys say things like that just to piss us off? Yes, that time of month. Which I know you knew already because you keep better track of those things than I do."

They'd been working together for three years before she realized that he never booked her a job the week her period was due. Even once she'd confronted him with it, and explained that she wasn't one of those females who couldn't function for cramps, he still gave her that week off, no matter what.

Their drinks and her fries were delivered just as Sergei looked at his watch for the first time. It was an old-fashioned, very expensive gold watch, one that required winding twice a day, and he was careful to take it off before they got into any kind of intimate contact, or he was going to be dealing with more than one lonejack....

He hadn't taken it off before going to the meeting. She felt a momentary burst of guilt about that, for not letting him know what he was walking into, then pushed it aside. It was still working, so no harm no foul, right?

"Didier."

That wasn't Andre's voice. It wasn't Andre, either, standing next to their table, but a very tall, slender, oh-so-leggy blonde. Exactly the sort of woman Sergei used to date, back before, when he was doing the whole Man About the Art Scene thing.

Wren waited for the old surge of jealousy to rise, but only felt a little ill this time. Maybe because Sergei didn't seem all that thrilled to see the woman?

"Bren."

He didn't make any move to introduce the two of them, so the blonde did it herself.

"My name is Bren. And you're Genevieve."

Wren hated her given name; the only people who got to use it were her mom, and Sergei when he was trying to make a point. But she didn't want this woman using any of her nicknames, either, so she just inclined her head in acknowledgement of the statement. Someone would tell her what was going on, eventually.

"You shouldn't be here, Sergei. And she *really* shouldn't be here."

"Free country. Public diner." Oh, he *really* wasn't happy to see the blonde, no. That made her feel much better.

"You know that's bullshit," Bren said, her face tightening like someone with too much BOTOX trying to grimace.

Sergei shrugged. "Tell me what I need to know, and we'll both go away."

"Are you *trying* to get killed? You, and her, and everyone who's ever touched you?"

Wren blinked, and got very, very still, the inherent skill that made her a Retriever effectively taking her off the radar of everyone in the coffee shop, even—for the moment—her partner. It was tougher to go away from him like that, but she could still do it. She didn't know why she did it, right then; some instinct that told her Not Being There was the right move.

Wren had learned the hard way to listen to those instincts.

"Tell me what I need to know, if Andre's too afraid to be seen with me."

"Andre doesn't know you're here. I intercepted the information before he got it."

"Why?"

"Because you walked away from *him,* Didier. So why should he come to you now?"

Wren's ears were definitely perked forward, now.

"What interest does the Silence hold with the *Cosa?*" Sergei asked.

"None. You know that. They don't approve of magic, unless…"

"Unless it's performed under their aegis." His gaze sharpened on her. "Bren. What is happening with the FocAS? Andre mentioned something, a while back. He was going to have Darcy look into it."

Bren sat down, almost shoving Wren aside, in her invisibility. "They're disappearing. You know that already. We thought, at first, they were leaving the Silence, that we were pushing them too hard, making them choose between loyalties…"

Sergei nodded, impatient. He and Wren had discussed this, gone over the possibilities. He had hoped that Darcy would be able to give actual names, so that Wren could check with the families themselves.

"That's not it. The ones who've gone, they're *gone*. Their families haven't heard from them at all. Even their Handlers are at a loss to explain it."

"Exactly when did these disappearances start?" If it coincided with the lonejacks who disappeared…

"As far as Darcy can tell, almost two years ago, for the first one."

Wren shook her head, forgetting that Sergei wouldn't

see her. The timing was off. KimAnn hadn't started anything active then; at least, not outside the Council itself.

"Two years?" Sergei, a former Handler, was outraged on half-a-dozen levels, and both Bren and his partner shied away from the anger in his voice.

"It wasn't noticed because, well, you remember what it's like. FocAS have more leeway than most, and their Handlers are…"

"Mavericks." Sergei was amused despite his anger; he had been one of those mavericks once, so much so that he'd left the game entirely. Or tried to, anyway. Not for the first time Wren thought that he'd Handled her quite nicely, if for their mutual benefit and enrichment.

"Idiots, is what I would have said. But then…some of them went missing, too. The Handlers."

"And nobody was bothered by this?" This time, Sergei didn't sound surprised or angry at all; he was on the scent of something.

"Andre was. Sometimes, I think Andre's the only one who gives a damn anymore." She played with the straw of Wren's soda absently, twirling it between two fingers of her left hand. "Sergei. You and I never saw eye to eye. I never understood why you got away with the things you did, why you left—and why they let you come back. Your partner's not as hot as all that, that the Silence couldn't survive without her."

Wren winced. That stung, but it wasn't untrue, or something the two of them hadn't wondered about, too.

"But recent events… Darcy's not the only one who can put two and two together and come up with fifteen. The only thing the Silence cares about is making the world better. Safer. More even-handed. And they do whatever it takes, use whatever they get, to make it so."

"You knew all this already. We all did." His voice sounded flat, uninterested, but Wren knew her partner. He was quivering on the edge of his mental chair, scenting blood in her words. Whatever he'd come here for, this woman was about to give to him.

"I think maybe they've gone too far." She folded the straw in half, then in half again, clenching it so firmly the tube was flattened. "I think they've become proactive."

Sergei went even more still, in a way that was almost Retriever-like. "Weeding out the unpalatable influences?"

"Possibly. Probably."

"How probable?"

"I don't know. Darcy might."

"Find out."

Bren looked as though she might argue, but his expression probably told her it would be useless. Or maybe she actually liked being given orders; some people worked better when told what to do; she'd seemed uncomfortable taking the initiative, coming here on her own, so maybe this made her feel better.

Whatever her motivations, she dropped the straw, wiped her hands on Wren's napkin, and got up and walked out of the diner without a backward glance.

Sergei sat there for a moment, then turned to where Wren was, silent-still, and seemed to focus on her again, even though she hadn't let up on the no-see-em.

"You heard?"

"I heard. I don't think I understand, though. What's so bad about being proactive? Isn't it better to prevent a problem, rather than solve it?"

"The Silence defines 'problems' as anything that causes trouble, or makes life difficult."

"Yeah, I got that."

"For humans. You hate my…what did you call it, fatae-phobia?"

"You're better, lots better these days," she started to protest.

"Yeah. I am. But the Silence isn't. From what Bren's saying, what Andre was seeing, it's getting worse. And they don't define human as human, Wren. They define it as *Null*. Talents—if they're FocAS, they can be used, but lonejacks? Council? A taint in the blood, an evolutionary path gone wrong. If they can be brought to the Silence's way of thinking they are allowed. If not…"

"And the fatae? Animals. To be harnessed, hunted, or eradicated."

"Like the vigilantes," Wren said, finally, only now, feeling horribly stupid, Getting It.

"Like the vigilantes," he said in agreement. "Come on. Bren was right. Being here is not the smartest thing I've ever done. Go back to being invisible. If anyone wants to take a potshot it should only be at me."

Wren didn't bother arguing. Unlike the warming spell, excluding him here would be more stupid than petty. But she didn't want to argue over it, either, and she didn't want to think about the fact that already she was breaking her vow not to touch him with current....

"Sway harmful intent;
Give them another target
For wrongful ire."

It wasn't as good as a bulletproof vest, and wouldn't stop anyone with a real mad-on, but if anyone was just idly looking, they'd keep going until they found someone else to be peeved at.

Sergei shivered as they stepped through the diner's door; the cantrip taking effect, although anyone observing them would think that he'd simply gotten a blast of cold air. She knew better. It was the same shiver he gave, the down-the-spine one, he made during sex, just before orgasm.

And how much damage did you just do to him there, with that one touch? How much current can his body handle? How much damage does it take, before his internal organs give up and break down? She needed to talk to a doctor, someone who could be trusted to understand, and give her a straight answer, and not spill…right. Good luck finding that non-existent paragon…

"You were used. Manipulated." The speaker tossed down a sheet of paper on the table in front of KimAnn, as though daring her to pick it up. She ignored it.

"Nobody manipulates me." They had arrived unannounced, without fanfare or the usual preparations that were required before one Council leader hit another's territory.

"Oh, I'm sure the original idea was entirely yours. It has all the hallmarks of your ego all over it—how only *you* could save us from the coming danger, the threats of Outside. But where did the coming danger come from? Who fed you that, Madame Howe?"

"Everyone knows…"

"Everyone knows that we have always walked a delicate line, a compromise between what we are and what Nulls fear. We have worked with governments, private agencies…we have made compromises and alliances, and we have always remained true to the Charter, without jeopardizing our existence—or threatening others.

"And then, suddenly, there is risk… and we must think that the risk exists only because of the belief you have, that *all* Talents must come under your sway." She started to protest, and he ignored her. "No one else heard of this risk. No other Council felt the need to take the steps you have taken."

There were four of them standing in front of her: Louise, from the Midwest Council, out of Chicago. Bee, the Tucson-region Council. Randolph, down from Quebec. And Jenne, elderly but hardly frail, to represent the Pacific Northwest. Missing were Lizzie from the Green Kingdom, and anyone from the Gulf Coast, which was still reeling from recent natural disasters. They had other things to worry about than what was going on out on the East Coast.

"And so you endangered us all. For what? For your own

ego—fine. We certainly understand the desire to expand your horizons, to enrich your holdings. And had it been merely that, we would have overlooked your recent alliance with the San Diego Council. But you allowed yourself to be influenced by outsiders."

"I repeat, that is untrue."

Bee stepped forward, forcing her to look at him. Bee was barely three feet tall, and oddly misproportioned, but the current inside him was unmistakeable. An opponent once said that being current-slapped by him was like getting stepped on by T rex. Not only did you have no doubt who it was, but you weren't getting up again anytime soon, either.

"You have not been alone in investigating this organization, the Silence. We too have been looking. And what we have found is that your spies were compromised."

"Impossible!"

He slapped one oversized hand down on the paper before her. "Read, woman."

Unwillingly, KimAnn looked down at the sheet. He removed his hand so that she could pick it up. Reaching with her left hand for it, her right picked up and unfolded a delicate pair of glasses and settled them on her nose so that she could make out the relatively small type.

It was a medical report, assessing the mental condition of one Mally Jones. The paper went on in rather graphic detail, describing the various forms of deprivation and reprogramming used on the woman, up to and including her most recent sighting, calling in to report to her masters on New Year's Day.

KimAnn didn't recognize the name, but that meant nothing. She learned very few names, now; her days of reaching out were over, now others reached up to *her.*

"This is quite sad, but otherwise…"

"This is proof," Jenne said, the only one who seemed genuinely regretful for being there. "Mally Jones was one of the people you based your reports to the Council on. One of the people you used to justify your actions, to build up the threat against us, the terrible danger all Talent faced.

"The only problem is that this report came—at great cost—from the files of an organization that bears us no good will.

"Your informants, your *trusted* sources, were members of the Silence, brainwashed into doing whatever their masters asked of them. In this case, feeding on your fears and suspicions, leading you directly down the garden path *they* chose."

KimAnn didn't crush the paper in her hand, but the tremor that ran through her wrist indicated she dearly wished to. "I will destroy them…."

"You will do nothing." Louise: solemn, but with an unmistakable undercurrent of satisfaction.

KimAnn looked up, and only then noted that the four had created a half circle in front of her—and that her own people had, somehow, at some point, been removed from the room.

"We have tolerated you because you are an elder, and powerful, and part of the Council tradition. No matter how you flaunted your disregard for the Charter, for the bonds which bind us all together, for the very reason the Council was formed—"

"To protect us!"

"To protect us *from ourselves.*" Louise was picking up steam as she spoke. "This organization, this Silence? They can harm us only if and when they know about us, they find us. This all can be laid at your door, Madame Howe. Had you not tangled with the lonejacks, harassed and attempted to intimidate them, none of this would have come to pass. The vigilantes would have been discovered and dealt with as so many others have in the past, and we would have weathered this storm and come out on top. We might even then have been able to use that occasion as one to bring the lonejacks to us, peacefully, within the bounds of the Charter. But you—you have made us visible. Have made us into targets. Not only your own people, crime enough, but ours as well. We have done what was needful, in order to put suspicion back where it belongs, but the damage has been done, and cannot be undone."

"In light of that, you have been judged, KimAnn Howe, and found guilty. The sentence is without appeal, the punishment swift and without malice."

There might have been time to run, to try and stage some defense, some kind of counterattack, but in the end, there was a certain dignity which must be maintained. Her position, her pride, demanded it.

She rose, meeting each of her judges' gazes evenly, without flinching, in turn.

"I did what I believed was needful. I did what I believed

was the right thing to do, the only thing to do in order to preserve our ways of life, our goals and our values. I would do it again, if the chance were offered again."

"And that is why you will never be given the chance again."

The four Council leaders didn't do anything as clichéd as hold hands, or even gesture. There was no sound, no indication of anything happening. But KimAnn could feel the heat increase in the room as current rose, generated not off the wiring, or even the power reservoirs mumbling to themselves in the basement of the building, but from the air itself, the electricity interacting with the biological matter of the Talent in the room, drawing on both; becoming a real, definable, physical presence beside her.

The Old Ones, the sources of wisdom, might have looked like this, she thought, her last thought before the presence grasped her tenderly by the face, and consumed everything that was important to her.

When it was done, KimAnn stood facing the four, her face still as proud, still as determined, and more than one of the judges felt a surge of pride in her strength, as though it validated their own, somehow.

They also felt a chill of fear. As she had been laid to waste, so might any Talent; burned out: the opposite of wizzing. Not too much current, but none.

"Your personal income remains yours," Bee said to the woman. "We will not interfere further in your life, or what you do with it."

KimAnn turned to stare at him, her gaze unblinking, the expression on her patrician face hard as stones.

"What life is that?" she asked. "Money? Belongings? You think they ever meant anything?" She didn't wait for any of them to answer, but turned away, moving away from the four to look out the window, her delicate hands resting on the old oak sill. The power which had always rested within her was faded, her core cold and empty, aching with loss.

"Go, now. You have what you came here for. Leave me to what is left to be done."

None of them could contradict her words, so they left her, alone.

twenty-one

By midmorning, everyone knew that there had been some sort of shake-up within the Council. The Mouthpiece, Colleen, had disappeared, was not answering current-pings, or knocks on her physical door. Even the Council members who had remained within the Patrol program were missing, come time for their shift, and across the city you could practically hear the slamming of doors and shooting of dead bolts as the Council turned inward, abandoning even the pretense of interaction with the rest of the *Cosa*.

"They're running like rats."

"They're not running. They're burrowing. When this is all over, they'll come back out… but we won't have forgotten."

The tone was grim to match the mood. The rental hall wasn't quite filled—there were too many among the *Cosa* who had been injured in the last Moot to risk another, and people were gun-shy about gathering now—but those who had appeared were wound up tight and fierce.

Wren had attended three Moots in her life, which was three more than most lonejacks ever got, and four more than she ever wanted to deal with. Moots were supposed to be last-ditch, the trumpet call to order, the summons to all, to deal with things that had to be faced.

One was bad. Two qualified for "living in interesting times." Three was apocalyptic in nature, and everyone knew it.

"We have neither option. We do not have the resources that would allow us to burrow…and where would we run to? This is our home. This is *our* home. We're New Yorkers, damn it!"

There was a grumbling of approval, and a rumble of dissent, and Bart backtracked slightly. "All right, no we're not all *New Yorkers*. You know damn well what I meant. Nobody but nobody makes us leave our homes unless we want to go. Anyone here want to go?"

The "no!" that answered him might not have been much by tent revival standards, but for lonejacks it was a clarion call.

"So what are we going to do about it?"

There was no platform, no balcony to observe from. Bart stood in the middle of the room, on a ladder-back chair, the other three members of the Quad nearby, supporting him, amplifying his voice to every corner of the space. Wren had commandeered a chair for herself, and was perched on the back of it, giving herself a little breathing room. Sergei stood near her; not by her side, but close enough so that anyone not carefully observing wouldn't notice anything off. When he moved too close, she got tensed up and nervous, distracted, and moved away. After the third or fourth time, he got the message and stayed a safe distance away. Everyone's attention was on Bart right now, anyway.

"All right, all right, everyone quiet down." Rick stood, speaking directly from the floor. Bart yielded to him as though it had been choreographed; it might have been— Wren wasn't going to underestimate the Quad any longer. They'd been through the fire and were still standing; that was more than the Council could claim.

"Fine. We can't count on the Council. Big deal. When have we ever counted on the Council?"

There was more muttered agreement from the floor, this time unanimous.

"We did something unprecedented this year—we came together. Not out of fear, or in a mad rush, but as an organized, rational whole, aware of our individualities but working toward a common goal. And not just lonejacks but fatae, as well."

All right, so that was a bit of an exaggeration; no more than you heard in any political rally charge-'em-up, and probably a lot more truth than in most. Wren was about par on the cynicism level of her fellow lonejacks; they knew they were being manipulated, they knew why, and they were letting it happen. Exactly what the Quad had planned on. Wren wasn't sure she was comfortable being led that way, even in a strong cause and by people she—mostly—

trusted, but there was no other option. If they splintered now, they would lose, and with far more at stake than merely their freedom from Council control.

"Now, we have to not only act together, we have to keep it together. That means working with information, with our brains, not from fear or misplaced aggression."

More muttered agreement, with some nervous laughter. Lonejacks were as known to rush into the fire as away from it; the Council had used that, almost successfully, against them just the summer past.

"So, to keep us all on the same page, and let it be known what's what, I'm going to turn the chair over to Nick Lawrence, one of the top dogs and co-founder of the PUPs."

Nick "Nifty" Lawrence was a mobile rectangle: square head, square shoulders, all the way down to oversized square feet. He didn't need to stand on the chair to get people's attention: he gathered it, in exactly the opposite way that Wren deflected it; naturally, and without conscious thought.

"People. Not going to waste your time here, none of us has the time to waste, least of all me. Not going to waste your time telling you what you already know: one of the angeli was killed in a dramatic fashion, left in a deeply dramatic fashion, without caring who found it or when—indicating that they had no fear of official reprisals or indeed any sort of notice at all."

"So much for New York's Finest," someone said.

"Hey, at least they don't discriminate. They hate *everyone*."

"People. Attention, please. We have since released the body back to the angeli—"

Wren did *not* want to know how that exchange had gone, since the angeli hadn't given permission for the PUPs to do an autopsy. Then again, this was the second of their kind killed by the vigilantes; they were probably pissed off enough to accept any means of getting back at…uh-oh.

did anyone put a stall on the angeli from taking matters into their own hands?

She sent the query out on a tight ping to the Quad; there was a faint delay, then she saw Michaela lean over to Beyl and whisper something. The griffin dipped her beak and said something in return.

they have been promised a share of the action so long as they do nothing until given word. Michaela's mental tone was weary, and carried with it the visual tinge of exasperation like a waft of red smoke. *Best Beyl could do.*

Wren forced her attention back to Nifty. The angeli would do as the angeli would do, as always, arrogant bastards that they were.

"We identified the trace as being true current—and no, I'm not going to explain to you lot how we did it. Not that any of you could understand, anyway."

Speaking of arrogant: the difference was that Nifty had earned the right. If he'd been Null he'd have MIT or Caltech in his résumé—he was pure inventive and intuitive genius. Who else would have thought to bring current to investigative sciences, to determine magical use or influence? More, who would have been able to actually do it, and then train others to follow?

"But it's confirmed within acceptable parameters that

the traces were in fact from current-use. A hundred percent certainty that the killers used that current to hold the angeli down while they cut him."

Not surprising, that. Nulls, enough Nulls, could swarm an angel, sure. But he would have made enough of a fuss that his brothers would have found him. And Wren didn't care how many Nulls you had on your side: a host of angeli were going to eat them on toast.

"The interesting thing was that, within a seventy-eight percent certainty level, the killers were neither lone-jacks…nor Council."

Wren frowned, as did half a dozen people in the room. Not everyone fell into the two categories, of course. Some Talent were disinclined to be lumped even with such a loosely knit organization as the lonejacks were…had been, she corrected herself. Some came from families that went their own way, dipping in and out. But most of those were low-level Talent, and certainly not the sort who would go up against the angeli!

But there was one type of Talent who might. A Talent who might be neither lonejack nor Council…who might have stepped outside of the *Cosa* itself, as far as they were accounted for….

Nifty was half a step ahead of her. "Some of you know people like this, who have taken jobs elsewhere, who never speak of what they do, never discuss their jobs, their affilia-tions…some of you have sibs, children, who took these jobs…and have disappeared. They were not victims of the Council's maneuverings, nor the anti-Fatae, antimagic movement…but their own employment. Their own employers, turning against them, using them…using them against us."

He was a powerful speaker, not for his voice, or his looks, or even his current, but the passion he took to each word, the faith he put in his information. Like an evangelist, you believed and followed because he believed and led. Wren suddenly thought, apropos of nothing, that this man could have been very, very dangerous if his goals had aspired higher than forensics.

"Who? Who was it?" A roar from the crowd, a bear of a voice, deep and scary-sounding. Others took it up, shouting, demanding to know who it was who had turned their relatives against them, to attack and kill an angel.

Beside her, even through the distance between them, Wren could feel Sergei shift uncomfortably. It was his knowledge that had brought them here—and his knowledge that had brought the Silence to them in the first place. Never mind that he hadn't known, hadn't realized…it was still going to be damning. He knew that, felt it in the crowd.

I'll protect you, she thought at him, as loudly as she could, as forcefully as she dared. She had the responsibility for him. She had brought him here, in all senses of the word.

Nifty shook his head, indicating that he could not answer that question. Bart took over, his grating personality best suited to building the bonfire that the Quad wanted burning brightly tonight.

Wren only hoped they'd be able to contain it.

"It does not matter who did this deed, but that it was

done, and under what orders. At first we stood by and waited, while our cousins the fatae were threatened, harassed by unknown humans. 'Not our problem,' is the first retort of all species, and while there may be shame in it, there is also a certain selfish honesty. Forgive yourselves that. When the time came to stand with our cousins, we were there. They know that. And they are willing to stand with us now."

Beyl came forward from the back of the room, her feathers sleeked back and her claws gleaming, every inch the warrior she was. Next to her, a nissanni elder, to represent the aquatic fatae. There were no fire fatae—most of them were in hibernation for the winter, just as Rorani the dryad and her kin were.

"For generations we have been passive. We have remembered that, just as the human Talent are our cousins, so, too, are the Nulls. They live, they feel, they are sentient and worthy of respect. We—the *Cosa Nostradamus*—have never struck out against them, even when such a strike might have been justified."

All right, technically that wasn't quite true. There was that whole "dragon" era of unpleasantness in Europe and Asia, and the Aztecs might have a few words about angry feathered flying gods…. But it made for good speechifying, Wren had to admit that.

"But we will not strike now, blindly. It must be a focused blow, a well-placed injury. And to do that, we must gather our forces, and determine the best way to do this. You may be called upon, individually or as a breed, to aid in this. For now, we ask your patience, a small while longer."

"I can't do that."

Sergei was holding his body carefully upright, muscles tensed as though he was afraid that he might step wrong and hurt someone. The irony of that, that he was surrounded by several of the most determined, if not the strongest, Talent in the tri-state area, not to mention several fatae who outmuscled him on a purely square inch basis, and *he* was worried about hurting *them?* Wren didn't know whether to laugh or shake her head in despair.

She'd probably do both, before the day was over.

"I don't understand." Beyl had settled herself on the floor, her wings folded around her in close approximation of a nesting pose. Michaela and Bart were seated on the sofa, while the other two members of the Quad paced the small room restlessly.

They had ended the meeting over an hour ago, and—after sending the bystanders and secondary commentators home—had gone into huddle mode. The Quad had expected that it would be a simple matter to get the information that they needed from Sergei; they had, in fact, expected him to take them by the hand and lead them to the Silence's door.

Wren didn't know what she had expected. Watching her partner now, she knew only that they weren't going to get anywhere, hammering at him like this. The more they tried to coax him, the uglier it would get.

"Don't you care?" Bart launched himself off the sofa and directly into Sergei's face, even allowing for the six inches of difference in their height. Wren, aware that the fuse had just been lit, wondered if the other lonejack liked the view up Sergei's nose. It was one she, another six inches shorter than Bart, knew all too well.

You're losing it. Tighten up and focus. Something's going to break, one of them is going to say or do something that will lead us out of here. This is what you do, you look for the openings, you find the soft spot. So do it, damn it. He's not your partner. These aren't your siblings, your cousins. It's a job. A scenario…

She took a deep, quiet breath, then another, pushing herself down away from the tension in the room, away from the physical awareness of her body, down the wide, flat slope into the core of herself, where the icy hot energy of current coiled like a nest if vipers. Fugue state; the best mode from which to observe. It was hell on her reaction time, but she didn't need to worry about that, here. She hoped.

"What about the bodies thrown down on their steps?" Sergei didn't step away from Bart's invasion of his personal space, but Wren recognized the look on his face, and in a less serious time she would have started taking bets on who would throw the first punch.

He looked around the room, meeting each of his opponents' gazes squarely. "Why does nobody care about that? These were human beings, possibly totally innocent beings. Members of the Silence, yes, but of no known blame in any of this. Someone killed them, branded their skin and dumped them with no respect. Because they're Nulls, does nobody care?"

"We care," Michaela said, still keeping calm, still seated in an almost relaxed pose on the sofa. "But we cannot let their deaths distract us from our own safety. For all we know, they were sacrifices made by this organization to further cast us into disorder, soften us for their final blow, whatever it might be. We cannot know. We cannot let it stop us."

"You're the only one who can help us," Beyl said, her feathers lifting and lowering in a nonexistent breeze, sign of her agitation. "Wren knows only some of these humans...you know them all. You know their thoughts, their ways. You can help us bring them down."

"You're asking me to help you destroy an organization that has done good for generations, that has saved lives, at great cost to themselves, because a few within the organization are afraid. How then are you any different than from them?"

"Is that what the Indians said about the Europeans? The Incas about the Spaniards? We're talking about our survival here, Didier. And either you're standing with us...or you're not."

Deep in fugue state, Wren suddenly couldn't breathe, couldn't swallow, couldn't bear the pressure against her skin, on her bones, weighing her down and buzzing like elementals on a bad bender. Too much current being roused outside, and she couldn't withstand it. Current swirled in her core in response, serpents of deep blues, reds, golds, and greens slithering around each other, rubbing staticky coils in a hissing, spitting noise that was giving her a headache. No wonder Talent didn't play together well. It was building, it was all building, in all of them, and it was getting out of control.

Is this what it feels like to wiz? I can't think, can't deal with this....

"Wren?"

Sergei, standing there in front of her. She always felt the urge to make tea for him, when he was coming home. Reached for him in bed, before she even woke up. Trusted him to cover her back, to bring her coffee in bed, to hand her the towel when she got out of the shower. Needed him. Wanted him. Loved him.

"Go." Her voice was sparse, hoarse, coming from miles away.

"What?"

"I can't... I can't deal with you. I can't..."

I can't be responsible for killing you. And I will, if you stay. You're being stubborn and you can't help being stubborn, but if they continue to direct all this current against you, even involuntarily...like calls to like and I can't keep it under control, around you. Not when it's used to resting itself in you.

"Just go, Sergei. Walk out of here, and don't look back."

"Zhenchenka..."

"Listen to the woman, Didier." Bart, standing behind her. She could feel him through the confusion, his current reaching out to hers even as his hand rested on her shoulder; safe, reassuring static, his own current now under control, if barely. He was at no risk from her own, he knew how to protect himself. She couldn't ground in him. She had no desire to ground in him. Around her, an entire room of people who were safe because she did not desire them.

"Sergei. Go."

He looked past her, at Bart. At the room around her. He didn't look at her.

And he went.

In the end, they went on what little they knew, what they could surmise, and a series of wild-ass guesses. Classic lonejack territory. There were five of them on point; more on call in an instant's ping. Two men, two women, and one fatae—Danny, muttering under his breath about crazy lone-jacks and crazier Nulls.

He stopped, and stared at the building, somehow menacing in its total lack of menace. "I thought it would be, I don't know...taller."

"Funny."

The ex-cop shrugged, unapologetic. "I thought it was."

"There's nobody in there." Rick shook his head in disgust.

"What?" Wren looked at him, then at the building for confirmation. It looked...she didn't know, like any other building on the street. Totally ordinary...and kind of un-nerving for being ordinary. Danny was right; she'd expected it to be...taller.

"There's nobody in there." He looked up at the moderate-height building, then past it into the leaden sky. "Gonna snow again."

"Can you please stay focused?" Bets was seventy if she was

an hour, and had been born short-tempered. She was also one of the few strong old-timers left, after the Council's heavy hand, and had demanded a spot on the sortie by right of survival. Nobody had dared suggest that she wasn't up for it.

"I am being focused. Feel it?"

Wren could. Not like a lightning storm forming: there wasn't any current swirling in the ether, but the air was alive with something nonetheless; a shimmering ugliness that had its own weird appeal, as well. You could get seduced by it, if you didn't pay attention.

Michael shoved his hands into the pockets of his parka, and tucked his chin into the scarf wrapped around his neck. "Your partner warned them."

"No. He didn't." Wren didn't know much anymore, but she knew that. "He wouldn't give us what we wanted…but he wouldn't go the other way, either. That's his hell. Being moral in the middle."

She knew that now: if he had been trying to play them, he would have. The fact that he didn't, that he walked away… The pain inside him was no game. None of this was a game.

She looked at the building, trying to feel the flow of current inside it. There was a faint trickle, but nowhere near what it should be. That was what Rick was talking about, not just that there weren't any people in the building, but that they had cut power. "They're many things, but they're not stupid," she said. "Never stupid." Without electricity, the lonejacks would have less to draw upon. It wouldn't surprise Wren at all if there was a sudden power outage

citywide any minute now, to ensure that they were handi-
capped. If it didn't happen Wren suspected that it wasn't
because they didn't want to, but that someone had stopped
them, and rightfully so. Too damn cold, too damn dangerous, for people to be without power with another storm
coming on.

"So, they're not here. Where?"

"Can't hunt 'em." A tiny, tinny voice at ear level. "Gotta
luuuuure 'em."

A piskie, one of the larger ones: almost two feet high but
barely five pounds, including its wild mass of hair. Wren
fought down the urge to swat at it when it hovered to close
to her face.

"Love them?"

"Luuuure them, idiot human. Lure them, not love them.
When you look like prey, the predators come. When you
look like easy prey, the smart predators come, even when
they know better. And then we give 'em something to be
really scared of."

"Like a bird dragging its wing." Bets understood. "We
give them a target they can't resist…but what wouldn't they
be able to resist?"

"The ones who killed those humans," the fatae said,
almost purring.

"We didn't—"

Wren nodded, understanding. "They don't know that.
They wouldn't believe that even if we told them a thousand
times, with iron-clad alibis and a witnessed confession from
the actual killer."

"How?" Bart asked, more to himself than anyone else. "And—where?"

The piskie grinned, showing off teeth that had been sharpened to even more unnerving-than-usual points, making it look like the rabid offspring of a kewpie doll and a vampire bat. "We gots us an idea."

twenty-two

"This is like a protest march!"

"What do you know about protest marches?"

"Hey, I watched the Million Metrosexual Man March on TV!"

Wren moved on, not wanting to hear where *that* particular discussion went.

It really shouldn't have surprised her; the piskies were historical troublemakers, and had the ability to prod other people into action. Of course, usually that action involved swatting piskies, not following them. But here it was, oh-fuck-early on a cold but thankfully dry Sunday morning, and there had to be over fifty lonejacks and fatae of various species gathered around the Christopher Street subway station.

The irony of this particular event starting a hop, skip, and wing beat from Stonewall amused the hell out of

Wren, historically speaking. She wasn't sure anyone else would be so amused.

She wasn't even sure she was all that amused, actually. It might just have been sleep deprivation making her feel so particularly flaked out right now. Or the fact that, with so many Talent trying to pull as much energy into their cores as possible before the event, current was stretched thin and sparse across the city now, so nobody was able to work feeling completely full. Lonejack brownout was not something she ever wanted to experience.

Rumor had it that every Council member who could, had gotten the hell out of Dodge, the moment they felt the drawdown begin. It hadn't been an official evacuation order, but KimAnn hadn't been heard to say yea or nay, so that was as good as a kick out of town.

Wren reached down and touched her own core, a reflexive twitch of nerves. She wasn't full-up, either, but her core was used to being asked for the impossible on a semi-monthly basis, and she had confidence she was up for whatever was going to come. A tendril of current coiled up her spine, green and blue static, and stroked the inside of her skull until she could practically feel her hair curl under the black wool watch cap she was wearing.

It had taken three days to get everything as organized as it was going to get organized, and she still wasn't confident that this was going to work. But nobody, God help them all, had come up with a better idea.

And there was a certain sort of nasty logic to it. Well, what other kind of logic did piskies have?

Wren found a bench to sit on, and sipped at the steaming grande coffee she had picked up along the way. The heat seeped through her gloves, making her fingertips feel slightly less numb. It was brass monkey cold out here, pre-dawn, and didn't look to warm up all that much.

"Lovely weather for it," she muttered.

"If it were happening in the summer, it would be ninety degrees and humid." P.B. sat next to her, the ice-cold wood of the bench seemingly not bothering his furry posterior at all. "Only luck we're catching these days is bad. Give me some of that coffee."

"No." Beside the fact that this was one thing she didn't let anyone mooch off of her, demon did not do well on too much caffeine. It was like giving a Yorkie amphetamines. It might be funny, but it was *wrong*.

"You think this is going to work?"

"The flutter-brains are right, it's too nasty not to." P.B. shrugged. "If you were the Silence, could you resist it?"

"Not a chance in hell."

"All right, people!" A figure wrapped in a full-length down coat was shouting into the crowd. Gender and species were muffled beyond recognition, but the voice had an authority to it that the crowd responded to, turning to face the figure and listening up. "If you don't have your assignment yet, see a Quad leader. If you know where you're going, go there! Let's move it, move it, move it!"

Slowly, the figures began to head downtown, some descending down into the subway, others walking. It was, Wren surmised, too cold to fly.

A jogger, braving the cold, went down the street, a huge black dog keeping pace alongside. The jogger didn't even stop to look, tugging at the leash when the dog paused to sniff at all these strange beings milling about.

"You got your assignment?"

"Yeah." P.B.'s face wasn't really designed for scowling—an evil grin, his muzzle could handle, and snarls and open-jawed astonishment, but not scowling—but he did the best he could. "I get to direct traffic."

"Poor baby," Wren sympathized, but was quietly glad that her friend wasn't going to be in the thick of things. They had no idea how this was all going to fall out. She had come home once to find him bleeding in a corner; she never wanted to go through that again.

Of course, she didn't want herself to get conked on the head or otherwise bloody, either!

"All right. Time to get this show rolling, then."

"See you downtown."

"No, you won't," Wren said, and disappeared.

P.B. snorted in amusement, and took the coffee cup from the bench where she had left it, chugging back the last few drops before getting up to join the exodus.

There was something going on. Sergei wasn't sure how he knew, but he knew. The air in the apartment was warm and comfortably moist. There was no reason for him to get out of bed at five in the morning, get dressed in warm, comfortable clothing and heavy-soled work boots, and go to his safe to retrieve his gun. There was no reason at all for him to do any of that, and then catch a cab downtown, telling the cabbie to keep driving until he said to stop.

No reason at all for him to rap once on the bulletproof divider and tell the cabbie to let him out on the corner of Elk and Chambers. None at all.

He stood on the corner, looking around. Narrow streets, quiet and still on a weekend morning, the small storefronts and restaurants closed up, the offices silent and still. He wasn't familiar with this part of town; he never had business down here, except maybe once every couple of years. Most of his dealings with city government were done on the phone, or online these days, and he was more often at Parsons than down at Pace University's city campus.

But something brought him down here.... Where? Where did the lure lead him to? Ground Zero? The Seaport? City Hall? Maybe.

He turned that way, looking at the old, still-impressive government buildings, thinking. What had woken him up, dragged him out here? What was he feeling? Up until now he had been operating on a purely instinctive manner, following a call. But now it was time to stop, study, evaluate.

He wasn't nervous. He should have been nervous, if only because he had no damned clue what was going on. But instead the annoyance of being awake and out in the cold was offset by a certain unnerving calmness, as though everything were going exactly according to plan. Not a front thought, but something stroking the back of his brain, almost like...

The way Wren described the urge she had to make tea,

when he showed up. He had never understood what she was talking about, until now. Less a feeling, or a thinking, than a *knowing*.

Something was going down. Something that involved Wren.

Trusting that knowing, he started to walk, a long easy stride that carried him down the street and toward the pale stone bulk of City Hall.

"Hell no, we won't go?" Wren shook her head, not sure if she should be horrified or amused.

"I like the History Only Repeats if You're Not Listening one, myself."

She and Bart were standing in the plaza in front of City Hall, watching the lonejacks choosing and trading their signs, milling about while others were trying to get organized. Some of the signs were old-fashioned placards on plywood sticks, while others were long cloth banners that took three or more to hold them upright and readable. The Christopher Street crew had been matched by at least as many coming in from the boroughs, about seventy percent human, thirty percent fatae. The fatae who had actual hands were also carrying signs, but they seemed to be content with whatever they were handed.

In the summer, the area in front of them was green, filled with rosebushes and daffodils, grass and people lounging in the sunlight; walking, in-line skating and cycling across the span of the bridge that stretched between the lower part of Manhattan and the borough of Brooklyn across the river.

Right now, it was bleak and dreary, the putty-colored government buildings around them managing by some magic of their own to be both ornate, and depressingly bland. The wind was cold, coming off the river and being funneled down the narrow maze of streets that made up the financial district.

Wren had warmed up on the subway downtown, but the wind was cutting enough to make her shiver, standing still. But neither of them made any move to get into shelter; things were going to get worse, not better, once the protest got underway, and being warm at the beginning simply meant that you would feel more miserable later.

"Who thought that a march past the police station would be a good idea?" she asked, already knowing the answer.

"We're not exactly marching *past* it. More like down the side street away from it. Anyway, we have a permit."

That surprised her. She would have paid decent money to see what the request form had said. "How did you—"

"We're a tolerance march."

Wren snickered. Well, it was true. Except they planned to enforce that tolerance in a particularly intolerant manner….

Wren watched a teenager test his sign, swinging it like a flag, then swatting his neighbor on the ass with it. "Equal Rights for All Genders? How old are these things? What, we raid Central Casting?"

"Pretty much." Bart shoved his hands deeper into his pockets, and hunched his shoulders until he looked like a blue-coated penguin, huddling over a chick. "Go get a sign, Valere."

Wren looked at him askance. "I don't think so."

"Valere…"

"Bart. I have to work hard just to not get stepped on in an empty room. Carrying a sign and singing protest songs isn't going to change that."

"So you can hit anyone who steps on you with your sign."

"If you try to make me march, I'm going to sing. 'Alice's Restaurant.' *All* the verses."

They matched stares, and he blinked first. "You're not that bad a singer, I'm sure I'd survive. But fine, go. What are you going to do?"

"Don't worry. I think I can cause some trouble here and there along the way…"

He just chuckled, and went back to watching his charges mingle and fuss.

She hated when people laughed at her, even though she knew it was mostly stress-release; the same reason she was flickering in and out like a lightning bug. Also, being invisible gave her a sense of security. If she'd had her new slicks already… But the order had only just been placed; she was going to have to wait at least another month for them to be made.

The light was beginning to change, in the eastern sky. Not yet sunrise, but false down, turning the dark blue sky into slate-gray to match the paving stones under her feet. The streetlights were going out, leaving the piles of dirty snow in shadows, the once icy whiteness now mixed with grime and soot.

"Up and at 'em! If you're ground patrol, get to your places! Air patrol, be ready! The rest of you, up and at 'em! We start in ten!" A human wearing a bright yellow snow bib and black boots stomped past, calling in a current-amplified voice. Why he didn't just carry a megaphone, Wren didn't understand. Sometimes, people got so dependent on their Talent, they forgot there were other, easier, less costly ways to do things.

But however he was doing it, he was getting heard.

The protest got started like a camel getting to its feet; slow, sluggish, and laughable. But once the banners caught the morning breeze, and the signs started waving, Wren had to admit that they looked almost impressive. Even more so was the sight of four griffins leading the horde, their eagle-tine heads raised above the rest of the crowd, wings tightly furled but still unmistakable. Almost any other fatae could and typically was overlooked; griffins got noticed.

People believed in them.

And nobody believes in you?

Smirking, she ran lightly beside the mass of pseudo pro-testers, until she was even with the griffins, then past them.

The plan was to circle City Hall once, make a reasonable if unnerving statement, and then start across the bridge into Brooklyn. At that point, fatae and lonejacks would combine to make a display that couldn't fail to attract the attention of anyone who already had a mad-on for anything non-human or Talented. A hundred-strong moving target—moving slowly, in plain sight.

It wasn't as risky as it sounded. That many bodies,

anyone nastily inclined would have to risk a full-out riot to do significant damage. And the lonejacks were on alert, this time.

The griffins peeled off at the entrance to the bridge, posing like sentries—which, in point of fact, they were. The humans continued on, waving banners and signs and generally acting like they were Boy Scouts out for an early-morning jamboree.

That was one thing you could count on, with lonejacks; someone somewhere in there had a flask of some warming liquid that smelled nothing at all like coffee, and they were willing to share.

As the protesters rounded the front of City Hall, staying clear of the tall wrought-iron fence and the police boxes at each entrance, someone in the mass started a singsong chant:

"Ain't your city
only, it's
Our city, too.
You want your piece of us, well
We got a piece of you!"

Slowly, other voices picked it up, deep human voices only, surging with the rhythm of their marching. *Ain't*—stomp—*your city only*—stomp—*it's*—stomp—*our city, too*—stomp—*You want*—stomp—*a piece of us*—stomp—*we got*—stomp—*a piece of you!*

It sounded like a particularly weak protest song, much

less impressive than the one Wren had threatened to sing, but it was far more than that; under the words, current surged from every lonejack present, formed by the words into a weapon. If you knew how to look, it was there, surging and roiling at shoulder level like low-lying fog, or a summer's thunderhead, dark red like molten lava, and faster moving.

You didn't need words to focus magic, not if you knew what you were doing, and were ready for it. But it helped. And when you were trying to pull a pranking that involved so many people, most of whom didn't know each other beyond a vague hi-howya-doin, it helped a lot.

Because that's what this was. The largest, nastiest, bloodiest pranking any lonejack had ever helped pull.

They were coming back around now, having picked up a single news van, rolling camera on the off-chance that it was a slow news day and they needed filler. Wren hoped that the van didn't get too much closer, as the current-cloud would turn all of their very expensive, very sensitive technology into a quivering pile of wires and blown fuses. Bad enough what they were going to do to the bridge— which was why the march was scheduled for this early on a Sunday morning. Later, or on a weekday or Saturday, and there would be too many people wanting to use the bridge. Here, they were probably just going to inconvenience a bunch of joggers, and a lot of public workers, who could at least then pull down overtime pay.

Not that Wren had thought of any of that; she wasn't a big-picture person.

She moved away from the crowd, scanning the surroundings. Up there in City Hall, a few window shades moved; probably cleaning people, as she didn't think any of the public servants would be in the building at that hour. Curtains were being twitched aside in apartments above the storefronts, but it seemed unlikely anyone would come out to watch; they simply weren't interesting enough to move anyone out of their heated apartments. Maybe two or three students, or someone still dressed from being out the night before, but it was unlikely enough that Wren didn't worry about them.

There... She paused, and then jumped onto the nearest lamppost, shimmying up the metal structure to get a better view.

Yes. Two cars had pulled up: dark sedans with New York plates. There were at least three people: two in the front, one in back, in each car. Probably more. And then two more cars purred down the narrow street behind her, cruising like sharks coming up on something tasty to eat, or lions readying to rush an interloper pack of jackals....

"Ain't your city
only, it's
Our city, too.
You want your piece of us, well
We got a piece of you!"

A higher-pitched chorus met them as they came around and up toward the bridge. The ground patrol—fatae set in place under the concrete and brick arches—and the air patrol, clinging to the cables and struts of the bridge itself. They were supposed to keep themselves in reserve, as the second wave, but the cantrip was apparently mindlessly catchy enough for them not to be able to resist.

Sometimes, all the humancentric stories about fairy simplicity and gullibility were truer than the fatae wanted to admit. But it shouldn't matter; the trap had been set, the bait about to be snatched up.

And then they stepped onto the bridge itself, and all hell came loose.

"God save us from fools and bigots...." Sergei had been in mob scenes before. He'd been part of the group of Operatives and Handlers who had to`clean up the kraken disaster of Nantucket back in '93. He'd even attended one Democratic/Libertarian joint fund-raiser, working security control for the extra money. He had never, in his entire life, seen the potential for disaster that was waiting in front of him.

There were at least thirty humans grouped in front of him. Dressed in heavy jackets and work boots, they clearly weren't out for a Sunday-morning stroll with the kiddies. From his position over a hundred yards away and behind a bakery delivery van, Sergei couldn't tell if any of them had handguns, but there were a number of wooden bats and metal staves in evidence, and the physical ease with which they were carried suggested that every one of them knew how to land blows.

More disturbing to him was the dark sedan parked in front of the men, and the two figures speaking earnestly with one of the thugs. He knew those figures. Knew them, one well, and the other not quite so well, but enough that he had no hesitation, no having to wonder.

Although he did wonder who else was in the car, waiting out of the cold, with them.

Taking his time, aware that nothing had happened as yet, Sergei surveyed the group in front of him once again, this time picking up details. Between the ages of twenty and fifty; mostly white, although there were at least two blacks, and a slighter build that might have indicated Asian or Indian ancestry, if he were able to see the man's face to confirm. Not that it mattered, except to highlight the fact that bigotry needed only one target; the old sci-fi movies of the fifties had it right: give us an alien to shoot at—or a pointy-eared elf— and all men really were brothers under the skin.

Previous fatae survivors had mentioned that there had been women and teenagers, even the occasional child among the vigilantes. He was relieved to see that the group in front of him was almost entirely older males. It was sexist of him, and it probably didn't matter when you had a metal weight coming down at you, but he fought easier against adult males, not women or children.

And with that, he realized that his gun was already in his hand; and that he had come here, not to observe, but to spill blood.

He had told Wren the truth: he had chosen his side. It didn't matter if she wanted him there or not, not anymore.

But he wasn't going for the thugs. The *Cosa* was more than capable of handling those miserable excuses for DNA, and more, they deserved the chance to do a little payback.

Sergei had his sights set on more rarified game.

And he was due a little payback, as well.

The thugs moved out, racing toward their targets, and Sergei stepped out of the shadows.

"Duncan. A word with you, if I may?"

The bridge was almost perfectly designed: two roadways on either side, one for inbound traffic and the other for cars heading into Brooklyn, with a walkway straight down the middle for pedestrian and cyclist traffic. Multiple concrete ramps led onto the walkways from the surrounding streets, and while traffic could become miserable at times, it never seemed to face the same sort of agony that was normal on the Jersey-bound side.

The marchers funneled up the middle walkway, waving at the occasional car passing them on either side. Almost without exception, each driver honked and waved back.

As they passed each light on the bridge, the current streaked up the wires, and snapped the light out with a glorious crack and waterfall of sparks, like miniature fireworks. Wren didn't know if someone was doing that deliberately, or if it was just a side effect, but it was a nice touch either way.

Then the chapel across and down the street sounded the hour: six gentle gongs in solemn procession, and the mood changed, just like that. Wren could feel it, a shiver than ran up her arms and down her back, under the skin, and had nothing whatsoever to do with the weather.

The griffins spread their wings and rose into the sky, beaks snapping at the air, their heavy bodies more than a match for the wind, where their smaller cousins would get blown about. Clutched in their great claws were heavy iron bars: Franklin poles, the *Cosa* called them, after one of the founding fathers of the American *Cosa*. Lonejacks on the bridge sent current up into the air, touching and sparking off the bars as it was absorbed and redirected back down onto the ground in flashes of red neon, like some fantastic lightning strikes out of the clear dawn sky.

That alone would get attention of anyone looking for current. It would also get the attention of everyone else who happened to be awake and looking up at that moment, but pity the poor soul who tried to capture the image with anything more advanced than a pencil and paper.

Magic wasn't meant to be captured. You just had to live in the moment.

Wren tore her eyes away from the display long enough to look around her, more than a little worried. By now, *someone* should have sent out an alert. There should be— and there they were.

Dozens of human figures appeared from doorways and alleys, swarming up the ramps on a direct intercept course with the lonejack "protestors." Within seconds, the battle was joined. Baseball bats and protest signs snapped and cracked over heads. Someone who had failed basic science tried to use a metal staff against an enraged lonejack, and fell to the ground, shuddering and shimmering from the current that ran up the metal length and into his unprotected flesh.

Idiot.

Wren, invisible, slipped through the crowd, tripping and poking the Nulls as she could, but more set on her own personal mission: to find someone who looked to be directing the action, or somehow connected to a leader off-site. Unseen, she would not be attacked, and so long as nobody accidentally swung at or stepped on her, she was in no danger, even in the thick of things.

She had told Sergei once that she could paint herself blue and waltz through Grand Central Station at rush hour, and not be noticed. She hadn't been exaggerating. Much.

The problem was, she couldn't do much of anything else, while waltzing. So every time someone did hit her, or step on her, she had to just swear and deal with it.

Frustrated, Wren reached the center span of the bridge a bit ahead of the battle, and looked back.

At some point, while she was sidestepping a swinging sign, the fatae had joined the fracas, giving the Nulls their preferred target. Occasionally a fatae would swing at the wrong sort of human—The Quad had ordered all lonejacks to wear a strip of dark red fabric on their shirts, to identify themselves just in case, but it looked like most of them had either forgotten or ignored the order entirely.

It was, she had to admit, an impressive sight even seen with Null eyes. Over the hundreds of milling bodies, four griffins still circled and wheeled, occasionally swooping to harry someone, or divert an assault. Smaller figures swooped lower, pulling hair and screaming insults and…

Wren almost laughed in the middle of it all, as she saw a slender, snakelike flying form very clearly take a shit on someone's head.

Occasionally, a body would be thrown over the side of the bridge. The crew assigned to under-bridge detail had strict instructions not to let any of their own people actually hit ground. They had been given no such instructions about Nulls. Wren just hoped they were able to identify them quickly—or err on the side of caution, rather than letting everyone hit the pavement.

Further out behind her, the nausunni had marshaled the water fatae. Anyone who tried to come in or escape by the water would meet significant—and deadly—resistance there. Comforted by that thought, Wren didn't bother to guard her own back, but kept scanning the crowd in front of her.

A loup-garoux ran on four legs through the crowd, biting the ankles of anyone who—as far as Wren could tell from the yelps—looked tasty. The beast came panting up to her, working on scent, not sight, and she kicked it away without hesitation, not waiting to see if it considered her friend or foe. It could stand on its hind legs like the rest of them, and look you in the face when it bit, not nip at your damn legs.

Okay, maybe she was a little shaky still over the hellhound thing. She had cause, damn it.

Shaking her head, she went back to observing the fight. Around and through the combatants, current raged. To

Talented eyes, the air was aflame with an orgy of crackling neon. But even the most hopeless Null would be able to see the current that was running up through the wires and metal rigging of the bridge itself, like some kind of post-modernistic Saint Elmo's fire, blue flame sparked with gold and silver running through every metal-touched element of the bridge, crackling and hissing with a corona that made religious folk cross themselves and pray for salvation.

Ohm's law, to the science geeks. Current lash-back, to lonejacks.

But in all that, she saw nothing that looked like a point of leadership. In fact, she saw nothing that looked like leadership at all, just a confused mass of swinging arms, kicking legs, and the occasional swipe of a sign or bat.

She grabbed a thread of current and sent it winging up into the air, searching for the psychic flavor she had imprinted on it earlier that morning, when they were getting their marching orders. The thread found the source of that flavor, and created a connection between them, like a semi-secure landline.

we've been played, she told it. *there's not a single person out here who has a clue about anything other than kill the monsters and their turncoat human allies.*

you're certain?

absolute. whoever's pulling the strings, they didn't come out to play.

we're going to have to up the stakes, the Quad-mind said grimly, then broke off contact.

"Up them how?" Wren asked the empty air, then used

some of Sergei's better Russian swearwords as she saw what was coming toward the bridge on the Manhattan side.

"Please God, don't nobody swing at a cop…."

"This is the New York Po—" The loudspeaker squawked and then died as current hit it. The truck rolling into the fray came to a stop at the start of the bridge, unable to move forward as the fight continued to rage. There had been a lot of frustration building over the past year, and the mere appearance of a dozen cops in riot gear wasn't going to slow that down.

Tear gas, though, did the trick. Within minutes, cops in gas masks had a dozen or more of the human population facedown on the pavement, most of them handcuffed to the railings. The smaller fatae slipped away, the cops either not noticing them or choosing—for whatever reason—to let them go.

Some of the force probably still remembered working with a partner who seemed more than a little…off, or unusual. The rest just didn't want to deal with the hassle of trying to book an illegal immigrant, no matter where they might have emigrated from. And at least one cop, when brought up face-to-face with a tall figure with a six-point rack of antlers growing from its head, made a shallow bow and then went on with his job.

Trusting her no-see-me, Wren slipped closer, then was driven back by the remaining fumes. Without a gas mask, going any closer in would end up with her flat on the ground, as well, and still invisible.

This was not how it was supposed to go, she thought

grimly. *Damn it, what are you guys planning?* She had to believe that they still had a plan, that their "higher stakes" hadn't involved the pulling up of, and buggering out.

Valere!

A cry for help, a warning, a hard slap between the shoulder blades; the ping was all that and a visual of a spear incoming, crackling with current-fire.

"What the he—"

The heavy thwap-sound of wings was the only warning she got before a great heavy shadow fell over her, and a griffin grabbed her, none too gently, in its talons. They were up off the bridge before Wren had the chance to draw breath. By the time she'd recovered from that shock, and could breathe again, the griffin swooped down in a dizzying dive, and dropped her. The landing, palms and knees on hard pavement, knocked the next breath out of her lungs, and she collapsed as though someone had landed a kidney-punch.

The blow of current *did* hit her in the kidneys, and sent her sprawling facedown onto the pavement. She rolled more from instinct than thought, her body moving when she would have sworn it couldn't.

"Wren, get up!" A voice—Rick's voice, urgent.

She got up, moving low and back on her heels, pivoting and scanning for the threat.

She hadn't faced off against another Talent since… since Max almost killed her, when she tried to prod the old wizzart into helping her. Not like this, not in a pure contest of current.

She pulled double handfuls of current up and formed a shield with it; trying to buy herself time to figure out what the hell that damned griffin had dropped her into the middle of.

The bridge loomed to their right, the possible escape of sidewalks and buildings blocked by a tall metal fence. She could maybe make it over, maybe not. Escape wasn't the point.

"You okay?" Rick asked.

"Stupid question," she said, feeling him take her back. They were surrounded by half a dozen…kids, was all Wren could think, although some of them probably weren't much younger than she was. Behind her, the biker-Talent's bulk wasn't as comforting as it should have been; the blood splattering on the ground wasn't hers, and it didn't seem to belong to their attackers.

"What the hell…" *Keep moving, Valere, keep moving…*

"I think we've found the ones who killed that angel."

"I think you're right."

They were under the bridge now, the pale red brick arching overhead, turning every sound into an echo. The ground underneath was bare; it was a gift, that no snow had been plowed into the alcove, or worse, allowed to melt and freeze into ice.

Out of the corner of her eye, Wren saw a figure move; part of her brain recognized it as Michaela even as a blast of current took the woman square in the chest, and she went down. The gypsy representative rolled onto her side, and didn't move again.

"Don't look," she said quickly, even as Rick started to react. "Don't look, don't think. Right now, it's just us here, us against them, and worrying about anyone else is going to get you—and me—killed. Do you have any defensive training at all?"

His snort was better than she'd expected. "Good. You do your bit, I'll do mine."

She could have disappeared. But that would have meant leaving him the only available target. *Escape isn't the point.*

Oh the bloody hell it's not!

He lunged away from her side, his arm and leg sweeping out in a move she vaguely recognized as some kind of kung fu judo-thing. It didn't take his opponent down, but it moved him past them, forcing three of the five to turn and deal with him, while the sixth was kneeling over Michaela, preparing to…

A shock ran through Wren's system, and she felt her gorge rise. *Oh Christ be merciful.* The boy was sucking her core.

It was anathema, like eating human flesh—worse than eating human flesh. Like consuming a person's soul, raping the essence of what they were, taking their power and their sense of self away, and feeding it into his own core…

Anathema not only for the harm it did to the victim, but for what it did to the taker, as well. Current was touched by the signature of the user; the longer the current was in contact, the stronger the signature. The core, the storage of all the power a Talent kept within herself constantly? It had a signature like John Hancock's. Taking that inside you, you ran the risk of losing your own self, if the person you ate was stronger.

Even as the shock was traveling through Wren's system, she was peeling off a strip of her shield and fashioning it into a weapon. The two remaining…whatever-they-weres, she couldn't call them Talent, not after what she'd seen them doing—moved toward her, and she shuddered at the expressions on their faces; blank, not angry or aggressive or happy or mad…not even hungry. Not even alive.

Stoking up the bright neon hum of her core, Wren dived into the solid mass of current, let herself be swallowed up in it, and came out the other side.

"Back off, bitches," she said to the nearest opponent, and slammed the woman with everything she had.

It wasn't enough.

"Sergei Didier."

Sergei had only met Duncan a handful of times, but he had heard about him from his very first day within the Silence. Duncan was the head of R&D, the memory and money of the Silence. He was fast, smart, ruthless, and above all loyal: rumor said that he was the handpicked successor of the original founders, the man chosen to hold the organization together on the daily level, while the top levels went about looking after longer-term goals.

Somewhere along the line, Duncan became the source of inspiration—and awe. He ran his department with a gloved hand that nonetheless could feel the pulse of every creature held inside it, from the newest, rawest recruit all the way up to the top floors where Andre worked.

Nobody feared him, exactly. But everyone was wary of him. And nobody crossed him.

Sergei had recognized KimAnn for what she was, because he had seen it in its final stages, in Duncan.

"You're far from your master, Poul," Sergei said to Duncan's companion.

Poul Jorgenmunder had the same training Sergei'd had; he didn't let the comment do more than roll off his back.

"Ah. I see." And Sergei did. Andre had been stripped of his right-hand man, at a time when he was trying to rally his team against the forces working against him. Forces, clearly, that Duncan led. Sergei wondered if the old man knew. And if he knew how futile his struggles would— inevitably—be.

When Sergei had still been with the Silence, Duncan had been a power to reckon with. A decade later, he had clearly gained even more control over the organization.

Sergei risked a glance down the street; the bridge was engulfed in what looked like fireworks. Current, he knew, and knew as well that there would be more than his purely human eyes could see. Sirens flashed and wailed in the morning light, and he had to look away, not be distracted.

"You've set all this in motion. Why?"

Duncan simply stood there, coolly watching him, but Poul was more than willing to respond. "You said it yourself." He recited, clearly quoting: "'Strange beasts, a variety of species. Considered an underclass of the *Cosa*, the

Council does not deal with them, and most of the lonejacks interact only sparsely."'

Sergei's own words; taken from one of his very first reports after meeting the fatae, years before.

"You memorized my earlier works. How touching."

Poul's expression tightened, and he would have moved forward toward Sergei if Duncan hadn't stopped him with a simple hand gesture.

Heel, dog, Sergei thought.

The car door opened. Sergei braced himself, but didn't look. The taptaptap of expensive shoes on the pavement came to him, and even before the third man came into his line of sight, Sergei knew who it was.

"Andre. So much for your attempts to help." He didn't even try to hide the bitterness in his voice: he had known that his former boss would try to use them, had accepted that. He hadn't thought the old bastard would lie to him. But then, why was he surprised? Nobody trusted anyone, it seemed. And with good reason.

Andre met his gaze squarely. "I agreed that we needed to discover who was behind all of this. Now I know."

"And knowing is all that's important?"

"Knowing is power, boy. You know that."

Poul smiled, seemingly reassured by having both of his masters to heel behind, and continued quoting Sergei's own words back to him: "'This country has enough problems without having to worry about these…animals, in our midst, using our resources and not giving back anything in return.'"

Sergei felt claws rip inside his rib cage, hearing his own youthful, stupid, ignorant—bigoted—words said back to him in Poul's voice, carrying with them a ring of conviction even he, the original speaker, had never been able to manage. A True Believer, he'd thought once about Andre's newest protégé. He hadn't known how true it was.

It was different now, for him. Those fatae had names, the species had characteristics and quirks attached to them. Piskies were prank-players. Griffins kept their young with them through young adulthood, and then sent them off to another herd to find mates. Nausunni could hiss even without sibilants. Demon were loyal. Rock dragons were not to be trifled with, for all that they were the size of Great Danes.

Some of the fatae weren't exactly brain surgeons. Some of them shouldn't be allowed to handle anything more advanced than a spoon. And some of them...

He thought of Shig, the Japanese fatae he had met over the summer. The lizardlike being was a shrewd businessman, with a wry sense of humor and excellent taste in artwork. He, and P.B. and Wren had spent an evening together during the summer, arguing about music, of all things, over dinner at Noodles. The little lizard had helped introduce Sergei to a number of influential dealers and artists in his native Japan, smoothing the way for an eventual business deal, down the road.

Shig. P.B. Rorani the dryad. The unknown breed that had saved them, when the vigilantes attacked the All-Moot. Beyl the griffin, and her gnome assistant whose name Sergei still didn't know. The piskies, flying pains in the posterior, but not animals, not if this...*thing* in front of him that looked and spoke like a man, was also not an animal.

They justified their actions on words...*his* words.

Sergei choked back the bile he felt rising, accepting the acidic burn in his chest as just payment for his once-ignorance.

Yes. Knowledge *was* power.

"You knew the truth once," Duncan said. "I don't expect you to fall into line now. There has been too much water under that bridge. But you need not destroy yourself trying to prevent what must be, what you yourself saw, so many years ago. Andre has kept you and your partner from falling into this morass. She is not with them out there on that bridge. You are not with them. Turn around and go home, let us clean this up. And all will be well for you both. My word on it."

"Don't be an idiot!" And P.B. was there, snarling, the thick fur around his neck hackling like a dog's as he glared at Poul and Duncan. Sergei felt dizzy, disconnected. How had the demon found him? Why wasn't he out there, fighting with the rest of his kind? And where was Wren? *Wren.* That was his focus.

"They're using you as justification for what they wanted to do anyway," P.B. said. "You're not part of them, not anymore. And neither is Wren."

"No..." The demon was right, Sergei knew he was right, but that didn't release him from his own guilt. Or his responsibility.

"You shouldn't be here," he said to the fatae, never taking his eyes off the three humans before him.

"You looked like you needed help." And the demon flexed his thick black claws to illustrate what he meant. "I can—"

"No," Sergei said again. Beyond them, the battle raged, and he couldn't do anything about it. And Wren was there, he knew it. Could feel it, no matter what Duncan said. His spies and scans couldn't see her, but Sergei could. He always could. But he couldn't go to her, not with this weighing on his hands.

"This is for me to deal with," he told the demon. "You have your own job to do. Go. Protect her. With your last breath, your dying body…"

P.B. looked hard at the human, his dark red eyes unblinking, then nodded once and slipped into the fire-lit dawn, leaving Sergei alone with the Silence members.

"So," Andre said. "What now?"

"We finish the job," Duncan said. "As we have always planned to do."

Maybe in the past, magic-users had fought glorious battles, throwing powerful thunderbolts around and laughing madly with a full accompaniment of flying monkeys or crazed warriors, or whatever it was they used to do.

Or maybe that was all Hollywood. If so, Wren was going to be witness for the prosecution that Hollywood didn't know shit.

Her jeans were torn in a dozen places, and her hair had

been singed so much that she was surprised her ears weren't smoking. Blood and sweat kept running into her eyes, and her palms were abraded from falling down so often.

Her only consolation was that, if she looked like the tail end of a bad knife fight, her opponent looked just as bad.

No. It's not a consolation at all.

The woman facing her wasn't all that powerful. No more so than Rick had been, before he'd been taken out by another of the…what did you call them? Enemy seemed too overblown, even if that's what they were. Evil wizards? Un-affiliateds? That was what the Council used to call lone-jacks; maybe it was time to pass the term on?

This woman facing Wren wasn't a match, on a basic power-level. None of them had been. But Wren had quickly learned that the empty expressions, the blank stares, were indicators that something—or someone—had driven these Talent to within a hair's breadth of wizzing, of overloading internally from current and going mad.

Once that happened, the Talent no longer has the sense God gave a gnat, and doesn't think to protect him or herself anymore. It created a passive death wish—but also allowed them to channel an obscene amount of current, because there was nothing there, not even the instinct to survive, to slow it down anymore.

What it meant, on a practical level, was that even the weakest of Talent could do amazing things, channel awesome forces.

It also meant, practically, that Wren was getting her ass kicked. The only reason that she was still standing was because—except for a few major blockages, like the one that kept her from being able to Translocate easily—she was almost as Pure as the woman facing her. And she'd had longer to learn how to use that much current.

But she also wanted to live, and in this particular knife fight, that was a distinct disadvantage.

Got to keep standing, she thought. *So long as I keep standing...*

The line of current running along her spine, protecting her limbs from physical assault, hissed and snapped like a downed wire, and she forced herself to strengthen it. But there was so little left to call on: current had to be controlled, and in order to maintain control you had to be firmly grounded. Manhattan bedrock was usually responsive, but the ground under her feet had too many lines already running into it, and every time she tried to reach for better grounding, her reach kept getting tangled in theirs. *Too damn much Talent in this city.*

And disturbing someone else's grounding might mean dislodging the only thing that was keeping them alive, those bodies still and bloody around her.

The ones who had been taken off by the police, the ones who had stayed on the bridge, were the lucky ones. They would live to see tomorrow. Whatever tomorrow brought, in a city where Talent had been turned against their own kind. But there was no such refuge for her; whether by external interference or random chance, the police hadn't come to the side of the bridge, focusing only on the humans actively fighting in plain sight. This battle raged without interference.

Overhead, too far overhead, a griffin wheeled. She wished it safe, and away.

"Die, witch," the woman hissed, and raised her arm to strike again. Current flashed from underneath her fingers, indigo and olive-green; muddy, ugly colors, but still damned powerful. Wren wasn't able to block all of it, this time, and only the sudden hard weight knocking into her ribs, pushing her aside, kept her from going down for the count.

ground in me

An intrusion into her brain, the voice unfamiliar and yet immediately recognizable, alien and a part of her she accepted, reached for instinctively.

where the hell have you been?

busy. Here now

Once before they had done this: in the basement of the Friesman Library, when faced with the forever-hungry maw of greed and vengeance given physical form. Then, Wren had hesitated. Now, she was grounded in the demon and on her feet before the other woman had time to react to the newcomer.

The question rose to the front of her mind, as it did the first time they had done this. *what are you, P.B.?*

demon he said, as though that answered everything. But she had no time to be frustrated; the battle was joined again. This time, with her core locked down and upheld by his unswerving support and dedication, buffered from outside blows by his love and affection, Wren was able to put the woman on the defensive, backing her up against the cold arch of the bridge and locking her in place with bars of current similar to the ones she had used to lock down the bansidhe, the one she had tested on the Nescanni Parchment, before that. Nothing was ever wasted, and nothing was learned in vain. If she survived this, what worse thing was this going to be training for?

stop thinking. You think too damn much

Agreed. Wren locked down anything extraneous, and focused back on her opponent.

The woman had been pretty, was still pretty, if you looked past the eyes hard and flat like slate, and just as lifeless. Only the mouth still showed any kind of life, twisting and chewing on dry air. Trying to speak with them hadn't worked before, but Wren felt obligated to try, one last time.

"We're *Cosa,* little sister. Family. Why are you so angry?"

That red mouth chewed more, the jaw working as though trying to produce some result. "You consort with animals, cause pain in this world…."

P.B.'s voice, not a tag but already inside her brain: *crazy. wizzed. way beyond wizzed.*

little damned busy, here

kill her.

no!

P.B. didn't understand. Grounded in his emotional bedrock, she found herself surrounded by a firm, unyielding pragmatism: survival above all. Demon. It was what he was, how he had been created; as much a part of him as the ability to survive the lashes of her current into his system.

But that wasn't how the *Cosa* worked.

You took care of the wizzed. You did *not* kill them.

"Little sister, listen to me." Wren said it with current as much as voice, focusing all of herself that was to spare into making herself heard. She dared not ping her opponent; the woman's sense of what was true and real had clearly been so badly twisted that getting tangled in her current would damage Wren even more than anything physical the Silence operative might do.

You took care of the wizzed. But you didn't emulate them. You didn't follow them. You kept your distance, as best you could, because they were crazy-strong in addition to being crazy-crazy. All the focus, all the will, and none of the self-preservation. That was why lonejacks were so selfish, why the Council was so cautious. Because if you didn't protect yourself from yourself, you ended up like this....

P.B. A sudden thought, communicated to him the same instant it occurred to her. *can you help her?*

she'd kill me the moment I tried. Or I'd kill her, in defense when she attacked. Or, both

Damn.

"I can't let you do that."

"You? Stop us?" Poul laughed. Neither Duncan nor Andre did. When Jorgenumunder realized that, he stopped, his gaze curious, but not worried.

"It's too late, Sergei," Duncan said. "I understand—I appreciate the fact that you feel your loyalties have been given, but there is a reality here you cannot avoid. We will win.

Humanity will prevail over these creatures. It is our right, and our duty to maintain our God-given place."

He sighed, seemingly saddened. "Had they only kept to their own place, in the shadows, in the darkness, perhaps none of this would have been needful."

Sergei doubted that. "There are more of them than you know. And the Silence, while strong, is finite. They will not go quietly."

"Oh, I have become quite aware of that. This city was our testing ground, a trial run. But we're not finished, yet.

"You say we are finite. True. But the outrage we can generate is not."

Sergei had no idea what the man was talking about. From the look on Andre's face, neither did he.

"Boss?"

Andre turned, his carefully patrician face suddenly showing concern as a tall, well-built blonde walked around the corner. "Andre? I got your message, and don't think it's not going to cost you, because getting past the cops out there was…oh."

Bren took in the scenario with a quick glance, and recognized that something was wrong instantly.

By then, Poul already had her in an iron grip.

Duncan turned to Andre. "You understand? You will see that it is taken care of?"

Andre nodded, his expression back to the cool façade he had perfected over his many decades with the Silence. Duncan nodded once in return, then walked to the car, getting into the backseat. The driver started the engine, and backed out of the alley, driving away into the cold winter morning.

Suddenly, Sergei realized that his fingers were freezing, even through his Thinsulate gloves, and his knees were creaky and painful, as though he'd climbed a dozen flights of stairs.

"Andre?" Bren was curious, a little nervous, but not frightened. Not even when Poul dragged a serrated blade across her throat, and her body dropped to the ground with a single gasp, did she display any fear.

Jorgunmunder calmly set the blade to her skin in five or six places, each mark looking like a jagged wound, the kind that might be created by the sweep of a tiger's claws.

Or a demon's.

Sergei let out a low moan of realization, and lunged forward, hands reaching for Poul's own throat, but Andre had a gun in his hand now, and it was pointed at Sergei.

"I am sorry, my boy. I saw no way to prevent it."

Satisfied with his work, Poul took a vial out of an inside coat pocket. About the size of his thumb, it was filled with a thick, black liquid. He sprinkled a little on the ground, creating a careful splatter pattern, then smeared some of it onto Bren's face and hands, as though she had fought her attacker off.

"Fatae blood," Sergei said, his voice dead.

"Exactly." Poul stepped back to consider his work, then added another smear to the palm of her left hand.

"She was a team member. A coworker. *A fellow Silence member.* Is this what the Silence taught you?" Sergei asked, too many steps beyond disgusted to remember his way back.

Poul didn't hesitate in his response. "The Silence taught me to do the right thing. Protect the innocent. Protect the weak. That means humans. *Real* humans."

There was a soft noise, and the vial fell from Poul's hands, the look of surprise and outrage on his face almost comical as he turned to stare at his mentor. "You…"

Andre waited until Poul fell onto his knees, then dealt him a solid blow to the side of his head with the butt of his pistol, hard enough to crack his skull.

Bending down, the old man took the blade out of Poul's pocket, flicked it open, and placed it in his protégé's hand, closing the cooling fingers around it firmly.

"Is there any of that blood left?"

Sergei picked the vial up, then shook his head. "No."

"Ah well. It will have to do. To all appearances, he killed her, and someone then killed him.

"Leaving out the important part, the part that the Silence has played in all of this." It wasn't a question: it was the only reason Andre would have been part in all this, to somehow, still, try to preserve the Silence.

"Lies built on lies, to protect the truth. This world turns on chaos, and we all fall into the fire." Andre looked down into the conflagration, water aflame with current, bodies scattered on the ground. "We do what we must. And I…will go back to the source of it all. Duncan will not trust me, but then, he has never trusted me. And in that lack of trust, I am still useful to him."

"Until…"

"Until this is over, one way or another. On the inside, I still have a chance to change things."

"You think you can survive long enough to oust him?" Sergei was aware of how macabre it all was, standing over the bodies of two former coworkers, two people Andre had chosen and trained, discussing what were, in effect, corporate politics.

"I believe in the organization," was all Andre would say. "I *have* to believe in it, or it's all been for nothing. Duncan is the power, but he was not the creator, was not the source of our mission. I will find allies, and I will fight back."

He looked at Bren's body, then Poul's, and for the first time in all the years Sergei had known him, the old man looked old.

"And you? What will you do?"

"I don't know," Sergei said, looking down at the base of the bridge. A short white form was there, barely visible in the sunlight. And leaning on him, limping but alive, was another familiar form. Something that had gone cold inside him started to warm again. "Gather the bodies. Make my report. Do what's required of me. Same as always."

Andre started to speak, then reconsidered. "Stay safe, boy."

"You, too."

His former boss, his mentor, walked away and didn't look back.

twenty-three

Everything was a blur, even now. Sergei had met them at the bridge, stepping over bodies to reach them. He had hailed them a cab, bundled them inside and sent them home. That had been two weeks ago. She hadn't seen him since then. P.B. had told her what he knew: the confrontation with the Silence, the dead bodies that were found in the aftermath. Wren had identified them both, Andre's second-in-command, the woman who had warned them in the diner; one enemy, one reluctant ally. Something had gone down, and gone badly.

She had left a message on Sergei's phone that day, but he had never returned the call. She was told that he had made a formal report, in writing, to what remained of the Double-Quad: Bart, his ribs taped and his leg splinted, Susan, still recovering from second-degree burns, and the nausunni elder, who had been protected by the river's depths. Beyl had taken a current-bolt through the lungs, and died that night, surrounded by the flock she had led for so many years. Gentle, mad-biker Rick had died of current overrush on the scene. Michaela was in a coma, and not expected to ever open her eyes again. Wren was too tired to mourn. There were too damn many deaths to mourn.

She didn't even have the strength to mourn Sergei, the death of whatever it was that had died between them. His fault, her fault. She only hoped that he would have the sense to stay low, stay out of sight. Stay alive. And not do anything stupid, jonesing for another rush of current.

Nobody trusted Nulls anymore. Nobody trusted anyone who might be part of the Silence, or their agents. Not after what they had done to the lost ones, the children, the Talent they had destroyed and turned into monsters.

The golden locket had been rescued from her pocket, but rather than replacing it in her jewelry box—a small wooden case—she had hung it over the edge of the mirror in her bedroom. In the night, when she lay in her cool bed, she would see glints from outside lights reflect in the metal, and wonder where her own innocence had gone.

It was February. Her bruises and cuts were healing. The wounds inside…she touched one, gently, and felt the pain like it had happened to someone else. It was there, it might always be there, but it was distant, observed more than experienced. Locked and sealed and not anything to deal with, anymore.

She had bought a rug, and a love seat for her apartment. Had hung framed and matted photos of her mother and grandmother on the wall. Kept the curtains drawn so that she could sleep in, and let P.B. fill her refrigerator with food, some of it even healthy.

She didn't miss Sergei. She didn't have the energy.

"When was the last time you slept?" P.B. finally asked.

"Every night, I sleep." Just not well, and not for long. She could have taken a sleeping pill, but she rather liked the edge exhaustion was giving her. She thought maybe she was going to need that edge.

"It's not over, you know." They were sitting on the new sofa, eating kung pao chicken and Jimmy's justifiably famous sesame noodles out of white cartons. Two fortune cookies sat in the center of the also-new coffee table. "All of it…it's not over."

"I know," P.B. said.

He had been gentle with her since they had staggered back into her apartment that god-awful morning. Had been treating her like handblown glass, rare and fragile. It made her want to scream, but she was afraid that, if she did, she really would shatter and prove him right.

"It's not over," she repeated a third time. "It's really only just begun. If what was in Sergei's report is true."

There was controversy over that; nobody was quite sure how much faith they could put in the words of a Silence Operative, someone who had been responsible, however indirectly, for the creation—the brainwashing—of the children who had been used against them.

Wren would never believe that Sergei had had anything to do with that, not after what they had been through, but she didn't argue. She was too tired of trying to be seen, trying to be heard. And she was just as glad that he was keeping his distance. She could survive anything, so long as she knew he was safe. And safe, right now, meant nowhere near her.

"It's not just us. It's not just this city, this coast."

The demon knew all this. He had heard her go over it before, in different words all leading to the same conclusion.

"The Silence... What they did to that girl, to the others... If we let it be, it will destroy us, down to root and stem. The Council—all the Councils—no longer have a choice about getting involved. This isn't only a regional squabble anymore. It never was."

"It's a new witch hunt," P.B. said, agreeing as he had agreed before. "Null against Talent. Null against fatae."

"Only this time, fatae and Talent are working together. God, P.B. Do you have any idea what we did? Did you *see?*" Fatae and human, marching together. Some of them arm and arm, singing. Carrying signs. Covered with blood still, staggering out of the police station the morning after. Someone had thought to bring a camera to the fight—idiot, but brilliant.

"What we were building...it can't be allowed to fall apart. Independently, we lose."

P.B. sighed, stretched, sucked garlic sauce off his claw. "We're gonna lose together, too. You know that, right?"

She knew. But she had to hold on to the victories of the moment, and hope that they would be enough.

"Shut up and pass me the dumplings."

P.B. reached, then paused. Scooping up the fortune

cookies, he got up and walked out of the room. She heard the window open, the sound of something being pitched into the snow, and then the window closing.

When he came back, empty-handed, some of the tension around his muzzle was lessened. She almost smiled.

Uptown, Blues played softly over an expensive sound system, a woman's voice crooning in French. Sergei Didier sat on his sofa, barefoot, wearing a pair of black dress slacks and a crisp button-down shirt. There was a glass of wine on the table in front of him, and a square cloth next to it. On the cloth, a number of metal and plastic pieces were laid out with surgical precision.

He finished cleaning the barrel of his pistol, and placed it down next to the cloth, the blued steel making a clink on the surface that barely disturbed the sound of the woman's voice.

She could think whatever she wanted to think. They could call him a traitor: God knew the Silence already did. But the flames that had surrounded the bridge last month were a portent of what was to come: her fortune had warned them about that.

He might not be wanted by her side anymore: he couldn't blame her for that. He understood. That didn't mean that he was about to let Wren go into this alone, whatever "this" might turn out to be.

I can survive anything, he told her silently. *So long as you're safe.*

* * * * *

Nobody said juggling a career and
a relationship would be easy...

bring
it on

On sale July 2006.

Valere's life as a retriever used to be simple, but now that she
and Sergei are in a relationship, things are getting much more
complicated. What's more, the city Valere loves is now at grave
risk. There's only one thing left for Valere to do—bring it on....

LUNA™

Visit your
local bookseller.

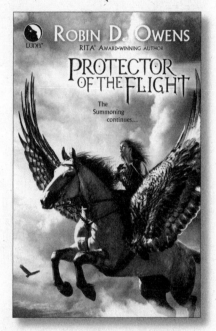